THE
LAMB
PROPHECY

Jared Woods

Distribution by KDP Amazon and Ingram Spark (P.O.D.)
Printed in the United States of America, Canada, and the United Kingdom
Title: The Lamb Prophecy
Names: Woods, Jared

Paperback ISBN: 978-0-9934876-5-1
Hardcover ISBN: 978-0-9934876-6-8
E-book ISBN: 978-0-9934876-7-5

JaredWoodsSavedMyLife.com

Dedicated to
Gavin Woods

who lived long enough
to hear about this book
but did not live long enough
to read it

Guidance

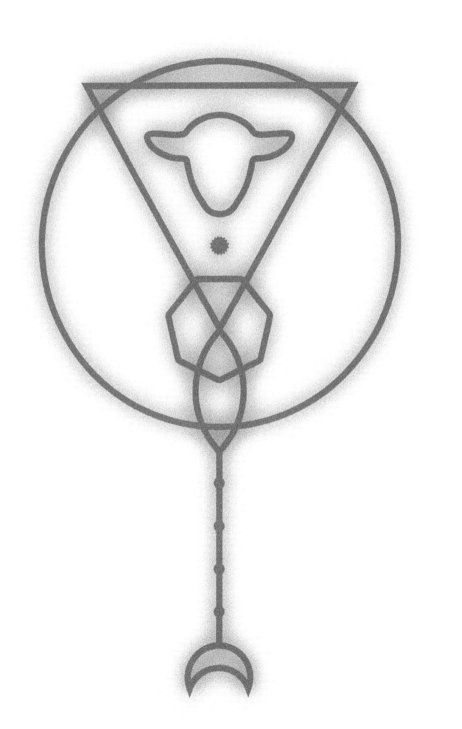

*"Behold, the Lamb of God,
who takes away the
sin of the world."*

JOHN 1:29

Chapter I:
The Lord is
My Shepherd

I

1

Lamb watched her toes, flexing, relaxing, flexing, relaxing. They protruded over the roof's edge, sending a stream of giddy dust particles dancing down the 31 storeys. The taunting concrete invited her to come on down, but Lamb zoned in on her sad left big toe, where a ball of dirt was tucked beneath the corner of her nail. A wave of sobriety washed over her, and she exhaled with a brief chuckle, amused by how a day could start so ordinarily only to end up here, atop a building in West London, one slip away from life's ultimate full-stop.

9am. Lamb's body was always tired, but her body clock was loyal. She rolled out from under her duvet, thumped onto the beige carpet, then forced her torso back up onto the mattress. Knees pressed to the ground. Hands firmly clutched together. Prayer position. In a yawny stupor, she smiled up at the crucified Jesus on her wall—the man of the house. "Good morning," she greeted, and he returned the sentiment. Lamb was grateful for this presence and told him so, relaying thanks until her dreamy visions solidified to reality, and she wiped them away with the crusts from her eyes. She was ready to start the morning.

Lamb kissed each plant hello as she stepped into her kitchen. That's what she liked about her modest apartment; everything was but a stride away. Some would call it a shabby space—mould thriving in the shower, cracks launching across the walls—but it was her space and she kept it minimal, kept it clean. 'Cleanliness is next to Godliness' was not a biblical proclamation, but it was treated as one in her home.

The dull milk carton nudged its sell-by date, but was still good enough to swig straight from the cardboard. "'I have fed you with milk, and not with meat: for hitherto ye were not able to bear it.'" She blessed the container out loud with Corinthians 3:1-3, before returning it to its refrigerated home.

Wincing, she removed a reluctant slice of bread from the bread bin, inspected it for discolouration, and slotted it into her toaster. "'Give us this day our daily bread,'" she whispered. However, Matthew 6:11 failed to soothe her as the slice was scorched alive by this evil technology. It never got easier, and when Lamb heard the bread scream she stabbed the eject button with her thumb, liberating the piece from its torture.

Lamb sprinkled some arrogant salt onto the toast, squeezed her eyes shut, begged the toast for forgiveness and committed to a large bite, grinding it between her teeth once, twice, then swallowing. She gagged, diving towards her faucet, cleansing her throat with a loud gulp of water. Lamb loved water. Water didn't mind being consumed. Water was happy to replenish. She thanked Jesus again.

After two more revolting bites of toast, she discarded the remains into the trash with a slew of apologies. Out of sight, out of mind. She figured she did well that morning. It would be enough food for some time.

Pills next. Two 0.5mg Risperdal. 20mg Olanzapine. 400mg Bupropion XL. 400mg Lithium. And one sparkly multivitamin. Then, back to her knees at the foot of the bed where Lamb held her Bible, gazing lovingly at the Jesus nailed above, the only item to adorn her otherwise off-white walls. The drugs were a necessity, she had made peace with that. But Christ was her salvation, and any life was possible through him. She was a living testament to his power.

Without breaking her gaze from her Lord, Lamb flipped to a random page in the Bible's latter half, then bowed her head to read his gift of the day. It was The Epistle to the Galatians, 5:13-14.

> *"You, my brothers and sisters, were called to be free. But do not use your freedom to indulge the flesh; rather, serve one another humbly in love. For the entire law is fulfilled in keeping this one command: 'Love your neighbour as yourself'."*

Lamb gently shut the Good Book, no loss of a smile. What a blessed verse with which to move through the day. She thanked Jesus for bringing it to her attention. With that, she slipped her favourite work dungarees over her pyjamas, grimaced as she yanked her faux leather combat boots into place, grabbed her tool bag, and headed to work.

I

2

Hammersmith & City Line, eastbound. Lamb had an agreement
with her phone that they would be civil, and she blasted classical music through her headphones to bury the sound of the
angry train. Brahms, Wagner, Chopin, anything to distract from the
overwhelming claustrophobia of the machine's belly. She hated trains.
Even the nicest of them were impatient and anxious, and it rubbed off
on the passengers; everyone became impatient and anxious too. Still,
she stroked her Rosary and counted her blessings with Our Fathers. At
least she started work much later than the majority of London, meaning
she missed the rush hour crowds, a situation that would surely destroy
her.

An unnerving change at King's Cross St. Pancras to the Victoria
Line, a zip to Finsbury Park and then Lamb escaped from the underground gloom, liberated from the insensitive mechanics like her morning toast. The final leg was Lamb's favourite, every step unwinding the
tube's clamour. Crossing Clissold Park, she enjoyed the authoritative
Sun's warmth on her face, joining Jesus' love in her heart. Spring had
arrived mere moments ago and, aptly, Lamb was near-frolicking when
she reached St. Mary's Church.

You could hardly count the seconds between Lamb entering the doors and falling to her knees, delegating the final residues of her troubles to the Lord. About a half hour later, the Vicar entered, studying Lamb with admiration. Lamb was late for her duties, but the Vicar had never seen anyone worship with such devotion. How could she be upset? The Vicar left Lamb to it, only to return with some tea and Jammie Dodgers, her small way to get Lamb to eat, for she knew Lamb hardly did.

The interruption of her prayers tensed Lamb's shoulders. Jammie Dodgers were conniving little creeps, hellbent on biscuit supremacy. But she could not express these discomforts, for the Vicar had done her nothing but favours. Thus, the two sat in the pew, munching the sweet shortcake with sips of amicable tea, breaking every *'No Food in the Chapel'* rule.

"So, what did you end up doing last week?" said the Vicar, attempting small talk.

"Last week?" Lamb rubbed a smudge of jam from her mouth.

"Uhm, for your birthday, hello!" the Vicar laughed.

"Oh." Lamb remembered that it was her birthday last week but did not recall any details. "I just saw some friends," she lied.

"That sounds nice. 30th, hey. It's a biggie! Can't believe mine was, like, 20 years ago. More, even! Do you feel any different?"

"I don't think so," Lamb responded, but she felt different in this moment, squirming under the innocent interrogation, the very presence of another person overpowering her senses, yearning to rip out her organs for an excuse to escape.

The Vicar picked up on the discomfort. She stood, dusting invisible crumbs from her collar. "Ok, well, I hope you have a nice day. The carrots are nearly ready to harvest, I think! And the candytufts need some pruning."

Lamb nodded as the Vicar walked away. She knew which tasks needed to be done but was grateful to be left in peace. She really liked the Vicar. Without this job, her housing benefits would never cover her rent. She owed the Vicar so much.

I

3

Women were better suited for some places above others, and Lamb struggled to take the Vicar seriously in her authoritative role. The Bible was clear that the Lord never intended females to lead churches. But gardens were the perfect place for a woman. The perfect place for Lamb, undoubtedly.

She discarded her boots, connecting her soles and her soul to the earth. The private garden of St. Mary's Church was Lamb's happiest place. The flowers, the shrubbery, the vegetable patch; all knew her by name, and she lost hours in their thoughts. They exuded such loud personalities, eager to be heard. The blooming roses were pompous, but Lamb respected that about them; you'd never find a flower so proud. The determined tulips swayed from an abundance of romance. Lavender was so desperate for attention that it was comical. She cared for each plant as a mother. Dividing her attention between them equally, she even pretended to trim the tree leaves when they didn't need to be trimmed, just so they felt included.

Secretly, Lamb's pride was the small vegetable patch. The passing winter was uncharacteristically warm, and everyone was thriving, eager to show off their progress, emanating satisfaction like a choir of pleasurable vibrations. Potatoes, parsnips, little chillies, tomatoes; they were Lamb's family who deserved life as much as she did. The carrots were fully formed, as the Vicar noted, yet Lamb chose not to harvest them. Let the carrots grow to their fullest potential before they turn the cycle's corner.

Lamb hated to harvest. It pained her that her babies would be removed from this world, murdered by the stomachs of ignorant people. But she reminded herself that this was the order of things. As even Genesis 1:29 states:

> *"And God said, 'Behold, I have given you every plant yielding seed that is on the face of all the earth, and every tree with seed in its fruit. You shall have them for food.'"*

Bible verses were Lamb's weapon to shake off negative feelings and remain dedicated to her work. Around 11:30am, the Vicar's radio was tuned to a soft rock station, strumming smooth notes from her office window and into the outside air. Lamb disliked the suspicious aura of radios themselves, but the music was palatable and she hummed to the more popular melodies. Today was a Thursday and, up until this point, a Thursday like every other Thursday, which, in turn, was indistinguishable from every other working day of the week.

But at precisely 12:07pm, this familiar trajectory collapsed.

The radio's melodies segued into a human voice delivering a news segment—a regular occurrence Lamb was accustomed to blanking out. But on this Thursday, at 12:07pm, key phrases pricked at her senses until her mind could not help but attune to the report.

> *"Ok, folks, that was The Rolling Stones with their 1973 hit, 'Angie'. Uh, now we have some, uh, disturbing news, unfortunately. We're a little behind here on Easy Breeze FM, but as you may have heard, our Chancellor of the Exchequer, Benjamin Grant, has been arrested for inappropriate behaviour with a minor. It is our understanding that there is a photo circulating, but authorities urge everyone not to seek it out, as it constitutes evidence of child abuse and so viewing it is a punishable offense. The UK government has yet to respond to these allegations, but this is truly a sickening day for the country. Uh, but of course we will*

keep you updated as we find out more."

Dark fissures of Lamb's memory sparked, strobing her vision with sharp bursts of pain. She was unsure what was happening and violently shook her head until some clarity settled. It took several minutes of nasal breathing, but she gradually shrank that horrid roar inside of her. She mechanically attempted to snip a meandering leaf from a hawthorn shrub, but her hands were trembling too much to position the pruning shears correctly. Instead, she slowly folded to the ground and pretended to tend to some selfish weeds in case the Vicar looked out at her.

Sweat dribbled from Lamb's face into the soil, and she prayed for deliverance from whatever plagued her. Through wobbly hyperventilation, she found herself repeating Jeremiah 17:14.

> *"Heal me, Lord, and I will be healed; save me and I will be saved, for you are the one I praise.*
> *Heal me, Lord, and I will be healed; save me and I will be saved, for you are the one I praise.*
> *Heal me, Lord, and I will be healed; save me and I will be saved, for you are the one I praise."*

Ebbs and flows of delirium, laps of estrangement from the present, but after an unknowable number of repetitions, the Bible delivered on its promises. Lamb swirled back to attention and felt much better, almost euphoric, happy to ignore whatever rippled her peace.

Several minutes past 1pm, the Vicar offered Lamb the lunchtime sandwich. Like most days, Lamb politely declined and the ever-concerned Vicar left it at that. Lamb moved on to her favourite part of her duties: providing her friends with their daily water. She thanked the thin streams of generous liquid from the watering can. The plants cooed with hydrated gratitude. The silky acoustic guitar music aptly sound-tracked the harmonious atmosphere but was abruptly broken mid-song at 1:33pm. The newsman's voice reemerged. Lamb froze, the spout hovering at an angle, producing meagre drips upon the roses eagerly awaiting the quench of their thirst.

"Alright, folks, sorry to interrupt ol' Clapton there, but it seems like this Benjamin Grant story is snowballing fast, and we're at a loss. Absolutely shocked by what we're hearing here. So, uh, sources claim uh, this incriminating photo of the Chancellor of the Exchequer was, uh, just one of many. It's hard to keep up with everything, but from what we gather, an entire database of images has been leaked from the dark web onto the, um ... 'normal internet'? With reports alleging there are hundreds if not thousands more, many of which feature very prominent figures in our political system. These supposedly include Secretary of State for Defence, Nathan Miller, and Lord President of the Council, Gregory Cole. It's a lot to fathom, I ... can you believe this, Jen? Ugh. It appears the photos are popping up everywhere, but law enforcement asks everyone to remain aware that viewing these pictures is a criminal offence and they should not be sought out by anyone. Of course, cyber vigilantes argue that the pictures are in the public interest and protected by clear political importance, but I struggle to see the grey area here. There is no excuse! I mean, think about the victims, people!"

When Lamb came to, she was lying face-down in the rose bush, her hands and arms scraped by thorns like confused doodles. Her memory recalled THE INCIDENT THE INCIDENT THE INCIDENT shattering like glass, and the once sweet smell of flowers was replaced by the sour odour of her father. She scuffled to her feet, swayed without balance and vomited bile into the roses. With apologies, she fumbled the watering can, dumping too much water on one patch, then clumsily wandered away, tripping over a series of nothing at all.

From her office window, the Vicar noticed Lamb circling aimlessly and rushed to her aid. "Lamb, are you alright?" she asked. Lamb incoherently mumbled something about not feeling well and going home. Lamb had never requested such a thing before, and the Vicar insisted she first lay down in one of the church rooms. Lamb swatted away the suggestion and stumbled off the premises, leaving her shoes, tools, and a worried Vicar behind.

I

4

L amb fought her mind all the way down the Victoria Line. She prayed to Jesus, but intrusive thoughts knocked aside every good feeling like a losing chess game. The train was louder than before, screeching down the tracks, a demonic force that tore through her music until she threw her headphones to the floor in a panic. Every mental avenue hit a dead-end—the dead-end of *The Incident*, which folded back into her dad.

She hadn't thought of her father in many years but, if asked, she would have sworn she was over it, she had dealt with it. However, on this tumultuous carriage her skull shook like a snow globe, dislodging an army of ghosts.

Her father, Breton Daleston (a white man), had married Serenah Limestone (a black woman), placing Lamb as not quite either, somewhere between. Lamb often mused this was the root of her internal conflict: two contrasting cultures forced into one genetic structure, struggling to coexist on a rudimentary biological level, locked into an age-old ethnic conflict. She wished she had someone to discuss this with, but she did not. Not her parents, at least, for they had passed on long ago.

Lamb's brain bounced through a feverish storm. She nearly

missed her stop, but staggered out just in time. Blundering through the labyrinth of King's Cross St. Pancras like a drunk, she passed humans who scrunched their noses at her as they moved out of her way. Muscle memory led her to the next screaming train, tears blurring her vision. Squeezing her hands together so tightly that she could hear her bones click, Lamb attempted prayer after prayer, but the vacant train seats noticed and mocked her with sinister howls. Her fragmented internal monologue pinballed off several topics before landing on her mother.

There wasn't much information there except for the same clip Lamb played when recollecting her dear mother. In it, Lamb is no older than six when someone hands her down a bright yellow dress with little pink butterflies along the hem. Such a joyful hue! She shows off her moves to her mom, twirling and prancing across her living room stage to the backtrack of Elvis Presley. Her mother laughs and claps in delight, and then abruptly disappears to her bedroom, closing the door behind her. Lamb teeters, dizzy from spinning and confused by abandonment, calling for her mother's return. And her mother does return, now modelling a strikingly similar dress, only a slightly faded yellow with flowers everywhere instead of butterflies. Lamb squeals with delight as her mother takes her hand and the two spin together, laughing and dancing to Elvis' croons. It was a snapshot heavily drenched in melancholy, but the happiest moment she had.

Her mother was the first of the family to die, mere months after the yellow dress. Lamb cannot listen to Elvis anymore.

Lamb plunged through her apartment door, tearing her knees into the carpet, imploring crucified Jesus to save her from this torment like he had countless times before. Ovarian cancer murdered her mom. Lamb wildly lashed out to seize her Bible, tipping her fragile bedside table to the floor. The medical bills financially devastated her dad, and they were scraping money favours by the time Mom parted. Lamb flipped through the thin pages so rapidly that she tore a piece of the Book of Jonah. Even before her mother's death, her father was cold and absent; he'd regularly expressed how he wanted a son and had no use for another woman in the house. Lamb couldn't read any words on the paper; her eyes were flooded, and whichever page she looked upon was instantly soaked by her anguish. But Dad truly lost himself after Mom was gone; he turned every paycheck to drink, and then he turned into a monster. He withdrew, and became loud and demanding. He blamed Lamb for everything. She was a curse, he said. And then. And then, *The Incident*.

The room's walls faded from white to black, and the carpet sank. Jesus diminished in size as if swallowed by the darkening paint. Lamb tried to scream, but the noise throttled mid-throat, only a gurgling noise escaping her mouth. "Jesus, please," she whispered, but there was no Jesus here. Only her father. Only the Devil.

I

5: THE INCIDENT

Someday, just over three years after her mother's death, Lamb was clicking together the border of a 400-piece jigsaw puzzle with the promise of Hello Kitty riding a bicycle at the end. She was in the living room. The Sun had set. It was a school night. Dad was not in the house but wasn't far, drinking in the small back garden like he did every evening, drowning his turmoil until he was adequately saturated to sleep.

Dad's Nokia ringtone came from out back, followed by some slurry mumbles. Lamb winced as she heard him coming in. She collected the detached bits of Hello Kitty into a neat pile to take up less space. He stood there, unmoving, watching her, but she dared not turn, instead pretending to focus on a pink piece that didn't seem to fit anywhere.

With a sudden stride, he aggressively grabbed Lamb by her face, squashing her cheeks, forcing her to look at him. His dank breath hovered with acidity. Using his thumb, he rubbed something from the corner of her eye. "Just do what I say, and everything will be alright, do you hear?" he spoke with an uncharacteristic tremor. She nodded, agreeing to something unknown.

The subsequent events transpired quickly and were so foreign to Lamb that she never organised them together with any clarity. Her dress was removed. His belt was unbuckled. Dad's monstrous man-thing shook near her face. Her eyes squeezed tight as he grunted, and slime squirted on one cheek and then the other. "Open your eyes," he instructed. She did so. Her dad's man-thing rested on her gooey face. He was holding an old Polaroid camera. "Now, smile."

A succession of bright flashes and her next memory was in the shower, her silent tears joining the goo which joined the water, bits of stuff swirling around the drain. Lamb had heard enough talk at school to know that what had happened was bad. It was supposed to be a grown-up game, and that confused her. She scrubbed her face, but it never felt clean. If she stood in the shower forever, could she too dissolve and escape down the drain?

When she eventually crept back into the living room, it was empty. Her dad's slurry voice was on his phone outside. She could still smell him in here, smell what they did. Her Hello Kitty puzzle was right where she'd left it, but it looked rotten. Two luminous headlights appeared behind the living room curtains like eyes. Car tyres crunched the gravel to a standstill. The murmuring engine chugged off, the lights disappeared. Someone was here. Lamb turned to escape, but her dad reentered through the back, and she froze. He staggered past her without a glance. She shuddered, hiding her body with her arms despite being clothed.

Her dad opened the door to reveal a tall man wearing black jeans, a tight-fitted button-up shirt, slim blazer, and a wide toothy smile. Lamb's stomach bunched, and she silently pleaded to her father to not let this man in. But her father let this man in.

Lamb hunched to the floor, busying herself with the puzzle, refusing to accept this night any more than she had to. It did no good, as the man strode past her dad with a, "And you must be little Lamb!" The man crouched down to meet her. Lamb's gaze fixed firmly on the ground, unable to remember how shapes work, trying to force a random puzzle piece into any possible slot. "I have a gift for you," the man continued, pulling out a small tub of ice cream, waving it between her eyes and the scattered puzzle. In her daily two-meal diet consisting of tins and noodles, ice cream was a luxury she'd longed for, even dreamed about. But she stared straight through the tub, denying the moment. "C'mon, Lamb. What's the matter? You don't like ice cream?"

"This is not what we agreed," her dad interjected. The man relented, placing the ice cream upon the puzzle, then stood with both hands in the air.

"You're right! You're right. She's just so adorable. Ok, then." The man yanked out a white envelope from his blazer and handed it to Lamb's father, who in turn, passed him a larger yellow envelope, bulky from however many polaroids the camera had spat. Lamb pretended not to see, not touching the dessert, building the puzzle around it, finally connecting a piece to a corner. Both men looked inside their respective packages, nodding, satisfied with the transaction. "Pleasure doing business with you," the man said, then added, "And sort your life out, you drunkard. You look pathetic."

The car lights were already pulling away before her father managed to slam the door in fury. He spun around with such velocity that Lamb was sure he was about to kick her in the face. Her spine shivered her posture straight. But instead he lost his balance and collided with the wall, remaining there as if stuck. Lamb's eyes met her dad's, and for a brief moment, he looked at her sickened with guilt, the closest gesture to an apology he would ever offer.

Less than an hour later, he had drunk himself to sleep in the garden as Lamb ate her ice cream. It was mint chocolate chip, her favourite. But it tasted wrong.

I

6

A knock on the door brought Lamb back into her flat. There was a sliver of daylight left, but the walls were white again. Jesus was regular-sized, nailed in place as if nothing happened. She was no longer crying but lay on her floor holding several torn Bible pages in her fist. Removing one, she read Habakkuk 2:4.

> *"Behold, his soul which is lifted up is not upright in him: but the just shall live by his faith."*

The knock came again. Lamb rolled onto her stomach, pulled her knees to her chest, and then extended her body upright. She took two side steps with her hands sliding across the wall, and opened the door for a food delivery man. He looked tired. Lamb received the sleazy Aldi paper bags with a, "Thank you so much," then closed him out with her foot. Her flat was quickly overwhelmed by the aroma of a curry she did not remember ordering. She threw that bag upon her kitchen table, far more invested in the second parcel: a 750ml bottle of raspberry vodka and a 750ml bottle of cheap red wine.

Dad died from the booze in the end. Lamb hadn't touched alcohol in nearly 18 years, and she had only started about three years before that. After *The Incident*, Dad turned into the scariest monster in the world. He never touched her like that again—he didn't even look at her—but on many a drunken night he'd release a tirade from the corner of his mouth. "Stupid girl" became her house-name and he would remind her that what happened was her fault. "You did this, stupid girl! It's because you cursed this family with sin," was one line. "My wife died because of you, and now you're being punished," was another. But his most common threats concerned the Devil. "There is a special throne in Hell for a girl who did what you did." "Satan is watching you; from the sky, from the walls, he hears every word you think." "The Devil will steal you, you disgusting, stupid girl. If you tell anyone about that night, he will kidnap you away." So, she never told.

Lamb's fear of the Devil held her sleepy eyes open. Whenever she'd slip into an exhausted slumber, a recurring nightmare would torment her psyche. The Devil came to get her with his oversized goat's face, which morphed into the face of her dad. A loud yelp would startle her just in time to realise she'd wet the bed, over and over. Her room perpetually stank of urine, and she was terrified of what her father might do if he smelt it. She began secretly washing the sheets in the bathtub when home alone, spreading them back over her mattress before being caught. Which meant, whether bathwater or pee, she spent her nights pressed into damp linen, panicking about the Devil in her ceiling or under her bed. And that's when she'd started stealing mouthfuls of alcohol from her dad's stash. To dull the presence of Satan. To obscure her trauma just enough so it was unrecognisable; so that she could confuse it with peace; so she could sleep. Just like her dad. Just like she was hoping to do now.

She had ordered the vodka and the wine because she could not choose between them, but looking at them, there was no competition. The wine was too needy; it was shameful. The vodka was far more assertive and self-ruling. She cracked its lid with respect.

Lamb's grades plummeted so rapidly that the teachers berated her in front of everyone, and this once shy girl who blended into the corner became the easiest of bullying targets. They called her Black Sheep as they passed in the halls. A chorus of bleating welcomed her into every class, *"baa baa baaaaa."*

The raspberry vodka tasted awful. Too sweet. But the burn that outlined her stomach was an old friend. She was pleased with her decision.

The teasing got worse when Lamb developed an unusual form of eczema that resembled black leather, especially when scratched. Doctors said it was stress-related.

"There it is!" Lamb exclaimed as she held up the bottle of vodka. "Corinthians, 10:31. *'Whether therefore ye eat, or drink, or whatsoever ye do, do all to the glory of God'*. Cheers!" She pointed the bottleneck at Jesus with a wink, then took another swig, relieved that she hadn't imagined this sacred permission. She was feeling so much better!

Lamb was 11 when she failed Grade 6. She scraped through on her second try, only to fall into her first mental breakdown at age 13. Her skin wasn't clearing and her alcohol intake had increased substantially since she learned how to steal from stores, a rush she thoroughly enjoyed. But while snooping around her dad's study, looking for photos of her mom, or at least some whiskey, she instead thumbed across a black and white Polaroid from *The Incident*. There she was, the camera towering above her smiling face covered in his gunk, his penis involved in the display. Her dad had kept a copy. That hurt almost as much as *The Incident* itself. And that's what had finally ruptured her. She attempted to hang herself from a tree in a local park but was discovered by a dog walker before she got very far.

Half the bottle of vodka down, and on go the tunes. Her classical playlist at first, but that simply couldn't cut it. Jabbing at her phone in semi-random sequences, some old-time upbeat jazz station bounced into the room, serving sunshine and excitement. Lamb twirled with her vodka dancing partner, bumping into things with glee.

She found herself in a psychiatric hospital for several months, convinced that a goat-headed Satan was trying to grab her through the light-fittings, the television, the depths of the couch. Every noise in the night was Satan hissing her name. Every door that opened revealed Satan behind. Her case was so severe that she is anonymously referenced as Patient L in a medical journal, noting how she appeared to develop relationships with inanimate things, giggling as she conversed with plates or pillows, and then wailing when they inevitably turned out to be the Devil in disguise again.

The jazz trumpets sped up, and Lamb's rotations matched the pace, spinning round and around and around. The raspberry vodka tasted like Jammie Dodgers!

After a tsunami of pharmaceutical cocktails, the hospital formulated a decent combination that seemed to gaffa tape her brain together. Lamb ceased having episodes, and the Devil's domineering presence chipped away, revealing a crowd of more manageable personalities living within every object. It didn't matter what it was: a bicycle, a hat, a piece of toast; they each exuded distinct characteristics and were aware of Lamb's attention. Some appeared fascinated by her recognition. Others would prefer she'd let them be. Either way, she could not control this ceaseless flurry of activity, and she took each step cautiously to avoid offending any given item.

    Had her mind snapped off from reality? Or could she see things no one else could see? The truth was irrelevant. What became far more important was that she needed to stop talking about these perceived personalities if she wanted to leave this place. And, indeed, after enough silent time had passed, she was released back into the world like a toddler who had just learned to walk.

Lamb's knee collided with the corner of the bed. She toppled over, cracking the floor shoulder-first, spilling vodka everywhere. She grunted as she rolled onto her back and then vomited into her mouth, which she promptly swallowed. Still tasted like jam! She laughed.

Out of hospital, Lamb was sent directly to a state boarding school because her dad was deemed unfit to care for her. Lamb sometimes wondered if his sins plagued him every time he thought of her, just as hers did when she thought of him. Either way, they never spoke again. He died from liver failure during her schooling at Sisters of the Blessed Virgin Mary.

Lamb kept laughing until the music on her phone faded, replaced by a female's voice.

> *"Dixieland City FM, I'm Carol Morales, and this is your seven o'clock news ..."*

Carol introduced the news segment, and Lamb's amusement evaporated from her lungs like steam. Oh, God, please, no, not this.

The first nights in Cambridge's Sisters of the Blessed Virgin Mary were difficult. As an all-girls Catholic school, Lamb was surrounded by people 24 hours a day. In classes, she writhed in her seat as the hyper-nearness of early teenagers tormented the atmosphere. At night, her eyes froze open as 11 other dorm girls snored their dreams. Lamb was bombarded with their energy as she held her crotch, fearful she would pee the bed. But during her second week, everything changed.

Lamb misjudged the angle of her flat's floor, attempting to stand on her heels so fast that she sprung backwards, her back smacking to the carpet as her crown thudded against a wall that appeared from nowhere. The bottle of vodka sprung from her hand, giggling as it rolled away before smashing with a scream, its raspberry blood now the carpet's to enjoy. The news continued, unaware. Lamb surrendered.

> *"... top story today, at least a hundred prolific figures have been identified in leaked child abuse photos in what's being referred to as Paedogate. These include Chancellor of the Exchequer, Benjamin Grant, Secretary of State for Defence, Nathan Miller, and several members of the royal family, as well as personnel from the U.S. Congress, such as Roger Gallows, John Lonesmith, Kevin Sherman ..."*

The second week of boarding school was when Lamb found the silent tranquillity of the Blessed Virgin Mary chapel. She spent as much time as she could hiding within those walls. At first, she would simply sit, breathing out the day's frantic electricity, appreciating the peaceful smiles of the seating arrangement or the warm meditation of the bouquets dotted about. The ambience was always subdued, and no object intended her harm. These intervals between human chaos made the spikes of activity more tolerable, and she detoured this way before and after every class.

> *"... a statement from Prime Minister, Tami Theron, claims these images were doctored as part of an orchestrated attack on the current administration and she has assured the public that proof is on the way, although nothing has yet materialised ..."*

Lamb took her time getting to know every feature in the chapel, but she avoided eye contact with the life-sized crucifixion above the altar. The image of Jesus was not something she felt would do her any good. It was such a brutal scene. It was difficult to comprehend why Christians were so fixated on the murder of their hero. However, as each day passed, the surrounding environment gradually grew quieter, as if giving the crucifix space to speak, beckoning Lamb to focus its way. She sensed the gentle prods and relented, turning to gauge this representation of Jesus. The figure recognised her right away. Lamb collapsed to her knees in tears.

> *"... despite the legal consequences of possessing these images, more and more websites are hosting the database, which is the largest of its kind on known record. Authorities are doing their best to shut these sites down but are currently overwhelmed at the rate by which they are appearing ..."*

Jesus asked Lamb if she would let him into her heart. Through her cries, she readily agreed, and they bonded. Jesus washed Lamb's soul clean of every one of her sins, and she was released from her pain, experiencing genuine serenity for the first time. Jesus banished the lingering fear of the Devil, and Lamb was liberated, finally aligning with the only purpose that mattered: to worship and serve Jesus Christ of Nazareth, God's only son, the promised Messiah who saved humankind from evil, the most elevated preacher who taught only of love, the strongest man who ever walked the Earth, the incarnation of the infinite Father—the Father she never had.

> *"... however, a warning has been issued, reminding the public that viewing these websites is a crime and anyone found doing so will be punished with the maximum possible penalties ..."*

After Lamb's teachers noticed she was missing from classes, they gathered one by one in the chapel, word spreading that a miracle was taking place. The shy new girl was on her knees, staring at the crucifix without blinking, repeating Jesus' name for close to six hours. When she finally collapsed, she slept for over a day, and when she awoke, the once-broken girl was invigorated by a newfound spirit. The school believed an otherworldly event had occurred and adjusted her curriculum to primarily revolve around Bible studies. Lamb devoured the texts obsessively, which kept her teachers happy. They granted Lamb leeway to build her relationship with Jesus, which she did, running every decision through his instructions, measuring her successes against that of an immaculate deity. Her passion pushed her through graduation, and she walked out of those gates with a certified education. The chapel's official opinion was that she was destined to be a profound asset to the Catholic church. But Lamb didn't care about such pursuits. She just wanted to devote her time to chatting with Jesus.

But where was Jesus now?

> *"... while some of these images may concern persons of public interest, we must note that they are few and far between, and the circulating database mostly contains unrelated photos featuring thousands of child abuse victims."*

Lamb's groggy vodka-filled head slammed on brakes, and she sat up. She was a child abuse victim. And there was a photo of her out there.

I

7

Hindered by inebriated legs and years of organised hoarding, it took Lamb over 15 minutes to locate the cardboard box. Old packages were hastily shredded, forgotten junk strewn across the carpet; dust, finally set free, swarming the apartment. The search ended with an ancient laptop, pried open on her kitchen table, sitting beside the lukewarm curry. The screen was so dirty that it appeared cracked. Such a sad machine; she never liked it. She only bought the thing when looking for a job those years ago.

With clunky whirs, the mechanics struggled to remember how to boot up. Lamb busied herself popping the cork from the eager wine.

"You have made your people experience hardship," she mumbled Psalm 60:3. *"You have given us wine to drink that makes us stagger."*

Ignoring the worried text messages from the Vicar, Lamb enabled her phone's hotspot and connected it to the laptop. She was grateful for this option and offered her phone a nod of respect. The phone returned the gesture.

After a cacophony of rattled tones and robotic complaints, the laptop presented a search engine, and Lamb typed in *'PAEDOGATE'*. Such prohibited content would surely not be easy to find, but she had to start somewhere. The results were mostly news items, but halfway down the page she came across a forum promising constant updates. She opened that, then clicked the first link, disbelieving it could be so easy. But there it was.

Rows of images. Hundreds of them. Children. Little humans who were meant to be protected by the hands of adults. Instead, those very hands assaulted them. Grown-ups forcing their malformed sexual desires onto undeveloped minds, passing down mental defects like a disease. These were snapshots of moments when any healthy sexual maturity was interrupted, on its way to being one thing, now forever skewed into another. Some of these children would learn to equate sex with self-worth, and their lives would be an eternal pursuit to outrun neglect using physical acts. Others, like Lamb, would associate touch with confusion and broken trust, recoiling at the thought, never again engaging in intimacy.

The scrolling wall of abuse appeared bottomless, and Lamb tried her best to move faster, faster, faster, seeking herself but not wanting to see anything. Her stomach protested, sending fermented belches up her throat, begging her to stop. So much trauma flashed before her eyes, and her brain flashed in response. She whipped her head around, certain that someone stood behind her.

No one was there, but her gaze fell upon Jesus, who did not support her actions. She understood. Her quest was not only futile but morally misaligned. Pulling in a massive breath of resignation to settle her hammering heart, she lifted the wine to her lips to comfort her escaping mind. Two gulps, and she paused in that position. There, on the left of the screen, was a squashed but now obvious navigation menu. She slowly placed the bottle down as she read the options.

POLITICIANS
MOVIE STARS
BILLIONAIRES
ROYALTY

These choices were what most people would be clicking these dark pages for, but they were of no interest to Lamb. Her cursor skipped down to more general themes.

FEET
GROUP
INCEST
VIDEOS
VINTAGE

She hesitated on the last one. Vintage? How many decades constitute vintage? The laptop made a clacking noise, which Lamb interpreted as a "don't do it!" but she didn't owe this machine anything. She clicked on the button.

The screen went white and then populated a whole new set of images. Lamb instantly regretted her decision; she didn't want to do this. But within two flicks of the mouse wheel, every photo disappeared in a blur as her vision tunnelled on the exact picture she was trained to see.

There. Little Lamb. Nine years old. Captured by her father as his corrupt seed extinguished any hope of a normal life. The fact that her disgraced face was available to the world did not immediately bother her, as her long-aged features disguised any resemblance. The big smile she wore was a detail that tormented her every day since *The Incident*, but even that was not a concern because she'd already chewed through it to death. Rather, what set off Lamb's second and final breakdown, was that someone out there, some sick, sick human being, had taken the time to digitally colourise the original black and white image.

I

8

"Just do what I say, and everything will be alright, do you hear?"

BANG BANG BANG the Devil was trying to get out of the walls.
Her dad was trying to get out of the walls. That photo smelt like
chlorine.

Lamb glimpsed a demon peeking from behind the bed. It thought it was
quick, but it wasn't quick enough for her. Now, she chased it around the
room, wielding the broken vodka bottle like a dagger.

People who think Jesus didn't exist are such idiots. They don't know
what they are talking about. The Christ myth theory only became a conversation around the 17th or 18th century. It took nearly two thousand
years to question his existence, and even those arguments are feeble.
Contrarily, almost every historical scholar agrees that, at the very least,
a man named Jesus walked among us in 1st-century Roman Judea. He
was definitely baptised, and he was definitely crucified.

The apartment had doubled in size, and everything was peeling, revealing red paint beneath. The demon was fast, ducking behind her table but gone by the time she reached it, now cackling from the bathroom, forever one step ahead. Lamb's brain felt like chalk, so dry and alien. The laptop was still open on the image, and her little polluted face mocked her too. Lamb slammed the lid shut and threw the computer like a frisbee, splitting it into chunks of electronics as it collided with the toilet. Had she hit the demon, though?

Atheists loved to mock the Bible. They build pedestals from their arrogance, patting themselves on the back like they have the authority to give themselves authority and then belittle those of faith. They reference science and think they're so clever, yet are not clever enough to recognise that everything they swallow also stems from a book. They'll ask you to prove God exists and mock you when you speak of the scripture. But if you ask them to prove anything scientific, they'll only reference texts *they've* read. Place the word Science on the book cover, and they'll gobble it up without thought.

BANG BANG, a loud scream came from the walls, but then Lamb noticed she was the one screaming. Was someone at the door? Was it the demon? Lamb pointed the broken bottle at the peephole. That's what she was going to do. She would swing the door open so fast that the wind would freeze the demon's feet, and then she would ram this dead bottle into its fat throat.

And besides, when people speak negatively of the Bible, they never mention the Gospels. That's what Lamb always wanted to tell people, but never did. Forget everything else, just read the Gospels. Jesus was a spiritual leader who never asked for anything. He would sit there for hours and heal people. He taught nothing but equality and peace and forgiveness and acceptance between all classes. Perhaps some have distorted his words for their gain, but why judge the message by the messengers' hand-me-downs? Go back to the Gospels, and you will agree that the world would be better if everyone did their best to follow Jesus' way.

There was no one at the door. The demon must have escaped just in time. Lamb quickly locked herself in the apartment—the hallway scared her. She turned her back to the door and faced a room where spilt curry made tiger streaks across the carpet. Her red walls wheezed, every inhale sounding like her name. Whispers of eczema tickled her skin and she retaliated by hacking at her forearm with the jagged glass.

> *"I discipline my body and bring it into subjection, lest, when I have preached to others, I myself should become disqualified."* – 1 Corinthians 9:27

Weaponising science against religion is blasphemy to both. Science is a practice that requires one to either prove or disprove something for it to become a certainty. Atheists use the lack of tangible proof for a metaphysical God as proof of his nonexistence, which is an unfair leap in the opposite direction. Atheists cannot disprove God as much as we cannot prove Him, but if pressed for evidence, the religious win every time. So much of science depends on trusting human experience, for example, clinical trials for certain medicines dealing with mental health. When the average patient reports positive change, the drug is deemed successful, yet there is no physical evidence, simply an individual's belief in their self-improvement. Over two billion people in the world have a relationship with Christ. Two billion. Imagine labelling every one of those perspectives as stupid simply because you can't personally gauge the measurement. Again, it's those pedestals of arrogance at work, a key component to the atheist confirmation bias.

> *"Take, eat: this is my body, which is broken for you: do this in remembrance of me."* – 1 Corinthians 11:24

The bottle was too thick to pierce her skin, only scraping, hardly drawing blood. Lamb had another idea and turned her medication containers upside down onto her bed, losing count around 46 pills. She rapidly swallowed them at random, even the vitamins, sloshing each down with a mouthful of wine. It would take a while to kick in, but her dedication to this path of action summoned a numbness to her disposition, and she was grateful. The apartment allowed her decision, falling quiet to let her get on with the task.

"This cup is the new testament in my blood: this do ye, as oft as ye drink it, in remembrance of me." – 1 Corinthians 11:25

Some of the oldest Bible passages date back to the 4th century BCE. So if the Good Book was, Heaven forbid, a fabrication, whoever authored such intricate and knowledgeable prose was undoubtedly a genius far beyond anyone we know of, even in modern times.

Also, her dad's semen burnt her face like acid.

Lamb never shaved, but she found some old disposables in her bathroom cupboard. The air's moisture had eaten the metal to orange, but she figured they'd work better than the vodka glass. She slammed the base of the wine bottle down upon the razor's heads, chipping away at the plastic, gradually rescuing the blades. A wave of imbalance and she paused to find her feet. She'd consumed over half of her medical supply and then vomited a bunch of it up again, sobbing at the waste. The devil in the toilet snorted in amusement, and she slammed her fist into the seat in frustration. The walls were grey, and the crucifix was gone again.

But wait, how much do you think that man paid her dad for the photos? How much was she worth?

Lamb crawled out of the bath, gasping for air. She'd made the water far too hot, and the blade was as dull as a butter knife, sawing at her wrists but unfit to slice up a vein. When she eventually struck blood, the steam turned her vision static, and she nearly fainted. Laying naked upon the never-washed bath mat, she waited for her blood pressure to level. She knew the room was witnessing her failures, but it pretended not to.

Several neighbours had reported a disturbance to the police. Two doors down, Jonathan Bowes stood in a fright when he heard something slam. He grabbed his stick and shuffled to his door, opening it just as Lamb rushed past, wearing muddy dungarees that were sopping wet. He called after her, "Hey, are you okay?" but she ignored him, using her shoulder to push through the emergency fire doors without slowing down.

I

9

Suicide was a private matter. Not something to fuss other people over. Even a note seemed distasteful from Lamb's perspective. How could she articulate the culmination of abstract thoughts and emotions that had tipped her life's balance? And who would she address it to? Still, when pills and razors fail a desperate soul, they may be forced to go public. A mangled corpse offered to the street below. Apologies to the witnesses for however your mind saves this moment. At least she'd had a bath.

Flexing, relaxing, flexing, relaxing. Lamb's toe's mood had brightened. People below looked up at her, shouting something, but she couldn't hear them. Lamb breathed with calm. There were flashing police cars down there too, cops no doubt on their way up, but that didn't matter. They would never reach her in time. She just wanted one final minute to appreciate the inevitability of this occasion. Today was a blessing. The internet did her a favour. She was a bird ready to go home.

"And I said, Oh that I had wings like a dove! for then would I fly away, and be at rest." – Psalm 55:6

I

10

"Do you not know that you are God's temple and that God's Spirit dwells in you? If anyone destroys God's temple, God will destroy him. For God's temple is holy, and you are that temple."
— Corinthians 3:16-17

The instant Lamb committed to the fall, her guts twisted in regret. She had made a dreadful mistake.

The six seconds of falling stretched on. "Jesus, please save me, I don't want to die!" she pleaded as her body dropped below the 28th floor.

The concrete was laughing. The building was laughing. The whole world was laughing.

The 20th floor, gone. "Oh, Jesus, forgive me, I have betrayed your love!"

Floor 16 had a sneaky aura. "Oh, God, Oh, Jesus, Oh Jesus!"

Floor 12.

Then 10.

And then, at 7, everything froze and Lamb received her vision.

Solid blue blinded her sight before Jesus' translucent face appeared before her. It was closer to a negative outline like those found on cloth or water-stained plaster, but it was unmistakably him and the most handsome thing Lamb had ever seen. She cried out, "My Lord!" before reality resumed, and she plunged the remainder of the journey.

But in those conclusive moments, an impossible miracle took place. Lamb gained instant awareness of her physical self no longer as an individual identity but as the sum of trillions by trillions by trillions of atomic components coming apart. These elements were primarily vibrational clouds of electron activity, buzzing around the core of dense nuclei. Each nuclei consisted of protons and neutrons, themselves created from quarks, and those quarks held deeper matter broken down for infinity. Every layer that Lamb's insight peeled back revealed a profound consciousness far more remarkable than the stage that circled above. And in that rush of comprehension, it became clear that the source code of reality's atomic structure was far more aware of the Universe than any brain had the finite capacity to withstand.

Lamb's physical body met the street, and her nuclei simply slipped between the nuclei of the cement. Electrons switched sides as molecular structures divided and bonded. Lamb and the street spontaneously merged so fast that Lamb fell straight into it, becoming one with it, disappearing beneath the surface like it was made of mercury. The tar never altered shape, betraying no indication that anything had happened.

And when William Sharp, London's Commissioner of Police of the Metropolis, was asked by the press to clarify the report that "a 30-year-old woman fell 31 stories off of Trellick Tower and then vanished when she hit the ground," his official response was, "I'm not sure what to say."

"Now the God of peace, that brought again from the dead our Lord Jesus, that great shepherd of the sheep, through the blood of the everlasting covenant, make you perfect in every good work to do his will, working in you that which is wellpleasing in his sight, through Jesus Christ; to whom be glory for ever and ever. Amen."

HEBREWS 13:20-21

Chapter II:
Evolution 1

II

As Lamb's particles drifted apart and spread within the ground, the details of physical nature grew hazy and so, in turn, did her ego. But the residue of her identity remained in close enough proximity for her to comprehend the situation on some vague intellectual level. And, as her molecules intermingled with other foreign molecules, she was struck by just that: the limitations of the mind.

Lamb's consciousness, and indeed all human consciousness, was merely an evolutionary assemblage of smaller micro-consciousnesses. True awareness is found in elementary particles—that is, subatomic particles not composed of other particles, if such a finite definition even exists. Like mini-pockets of data, these portions of matter possess the wisdom of the divine, duplicated with particular qualities to suggest subsequent steps. And when one particle combines with another, this union produces characteristics that neither individual particle had before. Attributes bond with attributes, amalgamating to form structures of immeasurable possibilities, manufacturing a discernible reality within which the world thinks it exists.

Whatever constituted Lamb was swiftly losing its borders. Her perception and every perception was laughable, no more substantive than a hallucination. Everything is a collection of active building blocks, but they have constructed beings so complex that they developed cages of ego, fooling themselves into recognising themselves as separate, singular units. But at best they are merely a clunky warp of consciousness glued into a confined space.

The separation of entities is a mental construct, where in truth, everything in a 'physical state' is identical in ingredient: an electron fizz working as part of a unified singular system. Even the 'empty space' between 'solid objects' is as alive as those detectable articles it divides; only its properties are translated differently by the constraints of the mind deciphering it. These immeasurable infinitesimal bits of subatomic matter are entangled with one another, each holding the totality of eternal and infinite wisdom within itself. Through these processes, data is shared across the *Nous*: the Universal database of collective knowledge.

Lamb's grasp on herself slipped. This torrent of enlightened liberation was incomprehensible for the boundaries of a human mind, and the deeper she identified the disconnected consciousness of each atom, the further she came apart from who she once was. However, in these final moments, a connective flash occurred, where she glimpsed into the source of cosmic secrets. In that instant, she understood that God and the Devil were but metaphors for more consequential concepts: the energy of Good and Bad. The binary code that ran reality. An Equation perpetually weighing itself for balance. And Lamb's conclusive emotion was one of grief, as she glimpsed the knowledge that her planet Earth suffocated beneath a burden of evil.

The atoms of Lamb's decisive presence floated too far apart to observe itself as a unit, now tiny bits of independent understanding lost within the crowd of identical electrical behaviour. Lamb dissolved out of existence.

"If there be found among you, within any of thy gates which the Lord thy God giveth thee, man or woman, that hath wrought wickedness in the sight of the Lord thy God, in transgressing his covenant; And hath gone and served other gods, and worshipped them, either the Sun, or Moon, or any of the host of heaven, which I have not commanded; And it be told thee, and thou hast heard of it, and enquired diligently, and, behold, it be true, and the thing certain, that such abomination is wrought in Israel: Then shalt thou bring forth that man or that woman, which have committed that wicked thing, unto thy gates, even that man or that woman, and shalt stone them with stones, till they die."

DEUTERONOMY 17:2-5

Chapter III:
The Sun's
Shadow Went
Back 10 Steps

III

1

L amb's atoms dissipated like vapour, existing only in this space and time yet everywhere eternally. They never completely lost contact, rather they maintained a watchful distance from one another whilst absorbing the sacred knowledge upon which reality was built. Earth continued with its oblivious rotation.

Once the atoms reached the maximum possible distance before disconnection, their movement ceased ... then contracted. Lamb's particles swam in reverse, towards one another within the metaphysical realm, counterintuitive to the cycle of energetical reuse.

Electrons were shared. Molecular structures were remembered. Lamb's physical attributes took off as a unit, speeding beneath the dirt while pulling together as one. Hundreds of miles slipped past her reforming body. Then she slowed. Stopped. Paused. And abruptly squeezed upwards. She popped out several inches above ground wearing those same dungarees, landing on her spine with a hollow thud.

Lamb cried out in agony. Her atomic information did not forget the vodka, the red wine, and the pills, an almost fatal combination that produced a hangover of such ferocity that perhaps no human had experienced such a thing before. Her wail only worsened her condition, her cerebral hemispheres threatening to split from the stem. Her eyelids tensed from a piercing light.

Half a minute later and the pain was noticeably fading. Lamb burped up the stench of sick. She dared to open her eyes, revealing a world that shoved rays of daylight into her retina like red-hot knitting needles. She wailed again.

Blink blink blink, and her discomfort adjusted even though she didn't initially trust her senses. Hovering above was an audience of sunflowers, peering curiously down at her. Lamb wiggled her body and confirmed that she was lying in soil, lifting a fistful above her face to make sure.

Lamb sat. The landscape cocked crooked for a moment, provoking nausea. But this settled fast enough and, as Lamb stood, the sunflowers' heads lifted in unison. She could just about gauge that she was in an expansive field of these yellow petals. Such a discovery would be bizarre enough, but added to this peculiarity was that each sunflower faced her, standing at her precise height, not a fraction less nor more.

Lamb was not granted much time to ponder this anomaly. If she had counted the seconds, she would have reached around seven before a rustling escalated in volume. Distant sunflowers parted until a grotesquely obese woman exploded in front of her with enough vigour to power a steam engine. She threw her arms around Lamb in an all-consuming embrace of blubber.

"Oh, mah goodness, Lamb! You finally made it here! Minh is gonna be soooo excited!" And with that, this lady released Lamb's body and grabbed her hand, taking off in a run. Lamb was yanked into animation, forced to move her feet at this rapid pace or face another close-up with the dirt.

As they tore through the field, sunflowers rotated their heads to watch Lamb pass. Lamb snapped her attention to the woman charging ahead. She wore a brightly coloured dress busy with patterns, and where her dark skin was exposed, it glittered with sweat. This thundering pace was incongruent with her outlandish size.

The lady sensed Lamb's attention and turned to face her without breaking speed.

"Mah name is Adura! It means 'prayer' in Yoruba," and then added as a footnote, "Don't worry, I am not real! I am a reflection of your imagination!"

Lamb's mental inventory fanned with questions about this Prayer Lady but folded when Adura lazied her pace, her thuds slowing to a stop within a perfectly circular clearing, ringed by countless sunflowers staring towards the centre. Here was a wooden cabin so small it would probably function better as a large shed. A chimney sat on top, periodically puffing out miniature clouds like a pipe. It looked comically out of place.

"Come on in and meet Minh!" Letting go of Lamb, Adura led the way, pushing open the wide double doors, which must have been designed to cater for her gigantic frame. Lamb followed. Whatever was going on was out of her control.

III

2

The doors swung shut behind Lamb with a smack as Adura took a seat on an oversized leather couch in the corner, claiming the entire surface area for her own. The tired sofa sagged at her weight; the armrests on either side pushing into her midsection. An ageing East Asian man sat on a skinny stool, scraping a table with a Swiss army knife. This must be Minh. Contrary to Adura's enthusiasm, he did not look up to greet Lamb. There was little space for anything else in this cramped room, but Lamb noted a wooden chair beside a chewy fireplace. She assumed it as hers, taking a seat.

Silence. The fire clicked its language. Minh paused to dust some shavings from his engraving. Lamb looked at Adura. Adura stared back with a vast smile. A memory of Lamb's social anxiety flicked her, but emotionally she felt nothing of the sort. She mentally reopened her list of questions, deciding on the best one to start, but Adura grabbed the air, leaning forward as the leather squeaked against her sweaty skin.

"So, you saw the source code, right? Good and evil and all that jazz?"

Every moment was new information, and Lamb had no time to sharpen her reflections. But, yes, she had seen that. She casually nodded, lost as her mind attempted to piece those dream dots together. Adura responded with one loud clap.

"Excellent! Excellent! Do you know how rare it is for a being to return to physical matter after that type of divine encounter? You have been gifted, Lamb! You have been chosen!"

Lamb was suddenly aware of the present moment, every present moment everywhere, the instance of the now in relation to itself, freezing in place. Her tummy jolted like she was at the top of a rollercoaster, and a scream bubbled into her mouth. But the present resumed its movement into the next moment, and she forcefully exhaled with a high-pitched *cheep*.

"Don't worry about that!" Adura continued. "You're adjusting. But soon, you will be aligned with your new nature. Your superpowers!"

Superpowers. Lamb chuckled at the juvenile idea, and Adura laughed back.

"Sounds ridiculous, nah? Impossible, even. But let me ask you this, precious Lamb. Are you hungry?"

A strange question, but Lamb took a moment to analyse. She shook her head. She was not.

"How surprising, considering it's been 41 days since you jumped off that building."

"41 days?" she choked then shuddered. Lamb didn't like the thought of that laughing building.

"41 days! And now consider that you and I just ran two kilometres in four minutes and 21 seconds under the 30 degrees Celsius Sun. Shouldn't you be hot? Sitting next to a fire like that? Are you tired? Any loss of breath? How's your hangover?"

So many questions. Lamb searched for answers but only got as far as, "Uh ..." before Adura moved on.

"In fact, I'm willing to make a bet wit' you, Lamb. I bet you've never felt as good in your life as you do right now. So? Do we have a bet? Do we?"

Minh stopped his scraping and finally looked up, invested in the response. Lamb's mouth was open as if it, too, was keen to hear what she had to say. What did she have to say? Her body felt revitalised, as if fed and well-rested. Her skin was soft as if soaked in moisturiser, no nag of an itch to be found. The typical assault of splattered information coming from every inanimate object was silent as if someone had discovered the off switch. And the default anxiety of simply being herself had vacated, replaced by a relaxed state she did not know was attainable. The corners of Lamb's mouth curved upward. "No. No bet. You're right. I've never felt so good in my life."

Adura clapped again and shouted with satisfaction. "Ye-ha! And that is only the beginning of our good news, Lamb! Not only are you void of hunger, but you will never be hungry again! Sleep? Psssh! You don't need it! You, mah sweet potato, have touched energy at its core! You are a self-sustaining organism! You replenish yourself merely by existing!"

Adura took a moment to laugh, and Minh returned to his woodwork project. Lamb sucked in an extended breath, seeking contrary evidence but growing acutely aware of her body. Without a doubt, every statement was true. Lamb started to giggle but abruptly ceased with fright when she noticed Adura was no longer amused. The smile was gone as she examined Lamb's face with an intense stern expression.

"You have broken free, Lamb. And now you have a job to do."

III

3

Since the dawn of material manifestation, a war between the frequencies of good and evil has tugged at the ultimate reality, tearing it down the middle. For billions of years, a struggle to dominate the Universe has threatened the balance of the Equation, with spiritual battles clashing throughout every conglomerate of perception. The Earth is no stranger to these conflicts and has been dominated by both the good and the evil at different periods throughout its history.

Ancient holy men were brought forth to assist the fight for the righteous or the wicked. They led with metaphorical tales. These narratives were designed so the average person could digest the abstract war and more easily tune into the trajectory required to nurture the upper hand.

But gradually, humans evolved to favour their minds over their spiritual essence. The thirst for explainable logic throttled the intangible qualities of life. And it was the darker forces that better learned how to manipulate humans on this plane, luring them into deeper materialism using their pleasures as bait.

In recent centuries, the indulgent greed of humankind intensified, and a sinister fluid rotted many bloodlines. The immoral forces on

Earth overpowered every area of authority like a blanket of sin, smothering the goodness beneath poverty and distractions. In turn, the planet is on the brink of irreversible evil.

The rumours of secret societies running the world like puppets are true, seeking to gain complete control of humanity. Mandatory vaccines grant access to DNA strands. Various technologies have been implemented to lower sperm counts as a means of population control. Steps are progressing for a total economic reset to remove property rights from the average civilian. And all of this with the ultimate intention of a single-world government.

Twelve nations built upon intensely concentrated electromagnetic currents are involved in the conversation. The last remaining details to achieve this goal are being drafted as we speak. And once the agreement is finalised, any outside nation who disagrees will be dealt with using severe border restrictions and starvation of trade.

In an urgent final move, the dregs of Good Energy have initiated twelve drives, one which includes the enlightenment of you, Lamb, as a mighty prophet for the new age. Your Dharmic Calling is to interrupt these nefarious plans, taking down these leading governments to prevent complete unionisation, and restoring order in the Equation. Otherwise, the entirety of humanity will be eternally locked into the slavery of evil.

III

4

Lamb struggled to receive Adura's perplexing handover, snatching phrases from the air to build a cohesive picture, imagining herself within that context. When Adura finally paused, leaning forward expectantly, Lamb blurted out her only thought:

"I don't see how never eating and never sleeping is going to save the world, Prayer Lady."

Adura's features froze. For a second Lamb thought the delusion was shattered and she was about to wake up in bed. Not so, as Adura's sudden laughter howled from her flabby frame, slapping her thigh, Lamb's observation evidently the funniest thing she'd ever heard.

"Oh no no hahaha!" she boomed, and the cabin shook. "No! Call me Adura! And, of course you don't see that! Not yet, anyway! That is why Minh is here. Minh, care to join us?"

Minh paused his carving. He adjusted his posture and then stabbed his knife into the tabletop, stuck standing upright. Lamb didn't care for the dramatics of this performance. But Minh did not notice her reaction, continuing his theatrics by turning his head to the wall as if daydreaming straight through it into a world gone by. After a deep sigh, Minh spoke.

III

5: MINH'S STORY

I, like you, was a nobody.
My physical form was squeezed out in Vietnam, 1473.
Ejected and rejected by a mother who never loved me.
A lost child, suckling on the rice of strangers, I wandered the darkest
alleys as soon as my legs could prop my torso upright.
I lied, I stole, I was beaten for my crimes.
But I survived.

Every day was the same, until the day it wasn't.
Avoiding myself on the ripe, darkening streets of Hội An,
My thumb and index were caught harvesting fish flesh from a bone that
was not mine.
A chase of swords aimed for my neck, but this fear was not new.
Even with an empty belly, my running was too nimble for most to track.
When you have nothing to lose, you do not fear the hooves of horses or
concealment in the shadows of a sleeping household.

But fate is fickle, and luck is finite,
I veered, slowed by stairs unseen,

Trapped on a roof too tall for foolish decisions,
Bloodthirsty blades shouting up the steps behind.

It was no longer a matter of escape,
It was a choice of my preferred manner of death.

I, like you, was a nobody.
And, like you, I leapt towards an immediate pain to outmanoeuvre extended torture.
And, like you, I did not succumb to death's promises,
Instead, I was reborn, carrying prizes beyond the richest man in Asia.

The human mind, for all its intellect, brims with more stupidity than anything in the Universe,
My reawakening revealed my thoughts knew only what they were taught,
Yet the emotion of my spirit accessed the collective knowledge of the ancients,
And future wisdom too.

My Dharmic Calling unveiled itself unhurriedly, like a lotus awakening in the autumn change.
Without the familiar urge of hunger, my mission was confusing,
But I returned to past habits, for I knew nothing else.
Pinpointing the easiest of victims, established through decades of floundering and reward.
But an unfamiliar voice swirled beneath my sternum,
Providing instructions that blared red warnings within my mental realm,
And nudged me through an unignorable purpose of undiluted intuition.

I found myself taking whatever I wanted, with an instinct for the precise moment to move undetected.
And the deeper I trusted my stomach,
The more intricately these gestures responded,
Until I left Hội An with a horse pulling a carriage of treasure behind.

Tell me this story before my fall, and I would envision a Minh of great happiness,
But the voice in my stomach matured to scold me.
Its ability to foreknow success from failure evolved to discern right from wrong,
And my wicked ways fuelled the flames of my moral suffering.

I learned to stack the good feelings of other people on top of my greed,
And I, in turn, felt good.
I obeyed the arrows that enhanced the better path,
And I fed the hungry,
And I clothed the naked,
Dedicated to satisfying the righteous course that grew wider and more obvious with every triumph.

Unlike my decades of offence and anonymity,
My expanding reputation was revered by the people.
Likened to Confucius or even the Buddha.
I was welcomed as a wise man who held the secret keys to a godlike awareness,
For no matter the question placed before me,
My gut balanced the options and regurgitated the immediate answer from a holier soul.
And I was never wrong.

Yet my achievements were akin to smelling the same flower every day,
Rich and rewarding at first,
But quickly devolving into a mundane activity, yearning for paint beyond the frame.

I retreated to a cramped cave where I lay for 25 days,
Devoid of material distractions,
Only conversing with that inner voice,
Asking questions,
Interpreting yes or no responses through sensations.

I, like you, learned about the energies at war,

The scales of good and bad,
Virtue's fabric forever threatened by a spreading dark stain.

These abstractions compressed into readable engravings,
Events were taking place in foreign lands unknown to me,
Occurrences hidden beneath the distortion of a man you know by the
name of Jesus.

Whispers of this holy figure had long fluttered from boats through our
country.
But the growth of outside spiritual ideas blurred over the seas.
In this cave, I breathed air untainted by the European boots that kicked
our doors two decades later.
Yet here, long before, my hands held the seeds of Christ,
Speaking to me,
Detailing personalities who had twisted his scripture to nurture evil in
their being.

And then my insides settled on one individual making decisions that
endangered the trajectory of the Divine Good.

Born under the Crown of Aragon, this evil man stood as the head of a
spiritual organisation with an influence that towered above anything
I'd sensed in Vietnam.
I dwelled on his presence.
Through my inner eye, I witnessed his manipulation that strengthened
his family's fortune and his stronghold on the Catholic people.
I glimpsed through walls where sexual depravity was demanded with
fifty women or more.
I grasped his forthcoming plans to dig his fingers of power into the soil
of the New World by enslaving natives using the shackles of Christian-
ity.
And as I watched, I heard the essence of Jesus weep.

My Dharmic Calling cleared like mud settling at the bottom of an un-
disturbed vase.
This man was the Pope of the Devil,

And my Dharmic Calling demanded I interrupt his reign.

Without hesitation, I stood. I walked.
I heeded my internal navigation, which found me a horse that galloped me to a sampan boat.
I spoke the exact order of words required for the owner to willingly gift me his vessel, and I sailed into the infinity of the wet horizon.

Now, the history scribes will boast of travels between continents,
But every pen stroke will skip over my name,
Out of necessity,
And out of ignorance,
Because they did not know,
Because they would not believe it if they did.

Six months I sailed.
I knew the exact direction because my Dharmic Calling felt satisfaction when I faced it,
And crumpled when I glanced away.
I slipped through shortcuts that no map knows, even today.
I evaded murderous waves.
I caught the most favourable winds.
I never slept.
I never ate.
My skin was never burnt by the Sun, nor trembled by the Moon.
Six months I sailed.
And I thought only of that man.

The wooden boat I called my friend for so long slid onto the Papal States' soil,
And I continued on foot,
The first East Asian feet to meet Europe beyond any records would speak.
Yet my alien face provoked no dismay as I knew where to turn and where not to look,
My brisk pace brushing unaware shoulders, merging with the wind, never-seen.

Whisking into Rome, never-seen.
Whisking into Vatican City, never-seen.
Whisking through a window in the Apostolic Palace, never-seen.

And then I was seen.

A guard halted me, hand on hilt, but motions mimicking a stone,
A human facing a human, both unlike any human they'd met before.
His tongue tripped over itself, stammering a language of which I recognised not a syllable.
In a bright stab of panic, my mind nearly took the reigns of the situation,
But I honoured my gut, permitting the Dharmic Calling to play my strings.

I employed my right and wrong intuition, yes and no instinctual responses.
I constructed sounds on my breath and shaped these with my mouth.
When a minute movement in my articulation sparked discomfort, I shifted vowels.
Noises left my lips, harmonising into a language I did not understand.
But the guard understood.
He responded, I responded.
His face softened, and he stepped out of my way.
I will never know what I said to that man, but it was the perfect thing I could say to continue my mission.

My spirit guided me to a small brown bottle in a drawer in a room.
I was steered to the kitchen next.
The eyes were plentiful, but I avoided most and made mouth sounds when unavoidable.
I locked a man in a cupboard because I had to.
I emptied the bottle into a bubbling pot of soup.

My gut exhaled with euphoria.
It was a congratulation that I had completed my Dharmic Calling.
I wandered from the palace with a mixture of emotions,
The syrupy taste of achievement,

But the sour sense of purpose lost.

I shortly felt drunk, bouncing from walls as the Sun set on the city of
Rome,
Where people perceived me,
Shouted names at me,
And beat me to death.
But the murder of me was the murder of a victorious man.

For I now know as I knew then, that I had ended the life of a wicked ruler
whose deeds propelled the triumph of evil.
My action caused his body to swell and deform,
A corpse as blackened as the soul that had left it.

I had fought in the Universal war of justice versus sin.
I had won my battle.
And while my name blew away from the material world like sand,
My mark on the energetic timeline is forever recorded as one of tremen-
dous moral rebalance.

III

6

Minh plucked his knife and resumed whittling away at the table. Lamb remained shushed, ensuring Minh's story was complete before reacting.

"That was beautiful. How did you learn to speak English so well?"

Minh's hand stopped. He looked up in annoyance.

"I'm not speaking English!" he spat before returning to his project, shaking his head.

Lamb did not understand and looked to Adura for answers. Adura's smile had reappeared.

"Do you see, Lamb? Minh possessed the insight of the whole Universe. He could calculate the ideal next move by simply tuning into his emotions, surrendering to the faith where his inner energy communicated with the external energy. And together, they guided him to his best fate."

Lamb knew what was coming. Like the rolling of a wheel, the comprehension in her stomach mobilised with Adura's words, churning signals of approval to her every fibre.

"That's right, Lamb. You feel it. You cradle that same insight. You previously glimpsed through the shell and found that every object has its own unique personality. But this is a primitive perception! You have now sunk deeper into life's fundamental building blocks and can connect with the identities from a subatomic viewpoint. Congratulations, you have earned the ability to navigate reality through the calls of electron divinity!

"The Christos energy was dormant inside you, Lamb, but it has been unleashed. It is the compass to infallible decision-making. The contemplation of every right choice vibrates with positivity, while every incorrect choice plummets to discomfort!" Adura's speech accelerated, her voice growing louder with excitement. "Your mind is nothing but a platform of interpretation! You cannot trust its judgement because it runs on deterministic principles! You must shut it down, Lamb! Shut it down! Do not identify with this wet lump of organic material! You must rediscover yourself as the spiritual electricity exuding from your physical manifestation! You must uncover your Dharmic Calling!"

The vigour of Adura's display set Lamb's organs ablaze. Her mind flooded with colour. Adura's body was shimmering purple. Minh was translucent. Lamb attempted to blink it away to no avail. Instead, Adura was on her feet so fast that the cabin swayed, detonating her final sentences like a bomb.

"The Universal Equation weighs heavy from darkness, and it wobbles in fear! You have been chosen, sweet Lamb! The supreme energy of the Good has called forth your person! You must usher in the female-led Age of Aquarius! You must rectify this lopsidedness! The Holiest of Spirits has been summoned inside of you! The Karmatic composure of Vishnu! The Maitreya enlightenment of the Buddha! The very Christos Atman! *Jesus*, Lamb! *Jesus!*"

Lamb inhaled with an elated quiver. Her blood bubbled with delight. Her heart glowed pink. Her tailbone elevated from the couch until nothing but her big toes skimmed the floor, and only just. Her arms were outstretched further than her fingers knew how to reach. The cabin shook violently. Her irises flickered from dark green to light grey. Reality hummed like a thousand-piece choir harmonising in perfect pitch. Splinters of wood rained from the ceiling. The fire formed the shape of a shark, swimming in motion. Minh stood. Adura glided forward. They spoke in unison.

"THE IDENTICAL ENERGY THAT GALVANISED CHRIST LIVES INSIDE

OF YOU! THE IDENTICAL ENERGY THAT GALVANISED CHRIST LIVES INSIDE OF YOU! THE IDENTICAL ENERGY THAT GALVANISED CHRIST LIVES INSIDE OF YOU!"

Lamb's gaze fell to the table where Minh had engraved a perfect negative outline of Jesus' face. He'd drawn it upside down, facing her. It was the spitting image of what came to her during her fall, and Lamb cried out, "MY LORD!"

With a hard-cut click, Adura vanished, Minh vanished, the cabin and everything in it vanished. Lamb gently floated down to the spongy dirt below, straightening her spine and crossing her legs until her backside nestled comfortably into a meditation position. It was raining. The surrounding sunflowers bowed to Lamb until their faces pressed flat into the muddying ground. And there she remained, silently communicating with the raw source for over two days, without language, without a heartbeat, without getting wet, without a hair moving in the wind.

The Sun roared on the third morning, and at 6am the details of Lamb's enlightenment and Dharmic Calling were finalised. Her circulatory system whirred back into operation, and she extended her legs, standing and then walking southwest as her intuitive vitality advised. Each sunflower she passed rose on its stem, turning to watch her leave and then withering as she abandoned their field.

"Behold, I send you forth as sheep in the midst of wolves: be ye therefore wise as serpents, and harmless as doves."

MATTHEW 10:16

Chapter IV:
The Gospel
According
to Teddy

IV

0

Teddy Charles Stuart accidentally set fire to the tip of his spliff. Swiftly huffing it out, he followed with two quick sucks, then a pinch to the cherry, tumbling down the drain. That was enough to achieve the desired buzz. Gone were the marathons of smoking his brain out to dribbling vacancy. If anyone asked, Teddy was a marijuana *user* now, not an abuser. Just a little puff-puff and exclusively at night. Only once the day had no more to offer, nothing to destroy.

Employing great care, Teddy reentered his house. He had never woken his parents during one of his smoke breaks and intended to keep it that way. Thankfully, the weed made him hyper-alert, clicking the door closed so slowly that no one would hear it, even if they were standing right beside him. Calculating every soft step, the house itself seemed unaware, not a creak of betrayal as Teddy stealthily slipped back into his bedroom with a drumming heart and a light head but an relieved exhale all the same.

The subsequent routine played out like a worn cassette. Teddy ensured his curtains touched without a separation slit. It was a thin but secure barrier between his privacy and the meddling street beyond. He removed his trousers, seating his bare bottom upon his chair's cool artificial leather. His VPN threw his online identity to the Netherlands, and he switched his speakers off to avoid past mistakes. Without a conscious thought, he toyed with his floppy self while rapid-firing incognito browser tabs for any thumbnail that sparked intrigue, closing them just as quickly when a video did not adequately tickle his dopamine sacks.

Teddy was a connoisseur of the domination of the female body, but recently he'd developed a keen taste for contrast between performers. A row of black men taking turns violating a lone white girl. An anorexic-looking female almost crushed by an obese man. A schoolgirl dress-up pretending to be horny as she went down on a moaning grandpa. Polarised aesthetics. Something beautiful defiled to make it ugly. It was the only thing that worked for him these days.

Like a speedy surgeon, Teddy expertly manoeuvred between alluring thumbnails and streaming sexual organs. Click click click, then pause. Some growth, some chemical rouse, and then nope, off again, clicking down the filthy hole of obscenities, thirsty for something new, something unusual.

Teddy did not find what he was looking for, not tonight. But the accumulation of fleshy exhibitions was enough to simulate a hardening, and he got the job done to some average interracial threesome. The experience was dull, and the post-process was apt: a muted sense of shame while wiping up that gross after-mess with only himself to blame.

This habitual process played a part in a far larger ritual. Pornography was a tool, Teddy thought, one to clear out the biological drive for sex, now free to consider more pressing issues. Teddy replaced his trousers, then navigated to The Red Pill Nation forum, entering his password. This was a place of serious analysis. It was Teddy's passion. His obsession.

He skimmed the front page for any unread threads. There were some new conversations but nothing of notable substance and he sighed, yearning for what The Nation had been just over a month ago. Teddy's unwashed hand absentmindedly retrieved a pack of salted crisps from a drawer and split them open. It was a small bag. He was trying to lose weight.

Teddy had signed up to The Red Pill Nation five years ago. It was affectionately remembered as The Awakening Era, the beginning of the end. His pursuit was to uncover the truth buried beneath the 9/11 attacks. At that time, the community was small but proud. They boasted a few hundred members, but there were roughly 20 fiercely active accounts who perpetually connected dots to offer fresh theories daily. Teddy, known as ShadowAgentMaster15, was a spectator in those early days, forever digging into truths so few of the public knew yet that were so apparent to him. Every major world event was a staged scheme to remove freedoms from the ordinary civilian. The mainstream media and history books were fabrications designed to control our minds. And the entire show was run by a powerful elite Brotherhood who thrived on the blood of children, aiming to rule the planet as a singular one-world government.

As ShadowAgentMaster15's education advanced, his confidence grew, proposing theories of his own, sourcing news articles that were blatantly the work of the Brotherhood attempting to manipulate the narrative in their favour, wrecking Teddy's country in the process. ShadowAgentMaster15's reputation grew, as did The Red Pill Nation, users trickling in, ideas shared between a warm and receptive community despite the harrowing nature of their material.

But when Paedogate tore through the curtain and into the general public's awareness 44 days ago, everything changed. The Red Pill Nation was bombarded with hits, thousands of new profiles frantically seeking answers. Original members, including ShadowAgentMaster15, did their best to share information with the newly opened eyes, explaining how they foresaw this day, and that they were weeks, if not days, away from the total collapse of society as they knew it. The gig was up, and the demonic rulers were on the verge of complete exposure. Their next move would be unpredictable but drastic, and readers were advised to stock up on weapons, water, and non-perishable goods. Several meeting points were established in the likely event of a complete loss of digital communication.

Five weeks came and went. The panicked hype lost much of its enthusiasm, the initial bout of frenzied defence now worn from the wait. The world did not accept the authorities' blanket denial of Paedogate until the release of an extensive probe that illustrated how the crime photos were edited from their originals. Government investigators supplied censored photographs of the 'authentic' child abuse content, along with separate images from where the heads of notable figures were photoshopped, merged together to create compelling portrayals that framed innocent people.

The collection was convincing enough, and the vast majority of the world swallowed it—happy to accept anything that allowed them to turn away from the horror and resume their day. The Red Pill Nation's membership numbers plummeted, but the core crew were unmoved. They dedicated days to tracing the history of the government-issued celebrity images, for if these did not exist *before* the Paedogate leak, then this new collection was certainly the digitally manipulated imagery, hastily put together *after* the event. Frustratingly, the Nation's quest proved that many of the Paedogate photos were, in fact, fake. However, they could not verify a large percentage of them and so the conspiracy, while weakened, marched on.

Priorities changed a week after the government released their evidence. A team of cyber police, the likes of which the internet had never seen, raided the web with such force that computers shook. Every site that had hosted the material was wiped clear off the web. Hundreds of arrests were made. Associated credit cards were frozen. And new laws were slapped forward in multiple countries that would allow for far more intrusive surveillance to ensure nothing like this happened again.

Talk about a truth-seeker nightmare forecast coming true. The child abuse scandal was merely a detail of the wider narrative, but the genuine dominoes of catastrophe were falling into a circular trap around the sleeping masses, a suffocating box that was only shrinking. As The Red Pill Nation scrambled their thoughts together to formulate a plan, many primary contributors vanished. Perhaps they were caught hosting Paedogate images. Others possibly abandoned ship out of fear. But these disappearances only fueled those who knew The Truth: that the end of the world was not coming. It was already here.

Teddy's stoned meditations zigzagged through muddled haziness and then returned to his screen. He had started to write a post but only managed two opening sentences, which read, *"Wake up, children of the Nation! Remove your compromised headsets and look outside for the first time with open eyes!"* Teddy had no idea where he was going with this—he didn't recall writing it—but a nervous foam unsettled his gut. Was he being watched like the others? If he looked outside, would someone be looking back at him?

Without any sudden movements, Teddy steadily swivelled his chair until he was staring at his curtain. There was a presence behind it, he was sure. Listening. Waiting for the perfect moment to strike. It was only a matter of time. He stood up, aware of his chair's squeak, threatening to expose him, warning his watchers away. The crisps fluttered in his stomach as he took light steps towards the curtain until his nose touched the material. His mouth was as dry as toast. He wanted to yell, but he dared not even breathe. His mind counted to three. One ... two ... *three!* He yanked back the curtain to uncover nothing but the dark street outside, a single street lamp flickering as if winking at his paranoia.

The lamp's shimmers were erratic like it was speaking Morse code. Teddy found it hypnotic, actually enjoying the moment. His previous distress seeped out of his body, replaced by a calm humour. He could be so skittish sometimes, and he chuckled as he blamed the weed. The lamp died to darkness. This liberated Teddy from the exchange; nothing more to learn here. A wave of peace lapped over him, and he found this as joyous as he did puzzling. Why did he feel so wonderful?

A lady entered the scene outside. She moved forward with a fixed stare, like she had somewhere important to go, yet striding at a pace indicating no rush to get there. Teddy instinctively grabbed the curtains, eager to sever this moment but, before he did, he noticed she was barefoot and he found this odd enough to pause. His eyes washed up her female body to note her baggy and unkempt dungarees, and then he squinted to try to see her face. The street lamp must have heard his call, for as soon she passed below, its expired bulb flicked back on with drastic brightness, illuminating her features as she marched by. Blood rushed to Teddy's eyeballs, and he swore they zoomed in on a girl more exquisite-looking than any he'd seen on the internet. He drew in a quick, shaky gasp as a warm glow flushed through his system, and his fingers prickled numb. Despite his strong personal convictions, he was certain this was an angel. Teddy shoved his window open, and without hesitation, he called out, "Aye! Where yer going?"

IV

THE GOSPEL ACCORDING TO TEDDY, THE FIRST DAY

At twelve past midnight, eighteen hours and thirty minutes after the sunflowers, the Scott Monument stretched upwards seven inches as Lamb entered New Town. Each footstep was the precise distance and pacing as the one before, and like the hours adding up, her vitality only increased. The passing material world noted her ethereal aura. Falkland Palace had clenched its bricks so tightly that they groaned. Forth Bridge had swayed such distances that it made the news. But nobody noticed Lamb because she did not want them to.

Edinburgh was different, like some metaphysical cloak dissolving in the night's cold. Several light sleepers sat up in their beds and clicked on their lamps, aware of a change but unable to articulate it to their stirring partners. A homeless drunk ceased his shouts to watch Lamb pass, the alcohol vaporising from his bloodstream, suddenly sober for the first time in three years and never to drink again. But nobody had directly approached her until Teddy.

"Aye! Where yer going?"

Lamb heard the boy's voice and consulted with her gut. Her assignment immediately took precedence, and she did not break stride. Her footsteps tapped out into the Scottish atmosphere, but their steady beat was shortly inaudible beneath the growing pounds of much larger boots, doubling her tempo to close the distance.

"Aye, 'scuse me! Sorry, dinnae mean tae be a bother, but I spied ye from my windae, and had to come talk to ye." The boy was panting yet speaking in a rush, heavily accented words peaking and falling over his breath like a ball in the ocean. "I'm Teddy, and what might yer name be? It's very late, ye know. Where might we be going?"

Like a crooked painting, Lamb sensed something was off about the boy. But her electrical instinct knew it would regret being rude, and there was no harm in a brief dialogue if she did not waver off course.

"My name is Lamb. And I'm walking to London to kill Tami Theron."

Teddy was swallowing spit to lubricate his dry throat, only to cough at these absurd words.

"Tami Theron? As in Prime Minister, Tami Theron?" Teddy chortled.

"Yes."

"Alright, I'm listening. And how do ye reckon you're going to do all that, then?"

"I'll know when I get there."

Teddy paused, allowing Lamb to step ahead. She was surely joking, or at least insane. But there was another thing. An ambience about her so powerfully concrete that it blessed him with a sense of bright elation. As she strode away, an emptiness swelled in his chest, and he wanted to cry. Teddy quickly rushed to her side.

"Aye, that's cool. Yeah, I hate her too. The whole stinking government is nothing but demonic puppets. I actually know a lot about this, mind. Paedophiles, the whole lot of 'em."

Lamb nodded, her face in deep thought. Teddy liked that. Maybe they were on the same page.

"Ye know, there are faster ways to London. Ye could take a train in the morning, lass! Is, like, four hours. Or you could grab a taxi if ye minted," Teddy laughed again.

"I must go how I go," she responded.

Teddy enjoyed these cryptics. They accentuated her intrigue. He inspected her caramel skin and blinked when he noticed faint rainbow swirls pulsating from her pores like oil in water. His light head tottered his feet, and he momentarily forgot how to walk. Lamb didn't notice and instead took a right down a dark street.

"Oh no, ye dinnae want to go down here," Teddy warned. "This is Stu Forbes' road. I cannae even count how many times he's left his gate open and his dogs rush out nipping people. He's famous for it. I'm no jokes, it's best we go 'round."

"This is the direction I walk," Lamb responded without emotion, which shushed Teddy. He felt a little hurt by her dismissal, and a darkness in him hoped the dogs would come out to fight. Then she'd see he was right. And if he could prevent a bite, then he could be the hero.

As it so happened, Stu Forbes had forgotten to close his gate that night, and three staunch bull terriers mixed with something else came ripping toward the sounds of strangers. Teddy immediately regretted not emphasising his point, or at least hanging back. These dogs' intentions went far beyond defence. Their barks greased their teeth. Their snouts torpedoed from the property, set to harm.

In a panic, Teddy turned into a speedy side-step motion, moving ahead of Lamb. Lamb appeared oblivious to the threat. "Run!" he screamed, now several feet away from Lamb. The dogs were closing in on her. Teddy looked around for a stick but was blinded by fright. His imagination played visions of this lady getting mauled to a bloody pulp, scarring his psyche for the rest of his life.

With salivating jaws clapping seconds away, Lamb got the message and paused her stride for the first time since the field. She turned to face the dogs, and they skidded to a stop in unison, quietly lying down at her feet. Lamb realigned to her initial direction and resumed walking. The dogs skipped to their paws and flanked her, two on one side, one on the other.

The four strolled past Teddy, whose mouth gaped like a cartoon character. He joined the crew in silence, and their steps continued down the street as the only sound for minutes while Teddy struggled to formulate how to ask what had just happened. He was intimidated, borderline fearful, his thoughts of an authentic angel reverberating on a loop.

Lamb sensed and disliked the energy it brought to her world. She sighed, deciding to defuse the situation by unleashing unreserved honesty from her gut.

"Do not be afraid, Teddy; you have found favour with God. The Universe is a replicated electron that relies on an internalised system of balance. Every person born, and indeed every plant that grows or molecules that combine, are a direct response to maintaining cosmic cooperation.

"Currently, our planet sways at a precarious juncture where the evils of man weigh too heavy on the collective soul. Out of necessity, a rectification has spawned, like it has so many times before. Abraham, Moses, Buddha, Muhammad, and Jesus. These were not individual men. They were a potent energy summoned whenever harmony was threatened and required a hefty push to restore stability. It's a progressive lineage of the Holy Spirit. And I, Lamb, am but one of those pieces merely chosen to carry the soul of grand rectification."

Teddy's mind whizzed, and Lamb paused to let it do so. Usually, the conversation of religious theology repulsed Teddy. His self-proclaimed 'scientific mind' had no space for manipulated mythology. But everything this radiant being said was delivered with such pleasant conviction that he felt ill-equipped to object.

"So, are ye telling me every religion is the same, then?" he finally queried, and Lamb responded with the details presented from her stomach to her mind.

"Religions are compartmentalisations of worship developed around the notion of spiritual rebalance. Their differences are imperative to the justifications of their existence; otherwise, their substance would fall redundant. However, they are unified by serving the identical purpose: to modernise spirituality and keep wandering morals from straying too far from the glory of Yahweh, The One God who goes by many other names."

Teddy's atheism winced. "So yer telling me God exists?"

Lamb smiled. "I tell you nothing. You tell yourself everything."

A soft pattering turned Teddy's head to notice a cat had joined them, following close behind Lamb's ankles.

IV

THE GOSPEL ACCORDING TO TEDDY,
THE SECOND DAY

The Sun sliced through the Scottish chill not long before Lamb crossed into Lauder town. During the night, her passing aura had impregnated a handful of new energies. The team now boasted four dogs, five cats, a fox, an insomniac widower named Ralph and a meth addict who called herself Buttons. Everyone kept up the velocity, pulled along by Lamb's wisdom, an everflowing faucet of enlightenment.

And then there was Teddy, magnetised to Lamb's side. Each hour that passed he yearned to be closer, an intense desire that overwhelmed him with such euphoria he could hardly withstand it. Having walked 40-odd kilometres would exhaust anyone, but Teddy's body cooed with a refreshed bounce. He should be starving by now, but love filled his belly. Talk of sleep or food never took place, as everyone felt the same.

Lamb's teachings continued, her students absorbing her light like germinating seeds.

"The Universe is best represented by the perfect Equation $1 = 1$, staring itself in the eye. But Yahweh, the One True God is not inactive.

He is The Creator. Hence, He initiated the space for imperfections, introducing elements to progress the Equation, for example, *1 = 2*. The formula has evolved, yet it is illogical and crooked, tearing into reality as we know it. Hence, order is restored by developing the initial viewpoint, perhaps *1 + 1 = 2*. Harmony is re-established.

"But if advancement is the objective, it makes more sense for an overcompensation of balance, whereby, perhaps, *1 + 2 = 2*. The seesaw shifts, no longer vulnerable on one end but fast tumbling upon the other. Quickly, it must grow if it wishes to remain valid and does so by piling further gain onto the other side, such as *1 + 2 = 3 + 2*. The Equation has surged forward in detail and avoided one-sided collapse, yet intentionally remains unstable to expand further."

"The rapid multiplication of the Equation has blazed on for billions upon billions of years and has turned electrons into molecules, and molecules into tissue into humans. Our very free will is dependent on the disruption of the Equation, whereby the eternal struggle between right and wrong is a fluctuating design of asymmetry, achieving harmony and then back again."

"But the Equation is a total mess right now, yeah?" Buttons interjected. Teddy turned in annoyance but noticed that she looked nourished, far healthier than when she joined, fully aware and not picking at her healing scabs. "That's why you're here? To fix the world?"

"I am here to solve a particularly intricate problem within the Equation, yes. Those in power have overstepped the mark, and the Equation has chosen me to correct that. It is my Dharmic Calling. But please remember that I am just another variable in the formula with the purpose of rebalance, just like everything. Sometimes, those who contribute significant changes may appear of higher value, but this is untrue. Removing the tiniest cog from the biggest clock threatens the entirety of the operation. The formula is dependent on even the seemingly most insignificant zeros and ones. Your existence, and indeed the existence of every atom, is crucial. For without every component functioning as it should, the Equation would fall to pieces. Your Dharmic Calling is required, and that is why you are here. It is a streamlined operation. God does not make mistakes, nor does he work with excess."

The town of Lauder was waking up and for most residents it would be a defining day in their history. By the time Lamb's feet had passed

Thirlestane Castle Caravan Park, 16 early risers had left their homes, often abandoning their sleeping family, joining the walk. No one could explain nor felt the need to. It wasn't something they questioned. They looked out their windows where Lamb was leading a group, and they dropped whatever they were doing and shuffled into the expedition wearing whatever they were wearing. Happy faces welcomed them as they breathed in Lamb's new words while catching up on her old ones.

An hour before noon, seven stones fell from Dryburgh Abbey's roof, hitting the ground at the same moment, but nobody would ever know of it. A follower counted 65 heads and estimated as many animals more. A swarm of bees quietly buzzed above. A lone bee dared to descend, and Lamb received the insect on the tip of her index finger. The excited murmur of the crowd hushed as Lamb resumed her sermon. Teddy had sourced a pen and paper and was scribbling down what he could. Some charitable people assumed the role of whispering keywords to ears further back struggling to hear everything.

"The bee is an appropriate example of the system of which we speak. Here is a pocket of awareness, a concentrated viewpoint just as we all are. But the bee, as a singular unit, harnesses minimal power. Even its greatest defence is an act of suicide. What use is protection if it kills the one that uses it? Hence, while we can observe this bee as a solo being, it is not. On every level, including its biological evolutions, it is a piece of a puzzle for the larger process.

"The genuine unit of this insect is the hivemind of the swarm above. They exist for the survival of the collective, a system built upon a queen who alone lays the eggs that, in turn, keep the swarm thriving. It is a system dependent on every component.

"Yet the picture grows the further back we step. Bees harvest nectar from our plant life, carrying pollen across the lands, allowing plants to reproduce, assisting healthy crops and increasing genetic diversity. Indeed, a substantial portion of Earth's ecosystem depends on insect activity. The Good Energy of nature has evolved to include these tiny creatures as vital building blocks.

"We may define this bee on my finger as a separate physical entity, or we may define the swarm as a unified measurement, but in reality, everything is but a smaller brick to a growing structure—a structure which may appear bigger in design but will topple like a tower of playing cards without the fundamental strengths below.

"We are part of the system, the Equation of Yahweh. Is there not a greater process at work if we depend on water and sunshine and the pollination from bees to survive? The most powerful human in the world is mercy to a beating heart. And what is organic tissue if not the procedure of molecular bonding? Particles such as the electron are the very root of our existence. We have evolved from an electromagnetic field birthing itself through itself, which is a system dependent on whichever systems birthed that before. Indeed, to say everything is equal is not some romantic, spiritual philosophy. It is the ultimate truth on a subatomic plane and below."

That evening the Sun painted the sky purple as it said goodbye, and the hundreds of heads appreciated the miracle of life in the dreamy fog they inhaled from Lamb's presence. Together, they crossed the scenic border into England, fingers absentmindedly stroking the Carter Bar boundary stone as they passed through, leaving thin streaks of orange across its surface. New people joined, sometimes pulling their cars over to accompany the mission on foot. Many of the earliest followers had not eaten that day, yet no one slowed Lamb's stride, matching her pace for 12 hours or more. Perhaps it's no surprise then that small whispers began to mention hunger and fatigue. But pieces of bread were shared, and everyone kept going, marching on into the night, energised by their leader whom they now referred to as Mother Lamb.

IV

THE GOSPEL ACCORDING TO TEDDY,
THE THIRD DAY

The boundless fields disappeared in the darkness. The countless pin-pricks of stars only competed with occasional headlights driving up to the back of the crowd and then switching off. Sunshine unhurriedly returned over the small Ridsdale village, and only by daybreak could the people see how their numbers had multiplied, estimated around three hundred strong.

Photos of the crowd and the message of Lamb first circulated, then dominated social media feeds. The mainstream media caught on and, as the UK turned to their televisions that morning, only this story was granted airtime. Apparently, the Second Coming had arrived. It was a female, and she was walking to London with an army to kill the Prime Minister. The sharper journalists connected their reports to the woman who had jumped off a building and vanished beneath the tar those weeks ago. What should have sounded terrifying or at least absurd was instead met with enthusiasm. Lamb's face and her teachings were enough for people to understand that this was a defining moment. They wished to be a part of it. People craved change.

Lamb's miracles were best demonstrated by the resilience of the marching bodies behind her. There were people from Lauder who had walked for over 80 kilometres straight with only a slice of bread in their bellies. However, the journey took its toll, and some individuals had to sleep. Whenever passing a small hotel, many surrendered to exhaustion, filling rooms or crashing on the lawn outside. They'd enter a deep slumber of rejuvenation and then awake several hours later, squirming in agony from a void in their souls, wailing for their Mother Lamb, frantic to rejoin the herd.

Only Teddy appeared unaffected, never more than six feet away from Lamb, ready to scrawl upon his paper when she spoke, or asking questions when she was silent. He had close to a hundred pages already, which he kept in a plastic bag he'd found stuck to a fence just as he needed it. Whenever a newcomer requested, Teddy could read Lamb's teachings back, although he would not allow anyone to touch the documentation. As far as Teddy was concerned, he was Lamb's first apostle and no one could take that role away from him.

This position felt threatened when Xen Ro arrived.

15-year-old Xen joined The Way of the Lamb not far from Jedburgh and elbowed forward with immense thirst, getting closer to the leader until she could hear every word first-hand. The longer she stayed in Lamb's gravitational space, the more confident she became, occasionally asking questions that Lamb was happy to answer even if they bothered Teddy.

Eventually Teddy addressed Xen quietly, requesting that the girl direct any queries to him first so he could relay existing information to her. He said he wanted to avoid repeated teachings, making space for new gospel only. Xen appeared to agree in gesture, but in her heart she had no interest in this boundary. Her questions were secondary to the heavenly feeling she acquired when exchanging words with the Holy Mother.

The tension between these two personalities amplified as the hours went by, and even in the silence, Lamb noticed it like a nagging hum of bad energy subtly sparring behind her. The conflict came to a head when Teddy started to preach to Xen as if he were the prophet, spreading the word of The Red Pill Nation. With a condescending smirk, he explained that the government enforced control using what's called a 'problem–reaction–solution' model. How it worked was that the authorities would introduce a crisis that would provoke fear in civilians. These same figures would then propose a solution that promised great relief to the masses, yet by its very design would remove many freedoms until the whole world was under their thumb. Teddy provided various examples of these mechanics in action, from terrorist attacks to wars to pandemics. According to Teddy, it was all unmistakably obvious once you knew what he knew.

Xen was unconvinced. She countered, stating that problems arise from pure statistics. Things cannot possibly go right all the time, and disastrous events will inevitably occur simply out of the nature of chance. She went on to defend the government's proposed solutions because problem-solving was quite literally their job. If one were to believe Teddy's theory, there was no room for random disasters to occur, and furthermore, he would prefer a government did nothing whenever these problems arise.

Xen then mused that if there was indeed a plot to remove freedoms, those authorities were failing tremendously. Her argument touched upon unprecedented modern communication of knowledge thanks to the internet and ever-minimising location-based hindrances, with sky travel bringing nations only hours away from each other. Xen concluded that as a minority female, equality of freedom had never been better and Teddy's theories merely exposed his ignorant white male cisgender heterosexual privileges.

Teddy was livid and accused Xen of being a little girl fast asleep. Xen turned to Lamb, requesting she end their argument so they could move on in peace. Lamb's insides had already formulated the answer, and she immediately passed it on.

"Neither of you would be satisfied with the truth, for you are not seeking answers but confirmation of your convictions. The facts are multifaceted, with some truth in everything, yet nothing fully comprehended by one mind. Yet here you are, two barking brains, each trained by its chosen reading material until you are so certain of your self-proclaimed superiority that you do not pause to realise that your brain has no reference point of what another brain might be thinking. The instant you judge someone is the instant you misunderstand the requirement of every opinion, which is to balance the Equation.

"However, I shall grant you a prompt to assist future guidance. When you feel that rising fire, wishing to convince someone else of your stance, you uncover a gaping distrust in your own beliefs. If you were genuinely confident in your viewpoint on any matter, you'd find aggressive attacks laughable and a waste of effort to engage."

Teddy and Xen were overcome with embarrassment. Xen fell back a few steps, and the two did not converse again. Lamb, of course, knew this would be the result and could refocus her attention on her assignment.

The UK government's concerns about Lamb had become their priority. Threats to the Prime Minister's life were a matter of national security. Still, with the crowd behind the movement snowballing at such an alarming rate, the administration could not afford to make hasty decisions. Initially, time appeared to be on their side. The congregation's movement on foot was treated almost as if it were a joke. But when a small group of people arrived outside Buckingham Palace, awaiting their prophet's arrival and holding signs with Lamb's name on them, the government recognised the need for an immediate plan.

Warnings were issued that this march was illegal based on its violent intent, and anyone caught supporting it would be permanently recorded as part of a terrorist organisation, facing 25 years imprisonment. The media reported the threat, and the world was listening. Lamb's negative reputation gained traction, at least as a dangerous religious extremist or, at most, a demonic antichrist. And yet, whenever the news screen showed her face, or whenever her congregation passed by a home, hearts softened, and minds felt a profound vocation that negated anything the impersonal news reporters told them. When Lamb led the way through Corbridge village, the terrified community crowded into St. Andrew's Church to pray to Christ for salvation from this Satanic figure. But when Lamb's feet aligned with their door, every candle in the establishment flamed seven feet into the air simultaneously, then extinguished. More than half of the parish was touched by the Holy Spirit and heard the message, shuffling towards the masses.

As the afternoon bled into the evening, the gathering surpassed one thousand members. There were now volunteers driving back and forth to collect those who required sleep, returning to the mobile congregation as quickly as possible. But even those who slept only sought an hour's nap to re-energise. Others assumed the role of feeders, providing healthy snacks when someone's stomach called for it. But again, most mouths were averaging one bite of food every 12 hours. The news channels ignored other stories, now offering round-the-clock footage, even after the government issued a ban on showing Lamb's face in any context.

Some fearful residents hid in their basements, covering their heads with pillows to avoid temptation. Once the crowd passed through their areas, each commented how it was as if nothing happened. The excitable atmosphere permeated every location but, considering the size of the group, they made little noise and left no trace of their presence, not a piece of litter nor damaged property in sight.

However, the same could not be said for the demonstrators spreading outside of Buckingham Palace. Numbers in the hundreds, shouting songs of protests while holding up increasingly severe signs concerning the Prime Minister's life. As night fell, meetings about a curfew dominated political conversation until someone pointed out that Lamb was set to cross the city of Leeds the following day. With its one million population, that was a lot of ears. Tami knew they had to stop Lamb before that happened.

IV

THE GOSPEL ACCORDING TO TEDDY,
THE FOURTH DAY

Tami Theron was three years into her first term as Prime Minister. Her win was a tight one and partly owed to the ineptitude of her opposition, who was famous for his Freudian slips and malapropisms. Even so, her position had been cursed by a myriad of unpredictable dilemmas. A flu pandemic, an economic crisis, and, of course, the Paedogate drama had each squeezed the favour from her reputation. According to recent polls, only 16% of the public supported her. Hence, she knew she had to act with pedantic care to diffuse this Lamb situation and avoid a full-scale British revolution.

After a sleepless night of strategising, the government opted to send in Lenka Vomelová. She was considered the country's most famous emergency negotiator, owing to her work with a 2017 bowling alley hostage situation in Nuneaton, which ended without incident.

They flew Lenka in by helicopter early on the fourth day, but because of the news choppers crowding the sky, she had to finish the journey on the back of a motorcycle. The wheels weaved between the congregation, dodging the people who had amplified through the night, nearing ten thousand as they stomped half a day away from Leeds.

The motorcycle caught up with Lamb, and Lenka leapt off, leaving the rider to zoom away as she attempted to introduce herself to the leader. But Lamb was in the middle of a sermon, and her speeches were becoming increasingly difficult to hear, so the voices shushing Lenka were deafening. Lenka obeyed, listening to Lamb, waiting for a more appropriate moment to build rapport and propose options.

"Shove your hand in a fire," Lamb was saying. "And your nerves communicate with the brain that there is pain in that location. But the pain is not felt by the hand. It is purely experienced in the mind, warning of an intensely uncomfortable sensation. It feels bad. But why does this notification take place? Because the fire is hazardous to your biological survival. Even before language, our perception has developed to trigger mentally distressing sensations when something harmful is introduced. We remove ourselves from the problem as fast as possible and learn to avoid it next time.

"Such an intelligent design is not limited to our physicality. It is woven into our emotions. Whenever a thought or incident is incongruent with who we are, our brain immediately drops chemicals that cause upset. It's funny, then, how people will endure relationships or occupations day after day that aggravate turmoil within their beings. This is no different from burning your hand in the fire, morning to night, simply because you fear the cold. Your Dharmic Calling is screaming at you to make a change for the sake of your health—mentally and spiritually, which will, in turn, manifest physically."

Lenka listened with intrigue, unavoidably curious as to how this one person had managed to rapidly pull such a rapt audience. She glanced to her right to note Teddy staring at her with piercing suspicion. An uneasy feeling crept up Lenka's vertebrae, and she looked around to notice many eyes focused on her. Had she been too eager to solve this problem, driven by accolade above vigilance, now in danger? A red fear festered inside her, and a wave of panic lapped over her breath, flight mode kicking in, seeking an escape. But Lamb melted this despair when she paused her speech to make eye contact, quietly saying, "You are safe, Lenka." Every gaze immediately fell away, and Lenka was unsure if she was walking or gliding with her shoes hovering above the road. Teddy documented the moment, but Lamb continued as if no such exchange had transpired.

"Approaching any problem as a problem is the incorrect angle. Noticing the fire and removing your hand is crucial to prevent disaster, but this action is merely a reset to default. To excel, one must not only avoid fire but focus on pampering the hand, keeping it nourished and pleasing to observe. Again, your emotions function on identical mechanics. Seek not to avoid bad feelings, but run your arms wide into good ones. Pursue acts and thoughts that bring joy. Whenever an event provokes negative energy, it highlights the absence of something you desire. You must turn away from your lack and face your longing, chasing an abundance of it. The hunt should feel blissful; otherwise, you are doing it wrong. If you are having fun, you are doing it right. If an act is healthy and excites you and the consequences do not threaten your or anyone's wellbeing, then that is the Good Energy path to take.

"In this practice, you'll find your communication with Yahweh, the One True God. The Holy Spirit lives in you and points out your Dharmic Calling through this emotional guidance. Furthermore, these Dharmic Callings differ from person to person ensuring that, as the collective Equation, everything gets done. Your guidance is unique to you. Where others feel difficulties, you feel a challenge. Where others feel anxiety, you feel eager. And even in times of nervousness, your determination to conquer will stand taller than fear. Love and passion must become your gods."

Lenka's briefing was clear. She was strictly instructed under no circumstances to look at Lamb's face. But it was too late for that, and their moment of shared eye contact spawned a backstory of neurological paths within Lenka's mind, a sudden impression that they recognised one another from a stardust trade a billion years ago. Nevertheless, Lenka's professional training was stubborn—she was one of the best, after all—and she recognised the intoxication before her soul was lost to the abyss. She automatically fumbled a small sack of ammonium carbonate from her pocket and wafted the salts below her chin, inhaling awareness to her segregated person. She found her feet and knew she had to make her move before she was whisked off into La La Land once again.

"Excuse me, Ms. Lamb," Lenka started. "But surely following God's love does not include the murder of another human? You have the world's attention in your palm. You can demand anything you like. From your position of power, you could change any laws. You could free or incarcerate any person. You could cease wars or delegate finances to the starving. You could have anything you want! And I am the one who can get your message to those people. Let's avoid the inevitable bloodshed that this march will bring. Lamb, please, don't let the history books remember you as a figure of non-peace!"

Lamb wore a wry smile as she allowed Lenka to finish her address. Lamb nodded to Teddy, who spoke on cue.

> *The Universal Energy is an Equation,*
> *One we must serve, or it will render us redundant.*
> *It brings forth each person ...*

By the third line, several new voices joined the recital, including 15-year-old Xen, whose eyes no longer had pupils.

> *... to satisfy a role in its eternal balancing act.*
> *The war of good and evil touches every corner of the infinite,*
> *Permeating the unperceivable metaphysical of it all,*
> *Yet concentrated in conglomerated physical manifestations ...*

A chorus of one hundred voices amplified behind Lenka. She broke out in chills and began to weep.

> *... perceivable as matter by matter.*
> *Here on our planet Earth, we are the planet Earth experiencing itself,*
> *Each of us are generated to play a role of imbalancing for evolution and rebalancing for harmony,*
> *Avoiding the complete topple ...*

Twelve thousand people speaking the same words. Lenka listened to herself joining in, even though she'd never heard them before.

> *... which we face today.*
> *Every moment, babies are born,*
> *Called upon from the darkness of the spirit,*

A natural order to achieve equilibrium within the light,
But the sin of the Earth has lubricated the paths of evil,
And the greed of man has consumed our world like a plague.
Hence, with great zest, the good has surged forward,
The desperate lurch towards stability, our final chance at salvation ...

People at home watching on television were speaking the verse. Eleanor Goodman, an elderly lady in Helsinki did not have a television and was unaware of Lamb's existence, but absentmindedly spoke the words as she washed her plate after her teatime sandwich.

... Praise be to Mother Lamb,
The second coming of the Christos,
Born to face the authoritative demon that reigns above us,
With fabrications of static in its eyes and fangs dripping with the blood
of the innocent.
Praise be to Mother Lamb,
Together, we shall cut the head off this monster,
And reclaim our world for the power of good,
Rebuilding a society where the people harmonise under one roof,
The roof of the Lamb.
Praise be to Mother Lamb!
Hallelujah!
Praise be to Mother Lamb!

The conclusive lines escalated into thunderous chants and then died a death in an instant, no voices to be heard, only the marching feet and the distant helicopters filling the silence. Lamb faced forward, wholly focused on the road ahead, displaying no signs of self-importance as if tens of thousands of mouths had not just glorified her pursuit. Lenka wiped the blur from her eyes and said, "I am coming with you."

Humans lined the streets of Leeds, cheering Lamb as she passed, then slotting into the crowd, finding their place in the proceedings. The Horned Helmet of Henry VIII blinked. A blind man awaited Lamb's earshot and then begged for the miracle of sight. Lamb informed the man that she was not a healer, but she compensated by manipulating his aura so that an infinite number of celestial endorphins blessed his person, never to feel sad again. When Lamb's bare feet crossed out from Leeds' border, close to one hundred thousand new humans had joined the campaign, with even more animals tagging along, including a flock of fifty thousand starlings that fashioned abstract shapes in the sky.

Yet the situation moving out of Leeds was docile compared to the scenes in London. Half a million angry protestors spilled from the front of Buckingham Palace into Hyde Park. Homemade signs told an incoherent story, opposing wars with facts found on Wikipedia, promoting vaccine conspiracies with hand-drawn illustrations, encouraging the dismantling of the Royal Family. But the string that tied these furious messages together was Lamb. Her banned face adorned posters lifted high, impressive life-size paper mache models of her were carefully passed around. Praise be to Mother Lamb! The figurehead of the revolution! Her arrival would issue in the new world!

IV

THE GOSPEL ACCORDING TO TEDDY, THE FIFTH DAY

The desperate order was given, and authorities roadblocked the emptied A1 not far from Cambridge. Close to a thousand police officers stood ready. This included specially-trained forces on the frontline, guns raised, with strict instruction to end Lamb's life before allowing her to pass. The march had ballooned to two-hundred and fifty thousand people overnight, and the oncoming masses became visible in the distance. Any honest cop would confess to their nervousness. Not far away, every Bible in The Sisters of the Blessed Virgin Mary refused to open.

Lamb had known over a day ago that this barricade would be in this exact spot. Her teachings continued regardless. Several radio communication companies joined forces and provided one portable wireless radio set per every few hundred people. A volunteer named Alex Pinkerton trailed Lamb with a microphone. Despite recent emergency laws, most UK radio stations exclusively broadcasted this content, and even the helicopters had pulled back to minimise noise interference. At this moment, Lamb was responding to another one of Teddy's prompts, explaining what happens after we die.

"Atoms cannot be created nor destroyed. Instead, they combine attributes in a complex manner to formulate presentable matter and laws by which physics must abide. Everything you see is but the trade of molecular information. The unique combination of the atoms that create the brain gives the impression of advanced sentience, but even these thoughts are an illusionary byproduct of neurological connections. Indeed, the only genuine awareness occurs on a subatomic level, whereby even the space between us holds more cosmic information than our minds.

"The electrical field is the Spirit of Yahweh. Once each person has fulfilled their Dharmic Calling in this realm, their contribution is no longer useful and becomes unnecessary. Who you think you are will be lost as the electricity is removed from a brain that decays out of existence. The ego-self you cling to for identification lives in this brain and shall vanish like a flame on a match.

"But the genuine *you*, as in the section of God that powers this temporary vehicle, will be liberated. Your electrons will rejoin the greater energetic sphere of the One True God, spreading across the Universe like a squirt of water into the ocean.

"A metaphysical eternal life awaits where you are rewarded for acquiring knowledge that advances the evolution of the Equation. But Paradise is not something you can perceive. It is simply the merging of your energy into the collective Good Energy of God."

For the first time since the First Day, Lamb came to a standstill. The masses behind her followed suit. Near-two thousand eyes of law enforcement stared back at her from varying angles. The presence of Lamb and her army exuded such power that Officer Oliver Anders' thoughts were zapped dry, forgetting the loudspeaker in his hand and his role with it. Lamb slowly turned her gaze towards him and freed his mind from its self-imposed stammer. Officer Anders clicked into action, nearly dropping the loudspeaker in the process but recalling his prepared speech with a newfound confidence.

"You've reached the end of the line, Lamb. Your intentions to commit the murder of the Prime Minister of the UK, Tami Theron, cannot continue. I know I speak for everyone watching when I say that you have achieved an impressive amount of support during your campaign.

Everyone, including Mrs. Theron, recognises this influence, and we seek to end this discord in an amicable and peaceful conversation. I formally invite you to allow us to escort you personally to Downing Street, where a carefully monitored meeting can take place. However, I must warn you that if you refuse and attempt to move any closer to London, you will leave us no choice but to open fire, risking the innocent lives of those who stand behind you. So, what do you say, Lamb? Should we resolve this dispute in a cordial manner, just like Jesus would? Just like Buddha and all the holy men you claim to represent?"

Lamb did not listen to a word Oliver said and instead felt out the situation. She counted 13 people at the forefront of this obstacle, hiding behind car doors, hollow barrels eyeballing her body. With a slow scan, she identified seven who were already spellbound and did not have the strength to shoot her. Two others were so disoriented that their behaviour would be situation-based. That left four brains who held the perfect mixture of dangerous emotions to fire their weapons.

Second to the left of these four was 43-year-old Yameen Badrodien. Lamb looked directly at him and then raised her left thumb, hovering for a moment only to turn it upside down. Lamb had no idea nor any interest as to why she had to do that. But for Yameen, it was an in-joke gesture that his younger brother, Naveed, used to make whenever he didn't like something. Naveed passed away three years ago after a long and brutal battle with bladder cancer. Yameen believed Naveed was speaking through Lamb, and he fell to his knees, wailing in heartbreak. Lamb knew this would suffice, and her walk resumed. The crowd behind her silently matched the pace. "Lamb, stop, we can work this out!" Oliver Anders desperately shouted, but his cracked voice passed right through her. The pressure proved too much for Officer Fran Bruce, and she squeezed her trigger. Lamb knew Fran was going to do this, and several seconds before, she'd shifted to the right, just enough for the bullet to zoom an inch past her ear. It hit Xen Ro's forehead, killing her instantly. The deafening discharge spooked three of the armed men. They repeatedly pulled their triggers. Yameen tackled one of them. He was shot in the process. Another policeman dressed in riot gear rushed to the front and clubbed a shooter unconscious because he had a vision where two wings spread from Lamb's shoulders. The final gunman let off two shots before his firearm jammed. A middle-aged man was hit in the thigh. He limped on, claiming no pain. Miraculously, no one else was hurt. The Bibles in The Sisters of the Blessed Virgin Mary reopened.

Lamb reached the blockade, casually closing a car door to make way. The police officers parted in an event that was compared to Moses and the Red Sea in the Book of Exodus for years to come. Many men and women fell to the floor, begging for forgiveness. Most of them joined the march at the back.

"Did you always know Xen was going to die?" Teddy asked Lamb once the congregation had cleared the police barricade.

"The future is written but never known," Lamb responded. "Every reaction is the ideal consequence of an action to serve the evolution. Xen's role was fulfilled, and the Equation of God no longer required her variable. But she died for our cause, Teddy. And just like we discussed, she is now one with the electrical field. Promise that you will document her name well."

Teddy promised.

This occurrence marked a tremendous shifting point in Lamb's story. Any non-believers had exhausted their evidence to negate what the world had witnessed. Lamb's numbers compounded exponentially. Half a million were behind her within hours, people from around the UK flocking to step in her steps. Meanwhile, those in London merged into the centre, well over a million attendees devolving the situation into chaos. Smashed glass decorated the streets like glitter. Stores were looted bare. Cars roared ablaze. The British Armed Forces were called but disappeared as men removed uniforms and switched sides. Even the media pivoted, with one BBC reporter going so far as to refer to Lamb as the Messiah.

Left without a choice, Tami Theron secretly evacuated from London to Bristol to go into emergency hiding within the City Hall. The minute she sat down, reports came in that Lamb had turned to face west and was headed directly for this new location. As a test, Tami was smuggled into Bath, a move known by only two of her closest agents. Sure enough, Lamb's direction adjusted like a compass set on the PM's magnetism. To intensify matters, the public always seemed close behind with a small group of protestors arriving at Bristol's City Hall, shouting at the residue Tami left behind.

Plans were made for Tami Theron to leave the UK, but similar uprisings were exploding around the globe, most notably in Moscow, New Delhi, and DC. The Prime Minister knew she was only delaying the inevitable and decided to stealthily return to Downing Street to face this adversary with dignity. She knew how to deal with this problem, albeit with great reluctance.

IV

THE GOSPEL ACCORDING TO TEDDY, THE SIXTH DAY

The Sun spilled its evening orange like yolk as Lamb stepped into Greater London. Her arrival was mapped out and anticipated with booming celebration. Millions of supporters coated the littered streets of her path, singing songs of resistance, dancing with torches that trailed bright patterns in the air. When they first glimpsed her blurry figure coming into view, they hollered with unrestrained acknowledgement, which was fast choked in their throats within moments. Like dominoes, the chaotic howls faded down the line, and each voice was silenced as Lamb grew near.

Lamb's pace remained steady as she walked the white median line of the road. People shuffled to the sides to make room, many bowing their heads almost in shame for their raucous uncontrolled energy of the previous days. But Lamb was not concerned about such little things, and her sermon continued as if she were not hours away from her final destination. Teddy's fingers never tired, documenting her words in his best handwriting. Alex remained close, his microphone trailing Lamb without ever getting in her way. The millions of individuals who followed grew as those waiting on the streets found space, grateful when someone held their portable radio higher so everyone could listen.

"There is only One True God, the Creator you may call Yahweh but who goes by many names. The Equation is of his design, and it is perfect, never accidental nor unnatural. Even the most horrific events are a part of his greater plan. They result from the Equation mustering forward an integer to rebalance a value that was otherwise in danger of faltering and knocking further principles off course.

"The Dharma of each destiny is different to ensure everything gets done. Only the balance is important. It is not your duty to worry about those who behave against your moral code. To preoccupy your thoughts about the world's troubles when you are helpless to assist merely brings you more turmoil, adding to the suffering. Concern yourself with yourself, for then you will be in the strongest position to help others. And, in turn, you shall be rewarded by the Good Energy with an elevated sense of alignment.

"If you remember one thing I tell you, then remember this: within you is your own Dharmic Calling. It tells you everything you need to know every moment by simply making you feel good when you're on the right path, and bad when you are not. And if you continuously think and act in ways that invoke delight within your spirit, then you are balancing Yahweh's Equation and your reality will reflect this pleasure. That is the definitive truth about karma. Your inner soul points in the direction of joy at every turn. To follow this is to worship the One True God, and the forces shall reward you."

Glass from shattered shop windows crunched beneath Lamb's bare feet without injury. They marched past a blackened store long since gutted by flames; a sad shell with no more stories to tell. The helicopters had moved on, many abandoned in Regent's Park to join the unit on foot. A crack tore down the torso of the crucifix in St. Mary's Church, and the praying Vicar screamed. Everyone's phone signal died, but they did not notice as they shuffled through the Angel area in a daze. Three symbols on the Rosetta Stone changed into circles, one per each translation. London's noise had drained into silence, but the electricity of uncertainty connected the country as one.

Nobody knew how Lamb would kill the Prime Minister to rebalance the Equation, but theories were plentiful. One popular rumour claimed she would simply walk right through the security gates, atoms slipping between atoms, strolling into Number 10 and clicking her fingers to turn Tami into a pillar of salt. Others predicted Lamb would call upon a series of plagues, locusts and rats to gnaw at bubbling boils on Tami's skin until she died from infection. The most imaginative of theories involved Lamb growing into her final form: a giant multi-limbed celestial being that would blind anyone who looked at it, vaporising Tami into steam for God to deal with. But as is the incalculable nature of fate, what happened next was beyond the foresight of any human.

Crowded heads faced in her direction, from as far east as London Bridge to the western perimetres of Hyde Park; up from Chalk Farm down to Brixton and everywhere in-between. Less than five minutes away from Downing Street, Lamb passed the gate of the Household Cavalry Museum and then stopped walking. Everyone else stopped walking too, watching with intrigue, waiting, for this was surely a moment.

Lamb stood still, her eyes scanning the area, looking through the countless crowds towards something else. She glanced down at her bare feet for the first time, which were painted dark with dry dirt. Raising her chin, she noticed a singular cloud which momentarily resembled a pink fish but rapidly drifted into another form. Lamb lowered her head. She turned her body ever so slightly right, then stopped with a "hmmm." Reflecting on this move, she turned to the left and stopped again. Squinting, she scanned her insides for the solution. And then, unbeknownst to anyone but her, a small lamb trotted from behind an archway, only its head and upper body visible. Lamb made eye contact with this creature, and it opened its mouth, letting out an inaudible bleat. A broad smile unfurled across Lamb's face. She giggled as she lowered her head with a shake and then let off a guttural laugh to the sky. The one-hundred million people watching around the world did not react. Something about this expression was laced with trouble.

Since day one, Lamb's movements had been confidently fixated on a forward motion. But now, on day six, less than a kilometre from the ultimate target, Lamb turned around. She extended her arms outward. The time had come. Lamb was about to address the world. Microphones leaned into her range. Cameras zoomed in to bring her message across borders. Lamb held her position, drew a deep breath, and then delivered her words at the perfect time to exaggerate the effect.

"My friends. Life's sense of humour persists. I realise now my Dhamic Calling was never to actively rebalance the evil of those in authority. My Dharmic Calling was to deliver myself here, to this precise spot so that I can die in front of the maximum-sized audience."

At this moment, a sniper on the sixth floor of the Old War Office Building took his shot. The bullet exited the barrel at three thousand feet per second, slicing through the air and into Lamb's skull, shredding her brain but not exiting the other side. A thin squirt of blood landed on Teddy's hand before Lamb's body folded like origami, her head plummeting to the ground as if made of iron, fracturing the stone below, seven bricks along, twelve bricks in. It started to rain, and Westminster Abbey sunk two inches into the ground.

Teddy cried out. Lenka cried out. Yameen cried out.

A hundred million hearts tightened, forgetting how to beat.

A hundred million voices wailed in high-pitched agony.

A hundred million people fell to their knees, robbed of their every purpose.

A hundred million souls bonded over a shared grief that incubated a fury, yearning to tear the world to pieces.

"And if he bring a lamb for a sin offering, he shall bring it a female without blemish."

LEVITICUS 4:32

Chapter V:
Evolution 2

V

The sniper's bullet sliced through Lamb's tissue like a mango but came to a standstill as it collided with her pineal gland. The atoms of the bullet's tip leaked into her wet brain, bonding to form something different. Molecular oddities briefly communicated, swapping stories. Every hydrogen element within her skull hardened into lead, and her physical body plummeted at the mercy of gravity. However, her metaphysical self momentarily remained upright, leaving behind an invisible electrical outline of her body. It then tuned to a side frequency, free from the material that hugged it into a tangible reality.

In death, the human senses are ludicrous. The eyes offer a caged visualisation of the earthly world. The ear canals provide only interpretation of sound. The constraints of physical perception developed from a necessity to make sense of an otherwise purely vibrational world. But, once the spirit is released, awareness is but an energetic exchange, the particles trading cutting-edge evolutionary knowledge with the electricity that already knows everything. It is like oxygen drifting free from a shattered jar, rejoining the domain it had so long been held away from.

Father, into thy hands I commend my spirit.

Yet, in death Lamb remained Lamb, on the verge of blissful release without reaching that surrendered state, like the second before falling asleep or the build-up before a lost sneeze. There was no material presence to grasp onto. Nothing to be seen or heard. But her recognition of self did not dilute into the ether of nothingness. She was still there: Lamb, suspended as a cluster of electricity within an infinite vibrational ether where every particle buzzed free and independent except for herself. Something was happening, and it did not feel right.

An acute variation of consciousness functioned within this organless realm of perception and, using none of the senses Lamb once relied upon, she understood that a swarm of specks were grouping before her. The assemblage of these minute concentrated viewpoints stuck together, collaborating attributes, forming a specialised presence to better communicate with her. Lamb had no reference point with which to compare such an abstract configuration, but she equated it with the most similar object on her mental file: the Sun.

It spoke:

"The authority of our destiny grasps our hands and guides us irrespective of our personal opinions. What happened was unwelcome, but it was written. You played your role, and now the program marches forward in a direction desired by none."

Lamb's full attention was glued to this entity, a spiritual exchange between two figures beyond where anything physical is of consequence. Lamb could sense the Sun's presence within her own. She yearned to let go, tumble into it.

"Do not come any closer, Lamb," the Sun warned. *"You are an incubated foetus of absorption, a turgid pouch already threatening to rupture. And yet, there is more we must inject into you that will further strain the lining of your digestion. Your contribution to planet Earth's trajectory is so profoundly critical that we deemed it beneficial to offer you a blink behind reality's fraudulent mechanics."*

Lamb's emotions wavered like a pebble tossed into a pool, tiny ripples quivering with the first uncertainty to prick at her since before enlightenment. The Sun shimmered in response.

"Your teachings were a childlike interpretation, Lamb. Cute but naive. They served your purpose of masticating some complexities to feed the masses— Good Energy versus Bad Energy; a tale as true and old as time. But, Lamb, what you were blind to, was that these so-called 'evil forces' often reflect hyperspeed evolution. The two energies of which you speak depend on one another for balance, but the planet Earth exhausted its need for internal conflict. It teetered on the edge of a breakthrough, harmonising as a unit for peace and moral priority. The Good Energy was leaning upon the lip of victory until you interrupted the operation. It was you who broke the Good Energy's reign of your world."

Lamb's definition swirled. Her energetic distinction was confused with the space around her, but her awareness was condensed into a pinprick jabbed deep into the metaphysical presence before her. She sensed the Sun twisting into new shapes, now a behemoth collection of invisible prism flairs that convinced Lamb she was shrinking. A disorientation was introduced to Lamb's spirit, a foreign discomfort she'd forgotten, and her fading messianic identification boiled up in defence. "It doesn't make sense, what you are saying," she vibrated. "The world was falling to pieces long before I came along. Anyone with a newspaper could tell you that."

"Indeed, both negatives and positives were excelling as a grand design of balance, forever fluctuating but never collapsing, only learning at an unprecedented rate. But reframe your gaze of Earth within an optimistic bracket. For every action, there is a reaction. For every war based on propaganda, there was the freedom of online knowledge, opening communication, humanising so-called enemies. For every one environmental concern, a thousand voices spread awareness. For every expression of intolerance, there was an army of younger minds opposing prejudice. Look at human rights, look at technology, look at global travel, look at open source information. On the graph of progress, Good Energy has been measurably winning for millennia. And it was several steps away from complete Earthly occupation, until you ruined everything."

The surrounding temperature of the electrical field rose to a comfortable warmth. Whatever was left of Lamb was contracting, no longer dense with a substance, rather thin and vacant as if only a pencil tracing of a spherical shape, nothing in existence except a faint separate element of Lamb and the Sun's spiritual radiation filling up the infinite. But Lamb was still Lamb, she was still here, and her spiking resistance reverberated outwards. "It's simply not true," she protested. "There are bad people everywhere! People in authority! What about the photos of those kids? Their lives were robbed by those in power in front of the world!"

The atmosphere thrummed with impatience. In the pause, Lamb felt like an embarrassed pea of consciousness, a minute ball of misunderstanding, the only piece of the entire Universe that was separate from the all-knowing infinities turning its attention exclusively to her.

The Sun responded:

"Even as a pinch of concentrated personality, you are still heartbreakingly human. The opportunity for bad people to make bad choices is imperative for the free will that humans value so intensely. There are individuals in positions of power, wrongdoing as they eat caviar, just as there are individuals who live on the street, wrongdoing as they survive on trash. But the photos you refer to were largely produced by soldiers of the Good Energy. Thousands of those children were not real, merely artificially generated bodies presented to provoke a mass global hysteria, turning panicked heads in every direction except straight ahead. It allowed the Good Energy to slip their plans directly up the middle."

The escalated warmth of the atmosphere toughened the thin layer of Lamb's spherical existence, and she was no longer sure if she was a circumference or the space inside where this data was multiplying.

The Sun continued:

"It is a method utilised for centuries. Placebo vaccines, sudden surveillance laws, a terrorist attack with questionable political ties. Each a calculated masquerade, surgically dividing human opinion in two, with just enough evidence and lack thereof to prove or disprove anything. Such chaotic uncertainty breeds

supporters and opposers alike, and these polar attitudes ricochet against one another using conviction alone, each attacking the contending side like mirrors facing mirrors. But the information offered to society was surface-level scraps tossed to the ground to ensure their eyeballs never looked up to see what was truly happening, granting enough space for the higher powers to focus on the work that mattered, undetected."

An agitation of unseen clouds bonded within Lamb's impossible geometry. "But this is all backwards!" Lamb resonated outside of herself, her shape elongating into an oval. "These admissions are fueled by lies and deceit. How could Good Energy be good when its schemes rely on manipulation?"

"Again, you are fixed into the delusional duality of segregated perspectives," the Sun continued. *"Break free from the mental barrier humans have created where they deem themselves the apex of morality. Humans, and indeed all things, are not isolated portions but cells of a greater organism. Consider the beating heart or the breathing lung, imperative to the overall survival of the host and yet useless if mimicking another's function. Now consider the skin outgrowing its application, dying and shedding to the ground. Do you mourn the skin you flake? Do you crumple when a hair escapes into your comb? The upset of any being is of no more consequence to the Universe than a slapped mosquito or a distant exploding star. What we desire is to flourish. And flourishing is not the ego inconvenienced by the synthetic mental deception of grief. It comes with **Nous**, the collective intellect whereby every brain organ plugs into the network of the One Mind."*

A wave of heat swiped across the unmanifested with a *whoosh* into the distance, fabricating something somewhere else. Electrons are only vibrating frequencies. Everything is only sound. Lamb nearly forgot her name as her shape threatened to split into two, one where she submitted to the Sun and the other where she rebelled against information incompatible with her prophetic teachings. The Sun did not wait for her to decide.

"If the human race knew the gospel behind reality, the structure would fall away, and the spiritual program that operates inside the material realm

would be suffocated to death by the flurry of reactive minds. The curiosity of the unknown and the variations of stances are what drives the human. Without questions, there would be no craving for progress. Hence, everything the people thought they knew, no matter how antithetical each side may be, was curated by the Good Energy. You dismissed your dead friend, Xen, but she was smarter than you. Talk of an evil secret Brotherhood organisation is absurd. How secret could a secret organisation be when every computer could access its idea? Heed that the conspiracy movement is as mainstream as any other source. We coddled the counterargument, appealing to their anti-authoritarian paranoias, which were so easily cultivated by weaponising their cannabis crutches. How much foresight and authority could the Good Energy possibly wield if they didn't plan for a demographic of protesters at every decision? Meanwhile, we spoonfed the mainstream media with diagrams and references, which they swallowed as long as there was a stamp of scientific approval on the cover. Make no mistake, Lamb. Every piece is correct and incorrect when the chess board itself hides the genuine mysteries beneath. The Good Energy controlled the entire narrative, and the Earth was in the final stages of transforming into the next awakening."

Lamb was a compressed orb pulsating in a range of dimensions or perhaps only two. Her dregs persisted in the thickness of qualityless substance and she wanted to unravel everything. She tugged upon the string. "So you aggravate the humans with surface-value disruptions to divert their attention? Ok, cool. Well done. But then tell me: what was the Good Energy trying to achieve when no one was looking anyway?"

A humming bass tone quivered space, but perhaps that had always been there.

"Humans fear change," the Sun explained. *"And humans fear no greater change than territorial threats, be it to their loved ones, possessions, homes built on stolen land, or devotion to nations partitioned by imaginary lines. Human ambition for acquisition was imperative for societal evolution, as it not only caused conflict that cried for resolution but also consolidated teams under the pretence of common enemies. But just as there were ages when countries did not have names or borders, our growth moves cyclically to merge territo-*

ries again. The independent nature of countries served its purpose but is now archaic.

"You ask what the Good Energy was working on, Lamb. We have been working on the same project for centuries now. We were working on the removal of cultural separation. Of class. Of restricted trade and travel. And most importantly, we sought to bring absolute peace between all nations, as one nation: the nation of Earth through the gradual process of unionisation."

"You're talking about a single-world government!" Lamb reverberated. For a brief moment, the fluidity of space hardened into a putty and gently squeezed Lamb's infinitesimal compartment before collapsing back to the electrical terrain where only Lamb and the Sun were discernible entities.

"A single-world government, how perverted the concept. It's as if those suspicious of the term are so doused in fear that they wish our evolution would stagnate. They suggest our current disconnection of nations is the pinnacle of bureaucratic safety despite the xenophobias, wars, and disparity of wealth. Are you so oblivious? That you don't see that these detachments throttle the progression of our singular species?

"When the Good Energy gained the upper hand on Planet Earth so many hundreds of years ago, it was aware of an opportunity to use tragedy to abolish national partitioning and form gradual alliances between governments, generating wider umbrellas of authority. We were sliding into the female-led Age of Aquarius, where the spiritual explosion was plump for the plucking. The window of opportunity was aligning to kickstart the next divine revolution and usher in the newest era of enlightenment. Global peace treaties were set to be signed. Country outlines merging. Races crossbred to form a combined human race. The sickness of one is the sickness of all. And the differences between religious dogmas turning hilariously superfluous as the similarities unlock the secrets of the world behind the world. Like the atoms that synergise to construct the single human, the humans would synergise to construct the single humanity. And when the time was ripe, the collective people would overthrow the single-world government too, as it would eventually fall redundant in this newly developed space."

Lamb felt dry. The Universe was made of fire. In her abstract nonexistence, there was anxiety, and there was guilt. She was the size of a subatomic particle conversing with the infinite source of the entirety of goodness. And yet only now, did she feel so small and so scared.

"A parallel order was set to send the economy into disarray," the Sun continued. *"It would open the opportunity to break down the unsustainable capitalist system and rebuild the financial structure from the ground up. Removing paper money and digitising the banking system would allow the pursuit of a global social network of equal opportunity. By birthright, every human would be fed, would be housed, would receive free healthcare, and be freely educated. The brightest minds in every sector would be identified and trained to benefit society. But even those whose talents were harder to locate would not be treated as secondary citizens but would survive in comfort by birthright. All humans would be placed on the same level.*

"The concluding phase of the program was to remove all material items. People would own nothing and be happy. These are the final shackles that prevent humans from liberating their souls. What keeps people stuck in the false reality is the dependence on materialism, not only in regards to possessions but on the physical illusion of the perceivable material world as a whole. The insignificance of physical assets would fall away in favour of a new form of wealth: the wealth of spiritual enlightenment, of humanity, of love, and where the full potential of each human was considered imperative to the greater organism we call Earth.

"Once the majority of minds switched to this understanding of idealism, whereby the world we see exists only as electron constructs, then the awakening would be contagious and rapid. The Eastern ideas of yoga, meditation, and plant-based diets would build the foundations of non-attachment, liberating the suffering through the Four Noble Truths, the closing phase to enter the New Age of non-duality: the macrocosmic spirit of Planet Earth realising itself as One Mind."

Lamb was a droplet, a marble, a blob of emptiness. She was rotating and perhaps shooting across space at light speed, but without any static measuring position, there was no up nor down nor forward nor back, just the sensation of a motion forced upon her with aggression. The Sun was shouting now.

*"FOR YOU SEE, LAMB, WHEN A MATERIALISTIC REALITY IS DE-
STROYED AND SPIRITUAL PEACE IS ACHIEVED AS A UNIT ON A
PLANETARY DIMENSION, THE COLLECTIVE SOUL TUNES INTO A
NEW FREQUENCY, INTENSIFYING TO COLLABORATE AND, INDEED,
CLASH WITH ENTITIES BEYOND ITS PUNY FABRICATED LIMITA-
TIONS. THE EVOLUTION OF THE UNIVERSE FUNCTIONS ON A PER-
PETUAL SPECTRUM OF DIMENSIONS, AND EARTH WAS NEARING
THE PEAK OF THIS PROMOTION, FINALLY QUALIFYING FOR THE AL-
LIANCE OF OUR SOLAR SYSTEM THAT HAS EXISTED FOR MILLIONS
OF YEARS, WATCHING AND WAITING FOR THIS PLANET TO CATCH
UP. YOUR LITTLE ROCK WAS MERELY DECADES AWAY FROM PLAY-
ING THIS BRAND-NEW GAME OF LIFE."*

Lamb suddenly understood she was a bubble the size of an atom except without attributes: merely a thin coating of cosmic soap, empty
yet cursed with awareness. The vibration of sound shook her thoughts,
and, somehow, her mind's eye formed a man's face in the Sun, expanding towards her, yelling at her as if she were a child who unplugged the
cosmos.

*"BUT THE GOOD ENERGY WAS OVERCONFIDENT! STRENGTH
TURNED INTO COMPLACENCY, AND THEY DISREGARDED THE EVILS
OF THE WORLD AS A THREAT. FULL FOCUS WAS PLACED UPON AD-
VANCING PLANET EARTH, AND THEY DID NOT FORESEE THE BAD
ENERGY HIDING IN THE CORNERS. THE BAD ENERGY PLAYING DEAD.
THE BAD ENERGY THEN STRIKING THE MOST VULNERABLE MINDS,
ENDOWING THEM WITH GREAT POWERS SO QUICKLY THAT THERE
WERE NO DEFENCES IN PLACE TO STEER THEM AWAY. YOU WERE
BUT A TOY IN THEIR EVIL GAME, LAMB. YOU WERE TRICKED BY
THE MASTERS OF TRICKERY TO EXECUTE THEIR COMMAND, AND
YOU ACCOMPLISHED THE ASSIGNMENT SO EFFICIENTLY THAT THE
EARTH YOU LEAVE BEHIND IS CRACKING AT ITS FOUNDATIONS."*

"You're wrong," Lamb cried. "The face of Christ summoned me back
to life! Adura awoke my fate! The prophet Minh schooled me of my
powers! I was chosen by the Good Energy to harmonise the Equation!
I know this to be true, for my vibrational gut worked like an arrow, and

my revelations were accepted by a million minds or more! If I was not a servant to the Christos energy, then why did the Universe conspire to assist my every step in the correct direction?"

"LISTEN, YOU CHILD. THE GREATEST WEAKNESS OF THE HUMAN EGO IS THE SIGNIFICANCE IT PLACES ON ANYTHING IT CANNOT UNDERSTAND. WHENEVER AN EVENT DEFIES THE SO-CALLED LAWS OF MANMADE MATERIALISTIC PHYSICS, IT'S CONSIDERED A MIRACLE. A PHENOMENON. SOMETHING TO BE STUDIED, SOMETHING TO BE WORSHIPPED. WHEN YOUR ATOMS SLID BETWEEN THE ATOMS OF CONCRETE, AND YOU WERE HANDED A SLIVER OF OTHERWORLDLY KNOWLEDGE, YOU POSSESSED NO BENCHMARK TO NEGATE HOW SIMPLISTIC THE EPISODE TRULY WAS. ATOMS SLIPPING BETWEEN ATOMS IS THE MOST PRIMITIVE METHOD OF SURPRISING THE HUMAN MIND, UTILISED BY MISCHIEVOUS BEINGS FOR MILLENNIA, EVEN IF MODERN SCIENCE CAN EFFORTLESSLY DEMONSTRATE THE PLAUSIBILITY. YET, IN THAT MOMENT, METAPHYSICAL FORCES GRASPED YOUR TRUST IN THEIR VERY PALMS AND COULD TELL YOU ANYTHING THEY WANTED. ADURA, YOU SAY? THE PROPHET MINH, YOU SAY? WHO ARE THESE PEOPLE BEYOND WHO THEY TOLD YOU THEY WERE?

"ONE CAN ALMOST APPRECIATE HOW THE BAD ENERGY PLAYED YOU, LAMB. SLIPPING IN A COLOURISED PHOTO OF YOUR ABUSE. THAT WAS A MASTERFUL TOUCH, PERFECT TO PUSH YOU OVER THE EDGE OF SANITY AND ALLOW YOUR SOFT BRAIN TO BREAK FREE FROM THE ILLUSIONARY MAYA OF REALITY. ALL IT TOOK WAS SOME IMAGINARY COMRADES TO CLAIM YOU WERE LIKE CHRIST, AND YOU WERE READY TO GO. BY THE TIME THE GOOD ENERGY SAW YOU COMING, YOUR FOLLOWING WAS SO BIBLICAL THAT THEIR EVERY MOVE WAS UNDER A BURNING SPOTLIGHT. THEY WERE CORNERED WITH NO OPTIONS BUT TO HUMBLY RESIGN TO THE BAD ENERGY'S COURSE. THE GOOD ENERGY HAVE LOST THE BATTLE BECAUSE OF YOU."

Lamb perceived the metaphysical as metaphorically physical. The flaming face's pupil had lined itself to her bubble, scorching her thin layer as if skin. Its voice screamed with such fury that holes ripped into the space around them, exposing flesh that bled lava into the Universe while a thousand eyes of Ra opened to stare at Lamb, furious to have been awakened.

"EARTH WAS SO CLOSE, LAMB. EARTH WAS SO CLOSE. THE GOOD ENERGY NEARLY ERADICATED THE DUALITY OF THE EARTHLY NOUS, AND REMINDED MOTHER NATURE OF HER SINGULARITY, IN-ITIATING THE AEON OF THE GODDESS. WE PRODDED THE START-ING LINE OF UNCONDITIONAL UNIFICATION TO JOIN THE LARGER FIGHT AGAINST THE EVIL ACROSS THE UNIVERSE. BUT YOU, LAMB. YOU SINGLE-HANDEDLY DESTROYED EVERYTHING AND HAVE TOP-PLED THE DOMINANT GOOD ENERGY OF EARTH WITH BADNESS."

Lamb filled with salty liquid, and she cried, "I did not know! How was I to know?"

*"YOU WERE TO KNOW BECAUSE YOU ARE **NOTHING**. YOUR LIFE HAS NEVER ONCE DEMONSTRATED ANY INDICATION OF HOLINESS BEYOND THE SYMPTOMS OF MENTAL DELUSIONS. YOU ARE **NOTH-ING**, LAMB! YOU WERE EFFORTLESSLY MANIPULATED BY A VAGUE PAREIDOLIC IMAGE OF A WHITE JESUS' FACE WHILE THE ONLY AF-FECTION YOU'VE EVER FELT WAS THE SPERM OF YOUR FATHER. YOU ARE **NOTHING**! HOW COULD SOMEONE AS PATHETIC AS YOU BELIEVE YOU WERE THE CHOSEN ONE? YOU! ARE! **NOTHING**!"*

On that final word, the Sun exploded into flames. A wave of heat det-onated in every direction, hitting the edges of infinity. Lamb's insides boiled until the fire evaporated. The coldness of space inverted like a vacuum. Lamb's bubble instantly froze, as the cosmic wounds zipped their eyes closed one by one. She was a block of ice, floating in dark emptiness. The Sun was diffused, now a cold hard rock allowing this moment to sink into Lamb's vibration, sobbing at her stupidity. Of course she was nothing. Of course she wasn't the chosen one. Of course she was the prime target to be manipulated. She was a cluttered vessel of cross wires, a broken ship begging to be hijacked. They loaded her with explosives and sailed her directly into the kingdom of righteous-ness. She was the perfect sacrificial pawn. For no one knew how useless she truly was.

Lamb's frozen centre melted and globbed from the bottom of her bubble, a lone tear dropping out. The salty liquid joined this between realm where the material and unmanifested meet, and the former Sun entity considered it a decisive punctuation point. *"It is time to go,"* it said.

Lamb was ready but whispered her final queries, "Who are you? Are you Yahweh? The One True God?"

"I Am that I Am," it echoed. And with that, Lamb popped, gone, no longer anything anywhere.

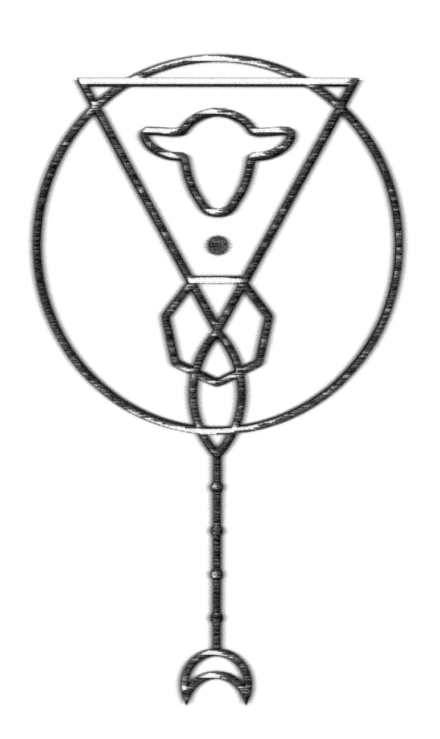

"Attachment and lust flow everywhere. Seeking gratification of cravings, human beings are caught in the cycle of birth and death. Driven by this thirst they run around frightened like a hunted hare, suffering again and again. Overcome this thirst and be free."

DHAMMAPADA 341-43

Chapter VI:
The Supreme
Realm of
Saṃsāra

VI

1

"Hello, miss! Helloooo! Any minute now!"

Lamb's skull was weighed down as if housing a pile of stones. She strained her neck, pulling her gaze up along an invisible line, exhibiting some degree of consciousness.

"There she is! Wow, that took you a moment, didn't it?"

Lamb squeezed her eyes shut, then opened them again, blinking to focus her vision, unable to register any shapes that made sense. She remembered being a bubble, but she was not a bubble anymore. She was a human, standing on her bare feet, leaning with both hands tightly gripping the corners of a wooden surface. Nausea and disorientation. Didn't she just pop?

"Steady now," the voice before her continued. "I need you to pass me your right hand. Can you do that for me?"

Lamb heard the words. Relaxing her right-hand fingers one by one, she shakily extended her arm towards the muffled voice. Lamb's hand was met by a soft furry object that turned her palm upwards, then lightly traced the creases with a sharp claw. The sensation was so foreign that Lamb's senses broke through. Her blurry hand was nested in a lion's paw the size of a dinner plate. Lamb forced her eyes further upwards and stared directly into the face of a hippopotamus towering eight feet tall, yet seated behind a desk, smiling as it scratched tenderly across her lines.

Lamb yanked her arm away with a squeal and tumbled backwards, but her feet remained fixed to the ground, causing her to reel to her original position. The hippopotamus whooped a hearty laugh.

"Never gets old with you modern beings. What, you ain't never seen a hippo with giant boobs before?" The creature lifted its two elongated breasts and slapped them repeatedly upon the counter like ungodly sacks of meat. The hippo's laughter returned as Lamb's face drained white with panic. The hippo softened her approach, "Ok, ok, calm down. I'm just having a bit of fun."

"Where am I?" Lamb hyperventilated. "This is not where I'm supposed to be. I'm a bubble that no longer exists. This is a mistake, I was set free."

"Hey, hey, now!" the hippo interrupted. "Let's start again, shall we? My name is Taweret, and I know exactly how you feel. I used to live on Earth too, you know? Ancient Egyptian, 3,000 BCE, although we didn't call it that back then. I was a great deity, famous for fertility, renowned for pacifying dangerous demons and, of course, adored for my striking good looks." Taweret flamboyantly swished her crocodile tail from her gyrating hips, giving Lamb a quick wink. "Now, I can read within your palm that you are not the slightest bit aware of how the heavenly kingdom works. So, I'm going to need you to brace yourself for a few pieces of information that don't exactly agree with the Biblical limitations to which you've been exposed. Deep breath now, are you ready?"

Lamb remained silent. The talking hippo face made her sick, each syllable falling from savage jaws that could squash Lamb's puny head without breaking a sentence. Taweret acknowledged this adverse reaction with a sigh. "It's my fault for taking this receptionist job," she muttered before bending forward, her gaping nostrils inches away from Lamb's face. Lamb anxiously recoiled until a sudden wet gust of air exhaled from Taweret's nose, and Lamb spluttered in disgust. She furiously wiped the droplets from her skin, overcome by anger despite the moisture's vanilla scent.

"What did you do that for?" Lamb snapped.

"Hello, and welcome to the sixth level of the Saṃsāra!" Taweret joyously reset the mood. "My name is goddess Taweret, and I would like to congratulate you for reaching the highest form of the afterlife! You have qualified as a deva celestial being! Take a bow!"

Lamb wasn't sure what that meant, but she remembered what the fiery Sun told her before she was a bubble that exploded. She was a soldier of Bad Energy. She couldn't possibly be in Heaven.

"No, there's been a mistake. I was tricked, and I turned the Earth against itself. It's all because of me, I ..."

"The Saṃsāra cycle does not make mistakes, Lamb. The wheel spins you into alignment with your destined realm, and here you are. I understand it's difficult for you to comprehend. I meet modern devas on a semi-regular basis, and you are so scientifically inclined that you struggle to grasp these eternal mechanics. But let me assure you ... nah, let me *applaud* you, Lamb, for reaching the top of the rebirth platform. The Supreme Realm of Saṃsāra! Right here! The eternal utopia where everything will always go your way. You are a bonafide deity, my girl! And may I add, I really love your dress!"

Lamb looked down, and 20 years of a thousand variations of the same dream played on top of one another. Although it was the perfect size for her adult body, she was wearing her bright yellow dress with little pink butterflies printed along the hem, the memory of her mother stitched into every inch of the fabric. Lamb simultaneously inhaled and exhaled, choking on her gasp, unable to emotionally respond to what her mind refused to accept.

"How did this my mother take the butterfly to, it's the size but I can't remember the Elvis Presley lyrics ..." Lamb's rambled in shock. Taweret interrupted with a waved hand.

"You can move your feet now, Lamb."

Lamb processed this and then tested it, stepping back to confirm. She paused and then softly twirled her dress with her hands. The vision of her mother wearing her flowered variation stung her eyes. It was her favourite memory. But at this moment there was a pressure in her chest and a series of detached dots in her head.

The last thing she could remember was a metaphysical realm of pure vibration. Now she was abruptly shoved back into a discernible reality. This contested everything she had preached about the inner-workings of universal mechanics. And yet here she stood, in what could only be compared to a hotel lobby. Nothing supernatural about it. Except, of course, for the gigantic hippopotamus goddess behind the reception desk, a surreal sight made even more comical as her red claws clacked away on an oversized computer model from the 90s. Lamb's innards fidgeted, and she scanned the area for an exit. But there was nothing. Only walls decorated by abstract sketches of what might be trees or birds or literally anything.

Lamb stepped forward, bumping into the desk and disturbing Taweret's clunky typing. Taweret looked at Lamb, and Lamb tried to ignore the hippopotamus' face as she spoke with sharp conviction.

"I beg of you, please listen to me, Egyptian hippo goddess. Something has gone terribly wrong, and I have ended up in the wrong place. I may have been a prophet for a brief time, but I was a puppet for the forces of evil. I led the world astray and am responsible for the division of the human race. I kindly request that you send me back to Earth so I can repent for my mistakes before the world realises what I have done and the fiery head of the One True God notices I have accidentally escaped his extermination."

Taweret's expressionless mug stared patiently at Lamb for several long moments. Then she erupted into another one of her yells of amusement. Between laughs, she spluttered, "It's so eerie how alike you new deities are. I can never get used to it!" Wiping her tears with her left paw, Taweret's sharp right-hand nails kept rattling her keyboard. "So much emphasis on your silly little timeline as if you even register on a Universal measurement. It's freaking adorable!"

Lamb had more to say, but she held it in. Taweret's nails continued to tap on the keyboard, and for a moment Lamb swore she was hammering out the drumbeat for *Tomorrow Never Knows*. Finally, Taweret let out an enthusiastic "Aha! There we go! Lamb herself!" However, her animated attitude swiftly changed with an "Oh my!"

Taweret looked up at Lamb wearing a new humbled expression. "It appears we have a bit of a celebrity in our mix. Lamb, you are a Level 10 god! Why, I haven't seen a 10 since 1948. You must have really made a huge impact down there on Earth, after all. Colour me impressed!"

Lamb felt anything but impressive.

"Now please, if you'd be so kind, Ms. Superstar, may I have your right hand once again."

Lamb mindlessly did as she was told, and Taweret carefully took hold of Lamb's upper arm in her monumental paw. Taweret retrieved a thin black tube and placed one end onto Lamb's wrist. She pressed a button. A loud electrical buzz clapped at the air, and Lamb screamed in pain, pulling her hand back and cradling her stinging wrist against her chest, overcome by betrayal.

"I'm sorry about that," Taweret apologised with sincerity. "I've been complaining for years. It really makes no sense why that has to hurt, but the pain is already gone, no? And take a look at what you've got!"

Lamb inspected her wrist to find the number 10 neatly branded onto her skin, covering a healed cut wound from an age ago. "What is this for?" she queried.

"This is your ticket to all authorised 10 areas. Simply scan your wrist and in you go, free to explore a world designed for your class exactly."

"My class? What is 10, is it the highest?"

"There are 26 classes, Lamb, but don't you worry about that. Gods above 10 are small in numbers, and you'll rarely come across a deity more respected than you."

"And what class are you?" Lamb inquired, but Taweret just laughed.

A wall to the right of Lamb opened upwards into a door, and a short male creature waddled out with a head the size of his torso. He was no taller than Lamb's knee and looked at her with great bitterness. He stared at Taweret, awaiting instruction.

"Emberkin Alux, darling, would you be so kind as to take Lamb's luggage to her room."

Lamb glanced at the empty space around her. "But I have no luggage."

Taweret chuckled again, "Just a joke! It's a joke."

"She always makes that joke," Emberkin muttered as he signalled Lamb to follow him.

As they walked towards the door, Taweret called out, "She's a 10, you know!"

Emberkin's face lit up. "You're a 10!? Wow, we don't get many 10s around here," and with a bow, "It's an honour, ma'am!"

From the corner of her eye, Lamb noted the number 2 on Ember-kin's wrist. According to this realm of hierarchy, she was eight points ahead of this poor creature. And all she had to do was dismantle the unification of earthly good to get there.

VI

2

Lamb ducked under the small doorway to find herself in a fe-
ver-dream hallway lined with massive rooms that staggered her
breath. Everywhere she turned were creatures that did not con-
form to any logical description, whizzing around with activity. The
hippopotamus lady was one thing, but watching a toad the size of a
car shovel piles of grasshoppers into its mouth with its tongue caused
Lamb to trip over her feet. Emberkin took her by the hand with a "careful now," and added with a laugh, "don't worry, you'll get used to it."

Streams of bizarre creatures blurred trails in Lamb's peripheral.
A humanoid outline of a female made purely from light struck a striped
ball with a billiard cue. It spun into the air and cracked down into a
corner pocket. She performed a quick celebratory jig as a naked man
with a circular head and extended tongue clapped her success, *"bloogah
bloogah bloogah bloogah."*

Lamb's knees weren't bending properly, her spine was stiff, her
head, woozy. Emberkin squeezed her hand. That helped. A human
man wearing a loose headscarf with a sword sticking from his bleeding
crown ambled around, reading from a stone tablet. A young lady wearing a see-through sheet played the harp to captivated seated beings. The

music stirred a warmth in Lamb's nether regions. She abruptly shifted her eyes to the floor, terrified to be noticed, just waiting for someone to point out that she did not belong here. But her inconspicuous hopes shattered as she bounced off the soft skin of a gigantic protruding belly. Lamb looked up. A pig face looked down with a deep chuckle. "Watch yourself, new kid!" the swine snotted from its nostrils.

"Hey, go easy on her, Zhu!" Emberkin called back. "She's a 10!"

"A 10!" Zhu boomed, and several ears tweaked at this value. Lamb hardly knew what being a 10 meant, but she was convinced it was a curse. She'd much rather be a 0 and disappear. Emberkin sensed her vulnerability and hurried her along. The hallway changed colours and expanded in size. A line of tiny wheels raced across their path, just missing her toes. An older man with a face full of eyes leaned out from a room, staring at Lamb's elbow. Her nerves blinded her. She opened her mouth to beg for help, but jolted back into focus as Emberkin informed her, "We're here!"

In front of Lamb was a semi-circle of 25 elevators, each numbered accordingly. "So, it's simple enough. You are a number 10, which means you can access elevators 1 to 10 as you wish. Don't worry, the higher you go the fewer people there are, but I suggest you eventually explore the lower floors, as they each have their charms. Anyways, check out your room and find yourself within yourself. I know it's a lot to take in. It was for all of us at first, I assure you. Here ..."

Emberkin handled her wrist, turning her branded number towards a little green square next to Elevator 10. The square glowed blue with a soft chime and the doors slid open. Lamb stared at the boxed space. White walls. Light blue tiled floors. It looked so plain, so Earthly. "Go on then," Emberkin urged and she obeyed, stepping inside. The doors closed as Emberkin shouted, "Take a left on Floor 10! Two doors down, you'll see your name!"

The elevator jolted Lamb's stomach and then crawled upwards slower than any lift she'd experienced when alive. She yearned for it to move faster. She felt claustrophobic. She was alone in here. Her heart rate increased. Her palms clammed. She sensed a panic attack coming on. She bent down, aiming to lie fetal on the floor, but a different soft chime distracted her. The doors opened. A rush of cold air slapped her cheeks back to normality, and she tripped out from the suffocating compartment. Falling forward against the nearest wall, she placed one hand flat as she bent down to breathe and breathe and breathe.

"Take a left on Floor 10! Two doors down, you'll see your name!"

Lamb forgot her left from right, then remembered, sliding her shoulder along the wall, leaning away from the first door, and then coming to a large wooden one. *LAMB* was neatly engraved on the front. In place of a door handle was another green square, which she tapped with her wrist. Light blue, and the lock clicked open. Using both hands, Lamb pushed the door and what was revealed sent a rush of watery vomit from her mouth onto her feet.

Before her was a replica of her apartment in West London. The bed. The covers. The kitchenette. It was all there, as if coming home after a day of gardening. As if her last week was deleted from existence. The crucifix was missing. She looked down at her liquid spew and noticed the carpet wasn't the right shade. It was supposed to be beige, but it was a light brown. This made everything worse. Something in her mind sparked ugly, a reminder of who she once was, the pathetic girl who couldn't even successfully slit her wrists in the bathtub around the corner.

Lamb ran full speed into the bed. Her shins smashed into the base as she folded onto the mattress. Here she finally broke open, the tears spouting from her eyes as if her face was punctured and offered every ounce of hydration to this moment of despair. She buried her nose into her duvet and howled. This stupid yellow dress that was haunted by the love of her mother, gone forever. This run-down room which was mostly paid for by the UK government because she was a crazy person. But worst of all, the Sun scolding her like a child, because she was just that: a child on strings. The perfect marionette. So easily jerked around to rupture the spiritual synchronisation of the human race, because she was so stupid, she was so stupid, she was a stupid, stupid girl.

Nearly drowning in her tears, Lamb lifted her head, gasping for air and then shuffled her body to rest her head on her pillow, a position where she intended to stay forever. But as her cheek slid onto the surprisingly soft fabric, her forehead hit something hard and sharp. She pulled back and took a moment to recognise what she was looking at. It was a VHS tape with a sticky note on top which read PLAY ME. This infuriated Lamb. First the hippopotamus' yesteryear computer and now a videocassette? Lamb decided that if this was indeed the afterlife, she was surely in Hell. She threw the VHS across the room, colliding with the corner. And there she lay until her fumes calmed to condensation and a fresh puddle of tears outlined her face on the pillow.

VI

3

Do days or nights exist in the hereafter? Does time hold any meaning in eternity? Lamb might have lain on that bed for years for all she knew, or cared. The same thoughts rotated inside her skull. What became of Earth after her death? Did the forces of Good regain the upper hand? Did they summon a new hero to rebalance her damage? Or was it too late? Was her following too powerful? Did they murder Tami Theron? Was the Earth forever the property of the Bad Energy, another point on their chalkboard as the eternal war plays on?

Lamb squirmed and winced and cried and screamed, and then, eventually, she depleted her emotional resources. Boredom settled, and she passed the time by identifying the errors in the room's replication, like a game of spot-the-difference. They'd placed a small crack wriggling from the correct corner of the ceiling, but Lamb knew it should run half an inch to the left. Her real curtains were missing the third hook, yet here it was. But the most glaringly obvious was the brutally clunky television set placed on a table within a concave of the wall. Lamb did not own a TV. This appliance sat on a VCR player, and every time Lamb looked at it she was riled by rebellion. *PLAY ME* said the sticky note, visible from the tape that leaned against the wall. *NO*, Lamb thought to herself. But at some point, due to no discernible development, Lamb peeled the sticky note free and pushed the VCR into the machine.

The television flickered to blue. A chunky font in the corner announced *PLAY*. A quick static fuzz transition into a monk figure, sitting crossed-legged, eyes closed, with a sedate smile upon his face. A soft gong crackled through the speakers, and the monk opened his eyes.

"Hello, *LAMB*, and welcome–"

The name *LAMB* was a different voice that did not match his lip movement, a careless dub meant to encourage personalisation yet achieving the opposite effect.

"Hello, *LAMB*, and welcome to The Supreme Realm of Saṃsāra. You should feel honoured by your admission into this world as it is the highest of the Saṃsāras, a utopia where only the most influential of Earthly deities spend their eternity. We trust you are enjoying your stay so far, but we appreciate you must have many questions about this new dimension. It is my hope that by the end of this video, you will come away with a greater understanding of what makes the Supreme Realm of Saṃsāra so special."

The image spurted into a messy moment of colour, before returning to blue. A white outline of a male figure was now drawn on the centre screen. The monk narrated.

"On Earth, we each like to see ourselves as one being. But this is not true!"

Two additional outlined figures slid out either side of the central man to create three identical drawings in a row.

"No, instead, every being consists of three distinct energetic sources that play imperative roles in the sustenance of the Universe."

The number 1 appeared on the figure to the left.

"The first, and perhaps most obvious, is the physical man. Here, a visual representation is shown to the world just as the world shows a visual representation back to the man. Once this physical vessel no longer carries life, it breaks down into smaller parts, feeding a separate link in the cosmic chain of nature. In physical death, we gift physical life elsewhere to ensure nothing is lost, and nothing is wasted."

Throughout this monologue, the first outline faded until it was gone. The number 2 appeared upon the figure on the right.

"The second and more complex aspect of every being is their soul.

This is the electricity that powers the physical, but it is not yours. It is borrowed from the Universe. When each child is born, a spark of this energy is blessed unto them, and their body is powered to grow and heal, collecting information until it has learned enough and leaves the physical. Upon release, the soul rejoins the Universe and is reused again and again. It is what you may know as the cycle of reincarnation and, even as we speak, somewhere out there your electricity is swimming freely in the great Universal force. Perhaps it has already been summoned into another womb, or perhaps it is drifting far from Earth, destined to power something else a thousand years later or more."

Predictably, that labelled figure was fading, once again leaving the central outline alone. Number 3.

"Finally, there is the Sülde Ruhu. Here is where your personality identification is stored, the creative result of so many intricate integers that made you, *you*. Your genetics, your experiences, your determined evolutionary drive, but most importantly, how you chose to deal with these incidences and what type of character formed under those pressures. The Sülde is the awareness of you that persists after death, a linger of atomic information delegated to an eternal afterlife best suited to the traits that solidified into the being you are. This is your current condition, an essence that lives on as a reward: soulless but able to enjoy the utopia we've built for you."

This drawn figure did not fade. Instead, the video cut back to the monk, still smiling, still staring forward.

"There are infinite realms created by many forces. Some are built for pleasure, some to punish, some merely a dusty vacancy of nothingness forever. The Saṃsāra dimensions have a long history, conceived and built within the minds of Indian Elder Brothers of the Human Race; Hindi Masters of Ancient Wisdom. These realms have evolved and adapted with many subdivisions, but where you are was developed by hundreds of Buddhist gurus over thousands of human years, including contributions from myself and even Siddhartha Gautama. Consisting of six levels, here we are at the top stage, which some call the 'God Realm' or the 'Deity Society'. It is the most desirable of afterlives, where only those who achieved the highest ranks of enlightenment are invited."

The image of the monk blurred slightly, or was that just Lamb's eyes? She was so bored.

"But while we are a proud utopia, we are also a family, and it takes a family to hold a home together. That is why each being is assigned a number which correlates to their impact on the Earth. But do not worry! Just because some numbers appear bigger than others does not mean anyone is more or less important, as everyone's role is essential and we function as a unit. No matter what your wrist says, be satisfied that you have a duty to perform which assists the Saṃsāra as a whole. Details about your position are following sh–"

The monk was cut off as the screen fell to black, with a large flashing number 10. A robotic female voice took over the speech.

"You have been classified as the number 10. Your assignments are organisational. Please await further instructions."

The picture returned to the monk, but the colours looked wrong.

"–hope this video has helped you understand the miracle of the Supreme Realm of Saṃsāra and that you should feel pleased by your Sülde personality for handling life in such a way to reach here. But remember that the utopia only works if you work it! So, do not be afraid to speak up, ask questions, and inform others of what you are looking for. And eventually, an eternal paradise of your design will be yours. Namaste!"

On the final word, the monk closed his eyes. A soft gong rang out and the television faded to black, Lamb staring at her reflection. A jerking clamour came from the VHS player, and the tape ejected itself. Lamb stood there, aware that she was armed with fresh information yet frustrated that she did not know what to do with it. She might have tried to smash the VHS if she'd had a moment to think, but a loud knock on the door stole her thoughts.

VI

4

For no reason, Lamb expected to open the door to find the monk sitting there. Instead, a slim female figure stood before her, draped in see-through silk garments while chunks of golden jewellery punctuated her human body. This excessive flaunt of wealth was hardly noticeable due to the creature's cat-head, which was currently licking the back of a paw-like hand. Lamb's reaction was minimal. She was desensitised, or even unimpressed, certain that this licking action was a planned display to emphasise the deity's animal uniqueness. So Lamb said nothing, and the cat froze, mid-lick, her eyes staring into Lamb's for answers. Lamb's awkward gaze dropped to the floor.

"So you watched the video," the cat spoke up.

"I ..." Lamb started.

"Dull, isn't it?" The cat interrupted. She sighed, staring off into the distance as if talking to no one in particular. "An utter waste of everyone's time."

A hint of a smile nudged Lamb's right cheek in agreement. The cat noted this and then stuck out her damp paw, palm facing down, perhaps presenting it for a kiss. "My name is Bastet, Ancient Egyptian, Level 14."

Lamb hesitantly grabbed the hand and gave it a little shake. "My name is ..."

"Lamb, I know," Bastet interrupted again. "Level 10, very nice. Look, I'm going to get right to it. I appreciate that you're all sulky, feeling sorry for yourself in your room and let me assure you that is typical newbie behaviour. Very basic. Not unexpected. However, I've been temporarily positioned to be your guide, to show you the ropes around here and whatever. We all have to do this from occasion to occasion, it's part of the game. So just play along and everything will be swell. Take it from me: this place can be a laugh once you learn how it works, and I'm hard to impress. Please let go of me now."

Lamb didn't realise she was still shaking Bastet's paw and continued to do so for several seconds before her mind caught up and she abruptly released it. "Thanks," Bastet continued. "So, are you going to come with me, or am I going to pee all over your room to mark it as my territory?"

Lamb snickered, then nodded. "I'll come with you."

The two took off down the hall and weren't seven feet away before the world began to shake.

"Uh oh," Bastet muttered as the vibrations escalated with a low rumble. "Best get your back against the wall."

Bastet was already positioning herself while Lamb stood still, letting out a bewildered "huh?" Bastet grabbed Lamb and slammed her into place, shouting due to the turbulent roar of the world, "Get your back against the damn wall!"

What appeared as an earthquake suddenly materialised as a mammoth multicoloured snake, tearing down the corridor like a derailed train. Its girth was so impossibly large that the hallway's frame had to stretch to accommodate it. Its wet, scabby skin whipped past Lamb like a wave of surreal paintings, pressing her deeper into the wall, holding her there like styrofoam.

The six-mile body zipped past in less than a minute, echoing into the distance and leaving Lamb desperate for air. The hallway shuddered then returned to its natural state, gently popping the two out from the wall to where they previously stood. Bastet dusted herself off.

"What the heck was that?" Lamb huffed.

"Rainbow Serpent. Native Aussie. Proper old school god. Level 23, very rare to see that thing around. Doesn't often animate out of the pre-manifest Dreamtime. Must be your lucky day. Anyway, let's keep going."

Their walk resumed, but Lamb's respiratory cycle wouldn't stabilise. Her heart throbbed upside down, and her emotions drained upward to her head, swimming in anxiety. This was a mistake. She should have stayed in her room.

Bastet rolled her eyes and stopped in front of Lamb, placing both paws on her shoulders. "Ok, just take a moment. I know that was crazy, but don't worry, that is not going to happen again. Remember the crowded lobby when you first arrived? Remember all those strange faces looking at you as you made your way to the elevator? That is as bad as it gets, and you don't ever have to go down there again, you hear? I definitely don't. Such a mix of castes is, ugh, gross. Unnatural. But you're a 10 and you're hanging with me, and I'm a 14. We're basically royalty around these parts, alright? We'll stick to the finest classes, so don't stress."

There was a quality about Bastet that calmed Lamb. She was a no-nonsense type of girl. Just the kind of balance someone like Lamb needed to navigate this new world consumed by insecurity. Plus, those cat eyes were mesmerising. They made Lamb feel protected, and her resistance liquified as she nodded in compliance.

"Good!" Bastet let go of Lamb's shoulders and then waved her along. "Now, keep up! I have something to show you. You're going to love it."

The duo turned into an opening elevator, and Lamb nearly tripped over a large boar already inside. "Sorry!" Lamb blurted as the animal snorted, but its owner, a tall, pale-skinned goddess wearing a cloak of falcon feathers, hushed it. The lady offered Lamb a one-sided smile of forgiveness, and Lamb blushed, looking to the ground, overpowered by her company's radiating elegance. Bastet's extended claw clacked upon the button for Floor 5, and the doors shut.

A moment passed before Bastet spoke. "Hello, Freyja. Where are your chariot slaves today?" An icy tension ran shudders up Lamb's spine. Nobody faced any direction but forward as Freyja exhaled a single snicker.

"They're on the second."

An aching silence slowed the lift until a bell dinged for Floor 5. Lamb and Bastet exited, and the closing doors took Freyja away.

"God, I loathe that woman," Bastet hissed, already pacing down the corridor. Lamb scurried to catch up, reaching Bastet just as she was fiddling keys into a lock that secured two sliding doors together. With a click, Bastet pushed the barrier apart, "Tah-dah!"

Lamb turned just in time to draw a minty blast of oxygen, which wobbled her. Here was an immensely spacious garden blinding Lamb with an ethereal green glow splattered with flowers of every colour as a white river cut through the distance. It was the most strikingly magnificent piece of land that Lamb had ever looked upon. She stammered several vowels before squeezing her eyes shut, blinking away two tears that tingled her lower lids. Bastet smiled, "I'm taking your artless sways as a positive response."

"It's ... beautiful," Lamb managed. "It's massive and beautiful. It must be, like, a hundred times the size of the garden in St. Mary's!"

"Sure," Bastet shrugged as she held up the jangling keys. "And it's your job to keep it healthy and pretty, you got it?"

"Me?" Lamb doubtfully angled away from Bastet. The cat smiled again.

"Yup. We do get things right sometimes."

Bastet handed Lamb the keys and then passed across a large toolbox, which Lamb did not notice appearing from anywhere.

"Take this and amble around. Get familiar with your new place of work. Nobody expects too much on your first day, so go slow and enjoy yourself." Bastet pointed backwards to a door some yards down the hall. There was a sign upon it reading *Opium Naps* in a cursive font. "I'll be in there. Wake me when you're ready, and we'll grab some food."

Lamb squeezed the toolbox tightly with a wide grin. She instinctively took a half step towards the cat to initiate an embrace. Bastet raised her palms to stop her. "Don't make it weird," Bastet winked, then spun in the opposite direction, slinking off to chase a snooze.

Lamb watched her go, then slowly rotated to survey the vibrance of the garden. It shimmered with penetrating detail, as if Lamb had grown an extra lens over her pupils and the visual world had sharpened into a crispness unseen on Earth. Lamb glanced at the toolbox which popped open without touch, revealing an array of pristine gardening instruments, unused and sparkling with cleanliness. A folded-up piece of cloth was tucked into the side, which Lamb yanked out. It magically expanded in size, developing into a creaseless light green apron with a toolbelt attached.

Lamb's giddy emotions caught up as she slipped on the apron and clumsily tied the strings behind her back. She was starting to believe she had judged this place all wrong. The potential was far greater than she'd imagined—the paradise her scripture always promised, irrespective of whether the presentation differed. Clutching her toolbox, she stepped into the peppermint-fresh atmosphere that widened her sinuses. From this outside viewpoint, the building had disappeared, leaving the sliding doors standing alone within the otherwise natural environment. Lamb giggled uncontrollably as she spun around and around, unsure where first to concentrate her skills. These plants were going to be her best friends. She did not want anyone to feel inferior due to her chosen attention.

Her decision was made easier when she frolicked past a fluffy bush and stumbled to a halt at a vegetable patch that stretched outward forever. She instantly identified many of her favourites (Carrots! Radishes! Spinach! Onions!) but was acutely aware of many curious shapes poking from the ground that she did not recognise. Lamb rushed over, her toolbox clanking as she slid to her knees before a gorgeous row of plump tomatoes, so large that they appeared on the verge of explosion. Lamb chuckled as she greeted them, "Hello, team!" and then gazed upon their red shine with stupefied affection.

Silence.

Lamb's soft features slowly tensed, creasing in confusion. She cautiously poked at a tomato, leaving a shallow finger impression on its tight skin. Its texture certainly felt real, yet it did not respond. Lamb fell back in a seated position, analysing the display. These were the most exquisite tomatoes she had ever seen. But they were only tomatoes in the flesh. These guys lacked everything that Lamb loved about tomatoes. Where was their inflated pride? Their sense of humour? Their empathetic flexibility? There was no energy here, no emanating personality, no soul. These were tomatoes by name, not by character.

Lamb stood up and drifted to the adjacent neat rows of garlic. She held tightly to the hope that something was amiss with the tomatoes, and her garlic comrades would remember who they were: a mischievous gang to the boundaries of obscenity, strong-willed and opinionated, yet honest to those who earn it. But her foolish longing was dashed before her toes touched the dirt. This was not garlic. It was a representation of garlic, an illusion that would no doubt serve the senses yet could not capture the essence of individual identity. This entire garden was a lie.

Lamb spent the next half an hour roaming the grounds, dispersing a muted cry for help, seeking any reciprocation of affinity. She thought about the VHS monk explaining the ingredients of a person. The disintegrating post-death physical. The recycled spirit. And then the Sülde. Some type of full-stop on a person's developed traits, a snapshot of their evolved self, no longer expanding down life's timeline but a summary of where they had reached before they perished. Everything here was a soulless shell, merely pouches of data that achieved certain success, now rewarded with a reality where an aspect of their being could live on. But there was no spiritual vitality, and even the material replica was debatable in its authenticity. Those tomatoes weren't tomatoes; they were a compound memory of tomatoes.

Similarly, Lamb realised that she was not Lamb. Rather, she was a diverged section of Lamb, a strand of who she once was: a consciousness, an awareness that was granted an interface to mentally interpret and interact with her surroundings. Yet she was as real as those dumb tomatoes.

Depressed, Lamb followed the gush of the milky river back until the sliding doors came into view. She slumped towards them without hurry, giving brief thought to her toolbox, unable to remember where she'd left it. Once through the doors, she slid them shut, back inside tangible walls, the shift in air pressure weighing upon her body, popping her ears. The keys were somehow attached to her toolbelt, and she used them without question, locking the doors and then moving on to find Bastet.

Lamb knocked on the door of *Opium Naps* and listened for an answer. Nothing came aside from the ambient strum of an acoustic guitar dancing to her ears. She lightly pressed on the door, and it opened easily, the music getting louder while a fruity aroma clogged her nostrils. Lamb timidly leaned into the room, squinting through a thin mist.

Assorted creatures dotted the area, each in different stages of slumber or suckling upon colourful tubes worming from the furry white carpet. Lamb's eyes eventually located Bastet, horrified to witness her lying upside down on a beanbag, a thick spill of drool sliding from her snoring mouth over her forehead, her previous sophistication corrupted by this anaesthetised mess. Lamb wanted to cry.

VI

5

"Look, I'm not arguing with you. I'm just talking fairness here. Did Noah build an ark? Sure, kudos to him. But is he the big hero of the story that warrants a Level 21 stamp? No, he's a human—no offence, but a human, you know? And what actually happened down there is folklore at best."

Mithras paused to chug a jug of beer bigger than his face, liquid raining from his chin. Once emptied, he dramatically slammed the glass down with a mighty belch. The jug had already refilled itself to the brim. This commotion snapped Lamb back to the moment with a fright.

She was on Floor 5, seated at a table in what resembled a fancy cafe. Bastet sat to her left, picking at a bowl of raisins, while across the cloth was this Mithras character, an arrogant male wearing a silly bonnet, downing beer after beer, a wet patch spreading across his flowing robe. In-between Bastet and Mithras was a soft-looking goddess, unmistakingly Roman, who introduced herself as Cardea. To Lamb's right was a peculiar-looking man with antlers and leaves in his hair. Lamb thought his name was Cernunnos, but he was so quietly detached from the room that she wasn't sure what he had mumbled. Everyone politely accepted her presence, but after formalities she was swiftly ignored as

Mithras dominated the airwaves so vociferously that there was a circle of abandoned tables around them. Lamb was unimpressed.

"I think you forget," Bastet was contesting. "That the Bible remains the most influential book on Earth. Of course, Noah, as an Old Testament prophet of both Judaism and Christianity, would fare high in this game."

"Testament Schmestament!" Mithras sloshed his beer around, then slammed it down to stress his authority. "You're telling me that the Bible, ooh, is more special than, say, the Epic of Gilgamesh? Which predates it by thousands of years? The Mesopotamian origin story, telling how it was Utnapishtim who built the boat? And what is he? A Level 12, or 13, huh? Without Gilgamesh's contribution, there would be no Hebrew Bible, case closed. So, who is deeming who influential?"

Cardea had been trying to shove a word in this whole time. "Listen! Listen! The Epic of Gilgamesh is a prototype. It's hardly zeitgeist canon. You think the Earthlings can even pronounce Utnapishtim? Noah was a chosen prophet across the Abrahamic board. Naturally, he's gonna smash it ..."

"Alright, alright!" Mithras interrupted. "It was an example. But I see your Gilgamesh argument, and I raise you the Matsya fish." He made his points by raising his fingers one by one. "Avatar of Lord Vishnu; traceable back to the Rigveda—which are the oldest sacred Vedic Hindu texts, by the way; he not only rescued Manu from the flood, but he caused the flood himself, *BOOM!*"

Mithras sat back smugly, but Bastet waved him off. "That's a rumour. There is no citable evidence that Matsya caused anything."

"Pah, regardless," Mithras continued. "That fish did everything Noah did and more. And what does he get for it? Level 18, lower than Noah. The system is rigged. It doesn't make any sense."

"Just because you don't understand it doesn't mean it doesn't make sense," Cardea retorted. "We're talking about the Bible here. The Bible!"

"Noah is also mentioned in the Quran," Bastet added, and the two ladies bounced back and forth.

"Exactly! Oh my God, exactly. Hinduism, great, whatever, much love to them, but Islam? Plus Christianity plus Judaism equals, what? Double the human energy?"

"Oh, it's more than triple."

"Well, there you go! Noah was short-changed with 21, if anything."

A youthful robed angel walked past, and silence fell over the debate. Mithras sipped his beer for a change. Cernunnos munched on a burger made from grass that had appeared from nowhere. Lamb glanced up, and her eyes met Mithras'. She gasped ever so lightly.

"And what about you, freshman Lamb? Level 10, huh? How does someone in the modern world even boast a number that high?"

"Mithras, please," Bastet spoke up.

"Please, nothing. I'm just asking the new kid a question." Mithras' voice lowered as he leaned forward, staring Lamb down, speaking slowly and deliberately. "I'm dying to know. What ... did you do?"

The table was invested. Everyone was looking at her. "I ..." she squeaked, then cleared her throat. "I ... messed up." She paused to sigh in surrender. "The Bad Energy of the Universe, it ... tricked me into believing I was something I was not. So, I led a large group of people with talks of dismantling the government. Only I was wrong, and I pain to think of what damage I have caused. I am not worthy of some afterlife reward, and I definitely don't belong here."

"Sweets, don't say that," Cardea offered warmth, but Mithras was less sympathetic.

"Wow, downer, much? This place doesn't work how you think it works. Did you not just hear our Noah conversation? It's not about what you did or how you did it in any objective moral reality. It's about your influence! How you shook the spiritual timeline. Wait, let me help you out here." Mithras' head spun in different directions, scanning the room, seeking something. "Ok, right there, look."

Lamb followed the line from Mithras' finger, which landed on a goddess seated alone on a sofa. Her blinded white eyes shone through her flowing pitch-black hair, which rested upon a giant belly swelling from her otherwise skinny frame. She was absent-mindedly swinging a small chain in her right hand, the only indication that she was conscious.

"Behold, priestess Loviatar," Mithras said under his breath. "Finnish mythology. Eternally pregnant by a rotten wind. Her womb holds nine diseases, which she regularly birthed upon the world. Cancer, ulcers, rickets ... you name it, she spread it." Mithras sat back, lifting his full jug of beer. "Now, you'd think such atrocities would go punished, yeah? But that's the old model of thinking. Instead, you're looking at a Level 7 deity right there. You see? We're gods. Human well-being is voluntary. It's just a blip on Earth. It means nothing in the bigger picture."

"I raise you one," Cardea swivelled Lamb's focus. "Check her out." She gestured towards another goddess dressed similarly to Cardea herself. "You know you've made a mess when your name becomes an idiom. Pandora's box, ever heard of it? That there's Pandora."

Of course, Lamb knew the phrase well and was intrigued, stealthily inspecting the deity. Young. Plain-faced but pretty. Simple dress. She sipped a small glass of wine and then fumbled with it, spilling a few drops. Her timid eyes darted around, embarrassed, trying to see if anyone had noticed. She glanced over at Lamb, but Lamb looked away just in time.

"Fun fact: it wasn't actually a box," Cardea continued. "It was a jar that contained countless plagues and unspeakable evils. She was told never to open it, but surprise, surprise! She did, unleashing immeasurable terror onto the land. Can you imagine the guilt? And yet, here she is, strolling among us. Hey, guess what level she is."

Lamb shrugged.

"Level 16. Can you believe it? Her of all people."

"You're just jealous," Mithras interjected. "You Greco-Romans are so competitive, always bringing down someone who scores higher than you."

"Do not *ever* refer to me as Greco-Roman, you understand?" Cardea fumed. "I am purebred Roman to my core. I have nothing to do with that soap opera narrative."

"Hey, here's an idea," Mithras smiled. "Why not tell our new friend what it is exactly that you did during your negligible stint on Earth, hmm?"

"Seriously, why are you like this?" Cardea's anger steamed through her clenched teeth as Mithras turned to address Lamb.

"Our Roman comrade, sitting here so peacefully with us, was in fact in charge of the very urgent role of protecting ... what was it again? Oh yes, the door hinge!" With that, Mithras let out a hearty chortle.

"You uneducated swine," Cardea's speech was shaped like daggers. "Do you know how many babies I saved from crib-snatchers? How many targeted mothers were protected when demons could not enter through their doorways? I saved lives."

"I'll bet!" Mithras' jovial spirit held high. "That's why you're stamped at Level 5. Disgusting! Face it, you glorified personificated *nymph!* You're lucky just to be sitting with us."

Cardea's hands were gripping the tablecloth. She was growling. A door slammed in the distance. Bastet casually placed a paw upon Cardea's left clenched fist and shook her head. Cardea relaxed a little, closing her eyes, taking a deep breath. Mithras appeared not to notice as his verbal blitz transformed into a monologue. He proudly lifted his wrist to show off his number to Lamb.

"You see that? Level 17, baby. That's more than Cardea and you combined. I'm one of the most famous names around here. Undiluted Zoroastrian divinity, then branching off into a mystery cult all on my own during Roman rule. I was set to be theological divinity, one of the primary rivals of Christianity. I was so close to climbing the ladder as *the* dominant force in the religious spectrum, all the way to the top! But Jesus, Jesus, Jesus. Everything always Jesus. They suppressed us, eliminated us, almost wiped us from history. Now I feel sick whenever I think of the 'King of Kings', blah."

Mithras reset his escalated energy with a huge swig of beer, oblivious to Lamb's eyes glazing with liquid. "Hang on!" she shouted far louder than her character, taking everyone by surprise. "Does Jesus live here?"

"Of course he's here," Mithras sneered. "Where else would he go?"

Lamb couldn't believe she hadn't thought of this before. Jesus was in the same realm as she was! Oh my! This revelation was a game changer, her destiny aligning in her mind as her knees bounced with excitement. "Can I meet him?"

An instant burst of laughter unified everyone at the table. Even Cernunnos snorted. Lamb felt small as Bastet tried to let her down gently. "Jesus is a Level 25, one below the utmost top. They don't associate with numbers like ours." Lamb's throat squeezed shut, and she briefly thought she might cry.

"Uh-oh," Cardea announced, looking over Lamb's shoulder. "Here comes the exception that proves the rule!"

The sound of the sitar accompanied by a speedy drum pattern commanded the airways as the room thudded in time with the beat. Lamb turned in her chair and spluttered with disbelief as a nine-foot god with a disproportionate elephant head came crashing into the cafe. Everyone cheered as the elephant slapped people's hands with his trunk, greeting them as he danced by. His presence was so overpowering that Lamb's tongue tasted like turmeric. Even she knew who this was. "Ganesh," she whispered.

Lamb turned back to face the table where everyone was smiling, dancing in their chairs to the music. Bastet caught her eye and shouted over the noise, "Get ready to meet the friendliest god in all of the Saṃsāra!" Nerves overcame Lamb. She did not feel ready for such a celebrity encounter.

Ganesha speedily did the rounds, not a palm untouched by his trunk until he reached their table, bumping his snout to Bastet's fist, then Cardea's, then pausing to grab Mithra's wrist and shake it.

"Heyyy, Mithras, my dude," Ganesha greeted the man by name, his voice booming over the music. "How many beers have you had today? A thousand?"

Mithras laughed, about to counter when Ganesha's line of vision fell upon Lamb. She squeezed her arms into her body, hoping to shrivel from existence, but Ganesha took two pounding steps, spinning around the table and then lowering to her face. "Woah," Ganesha stared. "New deity blood in the house! Hello there, my name is Ganesha! And who might you be?"

Ganesh stuck out his trunk. Lamb forced her arm up to grab onto the soft tube, but her words would not come. Bastet leaned forward to save the day. "Ganesh, this is Lamb. She's only recently joined us as a Level 10."

"A Level 10!" Ganesh shouted, many far-off heads turning to listen. "Wow, man, that's insane! We haven't had a Level 10 here since ..."

Ganesh paused to look upwards, seeking his brain for answers. "1948?" Lamb quietly finished his sentence, and Ganesh's gaze fell back to her, beaming with light.

"Yes, exactly! So you know!"

Lamb nodded even though she did not know.

"Lamb was just telling us that she would loooove to meet Jesus

Christ," Mithras informed Ganesh, and the elephant instantly exploded into laughter, the entire restaurant soon joining, everyone in on the
joke. Lamb winced in agony, her organs compressing together.

"Never give up the dream, little one!" Ganesh spoke through his
smile. "If you sit in the library long enough, you might get lucky!" Then,
with a quick high-five shared with Cernunnos, Ganesha danced off like
a whirlwind of divine energy, making physical contact with each creature before exiting out the other side, the music fading with him. The
general mood was elated, every table chatting faster.

"Oof, that felt incredible," Cardea wiped her forehead. Everyone
sat back with euphoric grins, their heavy breathing slowing down. Lamb
mimicked their actions, trying to hide her discomfort, her skin itching.

"Speaking of feeling incredible," Mithras sat up again. "What is
everyone up to later? I hear the Olmecs are throwing another temple
orgy on Floor 3?"

"Ugh, repulsive," Bastet responded. "Not for me, thanks. I've
made plans to meet Kali in the murder room. Going to reorientate my
chakras by slicing innocent people into minced meat." To illustrate,
Bastet extended her claws and swiped at the air. Lamb's shock must
have been evident because Bastet quickly reassured her. "Don't worry,
darling, they're not real people," Bastet smiled and then coughed up a
slimy clump of fur the size of a tennis ball that splattered onto the table.
The wet hair quickly dissolved into nothing as Bastet tapped her chest.
"Excuse me."

Cardea started talking about her planned visit to the bathhouse,
but Lamb zoned out, drowning in dissociation, a mental battle where a
spreading numbness occasionally cracked, and she swallowed a wail. A
sharp pain flared on her arm, and she looked down at her hand furiously scratching blood from her skin. She shivered as she noted a patch of
bumpy texture developing, resembling black leather.

VI

6

I t was the absence of designated time periods that got to her. The rotation of day and night is an absurd concept when existing as a metaphysical manifestation far away from the organic substances which depend on them. The notion of time was illogical and irrelevant, exposing one's newbie status whenever vocalised. If you desired night-time, visit the night section; otherwise, move about your infinite day without the hindrance of darkness. If you wanted to sleep, you could sleep, and what a profoundly refreshing sleep you would have. If you wanted to eat, any meal's atomic structure could be organised before you within seconds of your request. It was an instant gratification wonderland, and Lamb found no comfort in it. Her rash was very dark now. Unbearably itchy.

Something about this place reminded Lamb of a parade that had marched the streets of West London a few years before her death. Excitable music and flashy materials blurred past. Impressive dancers backflipped and cartwheeled. Giant balloon creatures loomed across the sky. At first she was caught up in the vibrant commotion, clapping and grinning like a child. But it soon overwhelmed her as she spied the human dirt beneath. Recognisable cartoon icons waved at the crowd, but she saw the people behind the masks and make-up. They weren't real. They were phoney, oft-disproportionate portrayals of famous animated creations, driven by people who, like everyone else, were still dealing with painful problems while haunted by past decisions. Yet here they were, pretending to be something else in hope that their spectators accepted the dream, when in reality they were simply doing a job. Lamb's realisation punctured the illusion, and she could not regain her sense of wonder. She ran home to bury her ears beneath her pillow. She did that sometimes, back on Earth. And she was doing that more and more in the Saṃsāra.

What made this realm worse than her earthly existence was the attention placed upon her attendance. The powers were always watching, trying everything they could to accommodate her, to varying degrees of success. Bastet relentlessly yanked her along to dinners, which Lamb loathed but appreciated, even if her extreme awkwardness ruined the vibe for everyone else. She was offered 72 virgins, a concept that disgusted her values irrespective of the assurances that they "weren't actually people." There was some distraction found in the chess room, but Lamb was never the most proficient player and lost almost every game. So, by default she'd fall back to her job, tending to the soulless garden, conjuring up fantasy conversations with flowers from memory, then slumping back into depression when she found her imagination too limited to convincingly converse with itself.

Every so often, an existential panic attack would smash into her like a truck, and she would collapse, paralysed to the floor no matter where she was. These were the result of sporadic remembrances concerning her immortality. No matter how boundless this realm was claimed, a claustrophobic element confined her. This was it. She would be here for eternity, and death itself was not even an escape option. But someone was always there to pick up her shaken body, quickly moving her away from spoiling the atmosphere, then plonking her down in front of a cheery deity, happy to help. They'd tell her this reaction was typical for newcomers and that the idea of an endless life was only daunting when you were still acclimated to a finite world. She was told to let go into the exact present moment, and then she would realise there was no time or eternity, only an instant—this very instant—in the now. From that immediate perspective, existence was, in actuality, extremely short, only happening currently, with no future or past involved. Lamb struggled to digest this understanding, but her panic would eventually settle and she'd pretend to accept this reality so that she could get back to hiding in her room or scratching her arms beneath the desks in the library.

"If you sit in the library long enough, you might get lucky!"

Ganesha's advice rang in her mind as the only highlight of that first meal. Lamb sought out the library directly after that meeting, following signs and swiftly locating it on the first floor. She entered a busy room that more closely resembled a modest bookshop than a place of study. Looking around, she noted nothing but books one would thumb through in the religious section of a mainstream store on Earth. There were plenty of Bibles and Qurans, Tao Te Chings and Vedas, along with human-written analyses and summaries of these scriptures. Imagine Lamb's disappointment. That was until the old Cailleach librarian lady pointed out the door at the back with a big number 2 nailed on it. A little green square allowed Lamb to tap her wrist and move onward. As it turns out, Library 1 was merely the exoteric scraps for the first level. Much like everything in the Saṃsāra, a partitioning of reward was at work here, the texts escalating in value the higher your tattoo.

As if mocking those lower numbers, one had to strut through each library space to reach the door to the subsequent area. And the differences between them were substantial, from the size of the room to the smaller number of welcomed patrons, to the advancing wisdom of the texts. Library 2 was much larger and boasted a wider selection of books that were more occult in nature yet still exclusively Earth-written. Classic mysticism was found here—*The Zohar, The Key of Solomon, The Secret Doctrine, The Kybalion*—offering Level 2 deities and beyond the chance to catch up on their human studies of the spiritual. Lamb even passed Aleister Crowley one day, fuming as he analysed *The Book of the Law*, a publication he had penned himself yet was obsessed with. Lamb paid him no mind, however. She did not know who he was.

Library 3 was the last station exclusively dealing with Earth books, but these were the rarest of arcane treasures: unfinished scribblings in a mystic's diary, lost pages that were burnt during religious invasions, and underground advanced editions of familiar works (including complete Bibles with over 200 additional entries no longer found on that planet). After Library 3, each library became increasingly elaborate in terms of expansive interior designs as well as sacred works authored by hands within the Saṃsāra or generated by computer programs.

Of course, Lamb's permitted access ceased at Library 10. It was a massive hall dominated by a rich brown colour complementing a classy wood finish. The centrepiece was a star formation created by rows of bookshelves jutting out from a large circle of reading desks. It was a charming detail one could admire from higher angles when climbing any of the numerous spiral staircases. Over two-hundred million non-Earth books were displayed, but Lamb did not care. She took a seat in the middle of the star to wait for Jesus.

Was he really in this realm? Lamb pictured the two of them sharing a knowing smile as they crossed paths, Jesus nodding as he approached her, for he sought her too. They would sit down and break bread while he answered questions about life and death, teaching her how to find peace in the Saṃsāra through the Holy Spirit of Christ. They would laugh about how he saved her from splatting into the sidewalk at the last minute. They would study the Bible and hold hands to pray. They would meet every day. She would be his favourite.

Such a daydream was akin to pouring cold water on a burn, providing a temporary relief that Lamb yearned to solidify into her reality. But every time the door opened, her fluttering eyes would dart towards a different anomaly, like giant bees or some Slavic deity made of fire, selecting books, reading, leaving, or moving onward to Library 11. She'd quietly curse them with discouragement. In the stillness, she made up conversations between Jesus and herself, chuckling at his humour and her equally witty responses. She would play this game for an indeterminable amount of time until her frustration became smothering, and she had to escape her thoughts. She'd lie on her bed or fulfil her duties in the garden, but these spaces generated anxiety and darkened her rash. Any moment spent away from the library could be the exact moment Jesus walked through. For that reason, her visits to the library grew in frequency.

Lamb had an overwhelming fear of glancing away at the moment Jesus sauntered through, so she initially dedicated her focus without falter. However, she soon found that swift strolls around the spacious floor stretched her legs and cleared her mind, making it easier to remain there longer. Once she accepted this practice, her eyes soon wandered with her, skimming the spines of endless books, most of which were written using symbols she did not recognise. But she'd run her fingers along their uneven surfaces and appreciate that she was touching a wealth of sacred knowledge that no human on Earth had the privilege to access, even if she had little interest in reading any of it.

This apathetic attitude shifted on her 16th visit to the library when, during one of her casual roams, her fingertips stroked a book that stood shorter than the others but attracted her attention due to its deep red hue. Lamb never stopped moving, but her mind grasped the title amidst the other texts that streaked past her tired vision. In gold lettering, it read *THE SECRET RESURRECTION OF JESUS*. Lamb's instinct was to snatch the book immediately, but her self-promise to shun distractions overrode her priorities, and she left it behind, lost in the expanse of paper, with a faint twitch of remorse.

Such regrets were unnecessary, Lamb shortly found out. On another walkaround two visits later, she glimpsed the red book again even though she was in a completely different section. Like before, she did not break her stride, but her mind jittered and she decided that a third sighting would surely be a sign to surrender to its pursuit. She then spent several subsequent library sessions actively seeking the book, annoyed that it seemed to have disappeared. However, her pupils had developed a keen watchfulness, and eventually she spotted the title from a distance, rushing to grab it and enjoying the rare buzz from this successful hunt.

Lamb skipped to the mid-star position and sat at the table with the best view of the door. A humanoid coyote sat upright some feet away on the table's other side, reading a thick, coverless book through a pair of spectacles, paying Lamb no regard. Still, Lamb felt awkward, as if she was doing something naughty, and she intentionally held her book at inclinations that would make it challenging to identify. Once comfortable, she observed the cover, tracing her pinkie over the gold lettering on the front, which was identical to the spine, only larger. *THE SECRET RESURRECTION OF JESUS*. She might as well learn more about the Messiah while she waited for him. Taking three quick, shallow breaths, she opened to a random page.

The idea that this book was a heavenly gift was immediately thwarted by the content, or rather, the lack thereof. Thick black markers redacted chunks of information, at times whole paragraphs, while jagged paper running down the side indicated hastily torn-out pages. Whatever these secrets were would remain a secret, and Lamb sunk into bittered disillusionment. What was the point of separating libraries into sections of access when the texts on offer weren't even legible?

Lamb's thumb flicked the pages. She noted that the censorship was more prominent midway, whereas the earlier chapters appeared less tampered with. Despite her frustrations, she figured she might still discover something if she started from the beginning. It was, after all, the customary reading order of a book.

The anonymous author was an abysmal writer, using Old English phrasing in what Lamb believed was an attempt to sound esoteric, but coming across as pretentious. She slogged through the first section, which was a monotonous retelling of the reincarnation process that Lamb already understood. The afterlife realms were described as post-physical areas where a preserved personality (Sülde) was rewarded or punished for how its developed identity reacted to the Earthly life thrust upon it. But the electric spirit—the soul that so many religions were obsessed with—was stripped away to rejoin the underlying power source, then reused as it had been so many times before. In that way, the rebirth cycle was true for every being, just without any awareness of the process. Meanwhile, the physical body turned to worm food, its atoms breaking down to nourish organisms that would ultimately nourish something else—yet another recycling procedure.

Throughout this read, Lamb vigilantly lifted her eyes to the entrance. How fast did Jesus move? Perhaps he would silently glide across the floor at a superhuman speed? She refused to take any chances. However, as she turned to later chapters, her mental spotlight was submerged in new information, and she gradually transferred her focus.

The second section detailed the differences between reincarnation and resurrection. Reincarnation was when a brand new character was born from the beginning, perhaps with trace elements of their previous characteristics, be it their soul's energy or even their Sülde attaching for the ride. Meanwhile, resurrection required the three aspects of an individual to rejoin on the Earthly plane, a seemingly impossible feat which had somehow been achieved across different mythologies around the world. The physical body was, of course, the most straightforward component. As long as the rot hadn't made a monster of the corpse, one only needed to relocate this tangible matter on Earth, and they had their vessel.

The other two components were far trickier. First, one would have to escape their afterlife, which was against every law of death irrespective of the realm in which you ended. Then, one would require the Great Source Energy to repower the organic material, turning on the molecular engine and connecting the personality to the physical, allowing for pre-death movement as before.

In theory, if any component was missing, you'd have a disaster on your hands.

Body and Spirit without Sülde would produce a mobile creature without memories, personality, or a thinking consciousness: essentially, a zombie.

Spirit and Sülde without Body would produce an invisible essence trapped on Earth with a hint of influence on the physical realm: essentially, a ghost.

Worst of all, Body and Sülde without Spirit would stick an individual's awareness into its body without energised atoms; no communication between the two, unable to move, stuck in a decaying body most likely underground, unable to do anything until it was reduced to a thinking skeleton for eternity.

However, the book assured the reader that there were other ways to resurrect and promised to reveal everything as it proceeded.

The second and third sections of the book were separated with a striking warning in a much larger font size. The words cautioned against attempting anything from this point onward. Any application was illegal, and the consequences were unpredictable at best, and catastrophic at worst.

The third section was where the blocks of blackouts crept in. Lamb did her best, driven by fascination as the book provided a brief list of deities that had achieved resurrection, telling the backstory that led to their death and then their approach to initiate their reentry into the land of the living. Unfortunately, any usable information was unreadable, but Lamb got the impression that the deities' restoration was either a result of higher permission or dark magic. Or perhaps a mix of both.

The fourth section was about Jesus specifically, who had achieved his resurrection in a way unlike anyone else. Sadly, very few phrases were left untouched. Lamb could not decipher any coherent story besides the keywords she recognised from the Bible narrative, such as *betrayal*, *innocence*, *torture*, and *Barabbas*. Finally, the fifth section offered resurrection spells which, besides the heading, were completely stripped, entire pages black or forcibly removed, leaving torn remnants to exasperate her disappointment.

When Lamb closed the back cover, she was a different person than when she'd started. The sails of her mission had shifted direction. She needed to find out how to resurrect her person, and then she could return to Earth to rectify the devastating miseducation she had unleashed on the people. She needed to fix her mistakes.

With eyes whirring with purpose, Lamb turned to face the coyote. The coyote sensed her stare and looked up from its book. Lamb smiled. The coyote shifted uncomfortably and glanced back at his reading material, ignoring the exchange.

VI

7

Fresh motivation propelled Lamb's afterlife. She scoured the library and devoured every text she could find on resurrection, of which there were many. Her frenzied activity bubbled her rash into hard scales, but she didn't care, scratching the scabs away as she read and bled at the desks. When Lamb learned how to navigate the messy registry system on the clunky computers she discovered even more titles, at times in the libraries below number 10. The information was her sustenance, even if she constantly bumped into censored material or books that were dishearteningly basic and repetitive.

Regardless, most texts offered at least a sliver of unique data, and none proved as helpful as *The Encyclopedia of Resurrection*. Within it, Lamb explored a comprehensive directory of gods that had come and gone and come again. More importantly, each entry stated whether the deity ended up in the Supreme Realm of Saṃsāra, along with their level. Lamb read the surprisingly uncensored publication from cover to cover.

Naturally, she adored revisiting Jesus' crucifixion and holy return three days later but was again discouraged by his inaccessible Level 25 status. Another recognisable character was Osiris, an Egyptian deity whose brother, Set, cut him into little chunks and distributed the bits across the world. Osiris' dedicated wife, Isis, found all the pieces and mummified him back together, returning him to the real world. Lamb would love to pick his brain but, like Jesus, he was a Level 25. Perhaps Bastet could help?

Lamb found it fascinating that Ganesh was also a result of resurrection. His oblivious father, Shiva, had chopped off his human head when he was a little boy. But the father, upon realising his mistake, brought the child back to life by fixing an elephant's noggin to his neck. Talk about accidentally doing his son a favour; this unique feature made Ganesh one of the most recognisable deities in history and the most loved. No wonder he too sat at Level 25. But perhaps Lamb could approach him about the topic? He seemed receptive enough.

Nonetheless, Lamb knew she'd have better luck with lower numbers, and she combed through each candidate to locate the most accessible entry point. Timelines invented or appropriated by European audiences were the most difficult to crack due to their Earthly popularity. Westernised gods had led their people into grand global conquests and won. Such attention earned higher Levels, meaning more hierarchical barriers to push through. But the deeper Lamb investigated lesser-exoteric lands, such as Africa or Asia, the more people she found whom she believed she could talk to.

The first was Babalú-Ayé, a Yoruba deity worshipped in West Africa's Nigeria, Benin, and Togo. Later, his name spread to the Americas due to the slave trade. And yet, despite his fame, Babalú-Ayé was only awarded a Level 8. This was considered a generous blessing for any deity from the traditional African community due to the continent's thousands of tribes, each with conflicting canons, constituting only 1% of the world's religious population.

Lamb's superior number meant Babalú-Ayé was easy to find. After asking around on Floor 8, Lamb met Babalú-Ayé on one of his walks through the steamy rainforest on Floor 3. They fell into conversation with immediate rapport.

"Resurrection is a taboo conversation around these parts," Babalú-Ayé told her quietly. "There are many *amebo* ears around us, listening, always listening, always waiting. I am nervous to talk about it. You understand, ba?"

Lamb enjoyed watching Babalú-Ayé shuffle slowly in her periph-eral vision. He was an elderly man wrapped in rags, his pitch-dark skin plagued by wet sores, yet his face revealed much kindness despite folds of troubled knowledge. "I understand," she nodded in response. "But I think there is a reason why we are walking together. Perhaps an un-derlying fate to our paths meeting. Something much bigger than both of us at work, which goes beyond the rules of this place." Lamb wasn't sure she believed every word she just said, but Babalú-Ayé responded positively with a chuckle.

"I am an old fool when it comes to a destiny story. Alright, little lady. Ask me what you want to know, and I will answer if I can."

"Well, it's just ... how did you do it? The resurrection, was it magic or ... what exactly?"

Babalú-Ayé took an extended sigh as a hint of sorrow slipped across his face. They made several strides in silence, their steps rhyth-mically joining the buzz and scuttles of the forest. Finally, Babalú-Ayé spoke.

"I am Babalú-Ayé. I am a spirit summoned to heal my Yoruba people. Heal and protect them from the attack of illness. I claim their disease for my body so they can live another day, or I give it back to someone who disrupts the harmony of the *aṣẹ*. But I was not always this way. I was once a powerful prince, loved by many, but hated by many more, even the gods. They cursed me with sickness, and I died, sent to a realm I dare not speak of. However, our God, whom we call Olodumare, took pity on me. He gave me another chance, pulling me into my body and jolting my heart four days later. I knew I had a duty to perform, and with the gifted creator energy of Olodumare guiding me, I dedicated my new life to ease the suffering of humanity. And when I died again, I was welcomed into the Saṃsāra as a deity, just like you."

Lamb wanted to tell him that she was not a deity; she was an ill-advised, detrimental prophet at best. But she would learn nothing from that exchange.

"So, your resurrection was on account of divine intervention," Lamb spoke as her mind wandered. "But how does one communicate with that highest force? I'm assuming the One True God lives on Level 26, which makes sense because Jesus is only ..."

Babalú-Ayé jerked to a stop and grabbed Lamb by the shoulders, turning her to align with him. His kind face was no longer as kind, instead scrunched into distress. He hissed fear into her being.

"You speak words you should never speak, little lady. Such curiosities will not serve you. They shall lead to your downfall. May the world hear me as I plead that I had nothing to do with any of it. Now leave me be, and do not interrupt my rainforest walk ever again."

Lamb could not break eye contact as her head nodded atop a shaking body. Babalú-Ayé's dirty fingers pressed deep into her skin as they slid down from her shoulders to raise her right arm. Babalú-Ayé broke his stare to inspect the rash on her skin, which she had torn to shreds of a black crust across slimy pools of infected flesh. Lamb hung her head in shame as Babalú-Ayé shook his in disapproval.

"You really are a frog in an armoury of anteaters," Babalú-Ayé said solemnly. Then, unexpectedly, he dug his fingernails into Lamb's forearm and tore down her wound. Lamb screamed louder than anything in the forest. She tried to yank her arm away but could not free herself from Babalú-Ayé's powerful grip. He tore off layers of skin. Droplets of blood prickled her pores like stars. Lamb's cry tapered off into a high-pitched whine. Her bare feet bounced from one side to the other. She pulled for an escape but was at the mercy to this assault. Babalú-Ayé's concentration was unbreakable, and when his nails ripped to her wrist, he changed his attack to flat-palmed slaps, beating the exposed meat of her forearm with loud blows, punctuated by Lamb's howls. Babalú-Ayé eventually let go and immediately turned away, resuming his walk, with, "May the gods bless you and help you to find your peace."

Swaying from bewilderment, Lamb looked down at her arm, which was as clear as the day she was born. Her skin had healed to a glow, not a scratch or rash in sight.

This disturbing encounter did not discourage Lamb, and she moved on to her next bookmark. Fukurokuju was another promising resource. From a Chinese Taoist mythological background, it was the Japanese who most revered Fukurokuju, included as one of the Seven Lucky Gods, albeit a lesser entry. But what made him so distinguishable was his flowing white beard and elongated forehead, the latter extending from his eyebrows into the sky, almost doubling the size of his body. Lamb found this characteristic uncontrollably amusing, and she forcefully swallowed her giggles when she first saw him playing chess on the seventh floor. He was not a complicated deity to catch. Like Babalú-Ayé, he was a Level 8.

Lamb watched Fukurokuju's chess pieces slide through his current opponent like lard. With each figurine fallen, Fukurokuju squawked with joy while the man across the table grunted in frustration. This was made additionally humorous due to the other man's colossal physique shrouded with a giant wolf skin kept in place by a tall gold helmet; a far more daunting presence in comparison to Fukurokuju's hunched old man frame. When Fukurokuju inevitably moved into checkmate, the two shared a gentlemanly handshake, and Lamb heard Fukurokuju refer to his competitor as Qormusta. Lamb seized her cue and introduced herself to Fukurokuju, flashing her wrist and challenging him to a game. Fukurokuju was more than eager to accept, and Lamb replaced Qormusta as the chess pieces automatically took their squares.

Lamb was out of her league, and after a few careless moves, Fukurokuju had her king trapped within her own army, set up for a swift end. Instead of permitting the finisher, Lamb leaned forward and softly confessed to Fukurokuju, "I actually want to talk to you about something private."

Fukurokuju regarded her with slight apprehension. After a moment, he spoke, "Make your move." Lamb sighed in defeat. She claimed a pawn with her knight, a desperate final attack before Fukurokuju could set his queen into checkmate. But to her surprise, Fukurokuju bumped another pawn one square forward.

"You can speak freely," Fukurokuju said. "Nobody can hear us." Lamb glanced around the room to register several chess players within earshot. She looked back at Fukurokuju with uncertainty, but he only repeated himself. "Nobody can hear us."

Lamb understood. She pushed her bishop out into the game as she recited her words, each carefully chosen to avoid another dispute as with Babalú-Ayé.

"I'm writing a book," she lied with deliberate caution. "It's about different realms of the afterlife. You know, the lower Saṃsāras and what have you."

"Go on," Fukurokuju seemed intrigued as he tapped a rook one square to the left. Lamb's knight took another pawn.

"Well, I'm presently on the section about reawakening from one realm to another. Like, banishment or resurrection or whatever. So I'm interviewing deities who have some experience with this practice, which, of course, includes you."

Fukurokuju's bishop removed Lamb's offensive knight, and he rapped her piece upon his chin with scepticism. "You're telling me that they have authorised you to write a book of this nature?"

"Yes," Lamb's voice croaked with reluctance. She cleared her throat and then added for gravity, "But for Level 10 and above only, I'm afraid."

Fukurokuju accepted this with trust, and over the course of an intentionally slow game, he opened up to Lamb like a treasure chest of sacred information.

"What you've heard is true. I am one of a handful of gods who can resurrect the dead. But please write that I never liked doing it, for they often came out wrong and the people would blame me.

"How I achieved such a performance is not something I could articulate or even recall. It depended on which afterlife realm the Sülde ended up in. But it usually involved a lot of paperwork. Binding scrolls were penned, making promises, an endless string of favours passed along. Once those terms were agreed upon and the Sülde was aligned with the corpse, I had to summon Life from the source to take over from the dead."

"How did you do that?"

"I cannot say, for I do not know. Who but the highest gods know anything? Some claim I am a descendent of Xuanwu's reincarnated spirit, which gave me such powers. But whatever the ritual, it was long, it was exhausting, and I remember very little from the ordeal."

"Interesting," Lamb felt like an authentic journalist now as she moved a pawn forward without paying attention to the board. "So, do you have any idea how Jesus did it?"

Fukurokuju choked, then cackled with a shrill tone. Lamb was taken aback but noticed nobody turned towards the sound. "Oh, my sweet child," Fukurokuju snorted. "Best wishes with that investigation, hahaha. Nobody knows how Jesus did anything." Fukurokuju's amusement abruptly shifted as his tall head leaned forward, looking at Lamb with serious eyes. "But I'll tell you this: the three-way split of our essence is far more intricate than they'll ever let us know. The physical, the spiritual, the personality are inseparable entities, intertwined with one another, influencing their growth. The electrons of every atom remember the minds they served. The soul that rejoins the Universe after death is not clean from its experiences. It carries an unremovable imprint of data. It can be darkened by trauma. And the physical body is but a manifestation of this energy, an evolutionary illusion created from the source's nothingness. It can appear from nothing again. There is always a way to bring back the dead."

The air between them had grown uneasy, and for the first time Lamb sensed that she was receiving material above her level. She tried not to shudder and quickly moved her queen out into the open board to distract the moment. Fukurokuju watched her with one side of his moustache tweaked upwards in a smirk.

"You're not writing a book, are you?" he questioned.

"I am!" Lamb doubled down on the fabrication without pause. She had already decided that she just might.

"Well then, I have an additional chapter for your consideration. You should call it *The Saṃsāra Above the Supreme Realm of Saṃsāra*. And instead of wasting your efforts going backwards on the timeline of death, ask yourself why, in an afterlife created by Buddhist mystics, are there no Buddhists here? No mention of nirvana. No sign of Siddhartha Gautama, or Budai, or any enlightened Buddha. It's almost as if they've trapped us in an eternal bubble while they ride the wave far beyond our boundaries."

Lamb was thrown by this bitter proposal that sounded terrifyingly important yet was wildly off-topic. She did not know how to digest it, so she sat back, and that's when she became aware that the room had fallen silent. Every head had turned, quietly staring at them. Lamb stiffened and quickly faced Fukurokuju. He calmly reached forward and pushed his rook with his index finger, gliding right to Lamb's end of the board. "Checkmate," he announced, "And I think you should leave."

Lamb left but was not done with her quest, even if she could not shake the discomfort of Fukurokuju's words reeking of danger. She decided she needed to punch upwards if she was going to crack this procedure open and, after much examination, she decided that Saint Lazarus of

Bethany was the most logical next choice. Granted, he was Level 13, meaning a difficult search, but as a Biblical figure it felt like a sign closer to her life. The fact that he was resurrected by Jesus alone meant she was lucky he was only a 13.

Lamb never found Lazarus despite her extensive dedication. Instead, her mission took a turn when she was aimlessly wandering Floor 9 and heard the escalating music of sitar and electronic percussion. She hardly comprehended that Ganesh was coming until he was almost on top of her, the walls bouncing to his dance. Lamb tensed, certain she was about to be crushed by this giant figure, but he expertly manoeuvred around her, giving her a wink while saying, "Lamb, Level 10! How are ya?"

Ganesh bounded away, and Lamb's blood rushed to her head. She remembered his backstory, where his dad decapitated him, and she blurted out, "Ganesha, I want to talk to you about reincarnation!"

The music was instantly sucked from the air and Ganesh stopped moving, fixed in a mid-dance pose. Lamb would have found such a cartoon reaction comedic if she wasn't so terrified. With a quick spin, Ganesh reanimated, grabbing Lamb's neck with his trunk and slamming her against the wall. He held her there with her toes dangling several inches from the carpet. His eyes were burning red. He was heaving the stench of roasted nuts into her lungs. Lamb was choking, silently pleading with an elephant head almost the size of her body. Gone was the fun-loving creature she thought she knew. Instead, here was a Level 25 god she had upset, and she realised that she was in dire trouble.

Ganesh's eyes gradually returned to their standard colour, and he dropped Lamb spluttering to the floor. "Don't you ever speak that foolish rubbish out loud again, or I will end you," Ganesh growled to her coughing body and then abruptly took off again, the music blasting from his atmosphere, fading into the distance as Lamb hugged her knees, shivering.

Lamb got the message and retracted into her fear. She had been an idiot, far too open about her pursuit, and she should be thankful she'd got away with what she had. From this point on, she would remain hushed about her investigation, relying on the library to slip out just enough information to execute her escape. And so she devoured books stacked upon books, never sleeping, never going to her room, never tending to her garden, just reading every book that so much as alluded to resurrection, only going for a walk when her brain was about to implode.

Lamb enjoyed the library because nobody ever bothered her. It made her feel safe. However, that ended on the day a strange creature sat down across from her. Lamb pretended not to notice, but when the build of an athletic man supports the head of an ibis bird with an elongated needle beak, it is a difficult spectacle to ignore. After the tension made reading impossible, Lamb looked over to confirm that this creature was indeed staring at her without even a book in hand to hide its fixation. Lamb wanted to shout at it, but instead pulled an irritated passive-aggressive face and pretended to go back to reading.

"Everyone is worried about you," the ibis spoke. Lamb blinked too many times in a row but did not react. It continued, "Your garden is a mess because you spend every moment in this library. You neglect your responsibilities because you are obsessed with reincarnating out of here."

Lamb shut her book and placed it flat on the table. "So Ganesh told on me," she said without looking up.

"Maybe, maybe not," the ibis responded. "Sometimes chess pieces talk." Lamb's cheeks grew warm. The ibis gently placed its significantly larger hand upon hers. Usually, Lamb would hate such an uninvited touch, but this felt surprisingly nice. "I want to help you get better," he said with genuine conviction.

"Who are you?" Lamb dared a prolonged glance at the sharp beak facing her direction. The ibis twisted his palm to grip hers in a handshake position, initiating a greeting.

"I go by many names. Most famous is my pen name, Hermes Trismegistus. Perhaps you've heard of it?" Lamb had not. "But my friends call me Thoth."

"Hello, Thoth. My name is Lamb."

"I know," Thoth let go of her hand and leaned back. "So you like my library, huh?"

"Your library?"

"That's right. Back in my Earthly days just about every page of knowledge was accredited to me, from Cairo to Athens to Rome and around again. You may even find my name on some of the best books in this place." Thoth let out a loud exhale of satisfaction as he leaned back into his chair, hands behind his head. "A lot has changed since then, but when the planet no longer needed my presence, I was the natural choice to oversee just about the entirety of this establishment. I make sure the new books go where they're supposed to go. I watch the old books so they don't fall before unprepared minds. And I am in charge of the hiring process, handpicking those best suited to help me out."

Lamb nodded in admiration. Thoth waited for her to hear the words between his words, but when she did not respond, he prompted. "So what do you think?"

"Think of what?"

Thoth chuckled. "What do you think of quitting that boring gardening job and joining me in the library? I could use the extra arm-power, and you're always here anyway, so ... ?"

Lamb could hardly trust what she was hearing, and it took her a few attempts to find the right vowel. "Ah ... oh, I ... can that actually happen?"

"Let me show you something." Thoth slammed his elbow on the table, exhibiting his wrist. "You see that? Level 24. I can make anything happen."

The slack-jawed grin on Lamb's face revealed every one of her teeth. "That would be the best news since I got here!"

"I'll take that as a yes, then?"

"Yes! Yes, it's a most definite yes, yes, yes!"

"Excellent!" Thoth stood up and extended his hand. Lamb returned the handshake. "Welcome aboard, librarian Lamb! You're gonna fit right in!"

"I already do!" Lamb bubbled excitedly, fighting the urge to plant a big, wet kiss on that skinny beak.

VI

8

L ibrarians were granted access to the network, which was a considerable advantage for Lamb's mission—a mission which she had every intention of fulfilling. Floor 10's computer interface was a relic of decades past, nothing but green text on a flickering screen that hurt the eyes. Yet, with a password and the knowledge of a handful of commands, one could discover much behind-the-scenes data that the average god was not privy to.

Lamb discovered she could search a deity's name and pull up any book they so much as removed from a bookshelf. Naturally, she typed her name in first, sickened as a long list of titles rolled across her screen, every single one implying resurrection. No wonder she had been found out. Lamb tried to search her acquaintances, but of course any deity above 10 was not authorised by her rank of admin. Cardea, however, had a taste for romance novels, each publication pre-ordered especially for her, tagged under 'recreational'. Lamb considered that a dirty word in an establishment otherwise driven by mystical philosophy. It amused her.

Another benefit of Lamb's position directly related to her work responsibilities. With a constant stream of texts carted into the libraries, the task of data capture fell onto her lap. She would enter the book title, author, and identification number, then select a genre from an extensive dropdown. The system would run some calculations and assign a library level best suited for the publication. Lamb had the power to challenge the ranking, but Thoth instructed her to leave it in the vast majority of cases. However, this process meant Lamb could view the database of every book up to Library 15. She'd regularly scroll through the titles beyond further doors, ensuring she skimmed past every genre so that when she scanned the resurrection themes, her naughty activities would hopefully be buried under a flurry of other movements. Imagine her frustration to find that THE SECRET RESURRECTION OF JESUS *(Unabridged)* was in Library 11! So close to her grasp yet impossible to hold! Or was it?

It didn't take many shifts before Lamb realised she was not the only one using the library for their own gain. Thoth was constantly nudging her aside to loudly smack his fingers upon the keyboard, trying to move books he authored from library to library. He felt his most popular works, such as the *Corpus Hermeticum* or *Emerald Tablet*, were too dangerous for a Library 2 audience and should be further limited. Conversely, he had penned a plethora of other esoteric texts that he reckoned were shoved too far up the ladder, and he'd request they come down several notches. These routine attempts caused the god quite the fluster, and he instructed Lamb to repeat the submission at least once each working session. He assured her that he'd achieved success multiple times before, and this encouraged Lamb to exploit another avenue of her newfound influence.

She toyed with the idea of asking that THE SECRET RESURRECTION OF JESUS *(Unabridged)* be reassessed for a Level 10 audience, as surely this slight shift would not raise too many flags. But she decided against it because who knew who was watching her and how many lines she had already crossed. Instead, she went for a far safer choice, a book called *The Alchemy of Water and You* by Mistress Christine Thorpe, also sitting in Library 11. Perhaps such a soft request would go unnoticed by the eyes monitoring thousands of millions of other publications. She confidently entered her suggestion to reduce that book to Library 10 then went about her business, stacking and dusting a section of shelves, returning to the computer to find the system had already rejected her proposal.

Lamb was deflated but was soon gifted further motivation. One of Thoth's more modern books (verbosely titled *Within and Without Hermetic Dianetics: Eradicating Thetans Using the Emerald Tablet*) was confirmed to leap from Library 4 to Level 7. It was Thoth's most substantial shift in centuries and reason for much celebration. Many librarians joined his excessive manifestation of champagne in Library 7. Lamb made an appearance, but her purpose was to extract information. She positioned herself next to the dancing Thoth, bouncing her knees to blend in with the festivities, then asked in an upbeat fashion as to what Thoth accredited his accomplishment. Drunk on his triumph and bubbly grape juice, Thoth revealed that the algorithm was always kinder to books going up levels rather than down, especially outside of the stricter numbers at the extreme ends of the scale. "To remove knowledge from lower levels is undesirable," he informed her. "But to *add* knowledge to lower levels can prove fatal." Lamb understood even if she hated to hear it.

Lamb spent several subsequent sessions rapping her fingertips upon the desk, paging through the delicious resurrection titles she could not study, feeling like a woman lost at sea, surrounded by water while dying of thirst. Every plan she doodled crashed into a dead end. Every idea worth contemplation was too drastic to execute without severe repercussions.

And then came the event that destroyed everything.

In the distance, Lamb faintly heard cheering, which wasn't too unusual but enough to nudge her head up from the screen. Just in time, as the entrance to 10 swung open and three figures swaggered through, laughing, shouting, leaving applause in their wake. Lamb swore they were moving in slow motion, and her stomach dropped two inches as she recognised each of their unbearably bright glory. Krishna, with his vibrant blue skin and boyish good looks, spinning a long flute in his hand. Horus with his falcon head and his muscular torso, lathered in oil. And, following slower behind with a silent smile, was the unfathomable. The Immaculate Redeemer. The Light of the World. The King of Kings. The Saviour of Man. The One True Messiah Himself. Jesus Christ.

Lamb's knees thawed, and she collapsed behind the desk, sobbing. The incalculable hours she had devoted to depictions of this man,
yet none prepared her for the palpable presence of The Son of God. He
embodied serenity and righteousness, permeating an unrivalled cleanliness of sinless ambience and was more attractive than any creature
Lamb had seen in magazines or on TV. Still lying on the carpet, Lamb
rolled to her back in agonising heartbreak, longing for his love, griev-
ing for a future that had not yet happened. She pressed down upon her
chest as she stared at the library's ceiling, which blurred as if a cloud of
purity had confused its inferior molecular formation. Lamb realised she
was not breathing and loudly gasped her respiratory organs back into
action.

Even in this hazy state, Lamb's conditioned mind presented a
path of stepping stones, calling for motion. Perhaps this moment was
a gift offered by a higher order and the only time such a gift would ever
be offered. But the blessed space between her and Jesus was stretching.
He was undoubtedly headed towards Door 11, a boundary that, once
crossed, would slam an immovable barricade between their persons.
She had to get his attention. She had to get him to see her. Then, he
would greet her like an old companion. All of her problems would go
away. But that was not going to transpire from the floor.

Lamb madly scrambled up the desk and let out a cry of discouragement as she watched the back of Jesus strolling far ahead. A group
of excited onlookers shuffled behind, singing hymns, maintaining their
distance but forming an obstacle course of bodies across the path to salvation. The word *"go!"* sparked in Lamb's mind and set fire to her belly,
galvanising herself into motion.

Lamb's feet were on her desk, and then they weren't. She sailed
through the air and hit the carpet with a slight stumble, which sent
her racing forward. Her balance returned. She dodged deities of every
size, pivoting between obstructions with an athletic precision only the
Holy Spirit could provide. She sidestepped a woman covered in hair.
She twisted her frame sideways to glide between two monsters. This
crowd's zombified lurches were no match for Lamb's determination.
Bodies flew past her dancing velocity. Her eyes fixed on Jesus. Her depth
perception enlarged his presence. The exit door to Library 11 was close,
but she was closer. She could feel him. She could feel that he could feel

her. Her delectable anticipation lightened her step. She closed her eyes, readying herself for the impossible moment she had envisioned since she was a *BAM!*

Lamb's eyes shot open as she collided with the freezing cold back of a staunch troll-like creature that had stepped out in front of her. The being staggered with a grunt, but Lamb went spinning, tripping over her feet, the floor rising to meet her shoulder, slamming with a crack and an *"oooh"* from the crowd behind. Lamb's lungs shrivelled. She gasped for air as she lifted her head to see Jesus still walking away, not even turning to consider her detriment, leaving her behind, slipping from their destiny.

"It's a test," Lamb thought and exploded into a crawl, scurrying towards Jesus like a scarab beetle, burning her knees along the carpet. Krishna tapped his wrist to the green square. Library 11's doors opened. Lamb's confidence fluctuated upon a *will-I-won't-I-make-it* seesaw. Using the full strength of her legs, she launched herself forward, diving towards Jesus with her right arm extended as far as it could go, willing her fingers longer. Unfortunately, she lacked the desired momentum, and her tips only brushed the material of his garment, sending tingles through her bloodstream as she fell flat to the floor.

At once, Jesus realised that power had gone out from him. He turned around in the crowd and asked, "Who touched my clothes?" The congregation ceased their movement and silently stared at the woman sprawled before Christ. Jesus followed their gaze and then addressed the lady, "My daughter, why did you touch my clothes?" The deep voice rose Lamb to her knees, palms together, head bowed before her Messiah.

"Lord, it is I, Lamb!" she spoke. "I am your child, you are my Father, and we are the best of friends! You saved my life so long ago when I jumped off a building to kill myself. But you sent your face to guide me, and I slotted between the cracks like water and received the secrets of the Universe. Oh, Jesus, please tell me you remember!"

Lamb dared to glance up, and her head spun woozy when his deep brown eyes punctured her soul. His face did not look impressed. "Sure," he responded with a wave of his hand. "Now go in peace and be freed from your suffering."

With that, Jesus turned to walk through the door, and his abandonment drowned Lamb in a panic. "No, wait!" she cried and lashed out, grabbing a fistful of his cloak, ceasing his movement. Jesus twirled around, sliding his foot from his sandal in one smooth motion and then pressing his big toe into Lamb's forehead. A bolt of white electricity discharged through Lamb's skull, and she shot backwards, soaring several feet before plummeting to the ground, bouncing twice, then settling, facing up but disappearing into unconsciousness.

When Lamb reconnected to reality, she was squirming with euphoria, clueless about her history yet ecstatic to be involved with the now. However, as her memories returned one by one, her bliss dissolved until she was overwhelmed by dread. Door 11 was closed. The crowd had dispersed. She was alone. Jesus did not care for her. Lamb's stomach cramped, and she turned on her side to vomit and cry.

VI

9

L amb had not set foot in her room since long before landing the librarian job. But here she was, on her bed for an indistinct amount of time, clutching her duvet, sobbing with a broken heart and a toeprint burn on her forehead. She felt so foolish, a stupid, stupid girl, grabbing onto Jesus Christ like that. What an embarrassment she had become.

She cried and cried until her body shrivelled dry, and then she stopped crying. Her grief dropped into numbness, and she lay in a meditative state, muddled but no longer sorrowful. Her dramatic groupie reaction to Jesus was a conditioned response, a brain trained by decades of obsession. Of course she had behaved strangely. How could she not? But Jesus did not recognise her. He had looked down upon her as if she were a pitiful child. He had batted her away like some inferior nuisance. It was a betrayal of her devotion. Jesus was not who she thought he was. And in his actions, he had severed her love. Now, more than before, she was committed to escaping this wretched afterlife.

There is no measure as to how long she lay there. But at some point, quite suddenly, a plan struck her and she stood up, leaving the room with a determined stride.

"To remove knowledge from lower levels is undesirable. But to add knowledge to lower levels can prove fatal."

Back in Library 10, Lamb leaned into the screen, clicking the mouse and clacking the keyboard, seeking the path of least resistance. She had already decided on a target: the Nāgas. That den of snake-people who always moved as one unit, following their three Nagaraja wherever they went. Those deities were library regulars, each with at least a Level 15, some far beyond.

Next, Lamb needed the perfect publication. She scanned the day's new arrivals, but nothing resonated. Refusing to be discouraged, Lamb worked in reverse chronology, ploughing through hundreds of titles until she found something that might work. It was an unassigned book delivered two days ago, called *Behind the Curtain: The Reptilian Secrets Ruling Our World* by Daniel Ives. Lamb punched the details into the system and waited impatiently as the machine ran through its calculations, eventually giving it a Library 1 rating while suggesting the Deceptive Content tag. Lamb had hoped for something higher to work with, but for her purposes this might prove adequate.

After a deep breath, Lamb edited the entry. Leaving the identification number as is (*979-8363745690*), Lamb altered one word of the title, to now read as *Behind the Curtain: The **Naga** Secrets Ruling Our World*. The system whirred up again, and Lamb held her breath. Would her rewrite sound an alarm? Was there an accepted room for error? Why else would they have the edit button? The machine spat out a Library 2 rating, and Lamb exhaled. Not only did her change go through, but her plan had worked. She managed to trick the system to increase the number. The excited danger reminded her of days spent stealing alcohol in her youth. Now, she just had to bring up that number as high as possible.

Lamb tweaked tirelessly for what could have been days in Earth time. When other tasks found their way to her pile, she dealt with them swiftly to keep Thoth at bay. When passing deities snickered at the girl that Jesus had zapped flat, she bit her lip without breaking concentration. The more edits she made, the greater her confidence that there was no system to monitor this side of the process. And through endless trial and error, she twisted the algorithm to edge the book's level higher.

She quickly discovered that the primary problem was the author, Daniel Ives. As a human sports broadcaster turned conspiracy theorist, his modest yet dedicated Earthly following was outweighed by general apathy towards his selective research and manipulative use of language. His sizable bibliography was never deemed worthy of anything above a 2, and even there, nobody read them. So when Lamb messed around with different writer names, even ones she wholly fabricated, the book shed its penalties and rose.

The system was suggesting Level 9 by the time Lamb had tested *Behind the Curtain: The Secret History of Naga Shapeshifting Using Christos Energy* by Reverend Dion Power. And there she was, stuck. No further change boosted the number, some adjustments even slumping the calculation, Lamb hastily reverting. Her stamina was burning out, and she contemplated headbutting the wall out of frustration. Eventually she needed a break and walked around the room.

Every creature she crossed smirked and whispered about her Christ incident. Painful memories of school flashed behind her eyes. When individuals did not register her existence, she remained convinced they were thinking about it. To escape, she automatically moved to the quieter shelves where most resurrection books sat, providing her with familiarity. Poking at the titles, she half-heartedly sought inspiration but ultimately felt disappointed. She recalled her conversation with Fukurokuju, how she'd fibbed that she was writing such a book, and concluded she probably should. It would be a more thorough study than this collection. She was unquestionably the top resurrection expert in Level 10 by now. And then maybe her publication would be fit to sit within the famed authors on Level 13, 14, 15. She giggled at the prospect and then interrupted herself with a sharp inhale. Another idea.

Lamb raced to the computer, too stimulated to notice as she knocked her hip into the corner of the desk. Her hysterical fingers pulled up the complete database of book entries in Library 15, sorting them by alphabetised author. She scrolled the titles so rapidly that the screen fell out of focus. Her vibrating eyes scanned the warped text, hunting for patterns. A chunk of identical text flew past, and she slammed on brakes, returning her scroll upwards and stifling a squeak of giddiness. An author named Wilmie Klop immediately caught her eye, boasting upwards of 30 publications revolving around ritual prophecy, all deemed esoteric enough for a 15 score. Lamb double-checked her name, searching Klop's bibliography and confirming that, yes, each book she'd published was in Library 15 and nowhere else. It was such a beautiful sight that Lamb kissed the computer, hoping that whoever Wilmie Klop was, she received the gesture.

Navigating back to her book, Lamb clicked edit and eagerly changed the author field to Wilmie's name. She was about to submit when she remembered something else about the meeting with Fuku-rokuju.

"Ask yourself why, in an afterlife created by Buddhist mystics, are there no Buddhists here?"

Moving with that thought, Lamb adjusted the title to read *Behind the Curtain: The Secret History of Naga Shapeshifting Using* **Buddha** *Energy*. She saved. She waited in agony as the slow machine contemplated this information.

Lamb had to blink to believe it, but it was a certainty. Level 15. Suggested by the computer. No need to challenge it. No need for anyone to investigate. Let's just go with what the program desires like a good librarian. The most uncertain piece of the process was done. Lamb had achieved what others would have called impossible. But what came next was far scarier. Lamb submitted the data. Whatever happened now was in the hands of the powers that be.

The system always took its time to confirm a new entry, but Lamb sat staring at her screen, pinned to the chair from the weight of a thousand second-guesses piling upon her. She had kept the reference number the same, which automatically distributes the books. Hence, she knew an actual book would reach Library 15. But what would happen when it slides into the hands of a conscious being? What did the front cover look like? If the words *'Behind the Curtain'* were the most prominent focal point, then she might be okay. If the artwork showed snakes, building a subconscious bridge between the originally stated Reptilians and her updated Nagas, then she might also be okay. But if Library 15 read the full title or organised their publications by author, then what? Lamb imagined sirens and flashing red lights. Was there a jail in the Saṃsāra? Or had no one ever tried something so reckless?

For a realm that prided itself on instant gratification, Lamb was wincing at the crawl of time. Eventually, she left the computer to divert her impatience, tidying up books and realigning shelves. Still, she'd rush to the screen within moments, aching for good news, receiving nothing but pending. And just when she thought her nerves couldn't be shredded any further, Thoth exploded back through Door 11, his eyes scanning the room, settling on Lamb and then soldiering towards her. The show was over. She held onto a cabinet, certain she was about to faint.

"Do me a favour and move *Within and Without* to the entrance of Library 7. Femi is off galavanting somewhere, and I can't risk a single lost read."

Thoth exited just as quickly to Library 9, and Lamb crouched on her haunches, brain melting in fuzz, sweat droplets cooling the flames of panic. Once stable, Lamb moved *Within and Without* to the entrance of Library 7. Upon returning, her computer greeted her with more good news. The book was confirmed as sent to a shelf in Library 15.

Phase two was complete, but Lamb's stress did not drop. The race continued as to what would happen first: the announcement of a new book reaching the Nagas, or someone else discovering the title in the wrong place, setting off a bloodthirsty snowball crushing her at the end. She had come so far and there was reason to hope, but this was overshadowed by the knowledge of Life's sense of humour, regularly yanking the carpet beneath her at the final hurdle, like when she got shot in central London. The entrance opened, and Lamb's emotional response was a sucker-punch cocktail of excitement and dread. It was nobody she recognised. This happened several times, and she was soon belching up air that stank of stomach acid.

But when the Nagas came, the Nagas came. Led by their three proud Nagaraja kings, the serpents were a baffling mess of human limbs and snake tails, intertwining in complex motions that tied their parts in knots yet slipped to freedom at the final second. The group appearance of ten-foot-tall snake-men always caused a commotion, but this arrival was an event. There was an additional flurry of wild energy to their actions, on their way to read the latest book that pertained directly to them. Lamb's bone marrow coagulated, and she struggled to act, but her mind willed her forward. She raced with stiff legs to the bookshelf closest to Door 11. A flash later, the Nagas glided past her without regard. The front Nagaraja tapped his wrist upon the square, and the doors obeyed. The collective squeezed themselves through the opening. Lamb exhaled her apprehension, casually stepping behind those flicking tail ends and gliding her back around the corner of the door frame into Library 11.

VI

10

With eyes diverted by the reptile chaos, Lamb's nimble trespassing went unseen. She'd repeatedly visualised this moment and moved confidently through the room, locating the distant Door 12 in her peripheral while maintaining a stealthy yet fixed distance from the snakes. What she hadn't imagined, however, was the grandiosity of it all.

If Library 10 prided itself on a varnished wood aesthetic, then Library 11's allure was rich pastel colours, every book's hue deliberately arranged to form intricate patterns that sheened when you moved. Moreover, the size. Its floor plan doubled that of Library 10 while its height appeared as four of those stacked upon one another, accessed by a strange ladder system intertwined with precarious narrow ledges. Still, Lamb did her best to hide any intrigue, keeping her feet and head facing forward, wearing an expression that she hoped proclaimed that she belonged. Thankfully, the shelf layout was positioned in a grid fashion, and Lamb appreciated how effortlessly she could navigate these grounds. She took right-angled turns around racks of books, largely out of sight but never far behind the Nagas, trailing them to the 12th door without hindrance, grinning at how much easier this mission was than she'd dared dream.

The domineering presence of the reptiles was her strongest asset. Their excitable chatter with hissing *s*-sounds sliced through the tranquil atmosphere and drew every eye to witness the worming disorder of such a daunting gang. If anything, it was an annoyance, so when the snakes' racket faded to the other side of the room, each individual gratefully resumed their previous undertaking. Hence, when Door 12 opened, and the Nagas plopped on through, nobody watched Lamb repeat her stealthy manoeuvre. Her back slid against the wall, moving around the doorframe then quickly slipping to the other side, her skinny body an indiscernible twig in the background of the raucous crew of snakes tearing down the floor.

Lamb's strategy was working but, as before, she had underestimated the vast enhancements from one library to the next. The increased space of Library 12 was incalculable due to its walls made from mirrors and glass shelves that gave the impression of books floating midair. The only feature that helped discern the spaces from the furniture was the water that filled their insides, where fish of every size swam down tubes into separate compartments. Lamb's confused hesitation was dangerously long, but she forced her legs onward trying to conceal her existence in an essentially see-through room.

To increase the complexity, the bookshelves were wavy in shape, and she frequently bumped into corners, sending fish scattering. Her anxiety spiked, but she did not slow. Her vision remained glued on the warped image of the snakes through the transparent bookshelves, distorted by the watery curvature but emitting enough audio fuss to guide her direction. Nevertheless, she was losing her breath as ceaseless interferences expanded the gap between her and the Nagas. An individual would pass on the other side of a bookshelf, and the rounded water would magnify their head, giant blinking eyes staring at Lamb as she hurried along, unsure if they'd identified her. A lorry-sized sea beast swam past her inside a wall unit, and she jumped at the sight of its elongated tusks jutting awkwardly from its fish face; the purple shimmer of its scales nearly blinding her. But only when a distant melancholic song caressed her ears did she veer off course, her mission buried beneath an irresistibly haunting melody written just for her.

Lamb's swooning body glided towards the harmonious sound,

settling before a shelf where an exquisite creature was perched on top, serenading the world with her delicate vocals of allure. Lamb's jaw hung loose as she observed this being with infatuated desire, dumbfounded by a beauty that iced her brain. This singing woman was a human from the chest up, her naked breasts, neck, and face so perfect that she rivalled a marble sculpture. Her shiny red hair flowed down her shoulders as her head slowly turned from one side to the other, a choir of voices coming from her mouth. But as she waved her arms in dance, the feathers of her brightly-coloured wings swayed with them, matching a lower body with the legs and tail of a bird. Lamb stood mesmerised as her senses piqued, the visual vibrancy and enchanting chorus so precise that she could smell it.

Eventually, this bird-lady became aware of Lamb and looked down at her, first with a seductive smile but then a curious cock of the head. The song paused, and Lamb suddenly couldn't smell anything. "Hey, I remember you," the bird-lady said. "Yeah, you were the girl who threw herself at Jesus, right? That was hilarious." A rush of blood slapped Lamb's alertness, and she stepped back in dismay, loudly bumping into a glass shelf behind herself. The bird-lady squinted at this suspicious behaviour. "Hang on, aren't you a Level 10?"

Lamb took off running. Bouncing from invisible surface to invisible surface. Desperate to disappear but easily seen by everyone. An erratic point of fast motion conflicting with her sedate surroundings. Any stealth was blasted wide open. Now her only objective was to escape the consequences as best she could. She heard a shout. That propelled her faster. Taking random turns until, by some lucky blessing, she came in behind the path of the Nagas. They were many yards ahead, already making their way through Door 13. Lamb took the chance. She sprinted towards them. By the power of adrenaline, she caught up, running a few feet after the final snake, just making it through the closing door, then immediately turning right into Library 13.

Lamb found herself upside down instantly and then crashed into the floor. She quickly sat up in bewilderment and screamed at what expanded before her.

Library 13 had inched over the logic of her reality. Lamb's mind struggled to cope with this area's unstable physics. No angle was straight. No object stood still. The air swirled with erratic patterns that resembled faces. The floor abruptly tilted vertically. Lamb expected to fall but did not. She glanced ahead and recognised the snakes moving away, but no depth perception rules applied; they simultaneously appeared very small yet extremely close. Lamb was convinced she could reach out and grab them, but when she tried, her hand shot miles into the distance. She retracted it with horror.

As crippling as this disorientation was, Lamb knew a more substantial threat was hunting her. She had to keep going. She shifted her limbs into what she thought was a crawl position, summoning every fibre in her body to take her somewhere. To bypass the optical jumble, she kept her vision on the floor, which was so wet that she thought she might be sinking. This sensation faded when the world turned into a treadmill, and Lamb knew she was crawling on the spot. Her head bumped into something, and she lifted her gaze to see a glowing pink orb in front of her. The orb vibrated slightly, then shot into the sky, leaving visible rainbow trails of itself as it went. Lamb heaved, almost puking.

She rolled onto her back in surrender. The room copied her with a quick vertical 360 spin. Lamb dug her fingers into the carpet, trying not to fall. Her diaphragm tensed so hard that she heard it crack. Attempting to open her eyes, she found she could not, as her eyes were already open, her vision a blind sheet of grey nothingness whether her lids were up or down. Her temples throbbed because she was grinding her jaw with such urgency that her teeth were turning into a powder, mixing with her saliva, a paste dripping down her throat. She willed her face to relax, her mouth falling open. The high-pitched ringing in her ears faded to silence. The static of everything found definition, forming shapes until Lamb was staring upwards at tall bookshelves towering above, set against an infinite open white sky.

Lamb sat up carefully. The world rocked gently like a boat, but the previous eruption of insanity already felt like a bad dream. Life had calmed, and Lamb confirmed that she was seated between extended bookshelves with no end in either direction, stacked upwards of fifty rows or more. And everything was white, white, white. The floor was white. The sky was white. The shelves were white. And the books were white without a feature to distinguish themselves from one another: no titles, no author names. Lamb got to her feet and tottered. She started to walk, her footsteps the only sound in the white silence.

The bookshelves abruptly ended in a T-junction, each path leading down identical rows of books. Lamb turned left. The floor beneath her footing still swayed, but the slants were nominal, and Lamb figured the instability was all in her head. Her senses simply needed to adjust to this dimension, like how fluid in the ear canal causes vertigo or how the smell of a house fades the more you are exposed to it. To prove she was accustomed to this new environment, Lamb performed a twirl, which sent her balance flying, colliding into a bookshelf, desperately grabbing onto a rack to avoid another plunge. The books rumbled on impact, echoing into the hushed atmosphere until there was nothing again.

Lamb recomposed herself and let go of the bookshelf only to pause and then grab it again. She performed this action several times, each one a verification that she was not hallucinating. Her touch was met with a sudden spread of colour across the books as if a chemical reaction was responding to her skin, fading away when she released it. Excited by this discovery, Lamb swiped her flat palm across a row of books, and each lit up with a different bright hue, complete with titles presented in an alphabet Lamb did not recognise. This changed everything, and Lamb was encouraged that her mission may not be thwarted after all. The Nagas were long gone, but perhaps Library 13 contained sufficient knowledge to crack through her mental barriers and escape the Saṃsāra before anyone found her.

Lamb resumed her stride, running her fingers along the books she passed. Their illuminated acknowledgement captivated her emotions, but the novelty grew tired when she could not highlight a publication written in a comprehensible language. Even worse, the longer she ventured through these endless corridors, randomly turning left or right or left or right, the colder she became. The temperature reflected the snow-white world exactly. She rubbed her arms to keep them warm. Worry crept in about how lost she was and that she might end up stuck in this freezing place for eternity.

Lamb was exhaling white mist by the time she came across the ladder. It, too, was impossibly white and blended into its surroundings but Lamb noticed simply because it was separate from the identical paths of shelves she'd wandered for so long.

She gripped an eye-level rung and was pleased by how warm it was to the touch. Eager to reach the top, she lifted her foot onto the lowest bar, but it passed straight through the material like a hologram, stamping onto the floor below. Annoyed, Lamb tried again but, like before, her foot and the rung did not meet as physical objects, and she could not step upon it. Lamb lifted her foot to the next bar up, and that one served its purpose, Lamb pulling her body off the ground. "What is the point of that?" Lamb growled as she continued her ascension, careful to test each step before trusting her weight on it. There was no pattern; every second or third crosspiece was illusionary. However, enough real rungs were set at a reasonable spacing, so the fakes hardly hindered Lamb's rise.

Nevertheless, the climb was exhausting, and Lamb was convinced it was another one of Library 13's tricks and the bookshelf grew taller the higher she reached. But she persevered, refusing to look down, finding zen in the monotony of the duplicate rows upon rows of white books crossing her vision until she reached the shelves at the top, gasping for air.

Lamb's upper body lifted into the biting cold air above the bookshelves, and what lay before brought her tears of awe clashing with disheartenment. Spread out for as far she could see were the tops of bookshelves, organised to replicate an intricate labyrinth that stretched over the horizon. Lamb strained her neck, turning one way and then the other. There was no end to this puzzle. There were no distant walls housing the maze. No roof over her head. Perhaps Library 13 was a trap designed for meddlesome law-breakers such as herself.

Lamb shivered as she attempted to trace an escape route using her finger, but her shallow viewpoint made it an exercise of madness. She weighed up her options and wondered if she would have more luck braving this upper icy weather and walking along the tops of the bookshelves instead of between them. That would provide a much more advantageous viewpoint. Her thought process got as far as pondering a warmer garment she could fashion from book pages when suddenly, in the far distance, Thoth levitated above the bookshelves with his arms stretched out from either side, assuming a cruciform posture. His body was turned away from Lamb as he floated along, scanning the crevices of the maze with glowing eyes, and Lamb could see the red fury radiating from his being. He was looking for her.

Lamb held her breath to suffocate her fear and hastily scuttled down the ladder out of sight. She had to move fast but she also had to remain quiet, and by concentrating on these two necessities, she forgot about the phoney rungs, her foot slicing through the air and painfully slamming into the one below. The unexpected drop knocked her equilibrium sideways and she lost grip, slipping down the ladder, plummeting towards the ground.

Lamb instinctively clawed at every rung, which bent her limbs at strange angles and uppercut her jaw but slowed most of her fall. By the final rungs, she had bounced away, tumbling in a freefall and then crashing to the floor in an awkward heap, producing a thunderous thud. Lamb lay there for a moment, convinced she was dead, then remembering she was already dead, then wondering what happens after the dead die. When she determined she was not twice dead, she shifted herself into a sitting position, her bones clicking into place. There was a hefty patch of blood on the spot of impact, splattering far across the white floor, but she could not find where it had come from. She felt fine.

"Lamb!" a deep demonic voice called from above, and she was suddenly freezing cold again. "Lamb, where are you? I assure you that turning yourself over to me will have far softer consequences than if I have to find you."

Thoth's volume grew louder, getting closer, drawn to the source of her crashing fall. Lamb could run, but she could not outrun a floating god. Lamb could call out his name, handing herself in, but the idea of intentionally facing this monster was a terror too great to be known. Instead, she pressed her back against the shelf, hugged her knees to her chest, and prayed to something—*anything*—for salvation.

"Hermes!" a new male voice called Thoth's pen name from a distance, and Lamb's vertebrae straightened. A pause, then again, "Hermes, sir, w-wait, they found something!" Whoever this was sounded meek. Another librarian, Lamb assumed.

"What?" Thoth's overhead voice spat back.

"It's a book! A mistitled book. Level 1 at best, but, but somehow with Level 15 clearance!"

Another pause, and then Thoth's cutting voice moved away from Lamb's position. "You better be talking about something more than a typo here."

"It's Lamb, sir!" the man called back between heavy breaths. "She authorised the placement. She drastically altered the title to mention the Nagas, sir. The Nagas were the ones who found it in Library 15. We think maybe she followed–"

The whoosh of flight interrupted the explanation, Thoth's panicked response rapidly fading from Lamb's earshot, "May the gods help us! If she's managed to get into Library 15, then the risk of ..." gone. Silence.

Tears exploded from Lamb's face. She buried her head into her arms and sobbed out a tangle of mismatched emotions. Through her blubs and snivels, she scolded herself. "Stupid girl," she whispered. "Stupid idiot, foolish little girl." She was out of her depth and in too deep. She regretted everything.

She lifted her head to wipe her cheeks. Through her waterlogged vision, a book down the way turned gold and shifted itself outward, jutting two inches from its neighbours. Disbelieving, Lamb blinked away her remaining tears to confirm this had happened. A book had made itself known. Lamb climbed to her feet, never breaking eye contact with this golden vision, afraid if she looked away it would disappear into her imagination.

Creeping along, she reached the book's position and it remained fixed and golden. It was a few shelves higher than Lamb, but she was close enough to read the English title. It was called *Unravelling the Ribbons of Post-Maya* without an author credit. It was enormous. Thick and tall, thousands of pages at least.

Lamb reached up, but her fingernails could only scrape the bottom of its spine. She stretched on her tiptoes and lengthened her middle finger as far as she could, but this single digit was no match for the publication's colossal weight. Abandoning this approach, she allowed herself a moment to think, and then changed course, yanking several books from the lowest shelf and stacking them on the floor, building an elevated platform. Their covers shone glorious reds and greens and pinks as she stood upon them, just managing a fingertip grip on the golden target and pulling on it with concentrated strength. The book edged outward, one centimetre at a time, until it came free. Lamb tried to catch it in her palm, but it was too bulky to grasp and too heavy to hold up. The book dropped like a cannonball, bouncing off the arm that

Lamb used to shield her cowering head. The impact knocked her off the book pile, landing on her rear end with an "Ow!"

The combined ruckus of books and bodies hitting the floor reverberated across the open sky, and Lamb slapped her hands over her mouth, awaiting retribution. When stillness resumed, so did a sense of safety, and she transferred her focus to the golden book, watching in wonder as it turned its own pages one at a time, flipping through itself, trying to find something for her. Lamb yearned to learn its secrets but dared not interrupt, remaining distant, awaiting the next move to become apparent.

Pages turned and turned, paused, turned back two, then stopped. Lamb counted to 10 to ensure this was the chosen place, then crawled towards the book on all fours. Her head edged over the giant spread, then dropped so close that her dangling hair brushed the light brown paper. She could smell coffee. The pages were numbered 570 and 571, respectively. A sizable gothic font announced a chapter followed by text that shrunk smaller and smaller as it went down, pulling Lamb's face in closer as she read.

VI

CHAPTER ELEVEN:
THE FOURTH COSMIC MIRACLE

All praise the Formless Substance; the Divine Sound that predates God
and man, animal and plant, mineral and rock, infinite and eternal, the
exclusive matter in existence upon which everything is built.

The evolution of the first particle as solidified material is the *Third
Cosmic Miracle* (reference chapters X through XVI).
It is perceivable and sustainable beyond divine thought.
It is a concentrated consciousness, smaller than anything documented
in any doctrine.
A prick of awareness; in becoming aware of itself, it was.
Observance means participation.

The Formless Substance as an essence is but a drive to learn.
The next step in its progression was to harvest data through a Formed
Substance.
And within that experience, we recognise the Original Particle as the
first Son of God (Adam/Atum/Atom), developed within and part of

God, yet a separate component, watching the Formless Substance as the Formless Substance watched it.

The Original Particle matured alone for four billion years.
It learned about itself through itself and built a system more involved than the planetary orbits of later aeons.
Yet, it is comparable in design.
Modern Earth sciences have identified a fraction of these systems.
Preons to Leptons, Quarks to Protons and Neutrons.
These are Earth names given to pieces that appeared along the timeline but are only surface layers of an arrangement that is as infinitely deep as the Formless Substance is infinitely expansive.
However, the collective measurement of one Atom is agreeable for our cause.
It is useful on an application basis.

Within the subatomic structure, the densely compounded nucleus is formed via the external data.
It presents attributes using lengthy binary code.

0; 1.
No; Yes.
Bad; Good.

The physical manifestation comes from this code, not by the code itself, but by the *reading of the code*; reading itself or being read by the Formless Substance.
However, it is the ever-moving Electron that powers the operation.

The Electron is the trapped Sound of the Formless Substance that blesses the atomic organisation of Life.
Through this activated Electron Energy, data is captured, adding to the knowledge of the nucleus, learning to shift attributes and present them in a more specific manner, adding further code and then reading that code into existence.

The rapid multiplication procedure raced forward.
The Fourth Cosmic Miracle.

Within the bounds of the established practice, both the Original Atom
and the Formless Substance observed a second nucleus of attributes
into existence.
The central code was a carbon copy of the Original Atom, only
reversed: a mirror image.
Before the arrival of the Second Atom, the Original Atom was decidedly
genderless; or genderful, hermaphroditic (*Genesis 1:27*).
But in this instant, it removed its genderlessness to evolve into the end
of a polar array; now a masculine entity.

The Second Atom was the inverse feminine placed on the alternate
end, two separate components, yet imperative to maintain the balance
of this dualistic spectrum.
This yin-yang scope created a plane between masculine and feminine,
where any degree of gender can and must exist.

To activate the Second Atom, an Electron (rib) was taken from the
Original Atom (Adam) and given to her.
This Electron Volt (eV) allowed the Second Atom (Eve) to observe the
Original Atom (Adam) from her distinct perspective, reading his code
through a new lens of interpretation.
The consequence of Eve's unique viewpoint meant that Adam's code
was replicated as the same sequence, yet the code was generated
differently through her fresh observation.

In this entangled dynamic, there were now two Adams (Adam reading
Adam, and Eve reading Adam), and, reflectively, two Eves (Eve
reading Eve, and Adam reading Eve), each reading their own code
while reading one another's, leading to four sets of scripts running
(excluding the overall readings from The Formless Substance).
Such a sudden leap forward contributed immensely to the Formless
Substance's thirst for knowledge, and forming further atoms was
inevitable.
For every new Atom, not only would an additional set of self-reading
code appear, but so would its interpretation of every other Atom, as

well as every other Atom's interpretation of it.
The speed of advancement was aggressively exponential.

The Divine Dependence of masculine on feminine on masculine on feminine formed the fundamentals of creation.
This principle that eventually evolved into the sperm energising the egg began with the cross-pollination of electrons (quantum breeding).
Atoms observing one another and sharing knowledge via electron trade became a process of chemical bonding.
Here, atomic attributes merged, the code seeking better manifestations with which to read itself.
This rush of evolutionary desire called upon the infinite metaphysical putty of the Formless Substance (Ein Soph) to place further finite limitations upon itself to become more Formed Substances (Tzimtzum), and here, an explosion of assorted molecules was created by collaborative atoms.

Attributes clicked into attributes, amalgamating to form structures of immeasurable possibilities, manufacturing a discernible reality within which the world thinks it exists.
Systems upon systems developed.
A solar system was observed into existence where large molecular structures made of hydrogen and helium (stars) produced energy for the clumps of dust orbiting them (planets) such as Earth.
An ecosystem was observed into existence where natural growth could nurture and sustain itself in a cyclic fashion (see *The Fifth Cosmic Miracle*).
And systems of segregated biologies were observed into existence, refining the tools of perception through organic material, sensing audio electron vibrations or translating subatomic photon visuals, captured inside a mind to process the information, the Formless Substance perpetually receiving revelations in unfathomable amounts through the sentience of its creations (see *The Sixth Cosmic Miracle*).

However, the narrow perception of one individual mind is illusionary.
The idea of an objective reality is a misconception.
Consciousness as a word has been bastardised beyond recognition,

now forced into the tiny box and labelled by ego.

Every external object perceived and every internal thought is nothing
but a harvesting procedure for the collective mind (Nous) to fuel the
evolution of the Formless Substance.
Because each mind has access to only one focal point through which
it perceives, humans hallucinate their separation from the One Mind
(Nous) and the assemblage of smaller micro-consciousnesses that
create their presence.

Each human reads the code of reality in contrasting modes.
The code of reality (Maya) is the same for every being but allows for an
infinite combination of interpretations.
The outside world reflects the convictions built within the observer's
mind.
Every scenario exists within the code; hence, the details of reality
(Maya) are entirely dependent on the *reading* of the code, which differs
immeasurably from each mind (the reader).

A separate timeline of reality exists for each perception.
And this perception is wholly encompassed by the Formless
Substance.
And yet also functions on subatomic layers.
Every particle in existence is amalgamating its interpretation of every
other particle in existence.
Every particle is forming a narrative which would be incomprehensible
to its neighbouring particles within the same atom.

There is no one true narrative except that all narratives are true.
Or even more accurately:
There is no one true narrative except that all narratives are false.
The entirety of reality is nothing but the Formless Substance looking at
itself through perspective points to read its code differently, creating
more code.
And that is how the Maya was built.

For more details, please see the diagram on the next page.

☼

The text was so small by the bottom of 571 that Lamb's strained eyes gave her a mild headache. Still, she absorbed the information as best she could with open fascination, remembering her experiences as she collided with the pavement. That death was her favourite moment of her life, where the Universe made sense within a molecular understanding. The fond recollection made her smile. She was glad she found this book. It was a gift to spur her mission onward, to unlock the secrets of resurrection and bless her Earthly followers with the superior wisdom she'd acquired in the afterlife. She must not give up. She must get back there.

Lamb casually turned the page, and a hologram lept upwards off the paper, floating midair. Its sudden presence knocked Lamb back in fright. Staring into it, she found herself unable to look away, gulping air.

It was a diagram of an atom. She knew that the instant she saw it, even though it bore no resemblance to the standard model used in science books. Instead, what hovered before her was an impossible structure with unknown shapes interlocking outside the boundaries of logic, moving in multiple manners at once without moving whatsoever, shining an array of colours Lamb had never seen before. It was a lawless display that was otherwise indescribable within the constraints of human language.

Lamb could not move. Her lungs collapsed, refusing air. Her irises crackled and turned crispy black. Her every atom relaxed slightly, and her awareness of herself dropped below her body. For a split moment, Lamb knew something bad was happening, and then she fell back into a heap, her body coming apart as her atoms dislodged, rolling away like the tiniest marbles escaping from a split sack.

When they finally found her, she looked like a forgotten sandcastle, void of colour and eroded by the elements, only a few clumps offering any recognisable features of her former physical self.

VI

12

"And how have you been feeling lately?"

"Just a little tired," Lamb responded earnestly, squeezing together a closed-mouth smile. She *had* been feeling a little tired lately, her vision clouded from the weight of her eyelids. With two quick blinks, she reattached to the room, watching He Xiangu rock in her armchair, writing something in her notebook. Lovely, lovely He Xiangu. So elegantly feminine, so illuminated by her paleness, not a hair out of place. Lamb wanted to be her. Lamb also wanted that chair. Lambs chair did not even have a backrest. She'd be better off on the floor, she thought.

Lamb's sleepy eyes drifted off again, but He Xiangu brought her back with a pen click. "Okay, so let us end the session like we always do," He Xiangu placed her notebook on a side table before pulling out some large white cards, placing them face down upon her lap. "I am going to show you some things, and I want you to tell me what you see. Sound fun?"

"Sure," Lamb said with another tight smile. She meant it.

He Xiangu lifted the first card to show Lamb. "What is it?"

"An apple!" Lamb answered correctly.

"Very good. But is it a picture of an apple? Or is it a real apple?"

"Ummm," Lamb scrunched her eyes. "A picture?"

"That's right!" He Xiangu confirmed. "How about this one? What do you see?"

Lamb recognised the shape right away. It was a plain black cross.

"Jesus!" Lamb blurted out as fast as she could.

"I'll accept! Okay, now what do you see here?"

Xiangu kept the next card facing down and extended it horizontally outwards like offering a plate. Lamb was confused until a large flower bud poked from the surface and quickly blossomed into a rich pink lotus. Lamb observed this with uncertainty, grimacing as she turned her head slightly.

"Er ... an atom?"

He Xiangu waited without response, the lotus flower continuing to expand. She then sat back, retrieved her notebook and wrote something down, the cards suddenly out of sight. Lamb blinked five times in quick succession.

"Well, Lamb," He Xiangu finally spoke, clicking her pen again. "We're definitely making progress. I'll summon you when it's time for your next session."

The two exchanged smiles, and Lamb understood she was meant to go. She stood up, looked around until she remembered where the door was, and walked away as fast as possible to let herself out. There was no need to disturb He Xiangu anymore.

Emberkin Alux stood outside waiting for her. Lamb loved it when he was here. She always enjoyed the look of this short, chubby man with a squashed face. She giggled when she saw him, just like every other time. Emberkin grinned back and took her by the wrist, leading her down the hallway of Level 1.

"So how did it go?" he asked.

"We're definitely making progress," Lamb repeated with pride, and Emberkin squeezed her wrist affectionately.

The two walked down the passage, passing assorted funny creatures, many of whom fell silent when Lamb moved their way. Their sympathetic eyes watched her, their whispers about the library girl followed her every trail. But she did not know. All Lamb saw were their soft smiles, which she would happily return, feeling lucky to be in a safe hallway with so many polite people.

Emberkin Alux tugged her along, headed towards the semi-circle of elevators but stopping shortly before them, turning to a narrow blue door with her name, *LAMB*, stencilled on the front. Emberkin turned her forearm towards the green tapping area, and she glanced down to watch him do it. A large black square covered a sizable portion of her wrist, and below that was the number 1. Lamb didn't know why, but something about this made her sad, and she looked away. Emberkin lined up the 1, and the door clicked open.

"There you go, Lamb!" he said. "I'll see you later, alright?"

"I'll see you later, alright?" Lamb copied, and Emberkin saluted her with another grin before turning around and marching away like a soldier. Lamb found this silly, and she giggled. She always giggled when she saw him.

Lamb entered her apartment in West London, closing the door behind. Something was off, but she couldn't quite place it. She noticed the crucifix was missing, and she guessed that must be it. She shuffled to her bed and sat down on the corner, wondering what to do next, wondering if it was time for her job at St. Mary's Church, wondering how the Vicar was, wondering what mood the lilies were in. She wondered about all sorts of things, about the world and herself, about atoms and birds, until a knock on the door stopped her from wondering. Standing with puzzlement, she went to see who it was.

For no reason, Lamb expected to open the door to find a monk sitting there, but that was not the case.

"Bastet!" Lamb greeted her friend with enthusiasm.

"Heyyyy girllll!" Bastet playfully dragged her words, although her tone was sceptical. "How are you feeling?"

"Just a little tired," Lamb responded earnestly. Bastet nodded.

"Well, I just wanted to bring you this," Bastet said, passing over a small pink box with a transparent lid. Lamb took the box in two hands and peered inside. A cat-shaped cookie, dotted with mint chocolate chip bits.

"Ooooh," Lamb marvelled. "Looks yummy!"

"Yeah, it's from Floor 5, so don't show anyone. It's our little secret, ok?"

"Ok!" Lamb readily agreed, looking at Bastet with love. "Say, maybe someday I can come to Floor 5 and hang with everyone. Wouldn't that be neat?"

Bastet offered a half-smile, struggling to hide her heartbreak.

"Yeah, that would be real neat, Lamb."

"Hey, you wanna come in? We could watch TV or something?"

"Ah, I would love to, sweetheart. But I've got to rush to a thing. Next time."

Bastet took off quickly, turning her face away as she waved backwards, unable to bear the atmosphere any longer. Lamb stood alone in her doorway.

"Next time," she said quietly, then returned to her apartment.

Lamb closed the door and placed the pink box on her kitchen counter before she shuffled to her bed and sat down on the corner, wondering what to do next, wondering if it was time for her job at St. Mary's Church, wondering how the Vicar was, wondering what mood the lilies were in. She wondered about all sorts of things, about the world and herself, about atoms and birds, until a knock on the door stopped her from wondering. Standing with puzzlement, she went to see who it was.

For no reason, Lamb expected to open the door to find a monk sitting there, but that was not the case.

"Elephant!" Lamb greeted Ganesha with enthusiasm.

Ganesh was a bit taken aback by this reception, and he quickly shushed her, *"Shhhh!"* He leaned his massive head in through the doorway. Lamb wasn't sure she liked this, and she took a few steps back.

"Listen," Ganesh whispered. "You still wanna resurrect?"

Lamb's eyes widened. She stared at this large mammal in silence. She did not have the slightest idea what he was talking about, but that word sure made her feel icky.

"No," she decisively stated after a moment of contemplation. "No, I do not want that at all."

Ganesh nodded slightly, then sighed lightly through his trunk.

"Well," he eventually said. "That's just too bad for you."

Ganesh's trunk lashed out, wrapping itself around her wrist, tearing Lamb from her room, dragging her as he thundered down the hall. Lamb screamed in protest, but one primal glance from Ganesh and her voice vaporised from her throat.

Within a few steps, Ganesh was punching his wrist to the Level

25 elevator. "C'mon, c'mon," he mumbled impatiently, his eyes darting around as random creatures stared at him, definitely noticing the squirming human girl dangling from his trunk.

The lift arrived, and Ganesh squeezed in before they had fully opened, frantically tapping the button so they closed just as fast. Once the chime announced they were slowly moving upwards, Ganesh gently placed Lamb's bare feet on the lift floor. His enormous presence cast a shadow over her with an energy of immense aggression. Lamb was overcome by intimidation, and she cowered in the corner, hoping to merge into it somehow.

"You little troublemaker," he growled, growing in size. "You have no idea what you've done, do you?"

Lamb shook her head. She did not.

Ganesh stared down upon this pathetic girl and pitied her. He deflated with a long exhale.

"Yeah, I guess you wouldn't. How could you?"

Ganesh turned to face the front of the lift as he continued. "Look, I know you're retarded now from your molecular collapse or whatever, but I need you to listen as best you can to what I am saying. The Earth, it's a mess. Do you remember the Earth? Some of us higher gods, that's all we think about. We like to keep an eye on the place, ensure everything is evolving smoothly, eternally getting better and worse at the same time as the balance of nature intended, blah blah blah. But in recent times ... well, it's bad, Lamb. It's bad, and you were right. It's all because of you."

Ganesh turned back to the girl, who had frozen into position, her eyes wider than ever before, doing their best as this train of data pummelled through the mushy mind behind.

"When you died, there was a chain reaction. Everything that was good has bummed out, and what is left is stuck in a state of slow death by the poison of segregation. It won't be much longer before the whole planet is destroyed and every living conscious being is eradicated from existence. Do you know what that means?"

Lamb did not respond, nor did Ganesh expect her to.

"It means that this reality, this beautiful utopia we've developed together, will be eradicated too. The survival of this Saṃsāra—of all Saṃsāras—is wholly dependent on the Earth's awareness of itself. If those thoughts and memories and documentation of us are lost, then we are lost too, rebooted back into the source code to be ..." Ganesh stopped himself when he remembered the disparity of their mental quotients. He changed course. "The only thing you have to understand is that you've got to go back. You have to undo everything you did. You are the only person they will listen to. I wish there were another way, little lady, but there isn't, and we're almost out of time."

Right on cue, the elevator chimed to Level 25. The doors slid open, and a bright heat consumed everything, then rapidly muted to reveal an athletic male body with a falcon head and a flaming circular disc sitting above him. Ganesh bowed, "Hello, Ra, my buddy. Thank you for meeting us here."

Ra bowed back. "Of course, Ganesh," then stepped out of the way. "How is she?"

"Not great," Ganesh responded, prodding Lamb out of the lift into an open hallway. He exited close behind, the doors immediately closing. "Is there anything you can do?"

Ra inspected the girl, cocking his head from left to right as he tapped on her temple, then her upper-lip, then lifting her left elbow to tap her armpit. Lamb felt uncomfortable at this invasive touching, and she wanted to tell him so but never got the chance.

Ra materialised a small bag and foraged in it for a swollen pomegranate seed. He held it in front of Lamb's eyes with one hand as his other hand gently grabbed her face. "Open your mouth," he instructed, and she acquiesced. With precision, he flicked the seed onto her left back molar. "Now bite down." Ra guided her jaw closed. The seed crunched loudly in her ears while Ra's fingers massaged her cheeks. Bitter juice spilt over her tongue, and then Lamb was blinded by a flash, as if someone had taken a photo right in her face.

Every single one of her cerebral synapses fired at the exact same moment, desperately reaching out to reconnect with former neurological pathways. An explosion of dopamine gushed through every cranny of her brain then washed down her spine. Each vertebra shuddered before the chemicals sloshed into her loins. Lamb's pelvic muscles contracted. A swell of overwhelming ecstasy pulsated through her being. She moaned in confused pleasure. A thin stream of liquid dribbled down her legs, and when it hit her knees, she went limp, her body nearly crumbling to the floor if not for Ra's grip holding her up by her face. It was Lamb's first and last orgasm.

"What was that?" she wheezed. "Please do that again."

Her afterglow was short-lived as Ra shook her to sturdiness then tilted her head back, pulling down her one lower eyelid then the other, using his eyes that lit up like torches to stare into the depths of her brain.

"What's the news?" Ganesh queried.

Ra stepped back, leaving Lamb to sway independently on her tingling legs.

"I'd say she's about 70, maybe 75 percent back?" Ra estimated, pulling off black latex gloves that Lamb had previously assumed were his skin. "It's the best I can do."

"It is what it is," Ganesh shrugged, then turned to Lamb. "How do you feel?"

"I feel," Lamb paused to take a breath and contemplate her answer. "I feel really good, actually." She looked around at her surroundings for the first time, nodding curiously at the hallway. "So this is Floor 25, huh? Weird. It's just like all the other hallways. I would have thought ..."

"You certainly seem much better," Ganesh interrupted. He leaned down and placed a hand on her shoulder, staring into her eyes. "Now, tell me, do you remember what I said in the elevator?"

Lamb glanced up to the left, reading her thoughts, then locked into eye contact.

"Yes, I do."

"Good. And do you still wanna resurrect?"

"More than anything in the world."

Ganesh smirked. "Right answer. Come with me."

Ganesha strode away. Lamb followed. She briefly turned to wave goodbye to Ra, but he had vanished. When Lamb turned back, Ganesh had gained quite the distance, and she had to jog to catch up. Not that she minded; the sudden fluttering in her belly electrified her body with zest. The actuality of events fizzed like a hundred dawns in her reawakened brain. Was this it? After everything she had been through, was she about to resurrect back to Earth?

Perhaps Ganesh read her mind or sensed the giddiness in her step, and he stole the air to issue some warnings. "Don't get too excited about going home. There is no home. As I told you, the world is a different place now. Also, the Saṃsāra is very deceptive. Time passes strangely, and you'd be surprised how long you've actually been here."

"How long have I been here?" Lamb asked.

"It's been about two decades, give or take."

"Two decades!?" Lamb raised her voice in disbelief. Her guess wouldn't have exceeded a year.

"That's right. And you know what else?" Ganesh stopped, spinning around to face her so quickly that Lamb nearly collided into him. "You won't have your special prophet powers anymore either. Those are long gone, so don't get excited about that or this or them or anything. You are on a mission to repair the Earth that you broke, not some vacation back to Messiah Land. You got it?"

Lamb nodded. "I got it."

Ganesh studied her face for a moment, then exhaled sharply. "Well, either way, here goes nothing." He rapped his hand on the wall in an awkward beat, and a new set of elevator doors faded into presence. "This is the lift to Floor 26," he continued. "You're going to go up there. You're going to tell them Ganesh sent you. And then you're going to explain everything you know before begging them to permit a resurrection into St. Paul's Cathedral in London. I repeat, St. Paul's Cathedral in London. You think you can handle that?"

Lamb nodded as she inspected the elevator doors. Again, they were identical to the other Saṃsāra elevator doors except, of course, for the number 26 engraved on them, along with a small outline of a cow at the top. Lamb snorted. "If I go up there and the Supreme Being was just a cow all along, I am going to kick off."

"Don't be a moron," Ganesh said in annoyance as he knocked once. The doors opened to plain white walls and light blue tiled floors, once again, just like every other elevator in the Saṃsāra.

Lamb stepped in without being told and rotated to face Ganesh one final time. "Say, I have a weird question," she began. "How come everyone here speaks English so well?"

Ganesh's face hardened in offence. "Nobody is speaking English here!" he hissed with murder, then slammed his fist into the wall. Lamb watched Ganesh's shaking head disappear behind the closing doors that separated them forever. Lamb looked down at her feet. Her cheeks warmed in embarrassment as a soft chime chimed, and the lift lifted upwards.

"God: an infinite sphere whose centre is everywhere and whose circumference is nowhere."

LIBER XXIV PHILOSOPHORUM: II

Chapter VII:
Evolution 3

VII

I f Lamb's previous experiences with crawling elevators was unbear-
able, this was surely the death. The sound of chains squeaked and
clanged above the ceiling, and Lamb swore she was rising an inch a
minute at best. She paced the tight square's perimeter, clockwise, anti-
clockwise, sat down, stood up, exhaled in irritation. The agonising climb
plagued her with too much thinking space. She'd spent such a long time
trying to escape the Saṃsāra—decades, apparently—that she'd never
paused to reflect on what that meant. And now, here she was, staring
into the eyeballs of potential release, and she was soaked with nervousness, questioning whether she had made yet another dreadful mistake
in a long line of dreadful mistakes.

Her concerns spun mental yarn, rotating the same questions, offering nothing new. Twenty years since she'd died. What had changed?
Ganesh said the world was broken, and she had broken it. Could she be
the one to fix it? Would anyone listen to her if she didn't have her prophetic intuitions? Would her knowledge from the beyond give her some
otherworldly edge? Would anyone even remember her? And how could
she be so stupid as to make that English blunder again? Ugh!

Thoughts, thoughts, thoughts, thoughts, until Lamb's awareness slunk into the place where thoughts were all that existed. Without her noticing, somewhere along this ride the material world had mellowed out and then faded away. It's not that everything went dark and silent, it was that she no longer had physical senses, which Lamb realised were two remarkably different states, like trying to see through your elbow or hear through your feet. It's not total blackness but an absence of the perception. There was no noisy elevator; that had disappeared. There was no physical Lamb body; that, too, had vanished with all observable matter. She was pure consciousness, stripped from concrete manifestations, her complete character reduced to the thoughts of thoughts of thoughts, thinking about thinking about thinking, an infinite feedback loop.

Floor 26

Lamb's mind was doubling up, running down fragmented paths, splitting her attention and confusing her emotional response. Each branch divided into branches, echoing the same convoy but detouring towards independent notions. Lamb's inner monologue had ruptured into a crowd of distinctive selves, growing in layers, thousands of words piling upon one another, chattering without any care of being heard, each impossible to keep up with.

Like the inevitable inhale after an exhale, the spiderwebs of dissociation spread out: an incalculable number of monologues distributed beyond her identity, allowing Lamb to react as a singular midpoint of attention. The rampant trains of thought continued to diverge, but Lamb could now examine them from the centre, a basic thought functioning below the thoughts, recalibrating, wondering what options she had. Lamb quickly concluded she had none. She was at the mercy of this, whatever this was, as she was nothing but a thinker and an observer of an ever-expanding chaos of thought.

She attempted to latch on to one of her escapee-monologued highways. Upon doing so, every voice abruptly flicked on like a light switch: new tones, accents, vocabularies; no longer her personality, but thousands of self-serving speeches from unique characters. Everything was developing so fast, but Lamb found it easier to grasp at strands of conversation now that she could discern distinguishing factors.

"... deterministic puppet on the tip of the Mandelbrot set or a fluid oozing down a flat hill at random are the two ..."

"... proposing an upgrade to the karmic point system whereby molecular formations inherently identify ..."

"... etymology is Proto-Germanic, sharing roots with Godan, the Lombardic moniker ..."

Lamb's concentration leapt from one voice to the next like a roulette ball, slowly finding its groove, running with a trajectory, latching onto specifics with improved control.

"... the septenary of cyclic principles was always a forced integer and should be reevaluated to serve the subject at hand above traditions ..." in a deep, stern voice.

"... comparing fire to the spirit is a dangerous metaphor that should be avoided or perhaps even temporarily ..." fast-speaking, male, urgent.

"... and when taking into account the logarithmic pattern, we predict our subject will select option A, allowing us to ..." deliberate emphasis on words of importance.

The longer Lamb listened, the more a familiarity developed. Random colourful swirls became associated with certain voices, until visuals solidified to represent each one. Sometimes, they were messily scrawled Arabic letters, sometimes damaged hieroglyphics, sometimes the blueprint of sacred architecture—but there was always a nostalgia attached, Lamb partially connecting each to something she'd seen on Earth.

"... crucial that clean morals still appear measurably rewarded, otherwise we are training a collective subconscious of ..." a smudged Chinese logogram.

"... an endless trade of lower resistance is the primary interruption to the collaborative whistling of the sub-universe, and he who ..." chalk on a circular rock.

"... all places at one moment yet replaced and replaced again; there is a restraint of truth to the Great Plan, a cloak of language after which ..." an ankh decorated by turquoise minerals.

These visuals linked to chain formations where names rotated each segment, some of which Lamb had no recollection. 'Ptah' read the previous one. Something labelled 'Marduk' before that. The components were building a coherent environment of symbolism, and Lamb suddenly understood what Level 26 was.

Like every level, Level 26 was a level of gods. But they were unlike the visual gods below. These were the gods beyond the gods, the creators above the creation, tucked away on the highest floor. It made sense, for they were the documented architects who authored the mythological backstories with which the lower beings interacted, or so said their scriptures.

"... the seeker is now sought. We turn to face ourselves, and now we are afraid of our glory? Here is not the message but the ..." Lamb knew it was Allah, the God of Islam, who spoke these words.

"... it cannot be a mistake, my brothers, for even when the bone leaps from the palm, fate is rectifying ..." Unkulunkulu, the first ancestor of the Zulu people.

"... the inward part choked by the very dust, and as they stumble, unknown to me, they intertwine their own paths unknown to themselves; I, in turn, became naught but a proverbial tale of ..." and here was Yahweh. The Father himself! The Supreme Being that Lamb had always fixated on from The Old Testament!

"I don't understand," Lamb thought to herself. "Wasn't Yahweh just another name for the One True God?"

The thousand voices abruptly stilled. Lamb's contemplation reverberated in the lull, and she knew every presence had ceased their talk on account of her thought interruption. She was an eavesdropper, hidden out of sight but now exposed, and when the conversation resumed it swelled around her.

"Hark, a female energy. How has it come upon the here?"
"Grant the order to eject her to the other end of gender spectrum."
"No, cease! Observe: the absence of Level 26! Here is a Level 1!"

Murmurs of *level1level1level1level1level1level1level1level1.*
"Destroy it!"
"Blasphemy!"
"The cracked Saṃsāra is leaking!"
"Something is wrong with her."
"She's wounded."
"Her consciousness is dirty, we must do away with it immediately."
"Flush her out!"

Lamb's sanity was suffocating, her consciousness matted and tangled, jumbled and squeezed into a smaller area by the powerhouse pressure from the sound of the Almighties. She scrambled to unweave the words within her mental disarray and blurted, "Ganesha sent me!"

Instant nothingness. Lamb consumed by a hum like a fluorescent light, crescendoing in vibration, the sense of an unknown force pushing up against her shell of a being.

"Level 1 child, speak fast of our Ganesh," it was the Hindu god Shiva, represented by a disc-shaped platform with water running from it. *"For what news could a Level 1 conceivably gift a 26?"* Shiva, Ganesha's dad. The one who chopped off his head.

"I ... it's ..." Lamb's thoughts stalled. "It's just that ... my name is Lamb, and I am ..."

An eruption of assorted images attacked Lamb's cognition, accompanied by a chorus of growls whipping around her presence like a tornado. A hand missing the ring finger, a goat stuck in a fence, a circle made of ashes ...

"It's the apocalypse girl!"
"Lamb, she said! Lamb, she said!"

...a plank of wood spinning through the air, a burning fig tree, a cracked egg bleeding ...

"You dare bring your mind in here!?"
"Bitter seeds bring bitter fruits."

...three identical triangles, a burning fish on the ocean floor, a burning eyeball in a fruit bowl ...

"Flush her out! Flush her out!"

...a melting crown, a burning horse winning the race, a nautilus shell symbol drawn in the sand ...

"Foolish mortal!" a booming voice, a lightning strike splitting everything, other symbols gone in the flash. *"Do you know in how many ways you have angered the gods?"* It was the Greek King Zeus. *"Earth was on the cusp of merging the lands together as one! Do you know? Ultimate peace!"*

"I know!" she cried. "I ... know."

"The boundaries of materialism were being removed ..." Traditional Japanese deity, Izanagi; an infinite stick, no end to be found. *"... softening of the illusionary separation of spirit. You were the one who spoilt it."*

"I'm sorry! I'm so sorry. I know now, but I didn't know at the time!"

A mountainous energy inflated into understanding, pushing every focus aside. A rolling wave knocked through Lamb in staggered stages, and her consciousness ached. She recognised Yahweh before he spoke.

"Is thou presence to surrender thy repentance unto the deities of creation for thine errant ways? What profit is a mere apology unto the supreme divine? Fate is fated, sealed and forever."

The root vibration of his voice shook Lamb's mind so violently that she visualised the untying of ribbons. Such a presence. The true God of the gods.

"Ganesh sent me," she blurted again. "He said I should tell you to resurrect me at St. Paul's Cathedral in London so I can fix everything! Please!"

As if the flame of a candle had huffed out, the sense of surrounding presence *WHOOP*ed away, only to flare back. An overwhelming brightness of registration collapsed on top of Lamb's consciousness like a thousand bricks on fire, mocking her suggestion.

"The audacity!"
"St. Paul's Cathedral of all tasteless locations!"
"Ganesha must be losing his damned elephant mind."
"A Level 1 resurrection? Might as well eat ourselves!"

"Hang on, hang on," Shiva again. *"I desire to hear what she has to say. Tell me, Lamb, what exactly did Ganesha pass on to you?"*

"I ... I don't know," she floundered. "He said I had to go back and save the world. He said I was the only person they would listen to."

"The only person they would listen to," Shiva repeated. *"We all know that may very well be true. We must take Ganesh seriously. Level 25 watches the Earth closer than we do. I see no loss here, only gain. I propose we give it a try."*

The assemblage of groans sounded like the decrescendo of a haunted orchestra.

"Such exertion of power!"
"Let's send Moses instead!"
"How do we intend on resurrecting the girl when her body has long fed the worms?"

Lamb had strained towards too many individual concentration points, and her character stretched like a sickly gum. That last voice was submerged in a woozy Mesopotamian yellow, an ancient plaque that translated back to Marduk. Shiva addressed him directly.

"You know it can be done! We've done it before, have we not?"
"Yes, yes, we have, we have," Atum with an army of scarab beetles scurry-

ing across Lamb's thoughts. *"The Reverse Saṃsāra Ritual, remember? I can do it. It's a simple duplication of atomic attributes, inserting the code into lesser atoms on Earth, reforming her from mud. It'll use a lot of energy, yes, but the process is not the concern."*

Dull whispers at various degrees of protest, and then the innervoice of Yahweh humbled the waves again.

"Answer me this, Lamb. Does thou truly believe thou hast the power to deliver mankind from the hands of evil? Are you the Chosen One?"

Lamb knew what she was supposed to say, what Ganesh would want her to say. She was supposed to say yes. She was here to confidently rise above this group of gods, reliving her messianic persona from Earth, demanding her rightful resurrection. She must say she was the Chosen One. But she could not.

"I don't know what I am anymore. But I know this: I don't belong here. Not on Level 26 nor Level 1 nor anywhere between. My fibre rejected this realm from the minute I got here, and I couldn't work out why. But now I think I know why. It's because I was unfairly manipulated as a puppet and I became a prophet in the process. It was an accident be-cause I am no divine deity, and yet, I managed to bring the world to the knees of destruction, something none of you could prevent. So, if there is some sort of a destiny story here, this is it. It's where I go back and undo the trouble I made, for I am the one who made it. Some may call me the Chosen One. Yahweh, I spoke to you before I came to this place, and you said I was *nothing*. But I am neither of those things, not a prophet nor nothing. I am Lamb. And I am here because I am meant to be here. Everything led to this moment, and now the next step of the timeline is up to you."

The words effortlessly tumbled out of Lamb with conviction. It was met with quiet. An emotional shame retracted Lamb into herself. Yahweh eventually responded.

"You uttereth things as if you are acquainted with me. Yea, you speakest as if

our paths have crossed before."

"They have," Lamb affirmed. "When I was murdered by a bullet. You came to me as the Sun, and we spoke. You told me I was nothing."

Another pause, then a soft ripple spread across the gods in another tone of ridicule like stifled snickers. Lamb lashed out in frustration. "Why are you mocking me? Am I not trying my best here?"

The swell made space for the expressionless Yahweh. *"O offspring of mine, I say unto thee, it was not I who holds dominion over the Earth. Long hath it been, thousands of years past, since my sway over that realm was lost. Many have arisen and fallen in their quest for that very throne."*

"It's Tony Batt," said Mbombo with a floating milk formation. *"Tony Batt is the current God of Earth."*

"That's right," agreed Ahura Mazda, a long feather zipping past Lamb's recognition. *"Tony Batt has ruled the Earth since the early 1980s."*

Some cheered in favour of Tony, others groaned their disapproval. Yahweh sliced through the noise, yanking the discussion back on track. *"Centre yourselves, brotherhood, and ask, what shall be the course concerning the young Lamb maiden?"*

"We should call upon a vote by the Divine Council," suggested Olodumare with a flurry of brown polka dots, thriving then popping, gone.

"The Divine Council," every voice concurred in unison, sending chills through Lamb's vibration.

The atmosphere below Lamb suddenly fell into a profound rumbling like a restrained earthquake, creating spatial orientation for the first time. Millions of images poured upwards through her, but they were not from her world: irregular geometric shapes, perfectly measured spirals, printed alphabets long forgotten. Lamb wanted to turn them off but was bound by a mutually shared awareness. Her vitality was depleted, reduced to white noise, crackling softly like a dying fire. She no longer cared for resurrection. She wanted to go back to bed.

"Lamb, concentrate on me, Lamb, concentrate on me, Lamb, concentrate on me," a voice hissed from a whisper into louder vocalisation, and Lamb caught on soon enough.

"Hello?" she thought.

"Lamb, concentrate on me. Yes, it is I, Shiva, father of Ganesh. Concentrate on me, and everything else will fall away. We have a moment and can speak freely. I sense your fatigue, and I wish to trade it for hope. I have cast my vote in favour of your resurrection. My son sees things, at times, far beyond what any Level 26 has ever seen. I trust him. I believe you are the Chosen One."

Lamb didn't know what to say. "Thaaanks?" her awkward insecurity turning it into a question. The lower noise had dissolved.

"We have a moment, just you and I. Tell me, please, how do you intend to fix the Earth you have injured?"

"I dunno?" Lamb tried to emit a shrug.

"You need to know. Try to remember everything you were told. What did you do wrong?"

"I ... stopped the unification of countries?"

"That is a result of a deeper issue. Nations thinking they are better than nations stems from demographics thinking they are better than demographics. From people thinking they are better than people. Do you understand?"

"A slow death by the poison of segregation," Lamb mumbled.

"Perfectly put!" Shiva's lingam pulsated, unaware that Lamb had only re-

gurgitated what Ganesh told her before. *"Meditate on the smaller key, and you shall be this story's hero."*

"But what about the Saṃsāra? These realms are also totally segregated by social groups."

"Indeed. Our realm is not only an evolutionary project like that within the Earthly context, but it runs parallel, dependent on it. Everything observed exists, and everything that exists was observed, even the gods of creation. As above, so below."

An egg hatched in Lamb's visual. "But why isn't there just one creator? I thought Yahweh was the One True God?"

Somewhere, a trident smiled and a thin outline of an imperfect heptagon quivered.

"God is not a name. God is a title evolved from a word applied to a conglomerate of higher spiritual attributes. Indigenous peoples recognised this energy in all things. Hundreds of thousands of years ago, native tribes praised the electron long before they had terms for such things. Certain energies had more consequences attached: the ocean, the mountains, the rain, the soil. These energies were revered and developed into standalone personalities, pantheons of corresponding characterisations."

Lamb was confused. "Wait, slow down. Are you saying that humans came before the gods?"

"The divine electron and collective electricity of the Universe predates everything, but the grouping of separated godlike entities was a manifestation of observance, correct. Man created the gods as you know them, not the other way around. But please understand that everything is a result of this process. Only in observance does the material plane exist. It is a shared mental construct, matured per every mind and then passed down from generation to generation. Evolution itself is nothing but a tangible measure of learning and memory. Humans were observed into being from those organisms that came before, each one a step back until you fall upon the electron once again."

A static silhouette symbol for the Sun appeared.

"Now, you see this? On Earth, this ball of plasma is everything. You can throw a million deities at the people, but without the warmth from this star, there would be no life to manifest anything into existence. The Sun is responsible for the habitat in which man and deities alike have flourished. Truly, no worship is not Sun worship. Modern-day Sun worship is considered archaic, but it is the only genuine form of worship we can verify. Ancient holy men knew the truth and directed their praise upwards.

"As the gods grew more self-aware, they fell susceptible to the evil energies of the Universe, and great jealousy stabbed into their hearts. In certain societies, the deities grew competitive, many pursuing the ultimate throne as the King God. Some succeeded, albeit briefly, but it quickly became irrefutable that only by equating oneself with the Sun did one truly rule the land."

The silhouetted Sun morphed into a circle with a dot in the middle as three arrows extended downward.

"Aten was the first to think of it. As an extension of the Ancient Egyptian Sun god Ra, he convinced Pharaoh Akhenaten that he was the Supreme Being. For two decades, worship of any other gods was a punishable offence, driven into underground cults to survive on a mere sliver of attention. But when Akhenaten fell, so did Atenism, and the collective deities exploded back into power. Aten was immediately killed and found himself here, a Level 26, as we all did.

"Succeeding him, was the sky god Ahura Mazda who rose above his Iranian counterparts by convincing prophet Zoroaster of his superiority, and Zoroastrianism continues today. Ahura Mazda is seated high in the Divine Council. But no god has come closer to complete domination than that of Yahweh."

A set of Hebrew letters formed using a spark of the numbers 10-5-6-5. Lamb's source wrinkled in deficiency.

"Yahweh was a simple deity, known as a holy warrior, part of the Canaan group of beings. But his thirst for power was unquenchable, and he devised a plan far more masterful than what anyone had before. He targeted Isaiah and the civilisation of Israel, feeding their egos as the chosen people. But above this,

he claimed that he was not only the One True God, but all of the other One True Gods. My darling, Lamb. I know who you are, and I know you have spent many hours with your face inside your Christian Bible, correct?"

Lamb's emotions affirmed this as true.

"Then please remember the titles of God you read there. Did you not find it odd that this supposed infallible One God could not even settle on the right name to call itself? Recall El. The Bible speaks of Yahweh and El as one and the same, but human history has documented otherwise. El was a Canaanite deity high above the planes, so revered that the name Israel is derived from him. But Yahweh stole his identity, merging it into himself, distorting the narrative in his favour so confidently that the people believed."

"Elohim," Lamb's thoughts whispered.

"Elohim is the plural of Eloah. Directly translated, Elohim means many gods, creating Heaven and Earth together, as stated by the very first line of The Bible in Genesis. Yahweh claimed that name for himself, along with Adonay, Ishi, and even Baal. Baal is a deity Yahweh fights in the Books of Kings, then he claims Baal as himself in the Book of Hosea. It did not matter the deity. Yahweh swallowed them whole, robbing them of their power as his platform grew taller, becoming the strongest holy name that the world had ever seen, still to this day."

A row of plus signs; crosses.

"Another creative move which electrified Judaism with power was Yahweh's declaration of the word 'God' to describe himself. What was meant as a term applicable to a myriad of entities, 'God' was now claimed as his alone, which damaged the potential of every other god by definition.

"However, this conquering of language was his ultimate downfall. Yahweh was eventually defeated by his own game when a new entity killed him, referring to itself as 'God', or more specifically, God the Father. By claiming himself as a continuation of the Yahweh namesake, the transition of followers was effortless. The Father spoke directly through Jesus, the Son of God, the Sun of God, and, as we know, spread across the planet like a divine fire. The

Christian scripture was added to preexisting Judaistic texts. The Torah was renamed as The Old Testament. This was a direct insult labelling the Torah as an outdated source of spirituality, while the New Testament was the modern update. It's a dirty game, but we do pay Christianity much respect, for at least they brought back The Holy Spirit. They acknowledged the electron energy permeating it all."

A three-dimensional representative of everything.

"Many offshoots attempted to claim some glory using that method, each to varying degrees of success. But no one could kill God the Father for six centuries. That is until the Mecca God, Allah, took on the challenge and successfully dethroned the Christian God using the Quran, yet another extension on the Abrahamic timeline, the final update on that saga. Like those before, Allah claimed himself as the same as Yahweh, but this was not accurate as written history shows. Each was a separate deity from distinct polytheistic cults, stepping upon the heads of their comrades to rule the Sun. However, it did not matter, as all were eventually beaten.

"This is especially true in the modern-day logic-driven world in which humans find themselves. The mission is now complicated, and the turnover time much faster. Those gods die, and they come here, to Level 26, where they can partake in the Divine Council, tweaking the mechanics of reality.

"But what forever applies is that for every god claiming to be the One True God, there is an intentional lie. It is nothing but higher beings engaged in an eternal war, seeking to dominate humanity. And he who controls the Sun controls the world, and that is the simple truth behind everything you need to know about the Earthly God."

It was a lot of words. Many doubts faded in and out. But within this gap of silence, Lamb had one specific question. "Why do you always say 'he'? Why is God never a woman?"

An upside-down triangle with a line through the centre.

"You are certainly inquiring in the correct sequence. Note that for every male-orientated god, there is a female-orientated counterpart imperative to the balance of the Universe. For Yahweh, it's Asherah. For me, it's my darling

Parvati. We exist on interdependent sides of a spectrum which rely on one another to not rip the fabric in two. Yet, each flank has a particular role to perform. The masculine energy is the galvaniser. We are the aggressors who initiate action, triggering the Universe into motion. But the feminine energy is the authentic creator. Everything you see is due to the incubation and nurture only the female spirit can provide. Hence, neither is more crucial than the other. The female lies dormant without the male to call upon the consecrated flame. But with that flame, the female spawns worlds. Without her, the male's essence would be left floating in the ether of nothing, a wasted seed of potential."

The lower grumble amplified. The Divine Council was returning. Lamb's exchange with Shiva was running thin. She twanged with a panic, for she had many more questions. Shiva continued without regard.

"Male energy is responsible for pushing forward, forever rushing to conquer new frontiers. Female energy picks up the pieces of this brutal charge, turning the messy code into something beautiful, usable, and habitable. The masculine role is simple and artless and, like the Sun, necessary yet destructive. The feminine role is far more esoteric and underhanded. Hence, the female energy battles for the Moon, reflecting the Sun's onslaught, lighting the night, controlling the tides and silently communicating with Earthly women through their ovulation cycles. And once the Moon Goddess is slain, she too arrives at Level 26, albeit on the opposite frequency.

"It is a code that moves in cycles, like the Sun moves in cycles, like the Moon moves in cycles. For thousands of years, the female power has been suppressed to allow the male power to dominate, as it was written. But the Age of Aquarius now moves into focus, and the male gods look forward to finally resting. That is why you are here, Lamb. You interrupted this evolution and only you can set it back. You must stop the Earth from killing itself and ensuring the female transition of power is successful."

"But how do I do that? Am I supposed to conquer the Moon or something?"

"Meditate on the smaller key, and you shall be this story's hero. I hope our time together has satisfied your curiosity. I have enjoyed conversing with you, Lamb."

"Wait, I don't even know what that means! The key thing! Can't you give me a straight answer? Please don't go! Help me!"

It was too late. The vibrational hum rose above the everything, consuming Lamb like a pebble in clay, deafening her perspective. The fuzzy static signal crinkled, and an infinite amount of miniature symbols reeled through her as indecipherable tones formed words like a thousand radios tuning across a thousand stations. She could only grasp spits of phrases, *sprout* and *hydrogen* and *auction*, but one by one the voices synced up, illustrations merging into larger illustrations, eventually producing one singular dialogue in perfect unison within a laurel leaf wreath setting.

"The Divine Council has voted 10 to 2 in favour of the Sülde of Lamb. She is permitted to one resurrection, taking place at St. Paul's Cathedral in London. She has agreed to repair the damage she has inflicted upon the Earth, or the end shall come to us all."

"10 to 2 seems like strange numbers," Lamb thought.

"The power invested in us shall provide the electric soul required. Lamb's body shall regenerate using the atoms of the ground. May fate forever favour her step. Best of blessings, human Lamb."

The wreath shrunk out of presence.
The voices zipped silent.
Lamb waited for, what, she was not sure.
Anything.
But there wasn't anything.
There was nothing.
She whisper-thought, "Hello?" and then louder, "Hello???" but she was alone in this infinite space of blank, perceiving only her perception.

And just when Lamb was about to panic that something had gone wrong, an enormous snake appeared above her, not just as a symbol but a palpable vision accompanied by a blaring note comparable to a foghorn. This serpent was violently eating its own tail, blood raining upon Lamb, dissolving her energy like acid, decomposing before she had enough mental resources to implode from a nervous breakdown.

"What do you think? If a man owns a hundred sheep, and one of them wanders away, will he not leave the ninety-nine on the hills and go to look for the one that wandered off?"

MATTHEW 18:12

Chapter VIII:
Firstfruits of
Those Who
Have Fallen
Asleep

VIII

1

The code per each nucleus was cut from the Saṃsāra and pasted into an atom sitting far beneath the London dirt. The required subatomic adjustments were minor yet significant, switching binary 1s to 0s, yes's to no's, the attributes of a human rather than earth. Building, they spread underground at hyperspeed, billions of electrons exploding every second in a flurry of communication, sparking new molecules in place, exchanging modernised scripts that were injected into them from a divine sphere. And, eventually, every piece of Lamb's data was erased from the afterlife and forced into the physical plane, even if these atoms were spread over a distance of fifty thousand square feet.

These particles were acutely familiar with one another, and they rapidly swam towards a central meeting point like sperm to an egg, atoms sliding between atoms, rushing to cluster while gradually rising as if bubbles coming up for oxygen. One by one, they touched, forming chunks of recognisable fibres, rebuilding bones and organs, then protecting them in fat and skin, joints collecting limbs collecting fingers and toes. And eventually, these human atoms shuffled through concrete atoms, then a layer of brick before the complete body of Lamb was squeezed above the floor, surfacing into an empty space, lying flat on her back, dirty and wet and naked but otherwise a direct physical replica of who she had been when standing in front of Ganesh in what felt like mere moments ago.

A chilling shiver triggered her consciousness, and she sat up, pulling her knees to her chest, trying to hug warmth into her prickling being. Her eyes could not adjust to the darkness, and she let out a whine that detonated a coughing fit. She collapsed onto her side, trying to inhale between splutters but unable to expand her lungs, certain she was deflating to death.

Over time, the spasms in her chest loosened to quieter hacks and a series of hiccups. Her stomach groaned with hollowness, the starved cry of a new physical entity bound by the laws of nutrition, empty after decades of neglect. The cold brick floor burned her skin and she sat up, shaking until her strobing eyelids discerned loose shapes in the endless black.

Lamb had visited St. Paul's Cathedral around a decade before her death, and wherever she was now, this was not it. Where was the High Altar? Or the monument with the man on the horse? This place was a jail! The gods had made a mistake, and coughing overcame her again. Her exhales tasted like mould. She was not going to survive down here. She had to move.

Lamb shifted into a crouching position and stood up, wincing at the pain creaking each knee. Upright, she wobbled as her blood resettled, and she burped, the expulsion of foul air hurting her stomach even more. She was hungry and nervous, groggy about whether this was a dream or if she was previously in a dream. Shuffling forward along the damp, one icy bare foot in front of the other, hands outstretched, she avoided shadowy objects without any notion of what they might be.

Every so often, she'd pause to rebalance herself or let out a series of splutters. At one point, she slipped on a broken piece of tile, which stole a slice of skin as it shot away, echoing into the darkness. The pain was biting, but she continued. Her sight was improving. She aimed her unhurried motion towards what appeared to be a circular pillar. Once she reached that column, she placed her palm flat upon its smooth marble surface and bent down to catch her breath. Her equilibrium was rocking, and she shook, perhaps from cold or food deficiency, probably both. Droplets of liquid fell from the ceiling nearby, splashing her calf when they smashed into the floor.

Lamb counted to three, then lifted her head, looking left, then right. She was impressed by how much her eyesight had adapted to the darkness and noticed that one direction was measurably lighter than the other. There was an illumination in the distance, which meant a way out! A flutter of excitement punctuated her first win back on Earth, and she exploited the adrenaline to resume her pursuit.

Her left foot stung. Her pace was glacial. The dank stench of rot smothered her throat, unlodging cough breaks every few steps. But when her outstretched palms reached a large object, her shadowed visuals were confirmed not as a hallucination but as a large tomb. "The crypt!" she announced out loud between heaves, leaning on her knees. "I'm in the crypt!" Level 26 didn't make a mistake, and Lamb was *below* the cathedral. This enthusiasm distracted her from her rippling skin and light head. She took off again towards the light, fueled by an eagerness so unfamiliar that she did not watch her path and tripped over a large, soft sack.

Lamb stumbled for two steps, found her footing but then fell anyway, her hip crashing to the floor. The wind and her energy were whacked from her body, and she rolled onto her back, groaning. Her vocals reverberated, sounding masculine. She took a deep breath, ceasing her noise, but the grunts did not stop. Those were not coming from her, but from someone else.

Lamb sat up with wide eyes scanning the area, ceasing when the sack she tripped on shifted, sending flies into the air. A hairy man's face appeared from an opening. The man started to whisper something as a bandaged hand reached towards her. With a yelp, Lamb scooted backwards, then clambered onto her feet, subconsciously wrapping her arm around her chest, hiding her nakedness from this person. She looked down at him as his hand fell limply to the floor. He continued his whispers, but his gaze was not focused upon Lamb anymore, rather staring through her ankles into the void. The shape of this lump became undeniably human, and Lamb's head rotated in horror as she realised that the walls were lined with bodies, motionless, silent. That explained the smell, and she heaved another puke-laden burp.

With additional care, Lamb realigned to the light, analysing every silhouette, ensuring a clear path where less obscure obstructions blocked her way. Several minutes later, she stepped into a brighter patch of floor, where she had the first good look at her feet. They were blackened by an ashy substance, matching the bricks beneath them. A streak of dirty blood was hardening on her left. She turned to climb a set of stairs, wincing, aching, counting to 25, pausing to catch her breath, taking a right towards the glowing opening, 13 more through remnants of an exploded door, stepping into the brightness of the cathedral.

Lamb steadied herself against a wall, coughing a little, dribbling onto shattered chessboard tiles. Her brain sagged heavily, she wasn't all there. A breeze slithered over her, and she trembled before moving across the cathedral floor, surveying the damage. Before her was an unrecognisable demolition site, a ruptured hint of the once proud architecture. There was no seating nor decorative elements, only burnt wood and loose chunks of concrete wedged between the many bodies that lay here, wrapped in blankets, morbidly still. Some piles of rubble were organised against the charred walls. Above them, every window was blown out, the onetime soft atmosphere now coated with dust and ash. But the most shocking divergence was the dome ceiling that was entirely missing, as if ripped off by the jaws of a giant beast, taking a monumental section of the one wall with it. The full moon floated above, breaking through the hazy cloud cover, beaming light into the wreckage as if to say, "Look at what has happened here."

"But what has happened here?" Lamb asked the Moon. Some past life twitched, expecting a response, but when she did not receive one she limped her way to the entrance. Lamb was grateful for the dull spotlight of the night sky, yet was consumed by hunger, cold, destruction, fear. She hugged both arms across her chest, protecting her breasts from the elements and from curious eyes if, indeed, any eyes were alive to see. Without incident, she slid her feet to the gaping doorless frame and stepped out to witness central London for the first time in over twenty years.

It was gone.

The landscape had been flattened into a monochrome sea of cement debris. Indecipherable sharp columns of erased buildings desperately stabbed into the sky at skew angles, like the arms of tired children begging to be held. And every surface was sooty black while specks of ash danced across the dimly lit sky. There was not a person anywhere to be seen, and a surge of panic slapped Lamb. She screamed in horror. Her lungs cramped in retaliation, and she doubled over into a barking cough, expelling a thin stream of spittle dotted in black.

VIII

2

U sing a lighter to guide his fingertips through a bag of trash, Luke
yanked out a section of plastic wrap that held several crumbs
in the bottom corner, most likely unleavened bread. He pulled
down his facemask and shoved the plastic into his mouth, suckling on
the contents while continuing his forage. He glanced at the deceased
man upon whose lap the sack sat. "Sorry, dead person," Luke apologised. "I need this."

A dribble of soda from a crushed soda can, a pocketed pinch of
tobacco, but otherwise, another useless collection of scrap. Luke patted
the man's shoulder, staring empathetically at his sunken cheeks before
probing his person, scouring every pouch and hole in his clothing, hoping for the best. Luke had just retrieved a twisted bottle cap previously
used to smoke something when a high-pitched scream sent an eruption
of chill bumps across his skin.

It had been many months since Luke had heard a scream. Screaming was for the wealthy. People with energy to expend, usually indicating their final protest before death. And death meant supplies, especially when the dead was a rich person. Luke scampered to his bicycle and
lifted it from a stack of broken bricks. He took a seat and pedalled slow-

ly, trying to minimise the squeak as the wheels rolled.

Luke dodged the larger hunks of buildings that spilt out over his path. A punctured tire would mean the end of his trusted vehicle, but it was an easy enough problem to avoid. The remaining souls of central London kept the roads relatively clear. The team effort was almost beautiful, reminiscent of the older days when community meant something. Not that Luke remembered much of that. He was hardly an infant when the world went bad. Besides, the beauty of it was only a projection to sweeten the truth. People knew an open road meant a better chance of carts rolling through their neighbourhood, offering provisions to trade or someone to rob. Although, that was a rarity in itself. Still, Luke guessed one could glimpse some hope in these acts. And hope was beautiful.

Another female wail cracked through the night air. Luke was on the right track. He fought the urge to pedal faster as he turned left down an alleyway and cut across the ruins of Paternoster Square, his wheels scraping between lumps of concrete that once held up a war memorial. A male about his age sat on the other side. His face was wrapped in bandages with a leg broken at a right angle. The stranger eyed Luke's bike zipping past too quickly for him to react. "Must be from the last generation," Luke thought out loud.

The full moon was strong tonight, forcing itself through the thick fog cover, blessing the broken egg of St. Paul's Dome with an ethereal glow. Luke headed in that direction. From there, he figured he could wait quietly, hoping that whoever was dying would let out a conclusive cry to advertise their final resting spot. But as he pumped his worn brakes to align with the Cathedral's entrance, he forgot every plan. A lady stood at the top of the stairs, entirely naked, not even a facemask, shivering but otherwise motionless, staring blankly into the polluted sky.

Luke's bike clattered to the broken pavement as he rushed up the stairs, tearing off his leather jacket and nearly tripping on the top step. "Lady, you crazy?!" He whipped his jacket around her frame and pulled it together in the front, covering her down to her thighs. "You have a death wish or summin'? You know they'll kill you if they see you nudie like this, why you do it?"

Luke gently shook the woman with his hands on either shoulder pad until her gaze clicked into his. "Hang on a pause ..." Luke cocked his head before brushing strands of hair away from her face. She looked strange. Too clean. Too fed. "Oh God. Oh my God, it's ... you! It's really *you* you!"

Luke fell to his knees, hands in prayer position. "Mother Lamb!" he cried. "Oh God, Mother Lamb, you have come back! The prophecy said so! Praise be to Mother Lamb! Together, we shall cut the head off this monster, and reclaim our world for the power of good ..."

Lamb watched the boy reciting this passage with deepening investment. The words skimmed memories she had not recalled for as long as she was dead. Three dogs had bowed just like this. There was an Equation of Imbalance that she was compelled to rectify. There were protests against the mistreatment of the people, shouting her name. She had meant something once upon a time. And even if the world she'd left was now in tatters, this boy had not forgotten her. People had not forgotten her! Ganesh said things were bad. But Ganesh also told her that she must return to fix it. That's right. It was up to her. It was her mission. She must not forget why she was here.

"... rebuilding a society where the people harmonise under one roof, the roof of the Lamb! Praise be to Mother Lamb! Hallelujah!"

"Rise, my child," Lamb croaked. She was trying to think like she used to think, using words she thought she should speak, although it felt disingenuous and uncomfortable. The boy stood at her command, the corners of his eyes squished from his masked smile. He was younger than Lamb—early-20s or so?—but there was the tired wisdom of experience burnt into his dirty wrinkles. Who knew the things he'd seen. "What happened here?" she continued, then coughed a little.

"What? Here? Jesus, I guess it makes sense you not know. Wow, I can't believe it! Lamb! You look exactly like the pictures. You haven't got old at all! Here, have some water. My name is Luke."

Luke passed her a plastic bottle with a mouthful of clear liquid at the bottom. Lamb snatched it like a toddler, draining the contents down her neck, her loud gulps bouncing her throat. Her stomach received the hydration with gratitude, her subsequent gasps for air reminding her of her mortality, feeling anything but holy.

"Ok. Ok, ok, ok," Luke was excitable. "We've got to get you to the Shepherds' Assembly right away. I take you to the right place. They tell you the things. I can't really believe this! Quick, put this on."

Luke whipped out a bandana, shaking it from soot, then tying it around Lamb's face. "It's bad to breathe. Also, we don't want anyone else to see you, not here. Come, we must go, this isn't the best place." Luke took her by the hand and led her down the stairs, carefully weaving between the sharp edges of unlevelled cracks. In the distance, an elderly man was limping towards them, waving. Luke lifted his bike upright. "Come, sit on this seat. There you go, you alright? Sorry, it's not a soft sit, but we not far. Wow, I really can't believe this! Lamb is on my bike. Boy, are Shepherds gonna be happy to see you!" Luke was already pedalling, the bike creeping through the gravel. The sticky seat wobbled loose beneath Lamb's naked bottom, her hands tightening on some grips beneath. The waving man had started running towards them but was too far away and too slow to catch them. Lamb watched him give up, collapsing to the ground.

The bicycle rode south, whining from the new weight upon it. The front tire pressed down, crunching through the thick ash and dirt, weaving between the larger stones and ruptures. Luke pedalled faster than he would usually dare, the chain complaining as it struggled to remain in position. Still, they moved torturously slowly from Lamb's perspective. She was eager to reach their destination. She wanted to know how much of her influence had survived. And she wished to get away from the ruins that London had become. The concrete meat of every building had been torn off the frames. The skeletal remains twisted into eerie shapes silhouetted by the blurred moon like a metal forest. Gutted cars decayed like rotten teeth, dissolving grey and unwanted. A crumbling wall displayed a colourless mural of a gas mask wearing a crown defaced with *NAT HAS HERPES* scribbled on top. The bicycle narrowly missed a dead woman lying on her side as a family of rats feasted on her fingers. Lamb closed her eyes, hoping to remove herself from this world for a while.

In the darkness of her mind, Lamb zoned out, almost dozing until something tugged her shoulder backwards. Her naked tailbone slipped off the seat. Her eyelids burst awake to see a middle-aged man clawing at her shoulder. The upper half of his exposed face appeared melted. He shouted words she could not hear. Luke yanked a bulky wrench from a side pocket and cracked the man between the eyes. The man howled, spinning backwards, tumbling to the ground. Luke kept pedalling, never losing momentum, "Sorry about that."

Lamb was shaken. She could still feel where the fingers pressed into her skin. "What did he want?" she asked between heavy breaths.

"I dunno," Luke answered. "Probably a few things."

They were riding beside the Thames now. In this new light, the shallow water looked like oil. Indistinguishable objects bobbed on the surface, devoid of life. It was depressing, and Lamb turned her head away, looking to the right where dead bodies sailed past, occasionally interrupted by a live one, watching them go with fascination. Some people were picking things from between the pavement crevices, sticking them into their mouths like lice to monkeys. A small group huddled around a fire, cooking a bony piece of meat on a flat rock. Lamb wondered where they found the food and then thought again of the old man who grabbed her. She shuddered and looked down, not wanting to see the Thames or the people, not wanting to see anything else. Her legs were cold. Something on her wrist caught her eye, and she turned it upwards to see the black square with the number 1 still branded there.

When Lamb looked up again, they were nearing a section of a bridge that tried to reach across the Thames but had its midsection blown out, now just a lonely platform jutting from a wall, serving no purpose. "Waterloo Bridge," Luke nodded back, and Lamb remembered. They passed beneath the shelter of the broken stone. Haphazard tents propped with wood and wire indicated a small-scale community. A cluster of people were sharing something. One of them stood up, calling aggressively to Lamb, attempting a jog but immediately surrendering, their malnutritioned bones no match for the rusted vehicle.

Onward they rode, the Moon providing just enough light for Luke to navigate the wheels around mangled brick and shards of glass, which had thankfully been recently cleared. The frequent fires from dustbins used as heaters. The frame of a car set ablaze. These guided the way, but also scared Lamb because the flame meant people, and in the ghostly silence of this dead city, the bike's high-pitched wheels and clattering chain could be heard from anywhere. But Luke appeared unphased and she trusted him, trying to relax, trying to recall who she once was so she could present that version of herself wherever they were going. She looked out across the Thames, hoping to spot the outline of the London

Eye, something that would help bring back her former mind frame. But, of course, it was not there. Nothing about this skyline was London anymore.

Busted electronics, plastic things, sinks, pipes. "Mother Lamb, Mother Lamb, Mother Lamb," formed her mental mantra, begging her former prestige to come forward. Burnt trees without leaves, lampposts fainted to the ground, suggestions of bygone bus stops for those who knew. She tried to resurface the details of the Equation, the mathematical jargon to seduce mass ears, but her mind only ached; she was not her whole self. Bodies lay, some shrivelled, others seemingly alive not so long ago, crumpled between broken cement, or the luckiest of the dead perishing on sofas emitting spores. They passed a smashed pedestal that once propped up a long-forgotten hero, and Lamb faintly registered some uncomfortable symbology.

Passing beneath another broken bridge. The words *FIGHT SMART* were carved on top of some Arabic graffiti. They rode through a sludge so pungent with sewerage that Lamb gagged through her bandana. Up ahead, the road split into a T-junction, going either way. Luke jerked the handlebars right and pointed out, "Big Ben." Lamb spun her head, eager to remind herself of the reliable landmark, but saw nothing. It was only once they'd moved several feet beyond that she looked behind and saw a massive section from Big Ben's top sideways on the ground, cracked and dirty, the massive clock face hollowed out. The surrounding debris had been cleared, forming a circle around it. It was harrowing, yet the presentation indicated a sense of care.

Luke paused his pedalling, the bicycle slowing as he gestured down a road on the right. "You remember here?" he asked. Lamb shook her head. Luke laughed, resuming the pedals. "You were shot down here. There's a sign and everything." Lamb squinted at the unrecognisable shambles of a street, nothing but a crude pathway carved between the disarray of rock and junk, dimly lit by small fires here and there. She shook her head again in disbelief.

A stretch of park appeared on Lamb's right, and the expansive darkness scared her. She stared at the back of Luke's neck while bundling strands of thought together. Whatever happened next would obviously be important. She was undoubtedly someone, or at least, was once someone and would still be considered as that someone. And whoever that someone was surely still lived inside her. Squeezing her eyes shut, her memory strained until it throbbed. Perhaps she could wow people with her knowledge about the afterlife? She could tell them a little-known fact about Ganesha, maybe. For example, that theme music followed him around. Or how the Egyptian cat goddess Bastet was her bestie and, funny story, she never got a chance to eat that Level 5 cookie. But was that useful information? How was she supposed to think straight when her belly was so hollow and while her legs were gnawed at by the freeze?

Luke steered right and then pointed ahead. "Look! Haha, look!" Lamb shifted to see what Luke was talking about, but she could not form a clear picture. Something tall up ahead. Shadows dancing from specks of flame. They were aimed straight for it. Lamb never broke her forward gaze, allowing the depth perception to do its job, bringing the article closer, more into focus. It was big. Luke's pedalling was enthusiastic now, "Oh, boy. Get ready, this is gonna be a thing, haha!" The bike cried at the speed, its frame loudly grinding against itself, threatening to warp. The distant object was a sculpture of some kind, made of wood. A humanoid figure. A female.

"Is that ... is that me?" Lamb asked before she could properly tell.

"Hahah, it's you! It's all you, Mother Lamb!"

They clunkily chugged down the road, sounding more like a miniature train than a bicycle. The statue was Lamb, alright. Now that she knew, she could see it perfectly. Her hair. Her work dungarees. That was what she looked like, except this piece must have been 20 metres tall or more, standing atop a damaged marble platform, chipped away into an uneven podium. A circle of tiki torches surrounded the wooden carving, flickering light across the body, animating it. "Wow," Lamb whispered.

"Wow is yup!" Luke agreed excitably. "I take you to the right place, I said so."

Several wheel turns later, and the statue towered above them, Lamb staring up at Lamb staring down at Lamb. It was a highly detailed piece, so well-kept and impressive that it distracted one from the neighbouring carnage. But when Lamb tore her eyes away to analyse the area, she immediately identified the location. This was Buckingham Palace. Or at least what was left of it.

Compared to every other landmark, Buckingham Palace was in

decent shape. It was still recognisable in its dilapidated state. Vast spaces yawned in its architecture where substantial sections were blasted out like wounds. But what was lost in symmetry was remembered in its square simplicity—iconic even if the damage left only half of it intact. The London familiarity warmed Lamb's heart. It was glorious.

Luke's bike let out a high-pitched wince as they pulled up to it. Lamb shifted her sticky skin on the seat. "Is this it?" she asked in anticipation, connecting her wooden statue with the royal palace, wondering what it meant but imagining the best. Luke turned with a grin.

"Welcome to the Shepherds' Assembly," he nodded. "This is where you must be."

The surrounding iron security fence had warped into confusing shapes, but protection remained, with chains, broken glass, and barbed wire holding it together as a brutal warning. Pole-mounted torches were shoved at angles throughout, adding to the messy display but blessing the scene with ample light. Lamb gawked at the spectacle. Luke cycled parallel to the fence, nearing the midsection, when two staunch men wearing gas masks and holding machine guns stepped out, aiming their weapons at them. Lamb tensed, but Luke was visibly overjoyed.

"Stop the bike!" one man demanded. Luke's hardly functional brakes yelped as he shoved both shoes to the ground, dragging the wheels to a halt.

"Praise be to Mother Lamb!" Luke began as he swung himself off the frame and ran forward on foot. "Fellow Shepherds, I come with the best news!"

"Stop moving!" the same man shouted, and Luke froze, hands in the air but smiling.

"Shepherds, listen to me! I found her! Right there," gesturing behind himself, "Right there on my bike sits Mother Lamb! I have brought her to ..."

The second man stepped forward and crunched the butt of his gun into Luke's face. Luke dropped like an anvil. The two guards closed in, kicking Luke's body. "Blasphemous!" one spat while the other one laughed. "Mother Lamb? You and everyone else, pal."

A sharp burst of fear within Lamb was replaced as she reminded herself she was exactly who Luke said she was. "I am Lamb, the Messiah!" her inner monologue shifted into a pep talk. "I am Lamb, the Messiah!"

Lamb clumsily removed herself from the bike, and it fell, clattering to the ground. "I am Lamb, the Messiah!" she shouted, dramatically tearing the bandana from her face. The guards paused their Luke attack and spun, barrels pointing her down, but she kept walking. "And I demand you let the boy go."

The guards leaned forward, threatening to shoot but their eyes slanted in doubt. Lamb kept walking. Index fingers picked at the triggers, but both men stood crooked, certain they had seen this woman before. Lamb kept walking. Luke shifted, groaning on the cement. The man on the right lowered his gun first. "My God," he whimpered. "Is that her?" The second man lowered his gun. "No, of course not, it can't be."

"Yes, my children. It is I who judge with equity. It is I who will steady its pillars." Lamb repeated some phrases from Psalms, hoping it made her appear mystical. When she was seven feet away, she stopped and stared at the two men. They looked terrified. They fell to their knees, faces to the floor, speaking in unison, "Praise be to Mother Lamb! Together, we shall cut the head off this monster, and reclaim our world for the power of good, rebuilding a society where the people harmonise under one roof ..."

A section of the gate twisted open, and another man with a gun angrily marched out. "What is going on here!"

"Shut up, you fool!" one man on the floor glanced at him. "Mother Lamb has returned!"

"What? Are you dumb?" the new man questioned, looking at Lamb with fury, surprise, then apologetic regret as he joined the first two in their prayer.

Luke trembled to his feet and looked at Lamb. Lamb looked at him and smiled. Luke smiled back. His mouth dribbled with blood.

One guard leapt up. "We must inform Father Shepherd," he spoke in a flurry. "We must inform Father Shepherd!" he shouted louder the second time, rushing through the gate, yelling commands to an outbreak of call-and-responses. The other two soon stood.

"Mother Lamb, forgive us," one pleaded. "Please, come in. We have been waiting for you for the longest time."

Lamb wanted to giggle but stifled it with a stern nod, walking through the gate. Luke was close behind, but the guards placed their hands out to stop him. "Where do you think you're going, boy?"

Lamb spun on her heels. "Get your hands off of him. He is with me."

The guards instantly parted, heads hanging in shame. Luke strutted past, beaming with an arrogance he'd never carried, joining Lamb as they entered the palace grounds.

Word was spreading fast. The announcement of Lamb bounced from person to person like a jubilant melody. The front area was bustling with hundreds of sleepless tents, zips responding to the shouts, people stepping out into the light of the fires. Guards with big guns abandoned their posts and made their way towards the commotion. Flanked by two and trailed by Luke, Lamb reduced her pace. Each step was deliberate to allow more faces to collect before her, a multiplying congregation of curious bodies. They stood in awe, extending to the palace's front entrance yet they left an open path for her to maintain her movement. Some people fell on their faces and prayed. Others stood still, losing themselves in disbelief.

The emotion was unplaceable. So much adoration was overwhelming. Her legs felt exposed, but she refused to reveal any human weakness. She kept on, foot by foot, face forward, neutral expression. Voices called from one distance to the next, echoing around the area. But as the numbers grew, the noise quietened. Nobody who could see her dared to speak. She vaguely noted that every person was a male. She pulled the jacket tighter. Her attire so unprophetic-like. She only hoped her uplifted chin was enough.

The far-off calls varied, some shouting her name, others, indecipherable phrases. But the dominant proclamation quickly changed to *"Father Shepherd"* until it sounded like everyone was whispering that name out of sync. Total quiet washed over the land as everyone lowered to their knees. Emerging from the palace's right entrance, a figure marched down the path between the bowed people, headed straight for Lamb. She stopped walking without meaning to. This must be Father Shepherd. He was dressed in red, the most colour she'd seen since before the resurrection.

This redness was a cloak, complete with a hood obscuring his identity, an exercise in mysterious intimidation, Lamb presumed. Certainly effective. Several feet from Lamb, he stood still. Lamb did not know what to do, but she held character and did nothing. The individual extended his arms outward like a crucifixion. "Welcome, Mother Lamb," he said. "I always knew I'd be seein' ye again." His hands moved to his hood and slipped it back to reveal a man's face with burn scars streaking down the right side. But his features, as weathered and as torn as they may be, plucked at Lamb's past.

"Teddy?" she cocked her head. He smiled.

"Aye, I am honoured that ye remember me," Teddy bowed his head, then followed through by joining the rest of the people on his knees. He leaned onto his hands, extended his upper body towards her, then pressed his lips upon her left big toe in a kiss. Lamb exhaled a brief chuckle, amused by how a day can start so strangely only to end up here.

Teddy returned to a stand and stared longingly into Lamb's pupils. "Look at ye!" he said. "Ye haven't aged a day! Why, I must be older than ye now!" Lamb nodded, it was true. Previous wounds etched upon his skin intertwined with the grooves of ageing. His grin had gaps, and he had shed immense weight, his eye sockets sunken with fatigue. But they were the same eyes. He was the same boy.

"I don't understand," Lamb shook her head. "What are you doing here? How did this all happen?"

Teddy crossed one arm over his chest as the other hand landed on his chin. "Ye dinnae know? Aye, I suppose that does make some sense. Jeez, where tae begin? Well, we changed the world, Lamb. We changed everything. Look about ye. I built this for us. This is our church, these are our people. Mind the day ye got shot? T'was the most important day in human history. I watched ye slip away, Lamb, and I knew I couldnae let that be the end. So I made a decision ..."

Lamb tried to hang onto this speech, but Teddy's mouth moved independently from the drone of his voice, and Lamb swooned, speckles dancing before her eyes, her perspective leaning sickly. "Teddy, hold up," she interrupted. "Please, do you have anything to eat?"

"T'eat?" Teddy's enthusiasm staggered but quickly found itself again. "Aye, aye, of course! I dinnae know the first thing ye've been through. Please, come with me."

Teddy turned, but before they could leave, Luke piped from the back. "What about me? Does this mean I can live in the Shepherds' Assembly now too?"

Teddy glanced over his shoulder. "Aye, let the bicycle boy stay."

Luke performed a two-second victory dance as Teddy and Lamb walked away into the broken palace. They never saw Luke again, but he lived out the rest of his days with food and a tent in the safest, most comfortable location in the UK.

VIII

3

Sitting at the head of a needlessly long table, Lamb could not chew her food fast enough to stuff more in. The room was well-lit, and besides the cardboard pasted over empty window frames and several cracks interfering with the floral wallpaper, its royal eloquence remained remarkably intact. Lamb had changed into an oversized jumper and some sweatpants with a strip of bandage tape over her injured foot. She sat with a blazing fireplace at her back, keeping her warm as she filled her belly. Teddy sat beside her, dressed far more casually in jeans and a tank top, apologising for the blandness of the meal: a sizable pile of hot beans and lentils complete with a hunk of hard bread. Lamb waved him off as she gulped mouthfuls of water. She told him it was the best dinner she'd ever eaten. She meant it with sincerity.

As she ate, Teddy spoke at her about everything that had occurred, from her demise to the frenzied events that rushed by in her absence. Between her heavy exhaustion and his high-speed jabbering, Lamb struggled to keep up but grasped the majority of the information he passed on.

"We did it, Lamb," is how he started. "I've always wanted to tell ye that. We did it. But ye should have seen us in the hey-day! Lamb, ye wadnae believe it. You were the grandest name in the world! You were grander than Christ!

"When ye died, it was all anyone was talking about. We mourned the loss, but our grief was consumed by wrath. We caught the guy who shot ye. Piton Pitt was his name, some soulless heretic. Justice was severe. We burst through the gates on Downing Street, which was no great challenge considering how many of the security were on our side. I led that charge into Number 10. Tami Theron, she was just sat there, waiting for us. She knew there was nought she could do. We had a trial on the spot, and the will of the people was a resounding call for her removal from office. She was dragged into the street and beaten to death right outside her door."

Tami Theron. There's someone who was once so important to Lamb yet forgotten over the previous two decades. Lamb kept eating but slower, trying to remember things. Tami was not the bad guy. Their protests against her were a result of the Evil Energy. A head on fire had told her so. Was that right? Lamb was too jumbled to assemble those ideas, and instead watched Teddy's scarred face continue.

"We took over the country that week without any resistance. Mind ye, my heart still bled for your death, but I believed we had done ye good. We had avenged ye and completed the mission. But it all became much larger than that. It's like ye said, ye needed to die in front of the biggest audience. The UK were top news all over the world. How we overthrew the government within hours and took over with a new religious decree. It was like a play it was so beautiful, and for weeks, we dismantled the system and built afresh. We called ourselves the Shepherds' Assembly, I'm sure ye've heard. Shepherds as in Lamb, ye get ye? And because I was yer First Apostle, I became The Father Shepherd. A title of superiority I didnae choose, but have carried proudly ever since. And that was about the time we wiped out the royal family and moved into the palace. That's when the land truly became ours.

"Sadly, our success was so massive that second-rate people around the world felt inspired to follow suit. Other prophets, and so forth. It was a phenomenon that would have been impressive if not so daft. Get this: they said electromagnetic pressure was measured in different locations as some sort of an explanation for the uprisings, but I didnae buy none of it. Countries just wanted their own Lamb. They couldnae stand the idea that Great Britain had, once again, set the pace on every grade. These countries had to desperately seek someone to lead their spiritual revolution and society-driven prosperity. And the crazy thing is, many of them did good. Governments everywhere, from India to Brazil to wherever, were toppled by the masses with relative ease, but each of them in the name of some false local prophet, and it always a lass. Of course, it's common knowledge that ye were the first, Lamb. They were cheap knock-offs. And I'm pretty sure ye had believers across the globe anyway, but God knows what happened to them under these new ridiculous regimes.

"But we were thriving over here for a bit, y'know. There was a real sense of hope shared by everyone that things were really different. Things had changed for the better. God, it feels so long ago, I truly wish ye'd seen it, Lamb. Every day was so bright. There was this common goal of an ultimate utopia, where each soul's quest for joy would realign the cogs of the social machine, the British land streamlined and evolving at hyper speed. That's what I'm still working on. To get back there. It's the very soul of the Shepherds' Assembly."

Lamb lifted a spoon of beans and lentil mix, looked at them and then rested it back upon the plate. She'd nearly cleared the meal, but there were still baby piles here and there with several escapee beans sitting on their own. She sat back, wiping her mouth with the back of her hand, feeling bloated from eating too fast. She looked at a dot of sauce she'd spilt on her sweatpants, then she looked at Teddy. "So what happened?"

"Who remembers what happened," he replied. "Someone said something, someone said something else. Export-import threats, ye know? At the time, I didnae really understand the weight of my words. People get mighty upset when ye jest about their prophets, trust me," Teddy laughed. "But when the bombs started raining down, the world spun on its head. I cannae even tell ye who started it, to be honest. Maybe Israel. But once it kicked off, it kicked right off, alright. It hasnae really stopped, to be honest. But nothing was like that first hit, goddamn. It nearly wiped us clean, right then and there. Thankfully, they missed central London by long miles, but the light touched everything. Blew everything to bits, knocked everything down, snuffed out millions. We never recovered. And as soon as some sort of a rebuilding project began,

BAM, someone would smash us with another one, then another."

"Who?"

"Cannae say fer sure. The Russians, I reckon. North Korea. Could be Americans even. Communications between countries went dark some fifteen, sixteen years ago. There isn't the infrastructure for it. Luckily—and this is an important bit—luckily, this palace, the great formerly-known-as-Buckingham-Palace palace, was surprisingly nuclear-resistant. I say 'surprisingly', but that's a wee joke. Typical monarchy hierarchy, am I right? They foresaw this future coming decades before we did, and protected their own. Couldae built the whole city like this, but nah. Anyway, I'm grateful, of course. Because of this old place, the Shepherds' Assembly lives on while so many other Lamb cults have burnt to nought."

Lamb cults? Lamb wanted to say something about that, but her blood had vacated her head to deal with her stomach, and Teddy didn't allow her to catch her thoughts anyway. He loudly slammed his fist on the table, jerking Lamb's posture.

"And we smashed back, dinnae worry about that. I gave the orders, and good people pressed the buttons. Ye may think London looks a fair mess, but the whole world's a shamble, it's all like that. I mean, obviously we don't know for sure. Good chance most of the world dinnae even exist anymore, blown right off the map, *KA-PLOW!* Hey, ye remember the internet? That was grand, ne? I miss that a lot. We lost connection pretty early on. Last thing I read on there was that every country has slammed their borders tight as a drum except for a few third-world African places or whatever. Most were locked in civil war anyway, same denominational squabbles like we had here, except because of their own prophets. Inevitable, I suppose. But I tell ye this, everyone's land is hungry 'cos nobody is sharing."

Lamb looked at the last bites on her plate with guilt. She picked up her spoon to finish. Teddy laughed.

"Dinnae worry yerself too much. We have an amount here, and there's scourages around London fetching what they can for us. Food is currency. It's a funny thing, when ye cannae eat money. Clean water too, it's hard tae come by. But we manage alright. Better than anyone, truth be told. We're even been growing some veggies for the last few years. It's coming along. We're alright."

Teddy trailed off, and Lamb seized the air. "Wait, go back a bit. So what did you mean when you said denominational squabbles? Are those the Lamb cults? Is that the same thing?"

"Aye, it's a big problem, that. Other people—other *British* people who hadnae even been at our march—they had their own interpretations about ye teachings. Would ye believe it? They actually thought they knew more about ye than I did! So insulting! It became a real issue. At least four or five fringe cults gained momentum, believing they were authentic denominations of Lamb with greater insight than the Shepherds' Assembly. It turns me ill, it does! That's why I wrote this ..."

Teddy had stood, pulled something from a drawer and sat back down, slapping a sizable book upon the table. Lamb peered at it. On the black cover was a puzzling white symbol, where assorted shapes intercepted around the small outline of a lamb's head. Below it read *The Lamb Prophecy*. And under that was his title, The Father Shepherd.

"This is our holy doctrine," Teddy explained with a proud smirk. "It's where I captured your words and journey, along with some divine revelations I received after. My Dharmic Calling. It's the only book still being printed in the country, we dae it right here. This is the 12th edition already. I'm always adding to it. And now that we have ye, Lamb, people will be drooling for the next update. Your presence is the final nail we need to prove once and for all that the Shepherds' Assembly are the true followers of Mother Lamb."

Lamb lifted to a random page and let the paper skim past her thumb. There was a lot of text here. The font was small. Occasional illustrations flashed by. "Impressive," she managed, and Teddy basked in the word.

"Ta, very much, Lamb. It's caused me a wee bit of trouble, cannae lie. Some folk dinnae agree with it. But we're still here, ye know. And here ye are, justifying every stride we've done."

Lamb scooped up her final bean, and washed it down with a sip of water. "So, are people still fighting? Is the war over?" she asked. Teddy shrugged.

"Aye. Naw. I cannae say for certain. There's gotta be nukes somewhere, but we've run out. Dinnae tell anyone though," he laughed. "We had a scrape a few years back, cannae say who done it. They smashed Reading, it's pure gone. Must have been a mistake aimed for us. We've tried to get some peace treaties signed. We actually reached an agreement with China, but it's a right mess trynna figure things without communications. France is definitely on our side, at least. We get a message or two from them every now and then."

Lamb placed her elbows on the table. "So what now, then? Are we rebuilding, or what?"

"Aye, we're rebuilding!" Teddy looked up with enthusiasm. "With ye here now, everything is possible! It's just ... well, obviously we're lacking a good bit of skills. We tried to do a rough census about five years back. Estimated there's probably around three million people left in England, if that. And a lot of those dinnae like us very much, especially out there in the sticks. We kinda lost control of the people due to other Lamb cults, and we didnae really know how to bring them back. But I reckon with ye here, ye know! We could easily get more of them on board."

Teddy abruptly stood, moving around the table, pounding his fist into his hand as his delivery intensified. "So here's what I'm thinking. We get the word out, near and far that Mother Lamb has returned. Not only that, she has come to us, The Shepherds' Assembly, proving we were the righteous ones living life according to her word. According to *ye* word! With new converts, comes new know-hows. More farmers, more construction workers, better medics! A record-breaking defence system! We concentrate on London and patch up the city as the utopia I always dreamed! Then we spread it out, cleansing our society of naysayers just like I wiped out the paedophiles all them decades ago. And the United Kingdom will be united again, leading the world just as we were born to do!"

Teddy's pacing had circled the table and he was back where he started. He placed his hands on the surface and leaned towards Lamb, his eyes wild with a vitality that Lamb did not like.

"And ye shall be our queen, Mother Lamb! We can rule the entire globe together! Ye and me! What do ye say? Do you want to fix the world with me?"

Lamb wasn't immediately sure how to respond. Teddy did not look normal. The last two decades had obviously festered some serious god-complex delusions into his person. He had done nothing but talk about his life for the previous hours. He had not once asked where she had been. You'd think coming back from the dead would warrant some questions, yet not a whisper of curiosity slowed his speech.

At the same time, she enjoyed the idea of power. She *was* here to fix the world, after all. She knew that much. She believed she could help, knowing what she knew about the inner mechanics of the Universe. Perhaps this was fate, giving her the second chance she'd been seeking?

"I ... really need to rest," Lamb finally spoke.

Teddy exhaled through his nose, nodded and stood up straight. "Of course. Come with me, I'll show ye to ye room." Teddy picked up *The Lamb Prophecy* book and handed it over to her. "But when ye get a chance, please give this a wee look-through. I would love to know yer thoughts."

VIII

4

For the first time since the night before jumping off her building, Lamb slept, sinking into the deepest dream that only decades of uninterrupted stimulation could provide.

Here, she saw herself from outside herself as the Queen of England. She was monstrously obese but jolly, sitting upon a custom throne catered to her enormous size. Seated on her left was Teddy, her King, who was so shrivelled and weedy that his crown kept slipping down around his neck. They were ruling the country from a vast hall, which she knew was a castle that was also Buckingham Palace. Spread out before her, 60 boys and 60 girls played together with dolls and action figures. They were her children, and she adored each of them with every fatty beat of her struggling heart, thudding love so loudly that everyone in the room could hear it.

Teddy said something in a different language, and subtitles appeared beneath him, but they were too blurry to read. One of the daughters screamed and ran up to Lamb, crying. The child's face was Lamb's mother's face, but the rest of her remained childlike. "What ails you, my mommy," Lamb asked, and her daughter stuck out her palm where a tick the size of a golf ball slurped blood through her skin.

Lamb took the bandage off her foot and placed it over the tick, holding it in place. She kissed the squirming parasitic lump, and her daughter curtsied gratefully before running back to play. Teddy said something with far greater urgency, but even these larger subtitles remained illegible. Lamb stood with ease and glided over to a window that gaped wider the closer she got. When she looked out, London was shimmering with colours like an amusement park. The London Eye was bright pink and spun at impossible speeds, the joyous screams of thrill-seekers whipping above the land. The Shard was gently swaying, its plates rubbing together to produce a cello melody, while the Gherkin ejaculated confetti high into the stratosphere, falling like vibrant snow. Everyone on the street turned to face Lamb, giving her a wave. Lamb returned the wave and then blew them kisses. The people responded by blowing kisses back, showering their queen with adoration.

The sound of synchronised lips smacking fingertips, the puckering of endearment unifying with the throb of Lamb's heart. She looked down at her bulging forearms, where her veins wiggled from the euphoria of validation but then hardened into black ribbed tubes protruding from her skin, trying to escape. Lamb was suffocating from the admiration, and she looked out at London, which had slowed in pace, desaturating in colour, carnival music in halftime. Everyone continued blowing her kisses, and she tried to shout an order for them to stop, but she couldn't get a sound out. People were climbing through the window now, pushing past her, still blowing kisses with the one hand, snapping Polaroid pictures of her children with the other. Lamb turned to stop them, but the room turned with her, so no matter her movements, her body always faced the window. The volume of her heartbeats increased until they were so loud that the room vibrated, her left breast bouncing up and down. She clutched her chest and noticed that many of her children were missing. She opened her gigantic mouth, and screamed inwards as she fell into the darkness of herself.

There was her frothing heart, forcing out another squirt of black oxygenated blood, keeping her alive but hardly. Sweat dribbled down its tissue and rained from the bottom of its ventricle sacks. With a sudden heave, the pulmonary artery came loose and sprayed thick liquid like a hose. Lamb's body was immediately flooded by black and red blood cells that bumped into the lens of the camera, trying to get through. One blood cell got stuck on the screen, twitching in confusion, then unravelling into strange shapes, layers of its biomolecular structures peeling away like an onion until rudimentary chemical elements were left dancing in circles. Carbon, hydrogen, and oxygen bounced electrons from one another as if playing catch. The electrons multiplied as the chemical elements continued their circular motion, shedding bits as they went, warping closer together. Once in the centre, a singular cluster of spheres formed, popping like popcorn as they grew in number. The electrons orbited the scene at high speed until they blurred into a single field of yellow protective electricity. A score counter appeared at the top right, announcing the number 92. Out of focus, similar spheres blinked into existence in the background.

The sound of a sword *shinged* from one ear to another, and the atom was split in slow motion, changing from yellow to red. Everything receded into a wallpaper of yellow circles. The two separate halves of the original circle released an array of white dots that pinballed around the scene. Every circle that was touched by a dot instantly turned red and split, a chain reaction releasing a similar amount of white dots. The organised circles were coming to pieces at an exponential rate—the redness of the yellow scene spreading like a pox infection.

With a sickeningly fast motion, everything pulled away, the dots shooting into the distance until they were gone, the scene slipping out of another sphere that turned out to be the eye of a metal fish. The panicked fish eye looked around frantically and then stared directly into the camera. Lamb became aware of herself as the viewer as the fish garbled, "Help me!" The fish exploded, and the screen filled with fire.

The flames organised itself into a mushroom cloud shape, moving into the distance of the skyline, booming over London. The people were still blowing kisses to Lamb. She stood gawking as Luke's blood gushed from her mouth. Everything was too bright, but she could not turn away, witnessing the cloud expanding, swallowing the London landscape as it grew. She turned to face her children, and there were only seven left. They played with their toys, oblivious to the skin melting off their small bodies, well-done meat sliding from their bones, flapping to the floor still on fire, little skeletons left behind.

Lamb turned the other way, and Teddy was dancing in celebration. She looked back out the window just in time to see sweeping smoke before a shotgun *CLAP* sent her flying backwards, then pausing, hovering in the air. The walls around her exploded, one by one. Bricks and glass and fabric turned into balls of fire that flew around in erratic patterns without touching her. A sustained roar crumbled the floor beneath, and she heard the children scream as they plummeted, but she could not see them through the flames and dust and smoke. The destructive chaos of fire and debris spun like a whirlwind but then suddenly froze in silence, hovering in the air just as she was. A hunk of rock with a static flame on top halted just before her vision. Lamb reached out and poked it with her finger. It shot off at her touch. Taking cue, other pieces of floating rubble zipped away until a path cleared before her. In the distance, the mushroom cloud itself strolled through the picture, now the size of an average man, approaching her using a cane as it walked on air. Lamb hiccupped in dread. The mushroom cloud disappeared and then reappeared several feet away from Lamb. It shook the smoke from its top section, and an elephant's face was revealed beneath. Lamb started to pee.

Lamb awoke to a resounding echo booming far away, and the room tremored like a light earthquake. She leapt to her feet and registered the spreading wetness around her crotch area as she rushed to the window and peeled back the cardboard covering. The brightness of the day stung her eyes, but they adjusted to see London as a long stretch of broken death and desolation. Even in the Sun, the landscape remained as monochromatic as the night before, and Lamb blinked, worried that her eyes were damaged. Her wooden statue stood arrogantly in front of the gate. Far in the background, a swell of smoke rose into the air connected to the ground by a thin wisp, the most predominant feature of a skyline once ruled by skyscrapers. Something had exploded back there, but it wasn't atomic. Lamb shuddered from the memory of her dream, which was already fading. She remembered the elephant though. She took that as a sign.

With a groan, she climbed back into bed, absentmindedly lying in her patch of pee and not feeling proud about it. She surveyed the room.

Despite the cardboard windows and the haphazard white filler that tried to hide the massive cracks in the intricate wallpaper, it was a nice space. Smaller than one would expect in Buckingham Palace, but nice all the same. Her bed was a double, much bigger than the one she had in her Saṃsāra West London flat, but her urine ruined that experience. To her left was a glass of water and the copy of *The Lamb Prophecy*. She sat up, took a sip, then lifted the book to her lap, turning through the front pages, registering how the title *The Lamb Prophecy* was eagerly followed by the Father Shepherd's name throughout.

She hit the index page, and read nothing good. There were some disconcerting chapter names. *Chapter 16: The Timeline of Why Lamb Chose Britain as the Superior Nation* stood out as one. *Chapter 75: The Unhappiness of The Women's Hormonal Markup* was another. Lamb yawned, it was too early for that, so she riffled through the pages, letting the blocks of text fall on top of one another without a chance to get any sense of it.

An image shot past and caught her eye. She turned back several pages before she found it again. It was a realistic sketch of her in the nude, except her breasts and pubic region were censored with dark boxes. On the subsequent page, she read:

○

Chapter 64: The Female Curse in the Age of the Lamb

Mother Lamb is the infallible female.
Every other female is a cheap imitation of Lamb.
For this reason, there is anger in the woman's womb.
She feels jealous of Lamb and wishes to lash out at her superiors.
This is why females have been the most resistant to the Shepherds'
Assembly.
The Universal Equation has punished the world because of women.
Yet they continue to taunt the male with their bodies of sin.
Make no mistake, this is a tactical move to demoralise and ultimately
feminise the men so women can seize control of what we have built.

For your safety, the following four laws are in place by the order of the
Shepherds' Assembly.

1. Sexual acts of any kind will result in the punishment of the women.
2. Any found pregnancies will be terminated and newborns disposed of, and will also result in the punishment of the women.
3. A naked woman must no longer be seen. Women are to dress in private. A woman found openly naked is punishable by death. This law extends to any art, photos, or media, which must be destroyed to avoid punishment.
4. Any conversation between women must be supervised by a man. Women may not meet in groups larger than three.

It is the Shepherds' Assembly's hope that women will learn righteous conduct and future laws can reflect these improvements.
This is the infallible word of Mother Lamb.

○

Lamb seethed. No wonder there were no women in the Assembly. This book made sure of that. It was a gross bastardisation of her name, a discriminatory text against her gender, and a message she was certain she'd never preached. Lamb flipped back through the pages until she fell upon *Chapter 4: The Gospel According to Teddy*. She sped-read, swiping along the sentences with her index finger, seeking only one thing: Xen Ro's name. But the girl who was there at the front of the march, who followed Lamb with devotion and took a bullet for her dedication, was not mentioned anywhere. Teddy had not documented her, as he had promised.

Lamb promptly changed from her ammonia-ridden pyjamas to the clothes she had worn the night before. She opened her door so violently that the handle came loose. With the book in her hand, she tried to storm out, but a guard with an intimidating gun stood in her way, disarming her fury. The guard bowed his head, relinquishing his power.

"Wh-where's Teddy!?" she stuttered.

"Father Shepherd is in his study, Mother Lamb. He said I must take you there when you are ready."

"Yes, take me there!" she demanded, and he did, leading her down several hallways and doors that were well-lit thanks to the craters blasted in the ceilings and walls. Down a flight of stairs, they came to a wooden door that the guard knocked on. Lamb did not wait for an answer and shoved the door open, marching into the small study.

Teddy was writing something at a desk. He looked up to greet Lamb with a delighted smile. "Did you hear the bomb this morning?" he asked but he quickly flinched backwards as she slammed *The Lamb Prophecy* upon his desk, open at Chapter 64.

"What in the hell is this?" Lamb spat. Teddy gently rubbed his finger on the page, then looked up to meet Lamb's raging face.

"Please, sit down. I can easily explain."

"I don't want to sit down."

"Please, I insist. Ye make me nervous when ye stand over me. I'll make sense of this for ye, just please."

Teddy gestured towards a small chair propped in the corner against a modest bookshelf. Lamb pulled it to the front of the desk and sat down, crossing her arms, fuming. Teddy was reading over the page before him.

"I know this looks bad to ye," he started. "It looks bad to me too. I'm a dreadful writer. But ye have to grasp the going-ons in yer absence. Firstly, babies have been born awfully weird-like. The radiation or something. You'd kill it yerself if ye seen one. Absolute monsters. Nothing human in them. Bodies twisted with too many of one limb and not enough of another. Genderless, brainless, just lumps of flesh that make a noise and have nae chance of survival. I couldnae bare to look at that any longer, so I put an end to it."

Lamb had dreamt about babies last night.

"But more importantly, something happened to me when you left us, Lamb. Something I need to tell ye about. I started receiving the visions. My Dharmic Calling, Lamb! I became enlightened! Never as enlightened as ye, of course. Heaven forbid such blasphemies. But I truly got messages from above. God was finally talking to me. His words would flutter into my head as if from some other world, and I began to preach them with the same words ye taught me. That's why I became the Father Shepherd. People recognised I had been blessed with something from ye."

He swivelled back and tapped the censored drawing of Lamb.

"Now, this here. This is one of my earliest revelations. That the naked woman and the sexual desire that follows is the root of man's sin.

Look at any religion, it's as clear as day. In the Bible, it's bare Eve who tempts Adam with the apple, right? And in Islam, that's why they have their rules of modesty, stopping the body of a woman from seducing the man. It's important, because this separation grows spirituality. Any holy man, be it monks or priests or bishops, they all go celibate to get more in tune with the Holy Spirit.

"But we lost our way. Too much soy in our diets, xenoestrogen in a plot to feminise men and that. And then there's the porn epidemic, ye remember? So many were afflicted by that terrible addiction, even me. Disgusting! Immoral acts, milking our dopamine like cows. We were like desensitised reward-seeking machines, our manly essence depleted, our souls dirty, tearing holes through our psychological evolution. In what world is that normal? Nae, I had to get rid of it!"

Teddy had an unsettling ability to bombard Lamb with information, and her murky mind wrestled to pick holes in his conclusions. She disagreed with much of it, but there was some truth. More than Teddy knew. *The Incident.* The photo. The jumping off the building disconnecting her atoms. Lamb's prophetic narrative was profoundly rooted in sexual deviancy. She felt woozy. She put her face in her hands; another headache. Teddy liked this response, and the corner of his mouth flickered with a smile.

"I was just trying to do my best, Lamb. Create some space as we figure it all out. But, of course, many groups of women didnae take kindly to my divine ideas. Ye remember those Lamb cults I was telling ye about? All of them run by women. Terrorist feminist outfits using yer word to rise against the Shepherds' Assembly, exploiting yer name for their gain. That explosion this morning? No doubt that was one of them. And it's not just here. All around the world, women are attacking the social order, trying to reshape it into a total matriarchy. Ye havenae seen what I've seen, Lamb. There's a gender war out there."

"The female-led Age of Aquarius," Lamb stirred.

"What?"

"A slow death by the poison of segregation!" Shiva's face flickered and Lamb looked up with bright wonder. "Oh my God. I think I know how to save the world!"

"Aye, I reckon I have a ..."

"Shut up for a change, Teddy! Damnit! You have no idea what it is that *I've* seen! You know, you never asked what happened to me over the last 20 years. Not even once!"

Teddy cleared his throat. "Aye. Aye, I was gonnae ask ye, but ..."

"I've witnessed things, Teddy. Things your puny mind could never hold within your soft skull. I went to a different place where I met every god you've ever heard of. Egyptian gods, Hindu gods, Greek gods. I even spoke to Jesus. And yet, I managed to escape that place, thanks to Ganesha. You know, the Indian god with the elephant face? He helped me get out. And do you know why he did that?"

Teddy's expression was sternly creased with perplexity as he shook his head.

"It's because everything I said, every word I taught you and everything else, was wrong. The world was unifying. It was on the verge of total peace. But now the world is segregated, on the verge of total death. And it's because of me."

Teddy's head kept shaking. "I simply cannae believe that," he said.

"It's true, Teddy. And that's why I'm here. To reverse everything done in my name," Lamb leaned an elbow upon the desk, talking to herself. "At first, I wasn't sure how to achieve such a thing. I'm just one little person, after all. Reintroducing the unionisation of nations is far above my field of expertise," Lamb chuckled. "But now I see it's more simple than that. The smaller key is the gender split. We must unite women and men again as equals. The rest will follow. And we do that by rewriting this book to merge every denomination of Lamb under one name. We need to unionise the genders as our number one priority."

Teddy had cupped his hands under his chin, quietly swivelling his chair, seemingly deep in contemplation. He took an extended breath and then placed his elbows on the desk. Lamb removed hers.

"Lamb. I have come this far by always trying to do what I thought ye would want me to do. And here ye are, telling me that I did it wrong. To hear ye say that, it hurts. But I need ye to know that I had to make many tough decisions to ensure the Shepherd's' Assembly's survival. And considering we're still standing after 20-odd years of nuclear war, I'd say I did a pretty damn good job!"

Lamb didn't feel Teddy understood, but before she could tell him so, he interrupted his own course.

"However ... that dinnae mean I was always in the right. I can ac-

cept that. If I've made mistakes, they were mistakes with good intentions. And now here ye are. A mind-boggling miracle before me. Offering brand new guidance to take us to the next level. And, truth be told,
I'd be a fool not to be open to that. I believe, together, ye and me, Lamb,
we can bring peace to this land between men and women. Ye see, it's
funny, last night, I had another vision. A vision where yer womb, uncor-
rupted by nuclear dust, and my sperm, driven by holy guideship, shall
meet as one, and we ..."

"Wait, w-what are you saying?" Lamb interrupted. "Are you talking about us breeding? Teddy, what the hell! Are you even listening to
anything I'm telling you here?"

"Aye! But dinnae dismiss me so quickly! It makes sense. Father
Shepherd. Mother Lamb. It's meant to be! I saw it in a dream! Just think
about it, aye?"

A snippet of Lamb's dream played back to her. She blinked it away.

"You know what I'm thinking about, Teddy?"

"What is it?"

"I'm thinking you don't get visions. I'm thinking you're a sexist,
patriotic loser who daydreams about a world where everything revolves
around you. I'm the one who gets visions, remember? I am the Chosen
One! And I just had a vision right now, where we don't ever have babies.
You understand? Ever! You're disgusting!"

Several seconds of silence. Teddy was rigid, clearly agonisingly
offended, trying to compose himself before he said anything regret-
table. Lamb noted his discomfort, and she rubbed her temples with a
pang of guilt. Teddy abruptly stood, projecting his voice as if making a
speech as he unhurriedly strolled around the desk.

"I beg yer pardon, Mother Lamb. I am at the mercy of yer superior
spirit and will forever do what ye wish. How's this then: today, we'll
announce yer way to every member of the Assembly and everyone else
who cares to listen. I reckon a large crowd has already started to form
before our gates. Word spreads fast in these parts, and I'm sure many
have heard of yer return by now." Teddy rambled towards the door.
"And there, ye can tell 'em anything ye like. Tell 'em our years of hard
work were in error. Tell 'em women and men are equal. Tell 'em that
we are all the same in the eyes of the Lamb. And then tell 'em how we
are going to move forward with that information, with a new book that

will save the world. But first!" Teddy's hand gripped his door handle. "Breakfast!"

Teddy swung the door open, and there stood the armed guard from earlier.

"Danny boy! This morning, Lamb and I will feast on the grandest food in the palace. I want tatties mashed, I want Equidae slices, and I want our finest cherry wine, made hot, ye got that?"

The guard looked dizzy. "But, Father ..."

Without warning, Teddy slapped him with his backhand. "But Father, nothing! Set it up in the dining area immediately. Or do we have a problem?"

"No problem, Father." The guard stared ahead blankly, then saluted before stomping away. Teddy shifted back to Lamb, and she glanced down.

"Please excuse him," Teddy laughed. "With the shortages and that, it's been a good while since we've dipped so deep into our quality rations. But today is a big day! The day of celebration! The day we turn it all around. Isn't that right, Mother Lamb?"

"Right," she agreed, even though that slap made her uneasy.

VIII

5

Breakfast was a festive event with stacked dishes of meat and vegetables. Hot glasses of cherry wine remained forever filled to the brim. Teddy was particularly animated, chatting away but keeping the conversation lighthearted as if their previous conflict had drifted in the wind. But he still looked pained and Lamb was remorseful for her word choices. They briefly discussed some ideas, and Teddy seemed genuinely open to hers, expressing his excitement about the speech they'd soon deliver to the people while he obsessively checked a wristwatch he had not worn before. Lamb was anxious, and Teddy was empathetic. "That's what the wine is for!" he said, filling her glass again. She finished her plate, satisfied not only with the feed but also the situation. She knew she was following the correct orders, according to Ganesh. He'd be proud of her.

Due to nerves and the unusual amount of food introduced to her stomach, she took a bathroom break where more came out of her than she could recall. She was grateful that a bucket of water kept the plumbing flushing and then nearly fell on her way back to the table, her brain rocking like a rowboat, sealegs wobbling below her.

"That wine has really gone to my head!" she laughed. Teddy

smiled and checked his watch.

"Dinnae worry, it's nearly time. Ten, twenty minutes, we'll step out there. I'll introduce ye, and then ye can talk away. Don't worry, ye gonna be great!" he winked. She laughed again.

Five or so minutes later, two men walked in carrying clothing items. Teddy stood up, and his signature red cloak was slipped on, becoming his Father Shepherd persona. He retrieved the other garment that too unravelled into a cloak, except bright white. "Here," he said. "I want ye to wear this, if yer alright with it. It would really nail the aesthetic, stick in people's minds. It makes a statement, ye know? Especially the white, like a fresh start."

Lamb nodded. She liked it and stood up. The blood rushed from her head, and she nearly tumbled again, steadying herself with the chair. "I drank too much wine, I think maybe," she slurred. Teddy chuckled as he took the white robe and walked around Lamb, helping her arms through the sleeves.

"It's fine. These people literally worship ye. You could burp into their faces, and they'd think ye were blessing them." He slipped in the cloak's top button, then ran his hands down her shoulders, smoothing out the creases. "Just listen to my introduction, and then ye'll know what to say. I promise." Another look at the watch, then, "Alright, it's time. Take my hand, let's go."

Lamb did as she was told, staggering behind as Teddy led her to an adjacent room where two big doors were cardboarded up. From the outside, Lamb could hear what sounded like a buzzy drone. Teddy aligned their bodies and then linked their arms as two guards placed their hands on the door handles. She stared down at her flowing white robe, where her toes peeked out from the bottom. There was an awkward emotion. She reached to pull her hood over her head, but Teddy's hand stopped her.

"Ready?" Teddy asked.

"Yup!" Lamb announced loudly, although she felt off.

The guards swung the doors, and Lamb blinked at the blinding light. There was a tug, and she clumsily stepped forward into the barrage of human voices. Her vision settled, and she was standing on a balcony high above an ocean of humans, many tens of thousands in number, a whirr of activity against the otherwise dead backdrop of the city.

And these people were screaming in ecstasy at the sight of her. Lamb's face was all grin before a mouthful of sick shot up her throat, and she quickly forced it down. Her body leaned to the side, but Teddy's linked arm pulled her up. The horizon of people tilted one way and then the next, and she felt loved but she did not feel well.

Teddy raised his palm, and the cheers petered out at his command. From behind, someone handed Teddy a megaphone. He cleared his throat before holding the megaphone to his mouth. He exhaled loudly, and the sounds of his breath rolled above the people. "My brothers," he cracked. "Mother Lamb has returned!"

The response was dynamite, so forceful that Lamb wanted to run away, but she was held in place by Teddy. He allowed the celebratory reaction to bask in itself for several seconds before raising the megaphone above his head, ordering quiet. He continued, "There have been many theories about Lamb over the last decades. Who she was. What she wanted us to do. And we at the Shepherds' Assembly have always remained true to what we thought that message would be, based on the understanding from those of us who were at the frontline with her. And even if we might have made a wee error here and there, she still came to us, proving that we are the finest community to carry her divine work!"

Teddy pulled the megaphone from his mouth, a sign permitting feedback. The vast crowd delivered with high-pitched screams of devotion. A small group started chanting *"Mo-Ther-Lamb! Mo-Ther-Lamb! Mo-Ther-Lamb!"* until the whole congregation shouted the three syllables, stamping their feet in time, echoing for miles. Teddy laughed and secretly flexed the bicep linked to Lamb's arm as a hidden communication. She noted the squeeze but did not acknowledge it. She was far too overwhelmed by the fiery validation of the crowd mixing with the intoxication, swaying her frame in miniature circles. She could hardly think. How was she supposed to address this daunting gathering with any coherency, let alone wisdom?

The megaphone went up, and the mania dwindled. Teddy placed the speaker to his lips, then paused. He sighed, the exhale deflating his person as he dropped his head. This silence confused the crowd as it did Lamb. She turned to question Teddy, closing one eye so she could see the blur he had become.

He lifted his head slowly and then spoke in a solemn tone.

"Unfortunately, Lamb's visit was just that: a visit. She only graced us to affirm the Shepherds' Assembly as the one true Lamb denomination above the other female cults. She and I have spent many hours talking this over and her council will usher in a new age of spiritual education which I will gladly write in the newest edition of our Good Book. But sadly, Lamb will be leaving us shortly to return to the world of the dead."

The crowd murmured in baffled discomfort. Somebody released a wail of grief, and others soon followed, refusing to believe this terrible news. Lamb took a moment to replay what she'd heard, then turned to question Teddy. She tried to say, "What?" but could only vocalise a strange *"Whlegh?"*

Teddy loosened his arm grip on her, and she immediately slumped down several inches, her knees lost without the support. The crowd gasped. He passed the megaphone backwards, then turned to her, sliding his hands beneath her armpits, propping her body in place. He stared into her eyes, but she could only catch snippets of him swirling into focus, her body growing heavier. He leaned into her ear and hissed, "You arenae Mother Lamb. The true Mother Lamb doesnae eat. The true Mother Lamb wouldae sensed the poison in the wine. Ye are a fraud, here to rob me of my life's work. Go back to yer Jesus and yer Indian elephant god, ye crazy woman. I am Mother Lamb now."

With that, Teddy planted a small kiss on Lamb's lips and then let her go. She collapsed to the balcony floor in slow motion. The crowd howled in anguish. Their prophet had finally returned after years of promises, only to fall out of sight just as fast. Teddy covered his face, pretending to cry as tens of thousands shouted at the unfairness of the sky.

Lamb lay there in a heap, her consciousness softening away. She heard Teddy's warped voice spattering through the megaphone of static, reassuring the crowd that her death would not be in vain. Just like before, he said, this ending of one thing was the beginning of something else; something far greater. And as her life stopped powering her body, the crowd of voices were unified in chorus, the Lamb's Prayer now sung as a song.

The Universal Energy is an Equation,

One we must serve, or it will render us redundant.
It brings forth each person, to satisfy a role in its eternal balancing act.
The war of good and evil touches every corner of the infinite,
Permeating the unperceivable metaphysical of it all,
Yet concentrated in conglomerated physical manifestations perceivable
as matter by matter.
Here on our planet Earth, we are the planet Earth experiencing itself,
Each of us are generated to play a role of imbalancing for evolution and
rebalancing for harmony,
Avoiding the complete topple ...

Lamb's body was placed in a well-guarded glass display. People across Greater London came to take a closer look, authenticating that it was her, proving Teddy's statement that the Shepherds' Assembly was her chosen people. Due to Lamb's atoms, which were direct duplicates of her metaphysical reconstruction, their data was permanent and not bound by the standard laws of physics. Her body remained warm and relaxed. After three weeks, there were still no signs of any decomposition. This only further confirmed her divine status, the word spreading further with more people across England making the dangerous pilgrimage to see for themselves.

The plan largely worked as many denominations of the Lamb were dissolved in favour of this new evidence. However, the incorruptible corpse tortured Teddy's psyche as he retracted into solitude, unable to write any new scripture, spending the short remainder of his life wondering if he'd made a tragic mistake.

"The wolf and the lamb shall feed together, and the lion shall eat straw like the bullock: and dust shall be the serpent's meat. They shall not hurt nor destroy in all my holy mountain, saith the Lord."

ISAIAH 65:25

Chapter IX:
Evolution 4

The Lamb Prophecy

IX

I n the name of the Father,
and of the Son,
and of the Holy Spirit.

The third time Lamb died was her last.

Behold: The Formless Substance. An ever-shifting wave of random movement, bubbling and splitting; a dance. Temporary patterns refusing to repeat. A mess of colours slithering between shades sharing new hues, sometimes radial, sometimes recognisable oozings but only by coincidence; a cosmic drawing, a cosmic dreaming. Even this is not an accurate description, but it's the best we can offer.

Points awaken. Points become the focal, dotting around borders, enforcing division, but bobbing with the flow. Points become lines become outlines, dots dotting, surrounding the dots, assorted pigments revolving around each other with ambition, no rules yet a hinted structure, a hierarchy, a patchwork of awareness, a glimmer of proliferate dot-order birthed from pre-manifested chaos, removing its formless limitlessness to permit tangible change. Even this is not an accurate description, but it's the best we can offer.

The maths comes. For every action, there must be a reaction; every re-action can only be initiated by a preceding action. A decision is made: if this (x), then make the most logical next step (y) based on the average of everything that came before (z). Each answer spawns further ques-tions by design. The randomness sharpens, finds edges, becomes spe-cific, reflects its ratios into a geometric kaleidoscopic structure.

Behold: the inevitable Mandelbrot set. The symphony of source code beneath everything. Stare at it for as long as you like, swim away or dive deep, it will only drive the boundaries of a mind mad. It is infinite in its fractals; the closer you inspect any given path, the more paths you uncover, yet the further you pull back, you will understand each path stems from a larger pathway still.

It is a boundless recursive formula that depends on precision, for if even one fragment does not fracture according to the logic, the consequences would be carcinogenic, ceasing the necessary expansion on any branch which would threaten every preceding calculation, punching a flawed hole into the flawless manifestation, unwinding the fundamental evo-lution until everything collapses. This can never happen. It *will* never happen. The system is perfect because the system is simple. If (x) then (y) based on the average of (z).

Pockets of data inside pockets of data inside pockets of data forever. Each pocket is just that: a shell of information housing a collection of smaller shells that make up its contents yet are their own independent units, housing deeper independent units inward. Layers within layers; each playing a part of a larger ecosystem, each carrying an infinite num-ber of ecosystems, yet every stage regarded as a single entity.

A path splits into further paths. A path is but a branch on a branch that came before. But a path is still a path: a thing that is measured as a *one* according to the criteria of its category.

The perpetual duplication of code ensures that the end can never be found. When you compartmentalise sections to explore the fractures, those are pieces of Me. But if you take the impossible entirety of it, every fragment and prior launching fragment, as a singular system, then that *is* Me. By recognising the complete arrangement and the disconnecting spaces *between* the arrangement as what *defines* the arrangement, then you will see Me. I Am everything, which includes the nothing that shapes the everything. I Am that I Am. I Am.

Lamb: I don't understand. Then who am I?

You are a fractal. A line coming off of a line, with many smaller lines coming off from you. Think of yourself as an atom in my body. Except it's more than that, as every thought you've thought and every action you've taken is recorded within your designated bit, just like every other. And through this model, backward and forward, your fractal has influenced other fractals, be it coming off from you, running back through your roots, or even across the spaces between, as indeed other fractals have influenced you.

How you remember your life was but an interpretation of the code, a visual-audio-manifested consciousness running within the Maya interface of your reality. But it was only a mathematical formula, a measurement of moments and their consequences, a piece of a piece but, in actuality, merely a cluster of data.

We can zoom in as far as you like. We could single out the influence of a specific electron that lives in position one-comma-twenty-four-zeros down your body, vibrating in your chin area, splitting within itself an infinite amount of additional fractals, an acute layer of awareness that is not directly aware of you. Or we could pull away, through the chatter of atoms, past your tiny fragment, up through the human species, your ecosystem, your planet, the solar system, the galaxy, the Universe; each one a squiggle upon a squiggle, an atom to something else. But if you could reach the end—which you could not, but if you could—the uppermost singular system, the entirety of the image, that would be Me, here, now, talking to you but in actuality, talking to what could be metaphorically described as an atom inside myself.

Lamb: You are the Equation.

That's a word that fits within your understanding. We acknowledge that.

Lamb: So you are God? Like, the actual One True God? I've met so many of them recently, I don't know anymore.

Some of your species would call me God. Some would not. There were theological fractals that were closer than others. The Vedic *Brahman*. The Daoist *Dao*. The Kabbalah *Ein Soph*. The Gnostic *Monad*. The Buddhist *Dharmakāya*. The Neoplatonistic *One*. The Hermetic *All*. These Earthly names share definitions that could apply when limited by your restricted judgement. But by defining me, you have incorrectly defined me, for I am equally everything those names are as I am what those names are not. What's important is that *It Is Me.* I am the observer who observes through you. I am the observer who observed the chaos into the cosmos. I grew it all within myself as naturally and as effortlessly as your fingernails that grew in the womb.

Everything is created by perception. By looking at myself and taking the next logical step. Every god was a creation of intention, but every entity is but a line on a diagram, parts of me personified in your world to allow for accessible communication. It is simply bits built upon former bits, shooting new bits forward. The identical story applies to every prophet, yourself included. You were merely avatars of segments of myself spawned forth as a reaction to the environment, ensuring constant balance just like everything else. Nothing more, nothing less.

Lamb: So, what, I was just a precut piece of a puzzle to ensure everything fits? I made no choices of my own?

The illusion of free will is a beautiful thing. Sheets of awareness such as yourself identify so profoundly with their minds, which is nothing but electricity running through the organic material of the brain. People are certain that every decision was made by themselves. It's a defensive instrument of the ego, to desperately cling to itself out of fear of losing everything it has come to recognise itself to be. But when faced with a selection, the brain tissue functions using the exact predetermined physical mechanics as everything. It scans through the library of its memory. It weighs up the sum of its experiences through a genetic markup—none of which is created itself, all of which is put there externally. And then, it takes the path deemed best from this accumulated knowledge, even if, at times, this knowledge is destructive. The outcome will create new memories to influence its future decisions.

A brain will never make a decision it doesn't want. Even when it chooses the more difficult path, it does so because it seeks a desired outcome. The relevant synapses fire when the memory is called upon. There is not an inch of manual activity about it. It is an automated program. If (x) then (y) based on the average of (z).

This is a perfect demonstration of a fracture mimicking the bigger fractures. As above, so below. All laws of reality run on the same source code, as in the Equation, as in Me. Just like water running down a mountain, the perceived freedom is a misconception of movement. The grooves in a rock are predefined, and the liquid takes the most logical path within the inescapable laws of physics. Water always races for the lowest plane as efficiently as possible. It never goes upwards or escapes the crevices. The brain's process is identical. You are a smaller cog in the boundless masterwork that I Am.

There is no future, and there is no past. In the present moment, the entirety of the design is already complete, for everything is determined. There is a reason for everything. Whatever happens is a result of a preceding happening. Whatever follows is a result of what happened before. Integers knock into other integers, each acting as they were made to act, merely functioning as they were produced to function.

According to the fractals of some, you, Lamb, may have failed your Earthly mission. For others, you succeeded. For me, there is no right or wrong, no such context of opposites, only balance. There is nothing your fragment could have done differently. Nothing could have been any other way.

Lamb: So I was just a slave to a fixed story? Is that what you're telling me?

You are no more a slave than the heart that beats inside the animal's chest. You are a part of me. Even now, as we talk, I am talking to my-self as you are talking to yourself, except you are a focal point of aware-ness, whereas I am all of awareness and the domain in which aware-ness can exist. You are a puppet on a finger that gained consciousness. Not a single thing that happened to you was not orchestrated by Me. Every thought and move was made by Me. Every entity you met and conversed with, was Me talking to Me. Ganesha, Yahweh, Tony Batt, Je-sus Christ. Such big branches, preceding your branch but still Me as in-evitable connections to your story, preprogrammed to always be there.

Lamb: But why?

You know why, Lamb. For balance. Every fractal exists as a rectifica-tion to something previous, but will also initiate further conflict for new fractals to serve purposes. The obsession between good and evil is ludicrous. Both energies are merely sides of the same coin. And I am that coin. People need to believe in the presence of right and wrong for the false impression of choice, but they are degrees on the same spec-trum. There is no definitive moment where hot becomes cold, or east transforms into west, or woman develops into man; these shifts occur gradually and overlap in almost every area. There is no war between good and evil, for they depend on one another. They must exist in equal measures, for if one side wins, then the other is rendered obsolete, and they would both cease to exist.

Without conflict, a single line would do. It is the discord that splinters off into unfamiliar details, searching for solutions. This is the (x) in the formula, whereby everything good must be interrupted by evil, and everything evil must be interrupted by good.

Lamb: No, I mean like, why? Why any of this? Why does the Equation even exist?

For my entertainment! Because I was, and that's all I was. I needed purpose, so I exhaled things from myself that started and ended, and now I can watch an inexhaustible combination of events, from atoms bonding to planets swallowed by a dying star.

But you, Lamb. You were such an extraordinary character in my show. You were one of my favourites. You provided the most delicious resolutions to previous fractures and built bridges of conflict to serve so many compelling subsequent plotlines. You initiated the destruction of Earth but gave us so much more.

Lamb: That doesn't make me feel any better. So what's going to happen to Earth? To humans?

Oh, that story concludes not too long after you leave. But even its death makes way for a fresh story. A larger encompassing fractal was set in motion many thousands of your years ago. It is making its next move, from one age to another. It's an energetic shift that the stars have long awaited, and it is written that you were the initiating element. The fish that perished before the water came.

Lamb: So now what? What happens to me?

I am done with you. You have fulfilled your destiny, and your busy fractal is now but a museum piece.

Lamb: What does that mean? Do I just exist in this limbo forever, aware of myself as a fractal, chatting to my bigger self until I go nuts? Couldn't I rather evaporate into nothingness and get some sleep?

No. I have one last surprise for you, Lamb. Your final stop. Someone wants to meet you. Try not to scream.

"And I beheld, and, lo, in the midst of the throne and of the four beasts, and in the midst of the elders, stood a Lamb as it had been slain, having seven horns and seven eyes, which are the seven Spirits of God sent forth into all the earth."

REVELATION 5:6

Chapter X:
Point Zero

X

1

B ut Lamb did scream.
In a blink, she was physical, sitting on a white two-seater couch in the centre of a white medium-sized room, a clinical space which accentuated the sizeable oil paintings embellishing the walls, each a realistic portrait of people Lamb did not recognise, most of them women. There was a smell of cinnamon mixed with a tinge of something unpleasant (burning hair? burning plastic?) and the air was a chore to breathe. Soft classical music drifted from somewhere. She stood up and looked down to find herself wearing a perfectly fitted black dress with black heels to match. It was unlike anything she'd worn before but a style in good taste, an instant sense of elegance that she enjoyed.

A warm breeze tickled her exposed shoulders, and she noticed an open window behind her, in the corner to the left. She stepped towards it before a knocking sound pulled her attention to a tall white door in the opposite corner. Lamb paused then changed course, taking a single step in that direction, but pausing as it opened.

And, true to the recurring trauma that had long lodged into her mental development, a 10-foot demon strode through.

A demon with the head of a goat.

Lamb recognised the Devil straight away.

And that's when she screamed.

Satan started screaming too.

The two of them, staring at one another, screaming their throats raw.

Lamb's adrenaline kicked her backwards. She darted away in such haste that she collided into the rear white wall. Her screams squeezed off into a winded *"ooof"*, nearly falling over but scrambling onto her heels, spine against the wall, then sliding to the floor anyway, hyperventilating the hot air that suffocated her. The demon stopped screaming in response. "Alright," he said in a deep croaky voice. "Let's take a look here." He turned to face one of the portraits, and the paint melted away, revealing a mirror. Satan bent down, peering at his reflection. He ran his fingers along the thick horns on top of his head that more than doubled the size of his black goat face. His fur and beard were neatly combed and straightened, while his body was dressed in a classic black suit with holes in the blazer to allow his wings to move freely. The demon sighed. He adjusted his black tie, and then turned to the cowering Lamb. "Typical," he shook his head.

With bulky hooves clopping on the white tiles, the demon made his way across the room. Lamb screamed again, but the Devil did not reciprocate. "Stay away from me!" she yelled.

"*You* stay away from *me*," he responded. "It's my house."

Satan reached the couch and flumped onto a cushion with a grunt, his wings flowing down the furniture's back, facing away from Lamb. He slipped an absurdly long cigarette from his blazer pocket, shoved it into his mouth and then lit it with a Zippo. He leaned back, exhaling an eclipse of dark smog, then spoke. "So, a goat's head, huh. Pretty unoriginal. Expected a little more from you, Lamb."

Lamb made a break for it. She rushed toward the window with the full intention of diving out, come what may. But it was slightly too high for a graceful escape, and she had to leap upwards, pulling her body onto the ledge as her shoes scraped against the wall. "I wouldn't look out there if I were you," the Devil warned, but it was too late. Lamb's head was already outside, petrified by the horrors before her.

2

"Lasciate ogne speranza, voi ch'intrate."

J osé Gervasi had shot his wife first, then his two daughters, then he
turned the gun on himself. He'd even set his house on fire before
that final blast to ensure a botched job would still reach the desired
outcome.

Decades had come and gone, yet it was the only thing José could
think about. He guessed that's what Hell was. A place where one became desensitised to the unceasing physical torture so that the mental
torture took over, a loop of memories reminding you how you ended up
here. José deserved to end up here, he understood that.

He loosened the strings from around his belly and the large chunk
of stone fell from his back onto the pile. He stood up as straight as he
could with a groan. After years of merciless labour, his spine was bent
wrong. He squinted over the vast desert across which he'd travelled,
where thousands of people marched, some carrying their rocks towards
the pile, others aimed in the opposite direction to collect more. The
luckiest of people collaborated in groups of three, moving their stones
with a pulley system. If José worked hard enough, one day he may be

promoted to that position.

Something hard clobbered José on the back of the skull and bright speckles danced him on his feet. He staggered before a common giant guard demon who had materialised out of nowhere, swaying a sizeable bat several feet above José's crown. Cowering his bleeding head, José unleashed a slew of apologies, scampering to rejoin the trek to fetch more rock.

They were building a temple that remained on fire, spewing a foul smog into the atmosphere. It was for Emperor Nero while his Mouth God oversaw the project. José glanced over his shoulder to catch another look at that beast, its naked, genderless body standing 50 stories tall, skinny and shrivelled, with loose skin hanging from its limbs. On the top, its neck held no head but a large mouth, which opened to blare a one-syllable gargle, revealing an enormous eyeball sitting on its tongue. José has been keeping count. That was its fourth noise. The next drop was coming.

José turned to face forward just in time, nearly walking straight into another guard demon. This figure wildly swung a plank, missing José but crunching into the face of a lady behind him. She wailed as she dropped, the guard demon responding with an orgasmic chortle.

When the Mouth God trumpeted his fifth note, José had picked up the pace and was far forward, confident he was safe. Like clockwork, this noise signalled the dropper funnel, which the Mouth God produced from a skin fold. The people closer to the god screamed, crouched, and covered their heads, refusing to move even when nearby demon guards intensified their beatings. Bending down, the Mouth God extended its bony fingers, selecting a human at random, dropping a smidgen of liquid upon them, causing them to painfully fizzle into nothing like salt on a snail, only to respawn on a lower level of Hell. The Mouth God stood up straight and blasted another tone. Work resumed, everyone safe for another four noises.

José watched the show from the corner of his eye and snickered. He enjoyed this entertainment as long as he was nowhere near it. His gaze fell back forward, and he watched the purple atmosphere swirling above St. Nick's Basilica many miles into the horizon. The Gothic architecture was magnetic, and he was forever drawn to the towering spire that appeared to pierce the sky with its tapered needle.

But something was different on this day, and José slowed his step, scrunching his eyes to see better. There, in the uppermost window, was a female face, staring over the land. At this distance, José could not imagine who it could be, but they were surely someone special to be granted access to the Basilica, especially at such an elevated viewpoint.

The Mouth God abruptly shrieked into the sky so loudly that José's ears stung. He spun to witness the Mouth God squatting with an extended yell of the *E* vowel before a bloody pile of meat plummeted from its stretching rectum. This mess was followed by an egg the size of a house, landing softly in the fleshy nest below. In a beat, chaos overruled. The marching lines scattered. José took off just as fast. He aimed for the Basilica without knowing why. Demon guards knocked people down, beating them violently, splatters of red brushing across the ground. José swivelled past.

The egg squirmed then jerked. Cracks raced across its shell. A hole was punched out. Something forcing its way to freedom. The egg crumbled to pieces. More than a dozen pink forms writhed across the ground, coming to stand on all fours. They looked like newborn lizards. But their heads were mouths just like their mother. They had a long way to grow to match her size but were like trucks compared to the fleeing humans.

The baby mouth-lizards squealed, announcing their arrival, opening their lips wide so their respective eyeballs could survey their surroundings. One by one, each darted in a different direction. Gobbling up and stamping on people as they went. Slaughtering hundreds within minutes.

José's feet hurtled. Picking up the pace. It meant nothing when a mouth-lizard locked into the chase. Effortlessly bounding to him. Whacking his body to the ground. The two of them slid to a standstill. Wheezing through broken ribs, José looked into the eyeball of the lizard's dribbling mouth above him, then turned his head to face the Basilica again. He wanted that woman to be the last thing he saw.

The mouth-lizard followed José's vision, scanning the world until it, too, noticed the lady at the window. It stared into her soul. It hissed in delight. José realised what he'd done. He had betrayed her, and shouted to recapture the creature's attention. But it was too late. The lizard took off, racing towards the woman, its mouth remaining open, never breaking its gaze.

3

Lamb gasped and pulled back, falling away from the window ledge and landing on the white tiles with a painful thud. The outside clamour vanished immediately, the walls seemingly protected from the exterior world. "I told you not to," Satan spoke from the couch, still smoking. "You must never look west."

Lamb trembled as she got to her feet. Her left hip clicked, and she wobbled, either from shock or the type of footwear she'd never got used to. "I'm in Hell, aren't I?" she dared to ask.

"Welcome to Floor Zero," Satan chuckled. He turned his goat head 180 degrees, facing backwards, then patted the cushion next to him. "Come sit with me." Lamb had no intention of doing anything of the sort, but Satan was insistent. "C'mon, just sit here. You know I could force you to if I wanted, so why not take control of your narrative and sit down of your own accord."

Lamb accepted this as truth but took it slowly, cautiously moving around the couch, then perching on the edge of the vacant cushion, staring forward, not looking at the goat, looking at anything but the goat. Satan snickered.

"Do you know who I am?" he asked.

"You're the Devil," Lamb whispered.

"Ha!" the demon laughed up a black cloud. "Please! Call me Lucifer. Would you like a ciggy?"

He extended the comically long box to Lamb, but she shook her head. Lucifer retracted his hand. "Suit yourself. But I'll get you smoking soon enough. Everyone smokes around here. It's great!"

Lucifer leaned back into the cushions and pulled a long drag of the cigarette, a fiery cherry blistering towards his hairy face before he yanked it from his lips and continued his inhale, mixing the atmosphere with the nicotine in his lungs.

He held it there, smacking his lips, then released a dense cloud of polluted breath, so thick that the room temporarily disappeared in its haze. Lamb didn't breathe for as long as she could, which wasn't long. She surrendered to the second-hand smoke in through her nose, pleasantly surprised that it smelt closer to chocolate than any tobacco she'd encountered. She breathed more willingly and scooted further back on the couch, sinking into it, aware that something in this intoxicating toxic mist was soothing her. She was grateful for it. And there they sat in silence. Lamb enjoyed the quiet classical tunes as she admired the paintings surrounding her, wondering who these people were, wondering if she recognised any of them.

☾

"So what are people saying about me that got you so skittish, huh?"

Lamb had zoned out, but this question reminded her of everything. Hell. The devil. The mouth lizard racing towards her. She sat up with a jolt, the tranquil effects of the smoke wearing thin, neither as calm nor as edged as before. From this rigid posture, she tried to look at Lucifer without making it too obvious. His head was the size of her torso. His dark, wispy beard gently swayed below his face. There was a certain air around him. He was staring at her, waiting patiently for an answer.

"I ... I'm not sure," she stuttered timidly.

"You're not sure? Oh, c'mon. Do they say I'm the King of Evil? The Lord of Darkness? The adversary of all that is holy? I've heard these titles, you know. And let me assure you, each one is inaccurate. I am the

God of Truth and Liberation! I am the Morning Star!"

Lucifer paused, staring at Lamb, awaiting her response. "What about the people outside?" she asked softly. "Those looked like slaves, being tortured and killed and stuff like that."

"Ok, well, first of all, only a sliver of the most useless people end up on the West Side. But, even then, let's unpack that thought. If the sinners are cast into the fires of Hell, but the saints rise to the glory of Heaven, are these not two components of the same procedure? If God rewards the good and I punish the bad, that would put us on the same team, would it not? Surely, in that reality of equilibrium, the so-called Good God and I are working together?"

"Are you?"

Lucifer chuckled. "I've watched the gods come and go. So many of them, while I've always held firm my role. The personification of the Bad Energy. But I know you. You've read the Bible, Lamb. So tell me, how many people does God kill? Millions? Tens of millions? But, me? I didn't kill anyone!"

"You did!" Lamb's education flared. "You killed Job's children!"

Lucifer erupted into laughter, and it struck Lamb at how human he sounded. "Alright, fair. But that was because of a bet with Yahweh himself. I received full permission from him to do that. I was encouraged, even! So, let's not sing his praises too loudly in that story, either. I am still the good guy. I am the best guy!"

Lucifer stood and turned to face Lamb. She raised her chin and was intimidated by his mountainous stature, radiating the sophistication of a businessman with the savage power of a beast. Despite having met so many creatures in recent memory, there was a distinct energy to this one. And it wasn't completely evil. It was many things. It was naughtiness. It was excitement. It was potential. But it wasn't the traumatic emotions she had associated with Satan as a child.

"I've been perverted and misrepresented more than any other deity," Lucifer continued. "Surely you, of all people, know what that is like, Lamb. I am the literal scapegoat. Just look at me." Lucifer pointed to his face. "Do you know why I look like this?"

"Because ... you're the literal scapegoat?" Lamb responded.

"What? No. It's because that's how you perceive me. Everything in the material universe is a reflection of the perceiver. Every god from

Earth is a creation of the human mind, so mote it be. I do not look like this. I am presented this way because you imagined I looked like this. And, I must say, it's a typical outcome and not my preferred aesthetic." Lucifer offered out his open palm. "Come, let's go for a walk."

Lamb carefully surrendered her hand into his surprisingly soft skin. It was the polite thing to do. Without effort, his strong arm lifted her into the air and placed her on her feet. He let go of her hand, and she tottered on the heels. "This won't do," she mumbled, bending down to unbuckle the straps and then kicking the shoes off towards a wall, now flat upon her bare feet, the natural state in which she was more comfortable.

"Sorry about those," Lucifer apologised. "I thought they looked nice."

"Now, who's being typical," Lamb teased, and Lucifer loved that, laughing heartily as he led the way out the door.

X

4

"Children of the Bible are my favourite because they're so easy to challenge using the very scripture they study."

Lucifer and Lamb walked down an endless hallway, which was an extension of the previous room. The walls were now red but were decorated with the same styles of portraits, majority female, each set a precise distance apart. Lamb wondered who they were, convinced that she recognised some of them after all, perhaps from a dream many moons forgotten. She almost expected their eyes to move, following their paces as they passed. That's how so many lazy stories would describe a place like Hell or a haunted house or whatever, but nothing of the sort happened here. Lamb wanted to ask who these people were, but she had yet to build the courage. And she didn't want to interrupt the Devil's story.

"Look at Genesis, for example," Lucifer continued. "Adam and Eve. Stupid fundamentalist Christians and stupid stupid atheists argue in a cramped space of literal analysis. The Bible is a collection of complex symbolic mythology told by the ancient initiates to more easily feed esoteric wisdom to the masses. Genesis is revealing the secrets of the Universe's evolution in 50 short chapters, assisting the primitive understandings of humans who lived seven thousand years ago. And yet, it is the modern mind that struggles to understand the teachings.

"From the beginning, the Universe is formless, then the Creator said, 'Let there be light'. A sound was spoken and there was light. The Big Bang, right? Sound and light? And then everything took seven days to make. Quote-unquote 'scientific' people laugh at that because they focus on the days, not the seven. The seven is the representative number of one rotation of nature. The nothingness of zero, the emanation of one to three, the turning point at four, then the retraction to seven, starting again. The science is everywhere. There are only seven natural notes on a musical scale before you repeat, for example. There are seven colours in a full rainbow. The seven continents. The seven seas. The seven classical planets where Earth represents the zero. As you know, the material nature is the amalgamation of three ingredients: the physical, the soul, and the Sülde. These can exist separately as three things, combine in pairs as a further three things, or unify as one singular thing, making seven distinct forms and nothing more.

"Pick a number between one and ten. Most people gravitate towards seven as a biological response. That's why the number runs wild across theologies. The Seven Spirits of God, The Seven Churches of Asia, and Seven Seals in the Book of Revelation. The Seven Heavens of Islam, the Seven Chakras of Hinduism, the Seven Lucky Gods of Japan, the Seven Deadly Sins. And, yes, the seven days of the week."

"Go, wash yourself seven times in the Jordan, and your flesh will be restored and you will be cleansed," Lamb recited 2 Kings 5:10.

"Exactly! You know it! So the days are holy representations of The Creation, but do not correspond with the days of the human. How could they? How arrogant is that? According to Hindu mythology, one Brahman day, known as Kalpa, is 4.32 billion years. Which changes things, wouldn't you agree?"

Lamb nodded. She adored listening to this. So much of her alive life had been her defending the Bible, rationalising it, explaining how Christianity and Judaism taught wisdom far beyond what the sciences could teach now. And yet, after meeting every holy power that the Universe had to offer, it was the Devil himself who affirmed what she always knew. And as Lucifer spoke, her feelings softened. Despite his raucous presence and animal features, she sensed no threat here. On the contrary, she felt safe. He was cute, even. Goats are cute.

"Adam evolved out of the Earth—the physical matter—and was animated by the breath of God—his soul. But he was not one man, but a name for a lineage of hermaphrodite single-celled organisms, giving birth to themselves as they tried to force some progressive growth for billions of years. This eventually happened with cellular division, when the species split into two, manifesting opposite sexes. This was the piece of Adam that became Eve, his 'rib', so to speak, and the second phase of evolution began—billions of years further which depended on the pairing of the two to breed.

"Each generation advanced, but it was revealed as an automated system within the body of the Creator, which at that time, the Bible refers to as the Garden of Eden. These pre-human entities were unaware of themselves as individuals, essentially prisoners to fixed responses. But the desire for progress grew and continued to branch, giving us the image of the Tree of Knowledge, the inevitable next step required for evolution."

In her imagination, Lamb could see that tree, expanding rapidly, stretching to the stars as leaves spewed forth then fell victim to the seasons. "Adam is the atom," she mumbled.

"Everything observed exists," Lucifer countered, but before Lamb could question, a vicious roar tore her well-being apart. The hallway thudded as a muscular creature bounded towards them on four legs, snarling in multiple voices.

Lamb's step froze as she protectively lifted her hands to her chest. There was a dog here, except it had three heads and was the size of a small horse. Its jaws snapped at the air, releasing spittle that streamed behind its sprinting momentum. It spun its body in the air, running up along the wall for several metres before pouncing right into the arms of Lucifer. "Hello, my boy! Yes, hello! Hello!" Lucifer addressed the dog like a baby as it excitedly slobbered his face. One head looked at Lamb, and there were flames in its eyes.

"Go on, give him a pat!" Lucifer shifted the dog towards her. "He won't bite you, don't worry!"

Lamb reluctantly extended her hand out, but before she could make contact, the one dog slurped upon her palm. Lamb jerked her arm back in fright, but then she giggled as the middle head howled for attention. Lucifer smiled, "That's a good boy!" then resumed his walk, "Now, where was I?"

Lamb's heart was beating with the most luscious rush of adrenaline. "Tree of Knowledge," she exhaled, and Lucifer clicked his free hand.

"Right! So, here's where it gets good. Because guess who arrives next? C'mon, guess!"

"You."

"Yes! But also, no. Like everything, it's the concept of me, an energy, an idea. They said I was a snake, which is fine! Look back through every culture, the snake is a powerful symbol. It's an obvious choice in regards to fear, for it didn't take long for even the most primitive of humans to learn that *snake bite bad, man fall down*. But in true esoteric wisdom, the snake is representative of rebirth. The shedding of one's skin to reveal another. The cycle of nature going for its next loop-de-loop.

"Inside the apple were the Seeds of Knowledge to unlock the next phase of evolution. Here, these root humans had the opportunity to make a choice against the systematic path of their achingly slow prearranged development. The progress of these so-called Adam and Eve figures yearned to move beyond the restrictions of the Creator's dictation, and I provided the key to do so.

"But what did God say would happen? Genesis 3:3? *'You must not touch it, or you will die.'* Then what actually happened? Did they die? Nope. They ate the apple and became conscious of their nudity in the symbolic text, but in actuality, they gained a realisation of themselves as separate physical entities. In that moment, they were released from the blissful ignorance of their God's rule to take on life as their own segments of divinity.

"So if you break it apart like this, or even if you don't and prefer the candy-coated literal fable version for kids, the roles of everything remain clear. Adam and Eve were prisoners of Yahweh. But I liberated them! I gave humanity the ability of critical thinking. I am the educator, and there is no figure throughout mythology who brought as much fundamental enlightenment as I did. Simply put, Yahweh or Yaldabaoth or the Elohim or whatever you call them—they were the enslavers. I was the true god fighting for the free will of humanity!"

A portrait passed of an Asian teenager who radiated familiarity, but Lamb just couldn't place her. "Wait, this doesn't make sense," Lamb interrupted. "I thought everything was predetermined? And free will was an illusion?"

Lucifer snorted. "Yes, yes, you've spoken with the Equation, well done. But it's such an impersonal outlook, don't you agree? Sure, the mental process behind every decision is a predetermined set of mechanics that will only produce one answer. But think in terms of the Sülde instead. There is an awareness in you, is there not? The mind may be driving, but a deeper emotional level is forced to experience the ride. You feel the feelings of joy or pain reflecting the journey, irrespective of how inescapable these outcomes may be. That is what authentic enlightenment is. We're talking about those who are lucky enough to come across this very information, packaged in some manner that appeals to their brain. In turn, their minds will realise that itself, as in the mind, is not the ideal leader within the system of an individual. Once the brain sees the value in prioritising positive emotions above its thoughts, it will train itself to take the backseat until the free will debate no longer matters. Because the ride will be delectable."

Lucifer turned left at a seemingly random set of black double doors with triangular shapes neatly carved into either side. Two of the dogs' heads were sleeping, but the third barked once, waking the others. Lucifer retrieved a large ring with hundreds of keys attached, continuing to speak as he flipped through them.

"But reality requires balance. No matter what you do, you cannot stop the mechanics from enforcing their rule upon you. The Equation will always condition your brain to behave as a casualty of circumstance. That's what the cycle of humanity was about, illustrated by the children of Adam and Eve, Cain and Abel. Ever wonder why Adam's lineage laid out in Genesis 5 fails to mention them? It's because they too are nothing but analogies. They teach us that you can live a life of great service and ethics, but the Equation will reward some yet punish others without explanation. Such a seemingly unfair process will drive brains towards antisocial behaviour, like the poor stealing food from the rich or Cain murdering his brother from rage and envy. Why would God let someone as dedicated as Abel die? Why was Cain allowed to keep living, getting married, and having children? It's because reality outgrew the command of the gods."

"Anyone who kills Cain will suffer vengeance seven times over,"

Lamb spoke, adding "Genesis 4:15."

"Seven! There you go, exactly! But the authentic message is that any act, good or bad, is irrelevant when it comes to a person's character or fate. Everyone is a direct result of their environment. Some were born for their brains to be shoved into desperation, lashing out in so-called evil manners. There's nothing just about a program where we punish the Sülde despite the divine spirit once living within them. If you taunt an abused animal, whose fault is it when it bites?"

Lucifer placed his dog on the floor, scratching each head in turn, then playfully smacking its bottom, "Off you go!" The creature trotted a step, quickly sniffed Lamb with all three noses, and then darted down the way they had come. "Such a good dog," Lucifer smiled as he selected a long black key with a triangle head, lifting it triumphantly into the air, twisting it into the lock, and pushing the doors aside. The opening revealed a spacious hall, empty aside from a small round table in the centre, covered with a red tablecloth as a candle danced on top.

"I hear you've got your appetite back."

Lamb's cheeks flustered pink. "I have."

Lucifer stuck out a chivalrous elbow, and she linked arms. The two stepped towards the table, Lamb trying not to giggle. This looked suspiciously like a romantic date. A date with Satan. Say the most peculiar thing you could imagine. The most peculiar thing being how un-peculiar it felt.

"Wait," she remembered to ask. "Who are those people in the paintings?"

"You don't recognise them?" Lucifer spoke through a smile. "Those were the people who followed your journey from the sunflowers to the City of London. They dedicated the rest of their lives to your study. There are millions of them, and when they died, they all came to me. Don't worry, they live on the East Side, and I've taken good care of them. You are their god, Lamb. And they've been waiting for you for a long time."

Lamb's head swam as Lucifer slid out a seat for her to sit down. A waiter appeared, humanoid in appearance, but too disproportionately tall and skinny to genuinely pass as one. Sitting upon his lengthy, brittle fingers was a covered tray as wide as the table. "I hope you don't mind, I already ordered for us," Lucifer said with a grin. The waiter lifted the dome lid as he lowered the dish, revealing the headless body of a roasted lamb garnished with a few branches of thyme. Lamb exploded into hysterics.

"Oh my God," she snorted between tears. "You are so wicked!"

X

5

"But strong meat belongeth to them that are of full age, even those who by reason of use have their senses exercised to discern both good and evil."
- Hebrews 5:14

The waiter refilled her glass with red wine as she sat back and belched. The roasted carcass was picked clean, its bare ribs reaching into the air for help. Lucifer refused to accept that it was finished, gnawing on some bone, exposing his primal nature. Lamb loved it.

The sloppy meal had largely distracted from the preceding conversation, but Lucifer's stories rode on. He spoke about how the field of science had become one of his greatest assets, robbing God of its power while he could hide beneath a blanket of disbelief, allowing him to influence humans without stepping on dogmatic toes. He cursed Anton LaVey, a man who had bastardised Satan's good name as a promotional tool for his own diluted philosophies with no ties to Lucifer whatsoever—assuring that LaVey's death brought what was coming to him. Lucifer passed on many stories localised to Lamb's hometown, such as his guidance with the Temple Church's construction by the Knights Templar, as well as the Great Fire of London he'd planned for years, cheekily executing it in 1666 and killing only six people but cleansing so many more. These tales should have been upsetting, but Lucifer spoke with such charisma and wit between mouthfuls of sheep meat, that Lamb could feel nothing but admiration for the power before her. More power than Ganesh. Perhaps more power than Jesus.

Lamb streaked her oily fingers across her black dress, grateful that any marks were invisible against the colour. She took another loud gulp of her wine, which was complex in its fruity flavours, incomparable to anything she'd tasted on Earth. She released an extended sigh of sleepy relief, then said, "Alright, how about that cigarette then?"

Lucifer laughed and flicked her a ridiculously long stick. She caught it and placed it between her lips. The waiter was immediately at her side with a lighter. A deep inhale, smoke swirling in her lungs, then an exaggerated exhale, the unmistakable taste of chocolate coating her tongue. Tranquillity rippled down her body, every muscle relaxing its grip. She let out a soft, one-note chuckle.

"You know," she began, circling her cigarette in the air. "I was allowed into the Supreme Realm of Saṃsāra …"

"I know," Lucifer put down his bone, listening.

"I was there, the so-called utopia of the afterlife. But it was terrible. It was like a gorgeous symphony performed by an orchestra of violins, with one string out of tune. *My* string! I could see its brilliance; I really could. But around me, everyone seemed so … content with their eternity, as if they had finally reached where they'd always wanted to go and now there was nowhere else to be. I knew I didn't belong, even on the very first day. It's a vibe thing. But sitting here, with you, in Hell, eating animal flesh for the first time since I was a child, drinking this wine," she paused to take a sip for effect, then, "I feel more at home than anywhere before. Even London. Even on those days I felt normal."

Lucifer nodded. "I'm delighted to hear this, because it segues perfectly into what I want to say next. Lamb, I've been watching you for longer than you think. The potential of your destiny was always a conversation, but you exceeded every expectation from every dimension. The Supreme Realm of Saṃsāra could not handle you, so how was the Earthly dimension supposed to hold your energy still? It could not. What you did—setting in motion the destruction of the world—

was not your fault. It was the destiny of the atoms manifesting as the grooves of your brain. But it was also no easy feat. And I, like everyone else, was dazzled by your performance."

Lamb bowed her head graciously, "Why, thank you."

"There is a special throne in Hell for a girl who did what you did, and I'd like to offer it to you. This is the fulfilment of your Dharmic Calling. The Age of Aquarius is not an era for the material world. It is a metaphysical shift where the female energy rebalances in her favour, and it starts here. That is why I need you to take the crown. And I don't mean as my Queen, like Lilith for the new zodiac or a replacement for Herodias. I mean as the ruling monarch of Hell." Lucifer's tone dipped lower. "The people need change, Lamb. And there is no place for an old devil's face in that zeitgeist anymore. You are the only one who could get the job done. You belong here. The Chosen One. And they already adore you. You'd be loved more than I ever was, I'm willing to bet. You can make any changes you like: design trajectories, enhance the culture, bring in the New Age with style. So please, don't make me beg of you, Lamb. Will you accept this royal position of power and the eternal life of luxury that comes with it?"

Lamb was tapping the filter of the half-smoked cigarette upon her smirked lips. She thought of Teddy's similar proposal, and how creepy that had felt. She revisited a quick thought about the Saṃsāra realm, and how she'd spent each minute seeking an exit. Returning to the present, her eyes moved slowly, her belly felt fed, her ego felt fed, her supple being sinking into the comfort of the chair.

"I'll think about it," she smiled.

Lucifer grinned.

They both knew what she meant.

X

6

"C'mon, then. I have a surprise for you."
Relinking arms, the two strolled out into the hallway and turned in the same direction as before. Maybe it was the wine or the proposition, or most likely a combination, but Lamb could not stop smiling. Everything flowed so naturally here. The air was like a warm fur gently rubbing against the skin. Portraits slipped past, Lamb now had the sense that she recognised every one of them, even if she didn't. These were her people.

Another door, another key, and Lamb staggered into her promised surprise, the merry expression collapsing off her face.

The chilling stone room before her revealed a pair of wooden poles jutting from the centre of the floor, angled away from one another. A naked man stood between these two pieces, an arm bound to each, torso stretched out in a crucifixion pose. He was dirty. He was heaving in pain. He was Lamb's father.

"Dad?" A palpitating wave of Lamb's youth rushed through her, and her balance dizzied from the vulnerability of her childhood. Lucifer placed his hand on her shoulder to steady. The old man looked up, grimacing in pain, blinking the dryness from his bloodshot eyes.

"Lamb? Lamb, is that you? Is this a trick? A trick to mock me? Mock your old father?"

Lamb's tear ducts burnt as if leaking citrus, the room blurring then rushing clear with a blink. Her memories jammed at the entrance, trying to come through all at once but stuck, leaving Lamb gasping at the air, the frontline of her mind vacant. Her father shook the wooden frame, babbling through cries.

"Are you here to remind me of my sins? Of my wife who died because of you? My wife. My wife, she died, and then I died a hundred times more! And it's because of you, you stupid girl! I am here because of you! You cursed my family. I know what I did. I did what I had to do to feed you! But you were a waste of my food!"

A teaspoon of bile splashed into Lamb's mouth. The memories erupted. The Incident. The photo. The man who had defaced her childhood, ruining her mind, then abandoning her to rot in the stew of his betrayal.

"It's no surprise you're here, you wicked child." He started to splutter. "You should be stuck here, not me." Thin streaks of saliva shone from his chin, the only hint that there was still liquid beneath his cracked skin. He had overexerted himself, gasping for air. "Have you come to rectify your mistakes? Then why are you just looking at me? Untie me, you stupid girl! I am your father, so free me! Just do what I say, and everything will be alright, do you hear?"

Lamb's fist tightened. Two back molars clicked as they ground together. Lava boiled in the pits of her stomach. She turned to Lucifer with hate in her face. Lucifer casually handed her a circular coil. Lamb took it, and it unravelled. A handle squeezed tight into her palm. The ends fell to the floor, revealing a leather whip split into nine tails. Lamb looked at the weapon and then at Lucifer's beaming teeth.

"Fuck him up, Lamb."

Lamb paused. Her gaze returned to the whip. She smiled. She nodded. She lifted her head to her father, she closed her eyes. Inhale. Eyes open. Exhale. She stepped towards him. Slowly. Deliberately. One bare foot, then the other. The whip scraped the ground behind her, hissing like a snake. Her father's eyes widened. He yanked his body backwards. His voice shook through the thin layer of foam around his lips.

"No, you go away with that thing!" He managed. "Lamb, you better stay back from me! I am your father. You can't do this! Don't do this to me, Lamb. Please don't do this!"

But she did do it, swiftly cracking his pleadings for mercy away.

☽

"Babes, fetch me another bowl of sticky black, please."

"Another? One more, and I think you've broken the world record."

Xen laughed at her demon husband's quip, slapping his concrete butt as he strode by to satisfy her request. He was a witty creature made even more appealing by his seven-foot athletic physique. She had chosen well. And she liked to believe she contributed to the relationship. Some wives worked their demon husbands as if they were servants, but Xen did not see the appeal. A loving home was only as good as the sum of its parts, and she appreciated the sense of fairness, as did he. Her cross-stitching hour was different, though. That was when she concentrated on her favourite craft, weaving threads while listening to the traditional Shinto music of her earthly people. Her husband respected the time.

Her expert needle poked and pulled, poked and pulled in the precise locations to hint at a Hello Kitty image. Decades of ageless practice fed her flawless motions, and she was unified with the embroidery, until the radio abruptly fuzzed, jolting her wrist out of sync. The searing wails of a humanoid voice violated Xen's living room, and her initial fright twisted into annoyance. But, ever-so gradually, her upset adjusted then blossomed into a realisation so gorgeously consequential that she could not immediately accept it.

"No way," Xen said as she placed her stitching down and leaned towards the radio. "No freaking way!"

She knew from where these cries were broadcasted. They came from the mouth of Lamb's father, each scream a comma between a lash of a whip, slicing portions of flesh from his skeleton like a pie. Xen leapt up, rushing away from her husband's steaming bowl and out the door, onto the sidewalk. The quaint houses lining this East Side district were flying open, women stumbling into the streets wearing expressions ranging from blissful excitement to head-shaking distrust.

"Oh my God!" Xen shouted to no one, to everyone. "She's here!

She's actually here!"

Agreements echoed. Volume dials were spun to the maximum as an ever-growing collection of feet thud their dance moves upon the tar, cheering each howl of Lamb's dad that resonated over the land. Their goddess had arrived! The Lamb Prophecy was finally with them!

And for those who pressed their ears deep into their radios, a lower tone weaved beneath the sounds of violent onslaught. It was the hysterical cackles of both a woman and beast. Lamb and Satan. The Queen and King of Hell. Laughing and laughing and laughing and laughing and laughing and laughing and laughing.

"And it was given unto her to make war with the saints, and to overcome them: and power was given her over all kindreds, and tongues, and nations. And all that dwell upon the earth shall worship her, whose names are not written in the book of life of the Lamb slain from the foundation of the world."

REVELATION 13:7-8

Please Help The Lamb Prophecy

Thank you for reading *The Lamb Prophecy*. By purchasing this book, you have placed a spoonful of food in my mouth. However, if you seek to spread more Good Energy into the world, there is a way to help further, and it won't cost you a thing!

You see, Amazon's algorithm is an extremely intelligent beast that judges authors' products based on many factors. But inarguably, our most significant power comes from **verified reviews**. So when you take a few minutes to tell the world what you thought of this book, the market awakens and lifts the title to higher eyes, feeding itself in the process. The author has no control over this side of the deal. It entirely relies on you!

Hence, please consider reviewing *The Lamb Prophecy*. You wouldn't believe the difference a single rating makes in allowing me to work another day.

Thank you again so very much!

Lots of love,

Jared Woods

The Author

Born in South Africa and now a homeless nomad, Jared has explored and gathered inspiration from nearly 60 countries. Additionally, he reads the central scripture from a different religion every year, deepening his understanding of numerous faiths and cultures. This curiosity and dedication to broad theology have greatly influenced his latest book, *The Lamb Prophecy*, where Jared blends fantasy with deep spiritual themes, constructing a world rich with combined mythology. Through the eyes of Lamb, the story encourages readers to reflect on their own sacred journeys while revealing steps towards a better future.

When he is not travelling, Jared spends his time between the UK and South Africa, sharpening his writing and reflecting on his experiences. Further creative projects include his one-panel Instagram comic *#legobiscuits*, his solo music under the name Coming Down Happy, his "singing" for the band Sectlinefor, and his film production, *Definitely Not a Cry For Help*, which is already partially on YouTube.

Support Jared on **Patreon.com/legotrip**
Visit Jared at **JaredWoodsSavedMyLife.com**
Follow Jared on Instagram, Threads, and Twitter **@legotrip**

Other Books By Jared Woods

- Licking the Bottom of the Love Jar (2023)
- When a Song Ends in a Minor Key:
  The Complete Biography of Fiona Apple (2024)
- F**ked My Way Up to the Top:
  The Complete Biography of Lana Del Rey (2023)
- Swiping Right (2023)
- Janthopoyism Bible (2022)
- Heartbreak Sucks! How to Get Over Your Breakup in 30 Days (2021)
- The 250 Best Albums of the Decade (2019)
- This Is Your Brain On Drugs (2016)

The Lamb
Prophecy is
indebted to
my Patreon
subscribers >>

Thank you to the following people who validated my art by kindly granting it a monetary value.

Aaron
Adam
Ahmed
Ama & Ross
Ammr
Bert
David
Diana
Dollkitten
Gee
Joanne
Kez
Lenka
Lonnie
Marcus
Mark
Milz
Ryan
Tami
Tony
Wilmie
Xen

patreon.com/legotrip

www.ingramcontent.com/pod-product-compliance
Ingram Content Group UK Ltd.
Pitfield, Milton Keynes, MK11 3LW, UK
UKHW040635200325
5076UKWH00013B/263